OUTSTANDING PRAISE FOR GAYLE LYNDS AND HER THRILLERS

THE BOOK OF SPIES

"Gayle Lynds is one of the best suspense writers in the world. *The Book of Spies* is a completely unique work, but for the purpose of inciting all of you to read it, let me say *The Da Vinci Code* meets *Bourne Identity*— which happens to be completely accurate."

—James Patterson

"A master of the espionage thriller...a thrilling, spy-laden, history-rich page-turner."

—*Library Journal* (starred review)

"Fast-paced and exciting."

—*Booklist*

"Hands-down the best book I've read all year. Grippingly paced, poignant, surprising with every turn of the page, this novel stunned me. Gayle Lynds has long been a master of espionage, but with this book, she proves that true masters only get better over time. Destined to become an instant classic in the field. In a word: Wow."

—James Rollins, *New York Times* bestselling author of *The Doomsday Key*

"Characters whose hidden depths are just starting to be revealed. When you begin a Lynds book, a roller-coaster ride is in store."

—*RT BOOKreviews* (A Top Pick)

THE BOOK OF SPIES

GAYLE LYNDS

St. Martin's Paperbacks

This is a work of fiction. All of the characters, organizations, and events portrayed in this novel are either products of the author's imagination or are used fictitiously.

THE BOOK OF SPIES

Copyright © 2010 by Gayle H. Lynds 2007 Revocable Trust.

Cover photograph by Scott Knauss.

For information address St. Martin's Press, 175 Fifth Avenue, New York, NY 10010.

ISBN: 978-0-312-94608-1

Printed in the United States of America

St. Martin's hardcover edition / April 2010
St. Martin's Paperbacks edition / March 2011

St. Martin's Paperbacks are published by St. Martin's Press, 175 Fifth Avenue, New York, NY 10010.

10 9 8 7 6 5 4 3 2 1

For Sophia Stone,
my granddaughter,
child of light and grace

ACKNOWLEDGMENTS

MY LIFE IS FULL of good and supportive people, many of whom helped with the writing of this novel. I'm particularly grateful to my extraordinary agent, Lisa Erbach Vance, of the Aaron M. Priest Literary Agency; my world-class editor, Keith Kahla, executive editor at St. Martin's Press; and my multitalented assistant and business manager, Tara Stockton, who speaks four languages and trots the globe.

I often consulted with novelist Melodie Johnson Howe, who heroically read and wisely commented on large sections of the novel. Authors Kathleen Sharp and Josh Conviser were generous partners in brainstorming international crime. Former CIA officers Alan More and Robert Kresge, who is also a fellow author, were remarkable sources upon whom I could always count.

My children and their spouses and one of my stepchildren discussed the book with me and provided details about geography and locations I was unable to visit: Paul Stone and Katrina Baum, Julia Stone and

Kari Timonen, and Deirdre Lynds. For those of you who have followed her story, my other stepdaughter, Katie Lynds, remains in a wonderful facility for the brain-damaged and is making good progress.

St. Martin's is my publishing home, and I love it there. Particular gratitude to Sally Richardson, Matthew Baldacci, Matthew Shear, Joan Higgins, John Murphy, Nancy Trypuc, Monica Katz, Brian Heller, John Karle, and Kathleen Conn.

Deborah Brown, bibliographer and research services librarian for Byzantine Studies, Dumbarton Oaks Research Library and Collection, Washington, D.C., was of tremendous help looking into the fascinating story of the Library of Gold. Others to whom I'm indebted include Kathleen Antrim, Barbara Paul Blume, Steve and Liz Berry, Ray Briare, Lee Child, Julian Dean, David Dun, Emily Erikson and Joe Ligman, Yogiraj Gurunath, David Hewson, Bones Howe, Randi and Doug Kennedy, Bill McDonald, David and Donna Morrell, Naomi Parry, M. J. Rose, Elaine and George Russell, Jim Rollins, Greg Stephens, Tom Stone and Alexandra Leslie, Steve Trueblood, and Diane Vogt.

As you read this novel, you might enjoy knowing that several of the characters have the real names of readers who entered a contest on my website. Much to my delight, they sent in e-mail waivers allowing me to use their names in the book whether for criminal or corpse or hero. No description is accurate, and certainly I won't tell you which ones are theirs. That's called suspense.

Thank you one and all.

PART ONE
THE HUNT

As he walked to the Senate, a note was thrust into Julius Caesar's hand. His spies had done their job, giving him a list of conspirators and their plans to kill him. Unfortunately, Caesar was in a hurry and did not read it. An hour later, he was assassinated.

—*translated from* The Book of Spies

In the abstruse world of espionage, it's not always easy to know when you are in on a secret.

—Time *magazine, January 9, 2006*

CHAPTER 1

A LIBRARY COULD BE A dangerous place. The librarian scanned the ten men in tailored tuxedos who lounged around the long oval table in the center of the room. Encircling them were magnificent illuminated manuscripts, more than a thousand of them, blanketing the walls from floor to ceiling. Their spectacular gold-covered bindings faced out to showcase the fortune in gems decorating them.

The men were members of the book club that owned and operated the secret Library of Gold, where the annual dinner was always held. The finale was the tournament, in which each member tested the librarian with a research question. As the books towered around them and the air vibrated with golden light, the men sipped their cognac. Their eyes watched the librarian.

"Trajan" challenged the international lawyer from Los Angeles. "A.D. 53 to A.D. 117. Trajan was one of the most ambitious warrior-emperors of old Rome, but few people realize he also revered books. His supreme monument to his successes at war is called Trajan's Column.

He ordered it erected in the court between two galleries of Rome's library—which he also built."

The room seemed to hold its breath, waiting. The librarian's fingers plucked at his tuxedo jacket. Nearly seventy years old, he was a tidy man with wrinkled features. His hair was thin, his glasses large, and his mouth set in a perpetual small smile.

The tension heightened as he mulled. "Of course," he said at last. "Cassius Dio Cocceianus wrote about it." He went to the shelves containing the eighty volumes of Cassius Dio's history, *Romaika,* compiled in the second and third centuries and transcribed by a Byzantine calligrapher in the sixth century. "The story is here, in volume seventy-seven. Most of Cassius Dio's work has been lost. Our library has the only complete set."

As pleased laughter swept the exclusive group, the librarian laid the large volume into the arms of the challenger, who stroked the embedded opals and sapphires on its cover. Gazing appreciatively at the golden book, he stood it up beside his brandy glass. Eight other illuminated manuscripts stood beside eight other brandy glasses. Each was a testament to the librarian's intimate knowledge of ancient and medieval literature and the priceless value of the library itself.

Now only the tenth member—the director himself—remained. He would pose the final question in the tournament.

The men helped themselves to more cognac. By design their yearly dinner was dazzling theater. Hours before the first martini was poured, ten wild ducks, freshly shot, had arrived by private jet from Johannesburg. The chefs were flown in from Paris, blindfolded of course. The seven-course meal was exquisite, including truffled sweetbreads with chestnuts. The alcohol was the best—tonight's cognac was a Louis XIII de Rémy Martin, worth more than a thousand dollars a bottle in today's market. All of the book club's liquors had been laid down by those who had gone before, creating a cellar of indisputable quality.

The director cleared his throat, and everyone turned to look at him. He was American and had flown in from Paris earlier in the day. The room's tenor changed, becoming somehow menacing.

The librarian pulled himself up, vigilant.

The director peered at him. "Salah al-Din, also known as Saladin. A.D. 1137 or 1138 to A.D. 1193. General Saladin, a Kurdish Muslim, was famous for his espionage network. One night his enemy Richard the Lionheart went to sleep in his tent in Assyria, guarded on all sides by his English knights. They poured a track of white ash around the tent so wide no one could cross it undetected. But when Richard awoke, a melon with a dagger buried deep inside had appeared beside his bed. The blade could just as easily have been stabbed into Richard's heart. It was Saladin's warning, left by one of his spies. The spy escaped without leaving a clue and was never caught."

Again the eyes watched the librarian. With every word, he had tensed. The door behind him opened quietly. He glanced over his shoulder as Douglas Preston stepped into the room. Preston was head of library security, a tall, muscular man who was an expert in weapons and took his work seriously. He was not wearing a tuxedo, instead had on his usual black leather jacket and jeans. Strangely, he carried a bath towel.

With effort, the librarian kept his voice steady as he headed across the room to another bookshelf. "The story can be found in Baha al-Din's *Sirat Salah al-Din: The Life of Saladin*—"

"Of course, you're correct," the director interrupted. "But I want another manuscript. Bring me *The Book of Spies*."

The librarian stopped, his hands reaching for the volume. He turned. The men's faces were outraged, unforgiving.

"How did you find out?" he whispered.

No one answered. The room was so silent he could hear the tread of crepe-soled shoes. Before he could turn again, Preston's towel slapped around his skull, covering his eyes and mouth. There was a huge explosion of gunfire, and pain erupted in his head. As he fell, he realized the security chief had given him fair warning by using a technique of the later Assassins—the towel was to cover the entrance and exit wounds to control spraying blood and bone. The book club knew that.

CHAPTER 2

Los Angeles, California
April, One year later

AS SHE WALKED INTO THE GETTY Center's conservation laboratory, with its sinks and fume hoods, Eva Blake smiled. On the sea of worktables lay centuries-old illuminated manuscripts, charts, and scrolls. Tattered and sprinkled with wormholes, all would be brought back to useful life. For her, conservation work was more than a profession—by restoring the old books she was restoring herself.

Eva's gaze swept the room. Three other conservators were already bent over their tables, lone islands of movement in the vast high-tech lab. She said a cheery hello and grabbed a smock. A slender woman of thirty years, she had an understated face—the cheekbones were good, the chin soft and round, the lips full—that resisted the sharp cut of classical beauty. Her red hair tumbled to her shoulders, and her eyes were cobalt blue. Today she wore an open-necked white blouse, white pencil skirt, and low-heeled white sandals. There was a sense of elegance about her, and a softness, a vulnerability, she had learned to hide.

She stopped at Peggy Doty's workbench. "Hi, Peggy. How's your new project?"

Peggy lifted her head, took a jeweler's loupe from her eye, and quickly put on large, thick glasses. "Hey, there. Seneca's worrying me. I think I can definitely save Aristotle, but then he's the one who said, 'Happiness is a sort of action,' so with that kind of Zen attitude he's bound to last longer."

Born and raised in England, Peggy was a gifted conservator and a longtime friend, such a good friend that she had stayed close even after Eva had been charged with vehicular manslaughter in her husband's death. As she thought about him, Eva's throat tightened. She automatically touched the gold chain around her neck.

Then she said, "I always liked Aristotle."

"Me, too. I'll see what I can do for Seneca. Poor guy. His toga's peeling like a banana." Peggy's brown hair was short and messy, her eyeglasses were already sliding down her nose, and EX LIBRIS inside a pink heart was tattooed on her forearm.

"He's in good hands." Eva started to leave.

"Don't go yet. I'd sure like your help—the provenance on this piece sucks." Peggy indicated the colorful medieval chart spread out on her worktable. "I'm waiting for the results of the date test, but I'd love to know at least the century."

"Sure. Let's see what we can figure out." Eva pulled up a chair.

The chart was about fourteen inches wide and twenty inches long. At the bottom stood two figures in rope sandals and luminous blue togas. On the left was Aristotle, representing natural philosophy, and on the right was Seneca, moral philosophy. To all appearances they were an unlikely pair—Aristotle was Greek, while Seneca was Roman and born nearly four hundred years later. Eva studied them a moment, then moved her gaze to medallions rising like clouds above their heads. Each medallion contained a pair of the men's opposing theories, a battle of ideas between two great classical thinkers. The chart's lettering was Cyrillic.

"The chart itself is written in Old Russian," Eva explained, "but it's not the revised alphabet of Peter the Great. So it was probably made before 1700." She laid her finger along the right margin of the parchment, where small, faded words were printed. "This isn't Russian, old or new—it's Greek. It translates as 'Created under the hand of Maximos after cataloguing the Royal Library.'"

Peggy moved closer, staring down. "I'm pretty sure Maximos is a Greek name. But which Royal Library? Russia or Greece? What city?"

"Our chart-maker, Maximos, was born Michael Trivolis in Greece and was later known as Maximos. When he moved to Russia, he was called Maxim. Does that give you enough information to know who he was?"

Peggy's small face lit up. "Saint Maxim the Greek. He spent a long time in Moscow translating books, writing, and teaching. I remember studying him in an Eastern history course."

"And that gives you the answer to your question—Maxim arrived in Russia in 1518 and never left. He died about forty years later. So your chart was made sometime in the first half of the sixteenth century in Russia."

"Cool. Thanks."

Eva smiled. "How's everything with Zack?" Zack Turner was the head of security at the British Museum in London.

"Distant, as in he's still there, and I'm still here. Woe is me—and he."

"How about going back to the British Library?"

"I've been thinking about it. How are you doing?" There was concern in Peggy's gaze.

"Fine." It was mostly true now that the Getty had offered Eva the conservation job to tide her over until her trial. She was out of sight in the lab—the press coverage of the car crash had been exhaustive. But then Charles had been the renowned director of the elite Elaine Moreau Library, while she had been a top curator here at the celebrated Getty. Charming, handsome, and in love, they were a star-studded couple in L.A.'s art and monied beau monde. His dramatic death—and her arrest and denials—had made for a particularly juicy scandal.

Being home all day every day after the accident had been hard. She watched for Charles in the shadows, listened for his voice calling from the garden, slept with his pillow tight against her cheek. The emptiness had closed around her like a cold fist, holding her tight in a kind of painful suspension.

"I'm so sorry, Eva," Peggy was saying. "Charles was a great scholar."

She nodded. Again her fingers went to the chain around her neck. At the end of it hung an ancient Roman coin with the profile of the goddess Diana—her first gift from Charles. She had not taken off the necklace since he died.

"Dinner tonight?" Peggy said brightly. "My treat for letting me tap into that big brain of yours."

"Love to. I've got karate class, so I'll meet you afterward."

They decided on a restaurant, and Eva went to her workstation. She sat and pulled the arm of her stereobinocular microscope toward her. She liked the familiarity of the motion and the comfort of her desk with its slide kits, gooseneck lamp, and ultraviolet light stand.

Her project was an adventure manuscript about the knights of King Arthur completed in 1422 in London.

She stared through the microscope's eyepiece and used a scalpel to lift a flaking piece of green pigment from the gown of a princess. The quiet of the work and the meticulous focus it required soothed her. She carefully applied adhesive beneath the paint flake.

"Hello, Eva."

So deep was her concentration, the voice sent a dull shock through her. She looked up. It was her attorney, Brian Collum.

Of medium height, he was in his late forties, with eyebrows and hair the gray color of a magnet and the strong-jawed face of a man who knew what he wanted from life. Impeccably turned out in a charcoal suit with thin pinstripes, he was the name partner in the international law firm of Collum & Associates. Because of their friendship, he was representing her in the trial for Charles's death.

"How nice to see you, Brian."

He lowered his voice. "We need to talk." Usually his long face radiated optimism. But not now. His expression was grim.

"Not good news?" She glanced at her colleagues, noting they were studiously attending to their projects.

"It's good—or bad, depending on what you think."

Eva led him outdoors to a courtyard of lawns and flowers. A water fountain flowed serenely over perfectly arranged boulders. This was all part of the Getty Center, a complex of striking architecture sheathed in glass and Italian travertine stone crowning a hill in the Santa Monica Mountains.

Silently they passed museum visitors and sat together on a bench where no one could overhear.

"What's happened?" she asked.

He was blunt. "I have an offer from the D.A.'s office.

If you plead guilty, they'll give you a reduced sentence.
Four years. But with good behavior you'll be out in
three. They're willing to make a deal because you have
a clean driving record and you're a respected member
of the community."

"Absolutely not." She forced herself to stay calm. "I
wasn't driving."

"Then who was?"

The question hung like a scythe in the sparkling
California air.

"You really don't recall Charles getting behind the
wheel?" she asked. "You were standing in your doorway
when we drove away. I saw you. You had to have seen
us." They had been at a dinner party at Brian's house
that night, the last guests to leave.

"We've been over this before. I went inside as soon
as I said good night—before either of you got close to
your car. Alcohol plays tricks with the mind."

"Which is why I'd never drive. Never." Working to
keep the horror from her voice, she related the story
again: "It was after one A.M., and Charles was driving
us home. We were laughing. There wasn't any traffic on
Mulholland, so Charles wove the car back and forth.
That threw us against our seat belts and just made us
laugh harder. He drove with one hand, then with the
other . . ." She frowned to herself. There was something
else, but it escaped her. "Suddenly a car shot out from a
driveway ahead of us. Charles slammed the brakes. Our
car spun out of control. I must've lost consciousness.
The next thing I knew, I was strapped down to a gurney." She swallowed. "And Charles was dead."

She smoothed the fabric of her skirt and stared off
as grief raged through her.

Brian's silence was so long that the distant roar of
traffic on the San Diego Freeway seemed to grow
louder.

At last he said kindly, "I'm sure that's what you re-member, but we have no evidence to support it. And I've spent enough of your money hiring investigators to look for witnesses that I have to believe we're not going to find any." His voice toughened. "How's a jury going to react when they learn you were found lying uncon-scious just ten feet from the driver's door—and it was hanging open, showing you were behind the wheel? And Charles was in the front passenger seat, with the seat belt melted into what was left of him. There's no way he was driving. And you had a 1.6 blood alcohol level—*twice* the legal limit."

"But I wasn't driving—" She stopped. With effort, she controlled herself. "You think I should take the D.A.'s deal, don't you?"

"I think the jury is going to believe you were so drunk you blacked out and don't remember what you did. They'll go for the maximum sentence. If I had a scintilla of hope I could convince them otherwise, I'd recommend against the offer."

Shaken, Eva stood and walked around the tranquil pool of water encircling the fountain. Her chest was tight. She stared into the water and tried to make herself breathe. First she had lost Charles and all their dreams and hopes for the future. He had been brilliant, fun, endlessly fascinating. She closed her eyes and could al-most feel him stroking her cheek, comforting her. Her heart ached with longing for him.

And now she faced prison. The thought terrified her, but for the first time she admitted it was possible—she had never in her life blacked out, but she might have this time. If she had blacked out, she might have climbed behind the wheel. And if she did—that meant she really had killed Charles. She bent her head and clasped the gold wedding band on her finger. Tears slid down her cheeks.

Behind her, Brian touched her shoulder. "You remember Trajan, the great ruler who expanded the Roman empire?"

She quickly wiped her face with her fingers and turned around to him. "Of course. What about him?"

"Trajan was ruthless and cunning and won every great battle he led his troops into. He had a rule: If you can't win, don't fight. If you don't fight, it's no defeat. You will survive. Take the deal, Eva. Survive."

CHAPTER 3

Washington, D.C.
April, Two years later

CARRYING A THERMOS OF HOT coffee and two mugs,
Tucker Andersen crossed into Stanton Park, just five
blocks from his office on Capitol Hill. The midnight
shadows were long and black, and the air was cool.
There were no children in the playground, no pedestrians on the sidewalks. Inhaling the scent of freshly cut
grass, he listened as traffic rumbled past on C Street. All
was as it should be.

Finally he spotted his old friend Jonathan Ryder,
almost invisible where he sat on a bench facing the
granite statue of Revolutionary War hero Nathanael
Greene. Tonight a call had come in from Tucker's wife
that Jonathan was trying to reach him.

Tucker closed in. A slender man of five foot ten, he
had the long muscles of the runner he still was. His eyes
were large and intelligent behind tortoiseshell glasses,
his mustache light brown, his gray beard trimmed close

to the jaw. Mostly bald, he had a fringe of gray-brown hair dangling over his shirt collar. He was fifty-three years old, and although his official credentials announced CIA, he was both more and less.

"Hello, Jonathan." Tucker sat and crossed his legs. "Nice to see you again. What's it been—ten years?" He studied him. Jonathan looked small now, and he was not a small man. And tense. Very tense.

"At least ten years. I appreciate your meeting me on such short notice." Jonathan gave a brief smile, showing a row of perfect white teeth in his lined face. Lean and fit, he had a high forehead topped by a brush of graying blond hair. He was wearing black sweatpants and a black sweatshirt with a Yale University logo on the sleeve instead of his usual Savile Row business suit.

Tucker handed him a mug and poured coffee for both of them. "Sounded important, but then you could always make sunrise seem as if it were heralding angels."

"It *is* important." Jonathan sniffed the coffee. "Smells good." His hands shook as he drank.

Tucker felt a moment of worry. "How's the family?"

"Jeannine's great. Busy with all her charities, as usual. Judd's left military intelligence and isn't going to reenlist. Three tours in Iraq and a tour in Pakistan were finally enough for him." He hesitated. "I've been thinking a lot about the past lately."

Tucker set the thermos on the seat beside him. They had been close friends during their undergraduate days at Yale. "I remember when we were in school and you started that investment club. You made me a grand in two years. That was a hell of a lot of money in those days."

Jonathan nodded. Then he grinned. "I thought you were just a smart-ass—all looks, no brains, no commitment. Then you saved my skin that night in Alexanderplatz in East Berlin. Remember? It took a lot of muscle—and smarts."

After college, both had joined the CIA, in operations, but Jonathan had left after three years to earn an MBA at Wharton. With an undergraduate degree in chemistry, he had worked for a series of pharmaceutical companies, then gone on to found his own. Today he was president and board chair of Bucknell Technologies. Monied and powerful, he was a regular on Washington's social circuit and at the president's yearly Prayer Breakfast.

"Glad I did the good deed," Tucker said. "Look where you ended up—a baron of Big Pharma, while I'm still tilling the mean streets and urine-scented dark alleys."

Jonathan nodded. "To each his own. Still, if you'd wanted it, you could've headed Langley. Your problem is you make a lousy bureaucrat. Have you heard of the video game called Bureaucracy? If you move, you lose."

Tucker chuckled. "Okay, old friend. Time to tell me what this is all about."

Jonathan looked at his coffee, then set it on the seat beside him. "A situation's come up. It scares the hell out of me. It's more your bailiwick than mine."

"You've got a lot contacts. Why me?" Tucker drank.

"Because this has to be handled carefully. You're a master at that. Because we're friends, and I'm going to go down. I don't want to die in the process." He stared at Tucker, then looked away. "I've stumbled onto something . . . an account for about twenty million dollars in an international bank. I'm not sure exactly what it's all about, but I'm damn sure it has to do with Islamic terrorism." Jonathan fell silent.

"Go on," Tucker snapped. "Which bank? Why do you think the twenty million is connected to jihadism?"

"It's complicated." He craned around, checking the park.

Tucker looked, too. The wide expanse remained empty.

"You've come this far." Tucker controlled an urge to shake the information out of him. "You know you want to tell me."

"I didn't have anything to do with it. I'm not exactly an angel myself. . . . But I don't understand how anyone could—" Jonathan shuddered. "What do you know about the Library of Gold?"

"Never heard of it."

"It's key. I've been there. It's where I found out about this—"

Tucker watched Jonathan intently as he spoke. He was leaning forward slightly, gazing off into the middle distance.

There was no sound. No warning. A red dot suddenly appeared on Jonathan's forehead and the back of his head exploded with a loud crack. Blood and tissue and bone blasted into the air.

Tucker's training kicked in immediately. Before Jonathan's lifeless body had time to keel over, Tucker hit the sidewalk and rolled under the bench. Two more sniper shots dug into the concrete, spitting shards. His heart pounded. His friend's blood dripped next to him. Tucker swallowed and swore. He had come unarmed.

Using his mobile, he dialed 911 and reported the wet job. Then he peeled off his blazer, rolled it thick, and lifted it to attract attention. It was a light tan color, a contrast against the shadows. When no more rounds were fired, he snaked out from under the bench. Hurrying off through the park, he headed toward Massachusetts Avenue, where he thought the bullets had originated. As he moved he considered what Jonathan had said: Islamic terrorism . . . $20 million in an international bank . . . the Library of Gold. . . . What in hell was the Library of Gold?

As he crossed the street, Tucker scanned the area. A young couple was drinking from Starbucks coffee cups, the man carrying a briefcase. Another man was pushing a grocery cart. A middle-aged woman in a running suit and wearing a small backpack jogged past and circled back. Any of them could be the shooter, the rifle quickly broken down and concealed in the briefcase, the shopping cart, the backpack. Or the shooter could be someone else, still tracking him.

When he reached Sixth Street, Tucker ran into the swiftly moving traffic. Over the noise of honking horns, he heard the distinctive sound of a bullet whistling overhead. Crouching between the lanes of rushing cars, he spun around and stared back. A man was standing on the sidewalk at the corner, holding a pistol in both hands.

As the man fired again, Tucker put on a burst of speed, running with the cars. More horns honked. Curses filled the air. A taxi was entering traffic after dropping off its fare. Tucker pounded the fender to slow it, yanked open the back door, and fell inside.

The driver's head whipped around. "What in hell?"

"Drive."

As the taxi took off, Tucker peered out the rear window. Behind him, the killer ran into the congestion, looking everywhere, his gun still searching for its target. A van entered traffic, and Tucker lost sight of him. When the van turned the corner, opening up the view again, he spotted the man three blocks back. A car slewed around him, horn blaring. Another car skidded. The man pivoted, and a racing sedan slammed into him. He vanished under the wheels of the car.

"Let me off here," Tucker ordered. He shoved money at the driver and jumped out.

Running back, he studied the stream of cars. They

should have stopped. At least they should be swerving around the downed shooter.

As two police cars arrived at the park, sirens screaming, Tucker walked up and down the tree-lined block. Both sides. Traffic roared past. There was no sign of a body.

CHAPTER 4

THE FUNERAL FOR JONATHAN Ryder was held in the Chevy Chase Presbyterian Church in northwest Washington. A somber crowd packed the sanctuary—businesspeople, lawyers, investors, philanthropists, and politicians. Jonathan's widow, Jeannine; his son, Judd; and assorted relatives sat in the front row, while Tucker Andersen found a spot in back where he could watch and listen.

After Jonathan was killed, the police had searched the buildings around Stanton Park and questioned all potential witnesses. They interviewed the widow, son, neighbors, and business associates, who were mystified why anyone would want to murder a good man like Jonathan. The police investigation was continuing.

Checking into Jonathan's last words, Tucker had found only one mention of the Library of Gold in Langley's database. Then he researched the library online and talked with historians at local universities. He also queried the targeting analysts in the counterterrorism unit. Thus far he had found nothing helpful.

"In Jesus Christ, death has been conquered and the promise of eternal life affirmed." The pastor's voice resonated against the high walls as he conducted the Service of Witness to the Resurrection. "This is a time to celebrate the wonderful gifts we received from God in our relationships with Jonathan Ryder. . . ."

Tucker felt a wave of grief. Finally the celebration of Jonathan's life ended, and the strains of "The Old Rugged Cross" filled the sanctuary. The family left first, Judd Ryder supporting his mother, her head bowed.

As soon as it was decent, Tucker followed.

THE RECEPTION WAS IN the Church, in Chadsey Hall. Tucker chatted with people, introducing himself as an old college friend of Jonathan's. It lasted an hour. When Jeannine and Judd Ryder were walking alone out the door, Tucker intercepted them.

"Tucker, how nice to see you." Jeannine smiled. "You've shaved your beard." A petite brunette, she was dressed in a black sheath dress with a string of pearls tight against her throat. She had changed a lot, no longer the lively wife he remembered. She was his age, but there was a sense about her of having settled, as if there were no longer any questions to be asked.

"Karen was in a state of shock," Tucker admitted with a smile. He'd had a beard off and on for years. "It's been a while since she's seen my whole face."

He shook hands with Jonathan's son, Judd. "The last time we met, you were at Georgetown." He remembered when Judd was born, Jonathan's pride. His full name was Judson Clayborn Ryder.

"A long time ago," Judd agreed genially. "Are you still with State?" Six feet one inch tall, he was thirty-two years old, wide-shouldered, with an easy stance.

Fine lines covered his face, swarthy from too many hours in the sun. His hair was wavy and chestnut brown, while his brown eyes had faded to a dark, contemplative gray. His gaze was rock steady, but a sense of disillusionment and a hint of cynicism showed. Retired military intelligence, Tucker remembered.

The State Department was Tucker's longtime cover. "They'll have to pry my fingers off my desk to get rid of me."

"The police said you were with Dad when he was shot." Judd spoke with light curiosity, but Tucker sensed greater depths.

"Yes. Let's go outdoors and chat."

They walked out to the grassy lawn. Only a few people remained, climbing into cars and limousines at the curb.

Tucker guided the pair to a spot in the shadow of the stone church. "Have either of you heard of the Library of Gold?"

"It was one of the bedtime stories Dad used to tell me, like *Lorna Doone* and *The Scarlet Pimpernel*," Judd said. "What about you, Mom?"

Jeannine frowned. "I vaguely recall it. I'm sorry, but I don't remember much. It was something Jonathan and Judd shared."

"Did the Library of Gold play a role in Dad's murder?" Judd asked.

Tucker gave a casual shrug. "The police think a copycat of the Beltway Snipers might've shot him." The Beltway Snipers had been responsible for a series of random killings a few years before.

Jeannine pressed her hand against her throat. "How horrible."

Judd put his arm around her shoulders.

"Jonathan said he wanted my help with something

related to the library," Tucker continued. "But he died before he could tell me exactly what it was. What did your father tell you about the library, Judd?"

Judd settled his feet. "I'll run through the basics. It all began with the Byzantine Empire. For a thousand years while the emperors were conquering the world, they were collecting and making illuminated manuscripts. But then the empire fell to the Ottoman Turks in 1453. That could've been the end of the court library, but a niece of the last ruler escaped with the best books. They were covered in gold and jewels. When she married Ivan the Great, eight hundred of the books went to Moscow with her." He paused. "The legend was born with their grandson, Ivan the Terrible. After he inherited the library he added more illuminated manuscripts and started letting important Europeans see the collection. They were so impressed they went home and talked about it. Word spread across the continent that only when you stood among Ivan's golden books could you really understand 'wisdom, art, wealth, and eternal power.' That's how the collection got its name—the Library of Gold. It was a good adventure tale with a happy ending that turned into a mystery. Ivan died in 1584, maybe from mercury poisoning. At about the same time several of his spies and assassins got sick and died or were executed—and the library vanished."

Tucker had found himself leaning forward as he listened. He stepped back and peered at Jeannine. "Is that what you remember?"

"That's much more than I ever heard."

"I checked into the library and came up with pretty much the same information," Tucker admitted. "The Byzantine court library existed, but many historians believe none of the books landed in Moscow. Some think a few ended up in Rome, and the Ottoman Turks burned a lot, kept some, and sold the rest."

"I like Jonathan's story more," Jeannine decided.

"Did you ask your father how he heard the story, Judd?"

"Never saw any reason to."

"Where did Jonathan say the library was now?"

Judd gave him a hard look. "The way I ended the story for you was the way Dad ended it for me—with Ivan the Terrible's death and the library's disappearance."

"Would you mind if I looked through Jonathan's papers?" Tucker asked Jeannine.

"Please do, if you think you might find something," she said.

"I'll help," Judd told him.

"It's not necessary—" Tucker tried.

"I insist."

THE RYDERS LIVED ON the prestigious Maryland State side of Chevy Chase. The house was a baronial white mansion in the Greek Revival style, with six towering columns crowned by an intricately carved portico. Jonathan's office was filled with books. But that was nothing compared to the real library. Tucker stared. From the parquet floor to the second-floor ceiling, thousands of books beckoned, many in hand-tooled leather bindings.

"This is amazing," Tucker said.

"He was a collector. But see how worn his chair is? He didn't just collect; he read a lot, too."

Tucker gazed at the red leather armchair, worn and softened. Returning to the task at hand, he led Judd back to the office. They began inspecting Jonathan's cherrywood desk, matching file cabinets, and the cardboard banker's boxes of his personal belongings sent over from his office at Bucknell headquarters.

"The Department of State is a good cover," Judd

said noncommitally. "Who do you really work for, Tucker? CIA . . . Homeland Security . . . National Intelligence?"

Tucker let out a loud laugh. "Sorry to let you down, son. I really do work for State. And no, not State intelligence. I'm just a paper pusher, helping the diplomats wade through the various policy changes that have to do with the Middle East. A paper pusher like me is perfect to go through Jonathan's papers." In truth, Tucker was a covert officer, which meant his fellow spies, operations, assets, agents, and the people who had worked knowingly or unknowingly with him could be endangered if his real position were made public.

"Right," Judd said, letting the matter drop.

When Tucker asked, Judd described the conditions he had seen in Iraq and Pakistan without ever telling him anything substantive about his own work.

"I'll bet you're being recruited by every agency in the IC," Tucker said. The IC was the intelligence community.

"I haven't been home long enough."

"They'll be after you. Are you tempted?"

Judd had taken off his suit jacket and was crouched in his white cuffed shirt and dark suit pants over a banker's box, reading file names. "Dad asked me the same question. When I said no, he tried to convince me to join him at Bucknell. But I've saved my money and have a lease on a row house on the Hill. I figured to do nothing until I couldn't stand it anymore. By then I should know what's next for me."

Tucker had been going through Jonathan's desk. The last drawer contained files. He read the tags. The end file was unnamed. He pulled it out. In it were a half-dozen clippings from newspapers and magazines from the past week—and each article was about jihadism in Afghanistan and Pakistan. He peered up. Judd's back was to him. He folded the clippings and stuffed them inside his jacket and returned the empty file to the drawer.

He activated Jonathan's computer. "Do you know your dad's password?"

Judd looked over his shoulder. "Try 'Jeannine.'"

When that did not work, Judd made more suggestions. Finally the date of his birth did the trick. As soon as Judd returned to the banker's boxes, Tucker activated a global search for "Library of Gold"—but uncovered nothing. Then he inspected Jonathan's financial records on Quicken. There were no red flags.

"Dinner," Jeannine announced from the open door. "You need a break."

They joined her for a simple meal at the maple table in the kitchen.

"Your place is beautiful," Tucker commented. "Jonathan came a far way from the South Side of Chicago."

"All of this was important to him." Jeannine made a gesture encompassing the house and their privileged world. "You know how ambitious he was. He loved the business, and he loved that he could make a lot of money at it. But strangely I don't think he could ever have made enough to make him really happy. Still, we had many good times." She stopped, her eyes tearing.

"We've got a lot of great memories, don't we, Mom?" Judd said.

She nodded and resumed eating.

"Jonathan traveled a lot, I imagine," Tucker said.

"All the time," she said. "But he was always glad to come home."

After coffee, Tucker and Judd returned to the office. By ten o'clock, they had finished their search, and Tucker was weary of the tedious work.

"Sure I can't convince you to have a brandy?" Judd asked as he walked him to the front door. "Mom will join us."

"Wish I could, but I need to get home. Karen is going to think I've gotten myself lost."

Judd gave an understanding nod, and they shook hands.

Tucker went out to his old Oldsmobile. He liked the car. It had a powerful eight-cylinder engine and ran like a well-oiled top. He climbed inside and drove the rest of the way around the circular drive and out past the electronic gates and onto the street, heading to his far more modest home in Virginia. Since he was working, he had not brought Karen to the funeral. But she would be waiting for him, a fire burning in the fireplace. He needed to see her, to remember the good times, and to forget for a short while the fear in Jonathan's voice for some impending disaster he had not had time to name.

Earlier, when he followed Jeannine and Judd's limo to their place, he had thought a black Chevy Malibu was dogging him most of the way. He had slowed the Olds as he drove in through the Ryders' gate, watching in his rearview mirror. But the car had rolled past without a glance from the driver, his profile hard to see beneath a golf cap pulled low over his forehead.

Now as he drove, Tucker went into second-stage alert, studying pedestrians and other cars. After ten blocks he made a sharp turn onto a quiet street. There was a car again, maybe *the* car, behind him. A dark color. A motorcycle turned, too, trailing the car.

Tucker made another sharp right, then turned left onto a silent residential avenue. The tailing car stayed with him, and so did the motorcycle. He hit the accelerator. Shots sounded, smashing in through the rear window. Glass pebbles sprayed, showering him. He crouched low and pulled out his 9-mm Browning, laying it on the seat beside him. Since Jonathan's death, he carried it all the time.

Flooring the accelerator, he felt the big eight take

hold, and the car hurtled forward into the night. Houses passed in a blur. No more bullets, but his tail was still with him, although falling behind. Silently he thanked the Olds's powerful motor. Ahead was a hill. He blasted up it, the front wheels lifting at the crest, and over. The front crashed down, and he raced onward, turning onto one street and then the next.

He looked around, hoping . . . there was an open garage, and the attached house showed no interior lights. He checked his rearview mirror. No sign of his tail— yet.

He slammed the brakes and shot the car into the garage, jumped out, and yanked hard on the door's rope. The door banged down.

Standing at the garage's side window, gun in hand, he watched his pursuer rush past. It was the black Chevy Malibu, but he saw only the right side of the car, not the driver's side, and could not quite make out the license plate number. He still had no idea who was behind the wheel. Immediately following, the motor- cycle whipped past, its rider's face hidden by a black helmet.

Tucker remained at the window, watching. A half hour later, he slid his Browning back into its holster and went to the center of the big garage door. With a grunt, he heaved the door up—and froze, staring into the mouth of a subcompact semiautomatic Beretta pistol.

"Don't reach for it." Judd Ryder's face was grim. He had changed out of his funeral clothes and was wearing jeans and a brown leather bomber jacket.

Tucker let the hand that had been going for his weapon drift down to his side. "What in hell do you think you're doing, Judd? How did you find me?"

Ryder gave a crooked smile. "You learn a few things in military intelligence."

"You put a bug on my car?"

"You bet I did. Why didn't the sniper in Stanton Park kill you, too?"

"I got lucky. I dove under the bench."

"Bullshit. You claim to be a paper pusher, but paper pushers freeze. They wet their pants. They die. Why did you set up Dad?"

Tucker was silent. Finally he admitted, "You're right—I'm CIA. Your father came to me for help, just as I said. After I got away, the sniper tried to shoot me, too. He was run down in traffic while chasing me. But when I went back, the body had disappeared. Either he survived and got out on his own, or someone picked him up. He'd seen me, which is why I shaved my beard—to make myself more difficult to identify. Someone just tried to kill me again, maybe the same asshole."

"What exactly did Dad say?"

"That he was very worried. He told me, 'I stumbled onto something . . . an account for about twenty million dollars in an international bank. I'm not sure exactly what it means, but I think it has to do somehow with Islamic terrorism.'"

Judd inhaled sharply.

Tucker nodded. "He was shot before he could say anything more than he'd found the information in the Library of Gold."

Judd's eyebrows rose. "He told the story about the library to me as if it were fiction. You're certain he said he found out in the library?"

"He said the library was key. That he'd been there." He saw a flicker of hurt in Judd's eyes. "Everyone has secrets. Your father was no exception."

"And this one killed him. Maybe."

"Maybe." An idea occurred to him. "Were you on the motorcycle behind me?"

"It's parked up the block. I got the license tag of the Chevy that was chasing you. I can't have it traced—you can. He lost me in Silver Spring, dammit." He slid his gun inside his jacket. "Sorry, Tucker. I had to be sure about you."

Tucker realized sweat had beaded up on his forehead. "What's the plate number?"

Judd gave it to him. Tucker walked back through the garage to the driver's side door of his car.

Judd followed. "Let's work on this together."

"Not on your life, Judson. You're out of the game, remember? You've got a row house on the Hill, and you're taking some time off."

"That was before some goddamn sniper killed Dad. I'll find his killer on my own if I have to."

Tucker turned and glared. "You're impetuous, and you're too close to this. He was *your father,* for God's sake. I can't have anyone working with me I can't trust."

"Would you really have handled it any differently?" Before Tucker could answer, Judd continued. "It's only logical I'd be suspicious. Maybe you were responsible for Dad's death. You could've tried to liquidate me, too. Look at it another way: You don't want to be tripping over me. I sure as hell don't want you in my way, either."

Tucker opened the car door and sighed. "All right. I'll think about it. But if I agree, you take orders from me. *Me,* get it? No more grandstanding. Now rip that bug off my car."

"Sure—if you drive me to my bike."

"Jesus Christ. Get in."

CHAPTER 5

AS SOON AS HE DROPPED off Judd Ryder, Tucker Andersen phoned headquarters.

"I'm coming in now."

Watching carefully around, he parked the Olds at the back of a busy mall outside Chevy Chase, caught a taxi, and phoned his wife. Then he hailed another cab, this time directing it back to Capitol Hill.

The headquarters of the highly secret Catapult team was a Federalist brick house northeast of the Capitol in a vibrant neighborhood of lively bars, restaurants, and one-of-a-kind shops. This sort of busy neighborhood provided good cover for Catapult, a special CIA counteroperations unit—counterterrorism, counterintelligence, countermeasures, counterproliferation, counterinsurgency. Catapult worked covertly behind the scenes, taking aggressive action to direct or stop negative events, both in triage and planning.

Tucker let the taxi pass the unit's weathered brick house with its shiny black door and shutters. The porch lamps were alight. The discreet sign above the door announced COUNCIL FOR PEER EDUCATION.

Three blocks later, he got out and strolled back as if nothing was on his mind. But once inside the fenced lot, he hurried past the security cameras to the side door, where he tapped his code onto the electronic keyboard. After a series of soft clicks, he pushed open the door. It was heavy steel, engineered to protect a bank vault.

He stepped into the hallway. While the exterior of the house was elegant with history, the interior was utilitarian and cutting-edge. The plaster walls and thick moldings were painted in muted greens and grays, and stark black-and-white photographs of cities from around the planet hung on them, reminding the few who were allowed to enter of the far reach of Catapult.

Glancing up, he noted the needle-nose cameras and dime-size motion detectors as he passed a couple of staffers carrying high-security blue folders. In the reception area, the office manager, Gloria Feit, reigned from behind her big metal desk. To his right was the front entry, while to the left a long corridor extended back into the house, where there were offices, the library, and the communications center. Upstairs were more offices, a conference room, and two large bedrooms with cots for covert officers and special visitors in transit.

Gloria's shift had begun at eight o'clock that morning, but she still looked fresh. A small woman with crinkled smile lines around her eyes, she was in her late forties. Once a field op herself, she and Tucker had worked together off and on for two decades.

Her brows rose over her rainbow-rimmed reading glasses. "You're on time."

It was a constant debate between them, since he often ran late. "How can you tell? I'm usually here."

"Except when you're not. Did you have good luck?"

"Luck is the result of preparation. I was prepared. But I didn't have as much luck as I'd hoped. Sometimes I think you know too much, Gloria."

She smiled. "Then you've got to quit telling me."

"Good point."

She had a remarkable memory, and he relied on her for details he occasionally lost in the barrage of information with which he dealt daily. Plus she was a walking encyclopedia of those with whom they had worked, both domestic and foreign.

"Why are you still here?" he asked. "You were supposed to go home hours ago."

"Now that you've arrived, I'll leave. Ted's taking me out for a late dinner. Karen called to check that you got into Catapult okay. You'd better phone her."

"Why does everyone worry about me so much?" But the truth was, Karen had spent too many years wondering where he was and sometimes whether he was alive.

"Because *you* worry, Tucker." Gloria turned off her computer. "The rest of us are necessary to make sure you're able to concentrate on worrying. It's a heavy job, but anything to serve the country." She grinned. "Your messages are on your desk. As soon as I saw you on the outside monitors, I let Cathy know you were here. She's waiting in your office. Have fun." She snapped up her purse, took out her car keys, and headed for the door.

Feeling the weight of Jonathan's death, Tucker walked down the long corridor. His office was the last one, chosen because it was quieter when the place was most active. As second in command, he got a few concessions, and his office was his favorite one.

He opened the door. Sitting in one of the two standard-issue armchairs in front of his cluttered desk was Catherine Doyle, the chief of Catapult.

She turned. "You look like crap."

"That good? Thanks." He shot her a grin and went to his desk.

Cathy Doyle chuckled. She was the same height as Tucker and dressed in a camel-colored pantsuit, her ankle boots planted firmly on the carpet. At fifty-plus, she was still a beauty, with short, blond-streaked hair and porcelain skin. She had been a model to support herself through New York University, graduating Phi Beta Kappa, then went on to earn a Ph.D. in international affairs from Columbia University, where Langley had recruited her.

"Gloria's gone home." He sat. "I can call over to Communications for coffee or tea."

"I wouldn't mind something stronger."

"That strikes me just fine." Tucker rotated in his chair to the file cabinet and unlocked the bottom drawer. He pulled out a bottle of Johnny Walker Red Label Scotch and held it up, looking back.

Cathy nodded, and Tucker poured two fingers into two water glasses. The spicy fragrance of the blended whiskey rose into the air, complex in its smokiness and scents of malted grain and wood. He handed a glass to her and cradled his, warming it between his palms.

"That license plate number came up," she told him. "It belongs to a Chevrolet Malibu reported stolen earlier today."

"Not surprising. Anything about the Library of Gold, an international bank, and jihadist financing?"

A slew of Washington's agencies—CIA, FBI, DIA, Customs, the IRS, the Financial Crimes Enforcement Network, the Office of Foreign Assets and Control, and the Secret Service—sent names of suspect individuals and groups to Treasury, which then forwarded them to a vast database of dubious financial transactions. The database compared the names to existing files and identified any matches.

Cathy shook her head. "Nothing yet."

"What about SWIFT?"

The Society for Worldwide Interbank Financial Tele-communication, SWIFT monitored international financial transactions on behalf of U.S. counterterrorism efforts, looking for suspicious transactions that might be for terrorist financing, money laundering, or other criminal activity. The problem was, the information SWIFT had was no better than that provided by the banks at either end of the transactions.

"Nothing," she told him. "If we had at least the name of the bank, we'd have something to go on. In any case, the usual suspicious transactions have turned up, and they'll be investigated thoroughly anyway. And nothing about the Library of Gold was there, either."

"What about Jonathan Ryder? Travel records, phone logs."

"Zero so far. We're still looking." She studied him. "What's been happening with you?"

He told her about the funeral and listening to Judd Ryder's "bedtime story."

"Interesting the father would do that," she said. "Shows he had a longtime connection of some kind to the Library of Gold."

"Exactly. Then I went to the Ryders' place, and Judd and I searched Jonathan's office. The only thing I found was a file in his desk—an unmarked file." He handed the clippings to her. As she read them, he said, "All are about recent terrorist activity in Pakistan and Afghanistan—mostly the Taliban and al-Qaeda. In terms of money, there's one about how difficult it is to track jihadist financing—finding a needle in a haystack is the cliché the article uses. Another talks about how subsidiary jihadist groups are funding themselves through fraud, kidnappings, bank heists, petty crime—just a fraction of what we know—and then tithing back to al-Qaeda central."

Decimated by intelligence agencies and the military, and largely cut off from previous sources of income, al-Qaeda's highly skilled, operationally sophisticated inner circle no longer could carry out attacks across continents. Now the major threat was the al-Qaeda movement—the numerous regional franchises and grassroots operations being born or refashioning themselves as affiliates.

"I'm eager to hear what the analysts think," Tucker said. "Several banks are mentioned in the articles. Right now it seems to me Jonathan was gathering research but didn't know precisely what he was looking for."

"My thought, too, although he was focusing on the two countries." She set the clippings on his desk.

"After I left the Ryders', I had another incident." He described the Chevy Malibu's chase. "I figure the guy spotted me at Jonathan's funeral, so he knows what I look like now. I can't drive the Olds again until this is over."

"Damn right. You can't go home, either. He may figure out where you live."

"I'll sleep here. It's cozy." He grimaced and drank. "Karen's packing. She's driving to a friend of hers in the Adirondacks until this is over. You have the adjustments to my cover at State set up?"

"I did that first. Probably an hour ago. Took you long enough to get here."

"I had to dry-clean my trail—you know the drill." He sat back, turning his whiskey glass in his hands. "I got a hit about the Library of Gold in our database. A few years ago a man who claimed to be the chief librarian managed to get in touch with one of our operatives. He said all sorts of international criminal activity

was going on with the book club—those are the people
who own it—and he couldn't escape. Unless we extracted him."

"What kind of activity?"

"He wouldn't be specific. Claimed the information
might be traced back to him and get him killed, but
he'd tell us everything once he was safe. When we
asked him to prove his bona fides, he smuggled out one
of the illuminated manuscripts—*The Book of Spies*. It
was created in the 1500s. We lost contact with him after that, and now Langley has the book somewhere in
storage."

She nodded thoughtfully. "You have a plan?"

"I'm putting one together."

"Okay, but it'll be hard to let you have any bodies.
I'm shorthanded as it is, especially if you're going to
work on this."

"No problem." He described how Judd had found
him in the garage where he had hidden from the Chevy.
"His full name is Judson Clayborn Ryder. I want to put
him on board as a private contractor. He's got the credentials, and I can use him."

"Bad idea. He's emotionally involved."

"True, but he calmed down quickly, and he's going to
look into it no matter what. This way I can keep my eye
on him, and he was military intelligence, so he's got
expertise."

She thought about it. Finished her whiskey. "I'll have
Langley check his background."

CHAPTER 6

Jefferson County, Missouri

THE NIGHT WAS CRISP and clear over Missouri's rolling hills as the man exited Interstate 55, heading west past farms and woodland. The truck was a Class-6 Freightliner with sweet power steering. His fingers bounced on the wheel as he watched the countryside pass by. On the seat beside him lay an M4 carbine rifle, the primary weapon for most special forces soldiers and rangers. It was an old friend, and when he moonlighted like this, he brought it along for companionship. He smiled, thinking about the money he was going to make.

The clothing factory lay ahead. It was squat, the size of a football field, encircled by a high chain-link fence and concertina wire. Stopping at the gate, he showed the credentials Preston had given him. The sleepy security guard glanced at them and waved him through.

Breathing a sigh of relief, he drove on, counting the loading docks sticking out like gray teeth on the south side of the building. When he figured out which number three, he circled the truck and backed up to it. The brakes huffed.

Once on the dock, he swore, staring at the mountain of crates. For two hours he labored, driving his dolly between the dock and the open maw of the truck, packing the boxes inside. It was a lousy job for one man. He was going to bitch to Preston about that. Who would've thought uniforms would take up so much room?

When he finished, he was sweaty. Still, at least this part, the most dangerous part, was finished. He climbed behind the wheel and drove sedately toward the guard kiosk. The gate opened as he approached, and he passed safely through. That was the thing about Preston. He knew how to plan a job. He grabbed his cell phone and punched in the number. Time to give him the good news.

San Diego County, California

THE YOUNG MAN PARKED his stolen sedan under the branches of a pepper tree at the distant edge of the sprawling truck stop off busy Interstate 15. He slid his FAMAS bullpup service rifle into its special holster inside his long jacket and got out, walking casually through the nighttime shadows along the rim of the parking lot, staying far from the brightly lit station with its restaurant, sleeping rooms, truck wash, and repair garage. With the trucks roaring in and out, the stink of diesel, and the taste of exhaust fumes, the place was an assault on the senses.

Scanning carefully, he headed toward thirty trucks parked in neat rows, their lights off while their drivers were inside tending to business, food, or entertainment. The truck he wanted was a Class-7 Peterbilt, a heavy eighteen-wheeler.

He found it quickly, then read the license plate to be sure. Satisfied, he glanced around, then tried the door. As expected, it was unlocked. He hiked himself inside. The key was in the ignition. He fired up the engine, noted the tank was full, and drove off. As soon as he was on the interstate, he phoned Preston.

Howard County, Maryland

AT LAST MARTIN CHAPMAN HEARD the car in his drive. He looked out of his third-floor window, the moon spilling silver light across Maryland's hunt country. His wife was at their château in San Moritz, catching the end of the ski season, and the interior of his big plantation-style home was silent. His German shepherds barked outside on the grounds, and the horses whinnied from the pasture and barns. The security lights were shining brightly, displaying only a fraction of his enormous Arabian horse spread.

He pressed the intercom button. "I'll get the door, Bradley. Go back to sleep." Bradley was his houseman, a faithful employee of twenty years.

Still dressed, Chapman glanced at the photo on his desk, showing Gemma in a long tight gown, diamonds sparkling at her ears and around her throat, and him in a rented tuxedo. They were smiling widely. It was his favorite portrait, taken years before, while he was studying at UCLA and she at USC, miles apart geographically, worlds apart economically, but deeply in love. Now both were in their early fifties. Full of warm emotion, he pulled himself away, a tall man with a head of thick white hair brushed back in waves, blue eyes, and an unlined, untroubled face.

Hurrying downstairs, he opened the door. Doug Preston stood on the long brick porch, golf cap in his hands.

Rangy and athletic, Preston radiated calm confidence. Forty-two years old, he had honed, aristocratic features. Little showed on his deeply tanned face except his usual neutral expression, but Chapman knew the man better than he knew himself: There was tightness around his eyes, and his lips had thinned. Something had happened Preston did not like.

"Come in," Chapman said brusquely. "Do you want a drink?"

Preston gave a deferential nod, and Chapman led him into his enormous library, where towering shelves lined the walls, filled with leather-bound volumes. He looked at them appreciatively, then headed for the bar, where he poured bourbon and branch water for both of them.

With a polite thank-you, Preston picked up his drink, walked to the French doors, and peered out into the night.

Watching him, Chapman felt a moment of impatience, then repressed it. Preston must be handled carefully, which was why he manipulated him with the same adroitness he lavished on his multibillion-dollar, highly competitive business.

"What have you learned about the stranger in the park?" Chapman asked, reining him in. Preston had run down the sniper with his Mercedes and pulled the corpse inside. The man had had to be eliminated; too many people had seen his face.

Preston turned and made a focused report: "I waited outside Jonathan Ryder's funeral, got photos of the guy who was with Mr. Ryder in the park, and ran them through several data banks. His name is Tucker Andersen. He works for State. I followed Andersen to the Ryder house, then picked him up when he left. I wasn't able to scrub him—the man drives as if he's a NAS-CAR pro. That kind of talent could mean something, but maybe it doesn't. So I called a high-level contact in State Human Resources. Andersen is a documents specialist, and he's scheduled to leave for Geneva tonight for a UN conference on Middle East affairs. It lasts three weeks. I checked, and he has a reservation at the conference hotel. Just to make sure, I've put a team on his house in Virginia, and I'll keep in close touch with my man at State. If Andersen doesn't leave, we'll know we've got trouble. I'll be ready for him and take him out."

Chapman heard the annoyance in Preston's voice. The failure to liquidate Andersen was difficult to swallow for a man who detested loose ends.

Still, all was not lost. "Good work." Chapman paused, noted the flash of gratitude in Preston's eyes. "What about the District police?"

For the first time, Preston smiled. "They're still not asking any questions about the library, and they would be by now if they knew about it. It's beginning to look as if Mr. Ryder either didn't or wasn't able to tell Andersen anything important." Chief of security for the Library of Gold for more than ten years, Preston was a man passionate about books and completely loyal, traits not only prized but required of library employees.

"That'd be a good result." Chapman moved on to his next concern: "What about the library dinner?"

Preston drank deeply, relaxing. "Everything's on track. The food, the chefs, the transportation."

Book club members had been flying into the library throughout the past month, working with the translators to find and research questions in preparation for the annual banquet's tournament. It was during Jonathan's visit to the library just days before that he had learned about Chapman's new business deal and become alarmed.

"Where are you with the Khost project?" Khost was

a province in eastern Afghanistan, on the border with Pakistan. It was there Chapman planned to make back his huge losses from the global economic crash, and more.

"On schedule. The uniforms and equipment have been picked up. They'll be shipped out in the morning. I've got it well in hand."

"See that it stays that way. Nothing must interfere with it. Nothing. And keep your eye on the situation with Tucker Andersen. We don't want it to explode in our faces."

CHAPTER 7

Chowchilla, California
Two weeks later

AT 1:32 P.M. TUCKER ANDERSEN finished briefing the warden of the Central California Women's Facility. She was a stout woman with graying brown hair and a habit of folding her hands in front of her. She escorted him out of her private office.

"Tell me about Eva Blake," Tucker said.

"She doesn't complain, and she hasn't gotten any 115 write-ups," the warden said. "She started on the main yard, tidying up and emptying trash cans. Ten months ago we rewarded her with an assembly-line job in our electronics factory. In her free time she listens to the radio, keeps up with her karate, and volunteers—she teaches literacy classes and reads to inmates in the hospital ward. A couple of months ago she sent out a raft of résumés, but none of the other convicts knows it. There's an unwritten law here—you don't ask an inmate sister what she's done or what she's doing. Blake has been smart and kept her mouth shut about herself."

"Who are her visitors?" Tucker asked as they passed the guard desk.

"Family occasionally, from out of state. A friend used to drive up every few months from L.A.—Peggy Doty, a former colleague. Ms. Doty hasn't been to see her in a while. I believe she's working at the British Library in London now. This is Blake's housing unit."

They stepped into a world of long expanses of linoleum flooring, closed doors, harsh fluorescent lighting, and an ear-bleed volume of noise—intercoms crackling, television programs blaring from the dayrooms, and loud shouts and curses.

The warden glanced at him. "They yell as much to give them something to do as to express themselves. We're at double capacity here, so the noise is twice as loud as it should be. Blake is in the unit's yard. She gets three hours every day if she wants it. She always does."

The warden nodded at the guard standing at the door. He opened it, and the raw odor of farmland fertilizer swept toward them. They stepped outside, where the Central Valley sun pounded down onto an open space of grass, concrete, and dirt. Women sat, napped, and moved aimlessly. Beyond them rose high brick walls topped with electrified razor wire.

Tucker scanned the prisoners, looking for Eva Blake. He had studied photos as well as a video of the court appearance in which she had pleaded guilty to vehicular manslaughter in the death of her husband. He looked for her red hair, pretty face, lanky frame.

"You don't recognize her, do you?" the warden asked. "She's that one."

He followed her nod to a woman in a baggy prison shirt and trousers, walking around the perimeter of the yard. Her hair was completely hidden, tucked up into a baseball cap. Her expression was blank, her posture nonthreatening. She looked little like the very alive woman in the photos and video.

"She goes around the yard hour after hour, loop after loop. She's alone because she wants it that way. As I said, she's smart—she's learned to make herself invisible, uninteresting. Anyone who's interesting around here can attract violence."

Impressive both in her attitude and her ability to be inconspicuous, Tucker thought.

The warden clasped her hands in front of her. "I'm going to give you some advice. In prison, male cons either obey orders or defy them. Female cons ask why. Don't lie to her. But if you have to, make damn sure she doesn't catch you at it, at least not while you're trying to convince her to do whatever it is you want her to do. You really aren't going to tell me what's going on, are you?"

"It's national security."

She gave a curt nod, and Tucker walked across the grass toward Eva Blake, catcalls and whistles trailing him. He wondered how long it would take her to realize she was his goal. A good hundred yards away, her strides grew nervy, and her chin lifted. She stopped and, in a slow, deliberate pivot, turned to face him. Her arms were apparently restful at her sides, but her stance was wide and balanced, a karate stance. Her reaction time was excellent, and from the way she moved, she was still in good physical condition.

He walked up to her. "Doctor Blake, my name is Tucker Andersen. I'd like to talk to you. The warden's given us an interview room."

"Why?" Her face was a mask.

"I may have a proposition for you. If so, I suspect you'll like it."

She peered around him, and he glanced back.

The warden was still standing in the doorway. Looking severe, she nodded at Blake. That made it an order.

"Whatever you say," Blake said, relaxing her posture slightly.

As she started to move around him, she stumbled and twisted her ankle, bumping into him. He grabbed her shoulders, helping her. Regaining her equilibrium, she excused herself, moved away, and walked steadily back toward the prison.

THE INTERVIEW ROOM HAD PASTEL walls, a single metal table with four metal chairs, and cameras poking out high from two corners.

Tucker sat at the widest part of the table and gestured at the other chairs. "Choose your poison."

Not a smile. Eva Blake sat at the end. "You say your name is Tucker Andersen. Where are you from?"

"McLean, Virginia. Why?"

She pulled his wallet from beneath her shirt, opened it, and read the driver's license, checking on him. She spread out the credit cards, all in the same name. She nodded to herself, put the billfold back together, and handed it to him. "First time I've ever seen a 'visitor' in the yard on a nonvisitor day."

He had not felt her pick his pocket, but her bumping into him had been a clue. As he followed her into the prison, he had patted his jacket and found the wallet missing.

"Nice dipping," he said mildly, "but then you're experienced, aren't you."

Her eyes widened a fraction.

Good, he had surprised her. "Your juvenile record is sealed. You should've had it expunged."

"You were able to get into my juvenile record?" she asked.

"I can, and I did. Tell me what happened."

She said nothing.

"Okay, I'll tell you," he said. "When you were fourteen, you were what is commonly called wild. You sneaked beers. Smoked some grass. Some of your friends shoplifted. You tried it, too. Then a man who looked like plainclothes security spotted you in Macy's. Instead of reporting you, he complimented you and asked whether you had the guts to go for the big time. It turned out he didn't work for the store—he was a master dipper running a half-dozen teams. He taught you the trade. You hustled airports, ball games, train stations, that sort of thing. Because you're beautiful, you usually played the distraction, prepping and positioning vics. But then when you were sixteen, a pickpocket on your team was escaping with the catch when some cops spotted him. He ran into traffic to get away—"

She lowered her head.

"He was hit by a semi and killed," Tucker continued. "Everyone beat feet getting out of there. You were gone, too. But for some reason you changed your mind and went back and talked to the police. They arrested you, of course. Then they asked you to help them bust the gang, which you did. Why?"

"We were all so young . . . it just seemed right to try to stop it while maybe we had time to grow up into better people."

"And later you used the skill to work your way through UCLA."

"But legally. At a security company. Who are you?"

He ignored the question. "You're probably going to be released on probation next year, so you've been sending out résumés. Any nibbles?"

She looked away. "No museum or library wants to hire a curator or conservator who's a felon, at least not me. Too much baggage because of . . . my husband's death. Because he was so well-known and respected in the field." She fingered a gold chain around her neck. Whatever was hanging from it was hidden beneath her shirt. He noted she was still wearing her wedding band, a simple gold ring.

"I see," he said neutrally.

She lifted her chin. "I'll find something. Some other kind of work."

He knew she was out of money. Because she had been convicted of her husband's manslaughter, she could not collect his life insurance. She'd had to sell her house to pay her legal bills. He felt a moment of pity, then banished it.

He observed, "You've become very good at masking your emotions."

"It's just what you have to do to make it in here."

"Tell me about the Library of Gold."

That seemed to take her aback. "Why?"

"Indulge me."

"You said you had a proposition for me. One I'd like."

"I said I *might* have a proposition for you. Let's see how much you remember."

"I remember a lot, but Charles, my husband—Dr. Charles Sherback—was a real authority. He'd spent his life researching the library and knew every available detail." Her voice was proud.

"Start at the beginning."

She recounted the story from the library's growth in the days of the Byzantine Empire to its disappearance at Ivan the Terrible's death.

He listened patiently. Then: "What happened to it?"

"No one knows for sure. After Peter the Great died, a note was found in his papers that said Ivan had hidden the books under the Kremlin. Napoléon, Stalin, Putin, and ordinary people have hunted for centuries, but there are at least twelve levels of tunnels down there, and the vast majority are unmapped. Its location is one of the world's great mysteries."

"Do you know what's in the library?"

"It's supposed to contain poetry and novels. Books about science, alchemy, religion, war, politics, even sex manuals. It dates all the way back to the ancient Greeks and Romans, so there are probably works by Aristophanes, Virgil, Pindar, Cicero, and Sun Tzu. There are Bibles and Torahs and Korans, too. All sorts of languages—Latin, Hebrew, Arabic, Greek."

Tucker was quiet a moment, considering. After a rocky start as a teenager, she had righted herself to go on to a high-level career, which showed talent, brains, and responsibility. She had muted herself to fit into prison, and that indicated adaptability. Pickpocketing him because he was an aberration told him she still had nerve. He was operating in a vacuum with this mission. None of the targeting analysts had found anything useful, and the collection of Jonathan Ryder's clippings had turned out to be little help.

He studied the face beneath the prison cap, the sculpted lines, the expression that had settled back into chilly neutrality. "What would you say if I told you I have evidence the Library of Gold is very much in existence?"

"I'd say tell me more."

"The Lessing J. Rosenwald Collection has loaned some of its illuminated manuscripts to the British Museum for a special show. The highlight is *The Book of Spies*. Do you know the work?"

"Never heard of it."

"The book arrived at the reference door to the Library of Congress wrapped in foam inside a cardboard box. There was an unsigned note saying it had been in the Library of Gold and was a donation to the Rosenwald Special Collection. They tested the paper and ink and so forth. The book's authentic. No one's been able to trace the donor or donors."

"That's all the evidence you have it's from the Library of Gold?"

He nodded. "For now it's enough."

"Does this mean you want to find the library?" When he nodded, she said, "What can I do to help?"

"Opening night of the British Museum exhibit is next week. Your job would be to do what you used to do when you traveled with your husband. Talk to the librarians, historians, and afficionados who've been trying to find the library for years. Eavesdrop on conversations among them and others. We hope if *The Book of Spies* really did come from the collection it'll attract someone who knows the library's location."

She had been leaning forward. She sat back. Emotions played across her face. "What's in it for me?"

"If you do a good job, you'll return to prison of course. But then in just four months, you'll be released on parole—assuming you continue your good record. That's eight months early."

"What's the downside?"

"No downside except you'll have to wear a GPS ankle bracelet. It's tamper-resistant and has a built-in GSM/GPRS transmitter that'll automatically report your location. You can remove it at night, to make sleeping more comfortable, if you wish. I'll give you a cell phone, too. You'll report to me, and you must tell no one, not even the warden, what you'll be doing or what you learn."

She was silent. "You opened my juvenile record. You can get me out of prison. And you can reduce my sentence. Before I agree, I want to know who you really are."

He started to shake his head.

She warned, "The first price of my help is the truth."

He remembered what the warden had said about not lying to the inmates. "I'm with the Central Intelligence Agency."

"That's not in your billfold."

He reached down and un-Velcroed a pocket inside his calf-high sock. He handed her the ID. "You must tell no one. Agreed?"

She studied the laminated official identification. "Agreed. If anyone there knows where the library is, I'll find out. But when I'm finished, I don't want to come back to prison."

Inwardly he smiled, pleased by her toughness. "Done."

Years seem to fall from her. "When do I leave?"

CHAPTER 8

London, England

THE WORLD SEEMED EXCITINGLY new to Eva—no handcuffs, no prison guards, no eyes watching her around the clock. It was 8:30 P.M. and raining heavily as she hurried across the forecourt toward the British Museum. She hardly felt the cold wet on her face. London's traffic thundered behind her, and her old Burberry trench coat was wrapped around her. She looked up at the looming columns, the sheer stone walls, the Greek Revival carvings and statues. Memories filled her of the good times she and Charles had spent in the majestic old museum.

Dodging a puddle, she ran lightly up the stone steps, closed her umbrella, and entered the Front Hall. It was ablaze with light, the high ceiling fading up into dramatic darkness. She paused at the entrance to the Queen Elizabeth Great Court, two sweeping acres of marble flooring rimmed by white Portland stone walls and columned entryways. She drank in its serene beauty.

At its center stood the circular Reading Room, one of the world's finest libraries—and coming out its door were Herr Professor and Frau Georg Mendochon.

Smiling, Eva went to greet them. With glances at each other, they hesitated.

"Timma. Georg." She extended her hand. "It's been years."

"How are you, Eva?" Georg's accent was light. He was a globe-trotting academic from Austria.

"It's wonderful to see you again," she said sincerely.

"*Ja.* And we know why it has been so long." Timma had never been subtle. "What are you doing here?" What she did not say was, *You killed your husband, how dare you show up.*

Eva glanced down, staring at the gold wedding band on her finger. She had known this was going to be difficult. She had come to accept that she had killed Charles, but the guilt of it still ravaged her.

Looking up, she ignored Timma's tone. "I was hoping to see old friends. And to view *The Book of Spies,* of course."

"It is very exciting, this discovery," Georg agreed.

"It makes me wonder whether someone has finally found the Library of Gold," Eva continued. "If anyone has, surely it's you, Georg"—now that Charles is gone, she thought to herself, missing him even more.

Georg laughed. Timma relented and smiled at the compliment.

"*Ach*, I wish," he said.

"There's no word anyone's close to its discovery?" Eva pressed.

"I have heard nothing like that, alas," Georg said. "Come, Timma. We must go to the Chinese exhibit now. We will see you upstairs, Eva, yes?"

"Definitely, yes."

As they crossed the Great Hall, Eva headed toward

the North Wing and climbed the stairs to the top floor. The sounds of a multilingual crowd drifted from a large open doorway where a sign announced:

TRACING THE DEVELOPMENT OF WRITING
SPECIAL EXHIBITION FROM THE LESSING J. ROSENWALD COLLECTION

She found her invitation.

The guard took it. "Enjoy yourself, mum."

She stepped inside. Excited energy infused the vast hall. People stood in groups and gathered around the glass display cases, many wearing tiny earphones as they listened to the show's prerecorded tour. Museum guards in dress clothes circulated discreetly. The air smelled the way she remembered, of expensive perfumes and aromatic wines, She inhaled deeply.

"Eva, is that you?"

She turned. It was Guy Fontaine from the Sorbonne. Small and plump, he was standing with a huddle of Charles's friends. She scanned their faces, saw their conflicted emotions at her arrival.

She said a warm hello and shook hands.

"You're looking well, Eva," Dan Ritenburg decided. He was a wealthy amateur Library of Gold hunter from Sydney. "How is it you're able to be here?"

"Do not be crass, Dan," Antonia del Toro scolded. From Madrid, she was an acclaimed historian. She turned to Eva. "I am so sorry about Charles. Such a dedicated researcher, although admittedly he could be difficult at times. My condolences."

Several others murmured their sympathies. Then there was an expectant pause.

Eva spoke into it, answering their unasked question. "I've been released from prison." That was what Tucker had told her to say. "When I saw there was a manuscript from the Library of Gold here, of course I had to come."

"Of course," Guy agreed. "*The Book of Spies.* It is beautiful. *Incroyable.*"

"Do you think its appearance means someone has found the library?" Eva asked.

The group erupted in talk, voicing their theories that the library was still beneath the Kremlin, that Ivan the Terrible had hidden it in a monastery outside Moscow, that it was simply a glorious myth perpetuated by Ivan himself.

"But if it's a myth, why is *The Book of Spies* here?" Eva wanted to know.

"Aha, my point exactly," said Desmond Warzel, a Swiss academic. "I have always maintained that before he died Ivan sold it off in bits and pieces because his treasury was low. Remember, he lost his last war with Poland—and it was expensive."

"But if that's true," Eva said reasonably, "surely other illuminated manuscripts from the library would've appeared by now."

"She is right, Desmond," Antonia said. "Just what I have been telling you all these years."

They continued to argue, and eventually Eva excused herself. Listening to conversations, looking for more people she knew, she wove through the throngs and then stopped at the bar. She ordered a Perrier.

"Don't I know you, ma'am?" the bar steward asked.

He was tall and thin, but with the chubby face of a chipmunk. The contrast was startling and endearing. Of course she recalled him.

"I used to come here a few years ago," she told him.

He grinned and handed her the Perrier. "Welcome home."

Smiling, she stepped away to check the map showing

where in the room each woodcut book, illuminated manuscript, and printed book was displayed. When she found the location of *The Book of Spies,* she walked toward it, passing the spectacular *Giant Bible of Mainz,* finished in 1453, and the much smaller and grotesquely illustrated *Book of Urizen,* from 1818. It was William Blake's parody of Genesis. A few years ago, on a happy winter day, Charles and she had personally examined each in the Library of Congress.

The crowd surrounding *The Book of Spies* was so thick, some on the fringes were giving up. Eva frowned, but not at the imposing human wall. What held her was a man leaving the display. There was something familiar about him. She could not see his face, because he was turned away and his hand clasped one ear as he listened to the tour.

What was it about him? She set her drink on a waiter's tray and followed, sidestepping other visitors. He wore a black trench coat, had glossy black hair, and the back of his neck was tanned. She wanted to get ahead so she could see his face, but the crowd made it hard to move quickly.

Then he stepped into an open space, and for the first time she had a clear view of his entire body, of his physicality. Her heart quickened as she studied him. His gait was athletic, rolling. His muscular shoulders twitched every six or eight steps. He radiated great assurance, as if he owned the hall. He was the right height—a little less than six feet tall. Although his hair should have been light brown, not blue-black, and she still could not see his face, everything else about him was uncannily, thrillingly familiar. He could have been Charles's double.

He dropped his hand from his ear. Excited, Eva moved quickly onward until she was walking almost parallel to him. He was surveying the crowd, his head slowly moving from right to left. Finally she saw his face. His chin was wider and heavier than Charles's, and his ears flared slightly where Charles's had laid flat against his skull. Overall he looked tough, like a man who had been on the losing end of too many fist-fights.

But then his gaze froze on her. He stopped moving. He had Charles's eyes—large and black, with flecks of brown, surrounded by thick lashes. She and Charles had lived together eight intimate years, and she knew every gesture, every nuance of his expressions, and how he reacted. His eyes radiated shock, then narrowed in fear. He tilted back his head—pride. And finally there was the emotionless expression she knew so well when confronted with the unexpected. His lips formed the word *Eva*.

The room seemed to fade away, and the chattering talk vanished as she tried to breathe, to feel the beat of her heart, to know her feet were planted firmly on the floor. She struggled to think, to understand how Charles could still be alive. Relief washed through her as she realized she had not killed him. But how could he have survived the car crash? Abruptly her grief and guilt turned into stunned rage. She had lost two years because of him. Lost most of her friends. Her reputation. Her career. She had mourned and blamed herself—while he had been alive the entire time.

As he scowled at her, she pulled out her cell phone, touched the keypad, and focused the cell's video camera on him.

His scowl deepened, and with a jerk of his head, he cupped his left ear and dove into the crowd.

"Charles, wait!" She rushed after him, dodging people, leaving a trail of disgusted remarks.

He brushed past an older couple and slid deeper into the masses. She raised up on her toes and spotted him skirting a display cabinet. She ran. As he elbowed past a circle of women, his shoulder hit a waiter carrying a tray of full wineglasses. The tray cartwheeled; the glasses sailed. Red wine splashed the women. They yelled and slipped on their high heels.

While guests stared, security guards grabbed radios off their belts, and Charles dashed out the door. Eva tore after him and down the stairs. The guards shouted for them to stop. As she reached the landing, a sentry peeled away from the wall, lowering his radio.

"Stop, miss!" He raced toward her, pendulous belly jiggling.

She put on a burst of speed, and the guard had no time to correct. His hands grabbed at her trench coat and missed. Stumbling forward, he fell across the railing, balancing precariously over the full-story drop.

She stopped to go back to help, but a man in a dark blue peacoat leaped down three steps and pulled the guard back to safety.

Cursing the time she had lost, Eva resumed her pell-mell run down the steps, the feet of guards hammering behind her. When she landed on the first floor, she accelerated past the elevators and into the cavernous Great Court. Thunder cracked loudly overhead, and a burst of rain pelted the high glass dome.

She saw Charles again. With an angry glance back at her across the wide expanse, he hurtled past a hulking statue of the head of the Egyptian pharaoh Amenhotep III.

She chased after, following him into the museum's Front Hall. Visitors fell back, silent, confused, as he rushed past. Two sentries were standing on either side of the open front door, both holding radios to their ears and looking as if they had just been given orders.

As Charles approached them, she saw his back stiffen.

His words floated back to her, earnestly telling the pair in Charles's deep voice, "She's a madwoman. . . . She has a knife."

Enraged, she ran faster. The guards glanced at each other, and Charles took advantage of their distraction to lunge between them and sprint out into the stormy night.

Silently Eva swore. The two guards had recovered and were standing shoulder to shoulder, facing her, blocking the opening.

"Halt," the taller of the two commanded.

She bolted straight at them. As their eyes narrowed, she paused and slammed the heels of her hands into each man's solar plexis in *teishō* karate strikes.

Surprised, the air driven from their lungs, they staggered, giving her just enough of an opening. In seconds she was outside. Cold rain bled in sheets from the roiling sky, drenching her, as she rushed down the stone steps.

Charles was a black sliver in the night, arms swinging as he propelled himself across the long forecourt toward the museum's entry gates.

"Dammit, Charles. Wait!"

The shriek of a police siren was growing louder, closer. Breathing hard, she raced after him and out onto Great Russell Street. Vehicles cruised past, their tires splashing dark waves of water up onto the sidewalk. Pedestrians hurried along, umbrellas open, a phalanx of bobbing rain gear.

As she slowed, looking everywhere for Charles, hands grabbed her from behind. She struggled, but the hands held fast.

"You were told to halt," a museum guard ordered, panting.

Another one ripped away her shoulder satchel.

A Metropolitan Police car screeched to the curb. Uniformed bobbies jumped out and pushed Eva against the car, patting her down. Frustrated, furious, she twisted around and saw Charles step into a taxi near the end of the block. As she stared, its red taillights vanished into traffic.

CHAPTER 9

THE POLICE INTERVIEW ROOM was a cramped space on a lower floor of the thirteen-story Holborn Police Station, just seven blocks from the British Museum.

"Well, there, Dr. Blake, it seems you weren't being truthful with me." Metropolitan Police inspector Kent Collins nodded at the police guard standing in the corner, who nodded back. The inspector closed the door behind him, sealing out the world. "You told me your husband was dead. You didn't tell me you were convicted of killing him."

He was a bristly man with a large nose and, despite the late hour, smoothly shaved cheeks. Tough, impeccable, and definitely in charge, he was carrying a crisp new manila file folder under his arm.

Eva's hands were in her lap, rotating the gold wedding band on her finger. She had not been able to phone Tucker Andersen because she had not been alone since the police arrested her. His warning to tell no one about her assignment was loud in her mind. But how was she going to get out of this? Could she, even?

"I said Charles was *supposed* to be dead," she told the inspector. "If I'd filled you in on the rest, you might not have heard me out. The man I saw was Charles Sherback. My husband. Alive." Then she reminded him, "I'm not the one who lied to the museum guards. *He* did. He told them I had a knife. They searched me. There was no knife."

Inspector Collins slapped down his file folder and dropped into a plastic chair at the end of the table next to her so they would be sitting close but at a ninety-degree angle. She recognized the technique: If you want someone to resonate with you, sit shoulder to shoulder. But if you need to challenge them, face them. The ninety-degree angle gave him flexibility.

He turned, facing her. "We're a little on the busy side to be searching among the living for a man who's dead and buried."

"Charles not only lied about the knife, he ran because he recognized me."

"Or he ran because he was some innocent bloke you were harassing."

"But then he would've complained to the guards about me."

The inspector lost his patience. "Bollocks. You—not him—assaulted the two sentries at the museum's entrance."

"I didn't have time to stop to prove I didn't have a knife and explain why I needed to catch Charles. And another thing—I have a black belt in karate. I could've hurt the guards badly. Instead I hit them just hard enough to make them step back and take deep breaths. Did either file a personal complaint?" She suspected not, since there had been no mention of it.

"As a matter of fact, no."

She nodded. "This is a lot bigger than just me. Charles

is alive, and someone else must be buried in his grave. Will you please look for him?"

Inspector Collins's expression said it all—he thought she was mad. "How do you expect us to find him? You don't have an address. Nothing concrete at all."

She picked up her cell phone, touching buttons as she talked. "I shot a video of him at the museum."

Positioning the tiny screen so both could see, she started the clip. And there was a miniature Charles, standing tall in his black trench coat against the churning background of museumgoers. He was gazing straight at her, above the angle of the cell phone, and scowling.

"You can't see his gait yet," she told him. "The way he walks is important. He's an athlete, and he moves like one, with a little bit of a slouch and a roll to his steps. His shoulders twitch periodically, too. It's really distinctive. He's also the right age and right height. The right eye color and voice, too."

In the video, Charles looked down.

"This is where he spotted my cell phone," she explained.

Charles lifted his hand to his ear, turned abruptly, and was swallowed by the crowd. Inwardly she swore. He had moved so swiftly she had no record of his walk. The video ended.

"That's it?" The inspector's focus felt like an assault. "That's all you have?"

"It's something. A beginning."

"You said other people were there whom you and your husband knew for years. If that were your husband—a dead man—they would've said something. In fact, I imagine they would've made quite a fuss." Shaking his head, the inspector opened his file, pulled out a sheet of paper, and slid it across the table. "The Los Angeles police e-mailed me this. Tell me who it is."

It was a portrait of Charles, shot for brochures for the Elaine Moreau Library. His refined features and glowing black eyes stared out at her.

"It's Charles, of course." Her voice was quiet. "After he disappeared he must've dyed his hair and had work done on his face."

The inspector jabbed a thumb at it. "This photo looks nothing like the man in your video." He gazed at her, challenging her. "I spoke to the prison. Is this the first time you thought you saw him since he died?"

She hesitated, then rallied. "Obviously you know it's not."

He pulled out another paper and read aloud: " 'In the first three weeks after Dr. Sherback died, Dr. Blake said she thought she had seen him twice. According to her account, she approached the men, who were friendly. But when she explained why she wanted to talk, they backed away.' "

The oxygen seemed to leave her lungs. "They looked similar to Charles." How could she get out of here so she could find him? She thought quickly. Then: "My husband and I were librarians and curators of ancient and medieval manuscripts. We used to fly around the world to attend openings like tonight's. Being back in that atmosphere again . . . perhaps you're right that I've made a huge mistake." She lowered her voice. "I miss him a great deal. I hope you can understand."

A flicker of compassion touched the inspector's bristly features. He peered at her, seeming to contemplate what to do.

Her entire body felt tight. She turned so her shoulder brushed his. "I'm really sorry to have caused so much trouble."

"Maybe you want him to be alive so you don't have to carry the guilt for what you've done," he said.

She gave him the answer he wanted to hear. "Yes."

There was pity in his tired eyes. Shrugging, he got to his feet. He pulled her passport from inside his sports coat and handed it to her. "Get on a plane tomorrow and go home. Make an appointment to see a therapist."

Eva gathered her things and followed Inspector Collins down the hall of the police station. As she listened to the breathy ventilation system, her mind kept returning to the man in the museum, the man she was certain was Charles, despite what she had told the inspector.

With each step, she reconstructed his profile, his height and age, the shocked recognition in his eyes. As they rode the elevator down, in her mind she replayed his words to the museum guards, hearing the familiar intonation of his voice.

The inspector left her, and she continued outdoors and stopped. As she stood in the shelter of the station house's doorway, she had a vision of Charles racing away through the stormy night. She could see his arms swinging at his sides. There was something about that. Something about his hands.

That was when she remembered. She took out her cell phone. She restarted the short video, staring hard. Freezing it, she pumped up the size of the image. Charles's left hand had been sliced badly in an accident at a dig in Turkey. If this man was Charles, there should be a long scar on his hand.

She half-expected to see smooth skin. Instead, her breath caught in her throat as she spotted it—a scar snaking blue-white across the top of his thumb and hand and then disappearing up under the cuff of his trench coat. *Charles.*

She jumped up and turned to go back into the station . . . and stopped herself. There was no way the police would help her. She considered Tucker Andersen. But he probably knew about the previous times she hoped she had seen Charles. He would not believe her, either.

But she needed to report in. She dialed his number.

There was no preamble. "What did you learn?" he asked instantly.

"I couldn't find anyone who knew anything new about the Library of Gold," she told him truthfully. "All of them have the usual theories."

"Pity. Go back to the museum tomorrow. Spend the day."

"Of course." She had bought herself some time.

Opening her umbrella, she walked through the sidewalk's lamplight, trying to gather her thoughts. Her marriage to Charles had not been perfect, but whose relationship ever was? With his death, the problems had vanished from her mind. She had loved him dearly, and she had thought he loved her. Fourteen years older, he was already celebrated in his career when they met. She remembered his walking into the classroom that first time; the long, confident strides. The handsome face that radiated intelligence and curiosity. He was the guest lecturer for an upper-division course where she was the assistant while working on her Ph.D. Quoting from Homer and Plato, he had charmed and impressed everyone.

"*Gratias tibi ago*, Dr. Sherback. *Benigne ades*," she had told him. Thank you. It was generous of you to come.

The crowd of admirers had dwindled away to just him and her.

He had peered down at her, taking her in. Then he spoke in Latin, too. "You remind me of Diana, goddess of the hunt, the moon, and protectress of dewy youth. Tell me, do you have an oak grove and a deer nearby?"

She laughed. "And my bow and arrow."

"Ah, yes, but then you're not only a huntress but an

emblem of chastity. No wonder you need your weapons. I hope you won't turn me into a stag as you did Acteon." The goddess had transformed Acteon when he saw her bathing naked in a stream, then set her hunting dogs on him.

"You are completely safe," she assured him. "I have no dogs, not even a teacup poodle."

He laughed, his eyes crinkling with good humor. "I like a woman who can speak Latin and who knows the ancient gods and goddesses. Will you join me for a cup of coffee?"

Colleagues, critics, and art lovers had admired him, and women had thrown themselves at him. But she was the one who had caught him. She had never suspected she was marrying a man who could pretend to be dead and send her to prison. But then, she like many others had been dazzled by him, by their lifestyle, and by her own dreams and ambitions.

As she moved along the street, the rain was a constant tattoo on her umbrella. She must find Charles. All she had was the short video. The inspector was right. It was not going to be enough. She took out her cell phone again and dialed Peggy Doty. Peggy had gotten back her old job at the British Library so she could be close to her boyfriend, Zack Turner, and Eva was staying with her while in London.

When Peggy's sleepy voice answered, Eva apologized, then said, "Remember the time I covered for you at the Getty when you took off for Paris to meet Zack for a few days? And the time I showed you the secret glue that's invisible and never fails? And then there was the time I blocked the sex-fiend tourist who was putting the moves on you."

There was a chuckle. "You must be desperate. What do you want?"

"It's a big favor, and I wouldn't ask if it weren't vital.

I need a copy of the security videos for the museum's opening tonight. Particularly those that include the people around *The Book of Spies*."

"What?"

"And I need them now. Right away. I'm walking toward the museum. I wouldn't ask unless I really did need them." With luck, they would show Charles chatting with someone she knew. Maybe he or she would have learned something useful.

There was a long silence. Finally Peggy said, "You want me to ask Zack." He was the head of security at the museum.

"He'll do anything for you. Please phone him."

On the other end of the line, a sigh sounded loudly. "I'll call you back."

Eva thanked her, following Theobalds Road, clasping her shoulder satchel to her side. But as she walked, she had a strange feeling. She peered back. A man in a blue peacoat was striding along about thirty feet behind. His face was in shadows. The man who had saved the museum guard from toppling over the staircase had also worn a blue peacoat. She looked again, but he was gone.

She headed north onto Southampton Row, then west onto Great Russell Street, where she found herself glancing at the cars speeding past. For a few heartbeats a bronze-colored Citroën slowed and paced her; then it rushed off. Uneasily she realized she had noticed it earlier. There was no one in the passenger seat, and she had been unable to see the driver.

At last the museum was in sight. She turned onto Montague Street, which ran along the massive building's east side and connected with Montague Place. The street was just a block long, one of the narrow lanes winding through Bloomsbury. There was no traffic, although parked cars lined the sidewalk. She peered back and thought she saw movement beneath the darkness of a tall tree.

Her cell rang. It was Peggy. Swiftly she asked, "Do you have good news?"

"Honey, Zack says he can't have copies made for you. It's against the rules. I'm so sorry. Come home. It's real late."

Eva closed her eyes, disappointed. "Thanks for trying. I'm sorry I disturbed you. I hope you can get back to sleep quickly." She touched the Off button.

Trying to decide what to do next, she was heading across the street when she heard the noise of a car's engine and felt the pavement vibrate beneath her feet. She peered left. The vehicle was rushing toward her, headlights off. Terror shot through her. She accelerated, but the car angled, keeping her targeted.

Ahead was the towering iron fence that surrounded the museum. Dropping her umbrella, she slapped the strap of her satchel across her chest and sprinted. With a silent prayer, she leaped high in a *tobi-geri* jump. Her hands closed around two wet rails, and her feet found two more for a precarious foothold.

Then she looked again. The car was a bronze-colored Citroën like the one that had paced her on Great Russell Street. But who—? She stared into the windshield. Charles? Oh dear God, it *was* Charles. His thick features looked frozen, his gaze vacant, but emotion showed in his hands. They were knotted around the steering wheel as if it were a noose.

With an abrupt movement, the Citroën jumped the curb and slammed along the fence. Sparks flew. The noise of the hurtling car, of metal screeching against metal, seemed to explode inside her head. She scrambled higher. The rough iron rails shook in her hands. As she fought to hold on, the Citroën blasted past beneath, enveloping her in a stench of exhaust.

As it careened off on the rain-slicked street, she released her hold on the fence and dropped to the ground, trying to absorb the fact that Charles had just tried to kill her. Filled with horror, she sprinted, her muscles pulsing as she pumped harder and harder, Charles's cold face burned into her mind.

CHAPTER 10

BY ELEVEN O'CLOCK THE BRITISH Museum was a dark fortress, massive and seemingly impenetrable. Surrounded by a great iron fence, it filled a full city block, dominating the narrow, quaint streets of the Bloomsbury neighborhood of London. Rain fell lightly. Nearby traffic had eased except on Great Russell Street, where it would thunder all night. There were no pedestrians in sight.

Four men in single file ran alongside the museum on Montague Place. They wore black nylon face masks and were dressed in black body suits, with large black waterproof backpacks snug against their shoulders. As they approached the iron gate, Doug Preston touched the electronic communicator on his belt. The click of the gate's lock was audible. He slipped swiftly inside, followed by the others.

The team hurried past grassy plots and open space until they reached a side door in the North Wing. It swung open, pushed by a man in a museum guard's dark blue uniform. They stepped inside, the door closed with a clang, and in unison all four pulled out towels from one another's backpacks.

"Hurry, Preston," the guard, Mark Allen Robert, said as they dried themselves. "I've bloody well got to get back."

"Is everything handled?" Preston demanded.

Robert peered nervously at his watch. "They'll be starting up rounds again through this wing in about twenty-five minutes. They'll be checking the floors and galleries for an hour. To be on the safe side you need to be back here in twenty minutes. No more. I'll control the security apparatus from downstairs." He rushed away, his flashlight beam preceding him through macabre shadows created by dim amber lamps installed high on the walls.

Silently the men changed into crepe-soled shoes. They mopped rainwater from the floor.

"We've got seventeen minutes," Preston told them quietly.

They raced off through the gloom without the benefit of flashlights. The museum's security lamps were enough, and each man had memorized the route.

But at the top of the north stairs, Preston smelled an acrid whiff of cigarette smoke. He gave a brusque hand signal that told his people to stand back. Besides being the chief of security at the Library of Gold, he was a highly regarded expert in both break-ins and wet work, and this could be a minor interruption. He hoped like hell it was minor. His orders were to go in, grab, and get out without leaving any hint that intruders had breached the museum stronghold.

Crouching, he found his nightscope, bent the neck, and aimed it around the corner until he could see. A guard, smoking languidly, was sauntering along the shadowy hallway toward them. Smoking was not allowed in the museum, so Preston thought the man likely had come up here to escape the rain, hoping no one would notice.

Preston frowned and settled back on his heels, warily watching as the guard closed in on the stairwell. He was about to signal his men to retreat to the next floor when the guard put out the cigarette, lit another, and ambled around in a semicircle to retrace his path.

Preston shook his shoulders to relieve tension. Beneath his mask, sweat greased his face. He hated not being able to take out the guard.

Another five minutes passed while the man strolled the corridor. At last he extinguished the second cigarette, punched the button for the elevator, boarded it, and vanished.

"Ten minutes left." Preston saw his men stiffen. "We can do it."

With a snap of his wrist, he signaled, and they sprinted to the events hall where the Rosenwald collection was being exhibited. As expected, the security gate was lowered, but the light on the electronic lock was green, signaling it had been deactivated. Preston liked that—it increased the chances the motion sensors inside the gallery had also been turned off.

Together they raised the gate three feet, slid under, and sped toward *The Book of Spies,* peeling off their backpacks. No alarms went off.

"Nine minutes," Preston said, relieved.

The high-security display cabinet had a frame of titanium without corner joints that could leak air. The top consisted of two pieces of tempered, antireflective glass, each three-sixteenths of an inch thick and fused with polyvinyl butyral, which would hold shards together and away from the manuscript if the panes shattered. The seals were made of Inconel, a nickle-alloy steel, and shaped like a *C* in cross section so the arms of each *C* fit into grooves to create a high seal. If someone did not know what they were doing, it could take hours to figure out how to open the case.

Their movements were slow but choreographed. Using special hand tools, two men opened the top seals and removed the first pane of glass and set it on the floor, while Preston and the fourth man slid a fake illuminated manuscript out of a backpack and unwrapped its covering.

As soon as the second pane of glass was hiked out, one man carefully closed the jeweled *Book of Spies* and secured it in clear archival polyester film and clear polyethylene sheeting, then wrapped it in foam. They slid it into Preston's backpack.

Keeping his breath rhythmic, Preston studied the display cabinet's interior, which had a jet-black finish. He was looking for the small pegs that indicated correct placement. Satisfied, he set down the fake book and opened it to the only two pages that were real—color copied and touched up by hand from photographs Charles Sherback had taken during the evening's showing. There were small seams where the pages had been glued into the book, but unless someone examined them closely, they were unnoticeable.

When he looked up, his men were wearing their backpacks. As he slung on his, the first two returned the panes of glass and closed the seals.

With a burst of satisfaction, he checked his watch. "Four minutes."

One man chuckled; another laughed. Preston gave an experienced look around to make certain they had left nothing behind, and they raced away.

CHAPTER 11

AS THE CITROËN SPED around the corner, Judd Ryder ran up the narrow street, following Eva Blake as she raced into the falling mist. Working for Tucker Andersen, he was in London to keep an eye on her and had learned two important pieces of information: First, she was alert to her surroundings—several times she had glanced over her shoulder, indicating she sensed she was being tailed. She had definitely spotted him once. And second, the man she believed to be her husband had just tried to kill her.

Still running, she hurled something beneath a bush. He looked and saw a faint glitter. Scooping up a wedding band and a pendant on a gold chain, he dropped them into his jacket pocket and accelerated past the Montague Hotel and around the corner. Traffic cruised past, and a scattering of people were on the sidewalks. He spotted her as she dashed into Russell Square Gardens.

Darting between cars, he entered the garden park, a manicured city block of lawns and winding walkways beneath the branching limbs of old trees. Although

April had turned chilly, the trees had leaved, creating black swaths where not even the park's ornate lamp-posts could shed light.

Blake was nowhere in sight. But he saw the Citroën on the east side of the park with the other traffic. It was circling. He took out his mobile and dialed her number.

A woman's breathless voice answered. "Tucker?"

He knew she thought only Tucker had her phone number. "My name is Judd Ryder. Tucker sent me to help. I've been following you—"

She hung up on him.

Swearing, Ryder hurried along a path, checking the shadows. Had he just seen movement near the Garden Café, inside the square's northeast corner? He stepped behind a tree. For a few seconds a wraith in a tan trench coat flitted in and out of the café's dark shadows. It was Eva Blake.

He kept pace as she exited through the park's wrought-iron gates and slipped behind an old-fashioned cabman's shelter to hide as the Citroën passed and turned west. As it continued around the park again, she ran across the busy intersection toward the historic Russell Hotel.

He left the park, too. She slowed as she passed the hotel and wove through the throngs around the Russell Square Underground Station.

Stepping off the curb, he sprinted along the gutter. Once he was in front of her, he hid in the lee of the *Herald-Tribune* newspaper stand and pulled out his black watch cap. As Blake rushed past, he grabbed her arm and used her momentum to swing her close.

"I'm Judd Ryder. I just called you—"

"Let go of me." She yanked so hard he almost lost his grip.

Her hair was rain-soaked, plastered against her skull, and her mascara had run, settling in dirty half moons under her eyes and gray dribbles down her cheeks. But it was her cobalt blue eyes that held him. They radiated fear—and defiance.

"I've got to get you out of here," he ordered.

She abruptly leaned away and slammed out a foot in an expert *yoko-keage* side snap kick. He stepped back swiftly, and the brunt of her blow hit only the loose front of his peacoat. Surprised to lose impact, she teetered and banged into his chest. Her hands pressed against him.

He jerked her upright and shoved his wool cap at her. "Put this on. Stick your hair up inside it. We've got to change your appearance—unless you'd rather risk your husband finding you again. Take off your trench coat. If you do exactly what I tell you, I may be able to get you out of here."

As commuters moved around them, she remained motionless. "Are you really working with Tucker?" she demanded.

"*For* him. Just like you are. That's why I have your cell phone number."

"That means nothing. Why didn't he tell me about you?"

"I'll explain later." He grabbed the watch cap and jammed it down onto her head and began to unbutton her trench coat.

"I'll take it off myself, dammit." She slipped off the strap of her satchel and shrugged out of the coat.

Catching both before they hit the ground, he rolled the coat into a ball so only the olive-green lining showed. She was wearing a black tailored jacket, a black turtleneck sweater, and tight low-slung jeans tucked into high black boots. Her dark clothing would help her to blend with the night.

"Push your hair up under the cap." As she did, he returned her satchel. "Take my arm as if you liked me."

Warily she slid her arm inside his. As they walked,

he patted her hand. It was ice-cold and tense. He dropped her trench coat into a trash receptacle.

She started to turn.

"Don't look back," he warned. "Let's keep the opportunities for your husband to see your face at a minimum."

As they continued on, the number of pedestrians lessened, which was both good and bad. Good because they could make quicker progress. Bad because she was easier to spot. He produced a palm-size mirror, cupped it in his hand, and examined the cars approaching from behind.

"I don't see the Citroën," he reported. "You're shivering. Button your jacket. We'll find someplace warm to talk."

"What did you say your name was?" She buttoned her jacket up to her throat.

There was no trust in her voice, but all he needed was her cooperation. "Judd Ryder." He reached inside his open peacoat for his billfold. His hand came out empty. Instantly he remembered her side snap kick and that she had bumped into him, her hands on his chest. Tucker had been right—she was a damn good pickpocket.

She pulled the wallet from her satchel, looked inside, and checked his Maryland driver's license, credit cards, and membership cards.

"Nothing says CIA." She returned the billfold.

"I'm covert."

"Then your name might not really be Judson Clayborn Ryder."

"It is. Son of Jonathan and Jeannine Ryder. Cousin to many."

"Credentials can be forged."

"Mine aren't. Here's an interesting idea—try being grateful. I'm the one helping you get away from your husband."

"If you really wanted to help me, why didn't you do something to stop Charles when he tried to run me down? You could've at least used your gun to shoot out his tires."

So she had found his Beretta. "It's a myth shooting rounds into tires makes them explode."

"Do you think Charles will try to kill me again?"

"Considering he was circling the park, I'd say he appears enthused about the idea."

Her expression froze, and she looked away.

As they turned onto Guilford Street, she asked, "Are you the one who saved the museum guard who almost fell over the stair rail?"

"He needed some help. I was lucky to be close."

She took a deep breath. "I'm glad you did."

They passed a row of businesses, all closed. Sitting cross-legged on the sidewalk in front of one was a homeless man, a dingy beach umbrella sheltering him and, in front of him, a hand-lettered sign:

MY DOG AND I ARE HUNGRY. PLEASE HELP.

Suddenly he felt her go rigid beside him.

"Charles!" she whispered.

With his peripheral vision, he caught sight of the Citroën approaching from behind.

"There's no time to run," he told her quietly. "Look at me and smile. Look at me! We're just an ordinary couple out for a stroll." He put his arm around her shoulders, took her over to the beggar, and dropped a two-pound coin into the man's hand. "Where's your dog?" he asked, playing for time as the car approached.

"I have a dog?" The man's words were slurred. He stank of cheap wine.

"Says so on the sign." He saw that the Citroën was nearly beside them.

"Bollocks. I left the bloody dog at home. Must be losin' my friggin' mind." The two-pound coin vanished into the man's pocket, and he stared blankly ahead as the Citroën rolled safely past.

Ryder peered down at Blake. "Our guests will be arriving soon, dear. We'd better head home."

She gave a curt nod, and they hurried on.

CHAPTER 12

THE LAMB PUBLIC HOUSE at 94 Lamb's Conduit Street was a classic old-school pub with dark woods, smoke-brown walls, and an ornate U-shaped bar topped with rare snob screens that pivoted to provide a customer with a modicum of privacy. The dusky air was pungent with the rich aromas of fine ales and lagers.

Relieved to be safely off the street, Eva cleaned her face in the bathroom and settled into a banquette at the back. She watched Judd Ryder at the bar, his long frame leaning into it as he waited for their orders and surveyed the room. The clientele crowded around the bar, shoes propped up on the foot rail. Ryder and she had attracted only a moment's notice, and now no one was looking at her, including Ryder.

If she had learned one lesson in prison, it was survival required suspicion. He had thrown his peacoat onto the leather seat. She searched the inner pockets. There were a couple of felt-tipped pens, his small mirror, a granola bar, a fat roll of cash, and a London tube schedule. She returned everything but the schedule and was just about to check whether he had made any notes on it when he picked up her tea tray from the bar. Instantly she shoved the schedule back inside his coat.

He walked toward her, his stride long. He was dressed in jeans, a dark blue polo shirt, and a loose corduroy jacket. She could not quite make out the shoulder holster that held his gun. His square face was weathered and had a rugged outdoor quality, as if it had been formed more by life than biology. His hands were large and competent, but his dark gray eyes were unreadable. He was athletic and obviously familiar with karate, otherwise he would not have been able to dodge her blow. He could easily be telling her the truth—or not.

She hid her tension and smiled. "Thanks. It smells delicious."

"Lapsang souchong tea, as requested. Heated milk and a warm cup, too." He put the tray down. "Drink. You're shivering."

As he headed back to the bar to fetch his stout, she grabbed the tube schedule and inspected it. There were no marks or notes. Next she examined the peacoat's outside pockets. Frowning, she discovered an electronic reader for some kind of tracking device. A small handheld computer with GPS capabilities, it was similar to those she had assembled in the prison's electronics factory. Tracking devices could be used to keep tabs on anything, while readers like this displayed an array of information sent from the bug.

She looked up. The bartender was setting a full pint glass in front of Ryder, and he was paying the bill. She had little time. Her fingers flew as she touched buttons, and the handheld's screen came to colorful life. She saw he was tracking two bugs. She keyed onto the first. Schematics flashed and coalesced into a map of London, showing a location: Le Méridien Hotel in the West

End. She was not familiar with the hotel, and she did not have time to check the other bug. She slid the hand-held back into his peacoat.

He was heading toward her, pint in hand, staring. As he stopped at the table, she saw his face had done a strange shift, revealing something hard and a little frightening.

She patted then smoothed his peacoat. "Forgive me. My nose is starting to run. I was just going to look for a tissue." The condition of her nose was true.

Without comment he took a handkerchief from his pocket, handed it to her, and sat with his pint of oat-meal stout.

"Thanks." She blew her nose, then wrapped her hands around her hot cup of tea. "When Charles and I visited London, we sometimes came here. In case you don't know, Charles Dickens, Virginia Woolf, and the Bloomsbury Group were regulars. Editors and writers still show up. The pub seemed to us the epitome of old Bloomsbury, the beating heart of London's literary world."

"You're feeling better," he decided.

She nodded. "Why didn't Tucker tell me about you?"

"You're not trained, and we wanted you to act normally. Some people can't handle being watched over. You wouldn't have known how you'd react, and we wouldn't have known either, until you were actually in the museum. There was only one opening night, and we were doing everything we could to maximize your chances of success."

"Is your name really Judd Ryder?"

"Yes. I'm a CIA contract employee. Tucker brought me in for the job."

"Then you're working for Catapult." Tucker had told her about his unit, which did counteroperations. "Why you?"

Ryder gazed down into his glass then looked up, his

expression somber. "My father and Tucker were friends in college. They joined the CIA at the same time, then Dad left to go into business. A couple of weeks ago he asked Tucker to meet him in a park on Capitol Hill. Just the two of them. It was late at night. . . . A sniper killed Dad."

Seeing the pain in his eyes, she sank back. "That's terrible. I'm so sorry. It must've been awful for you."

"It was."

She thought a moment. "But murder is a job for the police."

"Dad was trying to warn Tucker about something that had to do with a multimillion-dollar account in an unnamed international bank—and Islamic terrorism."

"Terrorism?" Her brows rose with alarm. "What kind of terrorism? Al-Qaeda? One of their offshoots? A new group?"

"We don't know yet, but he appeared worried some disaster was about to happen. Dad had collected news clippings about jihadism in Pakistan and Afghanistan, but so far they don't make a lot of sense. Of course Catapult is staying on top of international bank activity. The only real detail is where you come in—Dad said he'd discovered the information in the Library of Gold."

"*In* the library? Then the library really does exist."

"Yes. Dad also told Tucker some kind of book club owns it."

"Was your father in the book club?"

He shrugged uneasily. "I don't know yet."

"If your father was a member of the book club, it sounds to me as if he had a secret life."

He nodded grimly. "Just like your husband's."

She leaned forward. "You want to find out what your father was doing and who's behind his death."

"Damn right I do." Anger flashed across his face.

"Why didn't Tucker tell me any of this?"

"You didn't have need-to-know, and we thought your assignment would be simple."

"Both of us have personal reasons to find the library, but this is on a whole different level. So much bigger."

"It *is* personal for both of us." He set down his glass, put his hand into his jacket pocket, and slid her gold wedding band and necklace across the table. "I thought you might want these back."

Staring at them, she moved her hands away from her cup and dropped them into her lap. "I don't need them anymore. That was another life. Another person."

He studied her. Then he scooped up the jewelry and returned it to his pocket. "Tell me about Charles and the car crash."

"He was driving us home on Mulholland after a dinner party, and—" She stopped. In her mind she went back over the trip—Charles's carefree laughter, his playful weaving of the car back and forth across the deserted road. . . . She told Ryder about it. Then: "A car shot out from a driveway ahead, and Charles slammed on the brakes. Our car careened. I was nauseated and dizzy. And I lost consciousness. The next thing I knew, I woke up on a gurney." She hesitated. "Charles must've given me some kind of drug. Later the coroner found his wedding ring on the corpse, and the corpse's teeth matched Charles's dental records."

"That shows a lot of planning, money, and dirty resources. Could Charles have pulled it off alone?"

"No way. He was an academic. Someone had to have helped him."

"Who?"

She mulled. "I don't know anyone who could have."

"Where do you think he's been?"

"God knows. He's got a good tan, so it's someplace sunny."

"What kind of man was he?"

"Dedicated. Our world's small. Only a few thousand people are well-educated about illuminated manuscripts. Maybe a hundred are true experts. Most of us know one another in varying degrees. I suppose to outsiders we seem peculiar. We play card games from Greek and Roman times, and we have our own trivia contests. Our conversations can seem funny—we use Latin and Greek, for instance. Charles was considered by some to be the top authority on the Library of Gold. He was immersed in it, lived it, ached for it, and that's why he was so knowledgeable. It would've been hard for him to live with anyone who couldn't appreciate that in him."

"And you did?"

"Yes. It made sense to me."

He nodded. "Could his disappearance have been related to the library?"

"He was working awfully long hours before the car crash. He might've had some insight or uncovered something and felt he needed to disappear so no one would be tipped off while he closed in."

She followed Ryder's gaze as he surveyed the old pub. The polished brass fixtures glinted. A few customers had left; a few more had entered.

"I shot about an hour of video of the people around *The Book of Spies,*" he told her. "If there's a cyber café open at this hour, we can look at it together."

She pulled her satchel to her. "We don't have to go anywhere. I have my laptop with me."

They moved around the U-shaped banquette so they were sitting next to each other. As she put her computer on the table and turned it on, he produced a palm-size video camera, USB cord, and software disk from his jacket pockets.

Within minutes they were viewing the exhibition.

Ryder fast-forwarded until Charles appeared. She pointed out Charles's striking walk, described the changes he had made in his appearance, and identified the other people she recognized. But Charles spoke to no one, and no one spoke to Charles. And at no time did she see Charles make eye contact with anyone.

"That's interesting," Ryder murmured. He stopped the film and replayed it in several places. Although earlier he had been recording from a distance, he now was shooting close to the exhibit. "Look at how Charles is inching around the display case. Check out his right hand."

She focused on the hand. Charles was holding it near his waist, cupped casually. The hand rose and fell as he moved, and his thumb twitched.

She stared. "Is he secretly photographing *The Book of Spies*?"

"Appears to be. But why? The addiction of a wacko bibliomaniac?"

"Or it could have something to do with the Library of Gold—but what?"

"My question, too." He checked his watch. "It's late. We should go. You're staying with your friend Peggy Doty." He frowned. "Would Charles know that?"

Her throat went dry. She grabbed her cell and dialed.

At last there was a sleepy answer. "Hello?"

"Peggy, it's Eva again. You've got to get out of there. I know it sounds impossible, but I saw Charles tonight at the museum."

Peggy's voice was suddenly alert. "What are you talking about?"

"I saw Charles at the show. He's as alive as you or me."

"That's crazy. Charles is dead, dear. Remember, you thought you saw him before. He's *dead*. Come home. We'll talk about it."

Eva tightened her grip on the cell phone. "Charles tried to kill me. He knows I stay with you. You could be in danger. You've got to leave. Go to a hotel, and I'll meet you. Even if you don't believe me, just do this for me, Peggy."

When they decided on the Chelsea Arms, Peggy volunteered, "I'll make the room reservation for us."

Suddenly exhausted, Eva agreed and ended the connection.

Ryder drained his glass. "I'll have Tucker check into the identity of the man in Charles's grave and give you a status report in the morning." He related his mobile number and where he was staying.

They stood. As she slung her valise over her shoulder, he dropped his camera equipment into his jacket pockets and shoved his arms into his peacoat. Heading for the door, they skirted the drinkers at the bar and stepped out into the night. Glistening drops of rain floated in the lamplight.

"Will you be all right?" He hailed a taxi for her.

"I'll be a lot better once we've found Charles."

As a cab stopped at the curb, he gave her a reassuring smile. "Get a good night's sleep." Then to the taximan: "The Chelsea Arms."

She climbed in. As the cab cruised off, she turned in her seat to watch what Ryder would do. He was walking in the opposite direction. Pulling out his electronic reader, he seemed to be studying it. Finally he lifted his head and caught a taxi for himself. Glancing at the bug reader again, he climbed inside.

Suspicion flooded her. She leaned forward. "I've changed my mind. Turn around. Take me to the Méridien hotel on Piccadilly."

CHAPTER 13

CHARLES SHERBACK KNEW he had made a terrible mistake. He dropped off the Citroën at the car rental agency and caught a taxi, his mind in tumult. Ovid was right: *Res est ingeniosa dare.* "Giving requires good sense." And he had not simply 'given'; he had sacrificed for Eva. In fact, he had risked a great deal for her.

As the windshield wiper slashed across the glass, he stared out unseeing at the rainy London night. She was supposed to be in prison. How could she have been at the British Museum show? And now he had failed to eliminate her.

"We're here, guv'nor." The taxi driver peered into his rearview mirror. He had white hair, a sagging face, and tired eyes that thankfully remained bored.

Charles paid and stepped out of the cab and into the noisy din of Piccadilly. As cars and trucks rushed past on the boulevard, he dodged pedestrians and strode into the five-star Le Méridien Hotel, hoping Preston was not early.

He peered around. The lobby was spacious, two stories high, topped by an intricate stained-glass dome. The appointments were modern and refined, and the air smelled of fresh flowers. The hotel was elegant, just the way he liked it. It was also busy with people.

At the elevator, he stepped inside and punched the button for the eighth floor. The elevator rose with maddening slowness. As soon as the doors opened he ran along the hall, jammed his electronic key into the lock, and marched into the deluxe room. The window drapes were closed against prying eyes, and a hot pot of coffee was waiting on the low table in front of two upholstered chairs. There was no sign of Preston.

"Hello, darling." Sitting on the end of the king-size bed, Robin Miller clicked off the television. "I'm glad you're back. Are you okay?"

A moment of happiness flowed through him. "I'm fine." He peeled off his wet raincoat.

"Is she dead?"

Thick ash-blond hair wreathed Robin's face and draped in thick bangs down to her green eyes. Her mouth was lush and round, and her skin glowed with a ruddy tan. She was thirty-five years old. On the director's orders, all staff members had plastic surgery before they could go to work at the library. He had seen photographs of Robin from those days, and she was even more beautiful now.

"There were complications." He shook his head with disgust. "Eva got away."

She stared worriedly. "Are you going to tell the director she recognized you?"

He fell into a reading chair and poured a cup of steaming coffee. "It's safer for me to take care of the problem myself." He added sugar, then cream until the color turned to that of café au lait. He wished he had some good Irish whiskey to add.

"But what will you do?"

"I have to kill her." He heard the determination in his voice. He had come this far, and he had no choice. From the moment he had accepted the job of chief librarian at the Library of Gold, his lot was cast. He remembered the sense of destiny fulfilled. He had faced reality, banished any regrets, and thrown himself into his exciting new life.

"Maybe you should ask Preston for help."

He gave an abrupt shake of his head. "He'll tell the director."

They were silent, acknowledging the threat of it. He saw her hands were turning white from gripping the edge of the bed. He went to her and pulled her close. She laid her head on his shoulder. Her warmth flowed into him.

"I'm frightened," she whispered.

Robin was a strong woman. Until now she had not admitted being afraid. Because she had not told the director instantly, she could be in as much trouble as he.

"This is all Eva's fault," he assured her. "We wouldn't be in this mess if she hadn't recognized me. I love you. Remember that. I love you."

"I love you, too, darling." She wrapped her arms around him. "But you're not a killer. You don't know how to do such things. As long as Eva's alive, she's dangerous to the library—and to us. You need to tell Preston so he can take care of her. If you don't want to, I'll do it."

Four taps sounded on the door.

"Preston's here." She pulled away. "Give me a minute."

"Hurry."

She nodded and stood up, smoothing her hair and straightening her white cashmere sweater and brown trousers.

He crossed to the door, reaching it as another four taps began. He peered through the peephole. A distorted Doug Preston loomed in the hallway, a bulging backpack in his left hand. His right hand was hidden inside his black leather jacket, where he kept his pistol holstered. Everything about him, from his slightly bent knees to the sharp vigilance with which he was checking the corridor, seemed to radiate menace.

Charles took a deep breath and opened the door, and Preston strode into the room. Uneasily Charles watched as he scanned the interior. When he paused to peer at Robin, she nodded in greeting, her eyes wary. Charles focused on the backpack. He could postpone deciding whether to tell Preston about Eva because its contents were of immediate concern.

"You have *The Book of Spies*?" he demanded.

"I do." Preston set the pack on a chair and started to unzip it.

"I'll take over now."

Preston stepped back.

As Robin joined them, Charles removed the foam bundle. "Move the coffee, Robin. Leave the napkins."

She picked up the tray and carried it away. Although the table appeared clean, he used the linen napkins to wipe it. Then he set down the bundle and unpeeled layers of foam and transparent polyethylene sheeting. At last only archival polyester film remained.

He paused, feeling a visceral reaction. His throat full, he gazed at the illuminated manuscript glowing through the clear protective barrier.

"Ready?" He lowered himself into the reading chair and looked up.

Preston nodded.

"Hurry," Robin said.

He unfastened the polyester and let it fall to the sides.

"Oh, my Lord," Robin breathed.

"It's a beauty, all right," Preston agreed.

Charles stared, drinking in the sight of the fabled *Book of Spies,* compiled on orders of Ivan the Terrible, who had been fascinated by spies and assassins. Covered in gold, the volume was large, probably ten by twelve inches and four inches thick, decorated with fat emeralds, great rubies, and lustrous pearls—a fortune in gems. The emeralds were arranged along the edges of the cover, a rectangular frame of brilliant green. The pearls were gathered into the shape of a glowing dagger in the top two thirds, and beneath the dagger's point lay the scarlet rubies, shaped like a large drop of blood. The jewels caught the lamplight and sparkled like fire.

Awed silence filled the room. Robin handed Charles clean white cotton gloves. Putting them on, he opened the book and slowly turned pages, savoring the style, the paint, the ink, the feel of the fine parchment between his cautious fingers. Each page was a showcase of lavish pictures, austere Cyrillic letters, and intricate borders ablaze with color. He felt a thrill at the effort involved not only in gathering the knowledge but in creating such art.

"Six years of painstaking labor went into this masterwork," Charles told them. "Twelve months a year, seven days a week, twelve to fourteen hours a day. The crudest brushes and paints. Only sunlight and oil lamps to work by. No good heating during the brutal Moscow winters. The constant attack of mosquitoes in summer. Imagine the difficulty, the dedication."

Robin sat on the floor and leaned an elbow on the table to be closer. Preston pulled up a chair and sat, watching the turning pages. The paintings showed secretive spies, rotund diplomats, monarchs in furs, soldiers in colorful uniforms, villains with wily faces. It was a rich compendium of stories about real and mythical assassins, spies, and missions since before biblical times.

"You're sure it's authentic?" Robin asked in a low, excited voice.

"The style's correct, tending toward naturalism," Charles told her. "The final touches are in liquid gold— not gold leaf." Naturalism and liquid gold appeared only at the end of the Middle Ages, which matched the year the manuscript was finished in Moscow—1580. "What clinches its authenticity are the tiny letters beneath some of the colors. See? They're almost invisible. Even the best forgers forget that telling detail."

He pointed without touching the page. The letters stood for the Latin words for the colors the long-ago artist had been instructed to use to fill in the line drawings, which had been rendered by a previous artist. *R* for *ruber*, meaning red; *V* for *viridis*, meaning green; and *A* for *azure*, meaning blue.

"It was painted by an Italian who was working in Ivan's court," Charles explained.

"I remember the book well," Preston said. "The stories about spies are inspiring. Those who find the secrets and take them to their graves are the real heroes. That's what we signed on for when we went to work for the Library of Gold. Complete loyalty."

As Preston talked, Robin stared at Charles. Her eyebrows knitted together with determination, and her lips thinned. The message was clear: If he did not tell Preston, she would.

"We've got a problem." Charles steeled himself as Preston focused on him.

"There's no reason for the director to know about it, Preston," Robin urged. "You can handle it."

Preston did not look at her. "What's happened, Charles?"

He sighed heavily. "It started in the museum. I'd just finished photographing *The Book of Spies* and was walking away when I noticed Eva. My wife. God knows how she got out of prison, but she was there, and she recognized me." He rushed on, describing the chase through the museum and her arrest. "I rented a car. When the police released her, I followed and found a quiet street. Then I was almost able to run her down. But she got away. I drove everywhere, looking for her again."

"Does she know about the Library of Gold?" Preston asked instantly.

"Of course not. I never talked with her."

"What else?"

"She recorded me on her cell phone," he admitted. "I don't know whether it was photos or a video."

"Please don't tell the director, Preston," Robin pleaded.

Preston was silent. Tension filled the room.

Charles rubbed his eyes and sank back in his chair. When he looked again, Preston had not moved, his gaze unreadable.

"Where would she stay in London?" Preston demanded.

"There were two hotels we preferred—the Connaught and the Mayflower. When she came alone, she stayed with a friend, Peggy Doty. At the museum I overheard a conversation that Peggy had moved back to London. I don't have her address, but my guess is Eva's with Peggy. They were close."

Preston tapped a number into his cell. "Eva Blake may be staying at one of these hotels." He related the information. "I'll e-mail you her photograph. Terminate her. She has a cell phone. It's imperative you get it." He ended the connection, then told Charles, "I'll handle Peggy Doty myself."

Gayle Lynds

As Preston walked toward the door, Charles rose to his feet. He was sweating. "Are you going to tell the director?"

Preston said nothing. The door closed.

CHAPTER 14

AS HE DROVE TOWARD PEGGY Doty's apartment, Preston reveled in having pulled off the complex mission of recovering *The Book of Spies*. It had been like the old days when he was a CIA officer working undercover in hot spots across Europe and the old Soviet Union. But when the cold war had ended, Langley had lost the support of Congress, the White House, and the American people to properly monitor the world. Disgusted and heartbroken, he had resigned. By the time of the 9/11 attacks, when everyone realized intelligence was critical to U.S. security, he had committed himself to something larger, something more enduring. Something far more relevant, almost eternal—the Library of Gold.

Fury washed through him. Charles was self-important, and self-importance was always a liability. He had put the library in danger.

Preston speed-dialed the director.

"Did you get *The Book of Spies*?" Martin Chapman's voice was forceful, his focus instant, although it was past four A.M. in Dubai. The tirelessness of the response was typical, just one of the reasons Preston admired him.

"The book is safe. On the jet soon. And Charles has verified it's genuine."

As Preston had hoped, there was delight in the director's voice: "Congratulations. Fine work. I knew I could count on you. As Seneca wrote, 'It matters not how many books one has, but how good they are.' I'm eager to see it again. Everything went smoothly?"

"One small problem, but it's handleable. Charles's wife is out of prison and was at the museum opening. She recognized him, made a scene, and got herself arrested. Charles tried to run her down. Of course he failed. I'm driving to the apartment where he thinks she's staying. I just found out about all of this."

"The bastard should've reported it immediately. Robin was aware?"

"Yes." The library's rules were inviolate. Everyone knew that. It was one of the prime reasons the library had remained invincible—and invisible—over the centuries.

The director's tone was cold, unforgiving: "Kill Eva Blake. I'll decide later what to do about Charles and Robin."

PRESTON PARKED NEAR ST JOHN Street in the hip Clerkenwell neighborhood, around the block from Peggy Doty's apartment building. As he got out of the Renault, he pulled the brim of his Manchester United football cap low. The rich scent of Vietnamese coffee drifted from a lighted café, infusing the night. The historic area was full of a young, smart crowd involved in themselves and the evening's entertainment.

Satisfied he was clean, Preston walked quickly back to Peggy Doty's apartment building and tried the street door. It was locked. Finally a woman emerged. Catching the door before it could close, he slipped inside and climbed the stairs.

Peggy Doty answered his knock instantly, and it was clear why—she was ready to leave. She wore a long wool overcoat, and a suitcase stood on the floor beside her. Her apartment was dark and silent, indicating no one else was there.

He had to decide what to do. When he was much younger, he would have threatened her to find out where Blake was. But there was an intelligent, steely look about her that warned him she might lie, and if he killed her too soon, it would be too late to go back to her for the truth.

He put a warm smile on his face. "You must be Peggy Doty. I'm a friend of Eva's. My name's Gary Frank. I'm glad I'm here in time. Eva thought you might like a ride."

Peggy frowned. "Thanks a lot, Mr. Frank, but I've already called a cab." She was a small woman, with short brown hair and eyeglasses sliding down her nose. Her face was open, the face of someone people automatically liked.

"Please call me Gary." Since she had not asked how Blake knew she was leaving, it was evident they were in touch. "You live in a great neighborhood. Didn't Peter Ackroyd and Charles Dickens use Clerkenwell for settings in their novels?" He gave her a conspiratorial wink. "I'm a used-book dealer."

Her face brightened. "Yes, they did. Maybe you're thinking about Ackroyd's *The Clerkenwell Tales*. That's a terrific piece of fiction about fourteenth-century London. The clerk at Tellson's bank in *A Tale of Two Cities* lived here, too. His name was Jarvis Lorry. And Fagin's lair was also in the Clerkenwell area."

"*Oliver Twist* is a favorite of mine. Eva says you

work at the British Library. I'd like to hear what you do. Please let me drive you."

She hesitated.

He stepped into the silence. "Did you tell Eva you were calling a cab?"

She sighed. "Nope, I didn't. All right. This is really great of you."

He picked up her suitcase, and they left.

WITH PEGGY DOTY AT HIS SIDE, Preston drove south, heading for the hotel in Chelsea where she would meet Blake. Blake might already be there, and he wanted this small brunette with him to ensure he got access to the room without drawing attention to himself.

"So Eva sounded upset to you, too?" he prodded.

Her hands were folded in her lap, pale against her midnight blue coat. "She says her dead husband's alive. That she actually saw him. Can you believe it? I'm hoping she'll have recovered her brain by the time we get there."

"I'm sure she will," he said, and they drove on in silence.

At last he parked, tugged the brim of his cap low over his eyes, and walked with her into the hotel, carrying her suitcase. As she registered, he noted she was right-handed.

"Has Ms. Blake checked in?" she asked.

"Not yet, miss."

Her face crumpled. They took the elevator up to her room. It was full of fussy chintz and the hideous line drawings of horses standing around on hills one saw in tourist hotels in London.

She peered at the emptiness. "She should've been here by now, Gary."

He laid her suitcase on the valet stand. "Would she have stopped someplace first?"

"I'll call her." She tapped a number into her cell and listened, her expression growing grim. Finally she said, "Eva, this is Peggy. Where are you? Phone as soon as you get my message." She hung up.

"Was she with anyone when you talked before? They might've gone someplace together."

"All I heard was a noisy background." She sighed heavily. "I hope she's okay."

The time had come. Fortunately because of what he had learned from her, he now had a way to liquidate Eva Blake.

"Peggy, I just want you to know you're a nice woman."

She looked at him, a surprised expression on her face. "Thanks."

"And this is just what I do." Swiftly he leaned down and removed the untraceable two-shot pistol from his ankle holster.

Staring at the gun, she took a step back. "What are you—?"

He advanced and grabbed her shoulders. She was light. "I'll make it fast."

"No!" She struggled, her fists pounding his coat.

He pressed the gun up under her chin and fired. Skull and brain matter exploded. He held her a moment, then let her fall to the floor, limp in her big coat.

Pulling on latex gloves, he cleaned his black jacket with the special tissues he always carried. As he wiped the gun, he listened at the door. There was no sound in the corridor. He ran back to her, pressed both her hands around the gun's grip and muzzle, and then put the grip into her right hand and squeezed her fingers around it.

Snatching up her cell phone, he debated with himself, then finally decided the police investigators would be suspicious if the phone were missing. He memorized Blake's cell phone number, turned off Peggy's cell, and left it in her coat pocket. Then he wiped off the handle of her suitcase, used the wipes to take the suitcase to her, pressed one hand and then the other around the handle, and laid the suitcase back on the valet stand.

Outdoors, the night seemed warm and inviting. Striding down the busy street, Preston dialed out on his cell to his men in London. "Eva Blake is due to arrive shortly at this address." He relayed the hotel's information and room number. "Terminate her."

THE TEMPERATURE IN THE ROOM at the Méridien hotel seemed to have dropped ten degrees. As soon as Preston left, Charles had taken out his Glock and laid it on the coffee table next to *The Book of Spies*. He watched as Robin methodically packed their things. He was chilled, and his hands ached from knotting them. It seemed as if the world were shattering around him.

"You're not angry with me, are you, Charles?" she asked finally.

"Of course not. You were right—Preston will find Eva and take care of the problem. You've forgotten to scan the manuscript."

"I guess I'm a bit rattled."

She unzipped the suitcase and found the key-chain–size detector. It had a telescopic antenna that sniffed out hidden wireless cameras, audio devices, and tracking bugs. As soon as she turned it on, a red light flashed in warning.

Charles swore and sat up.

Brows knitting, she moved across the room, looking for the origin. As she approached *The Book of Spies,* the light flashed faster.

"Oh, no." Robin's face was tense.

She moved the detector over the cover of the illuminated manuscript until the light held steady. It pointed
to one of the emeralds rimming the book's gold binding.

She read the digital screen. "It says there's a tracking
bug in this emerald." Stricken, she peered at Charles.

"Maybe the museum or the Rosenwald Collection
planted it as a security measure," he said. "No, that's insane. They'd never violate something as precious as *The
Book of Spies*. It had to be someone else—but why?"

"What do we do? How can we tear off one of the
jewels? We'll destroy the integrity of the book. It's a
sacrilege."

They stared down at the manuscript.

At last Charles decided, "The integrity has already
been destroyed because that 'emerald' can't be real."
He took out his pocketknife and pried off the fake
jewel, leaving a gaping hole in the perfect frame of
green gems.

She groaned. "It looks awful."

Sickened, he nodded, then jumped up and ran into
the bathroom. He flushed the bug down the toilet.

CHAPTER 15

JUDD RYDER WAS PUZZLED. He walked west down the wide boulevard in front of the Méridien hotel and crossed Piccadilly Place, then Swallow Street, studying traffic. According to his electronic reader, *The Book of Spies* was in the middle of the boulevard, still moving, but more quickly than the vehicles. How could that be? He checked the altitude—and swore.

The bug was belowground. Sewer lines ran beneath the boulevard. Whoever had *The Book of Spies* had flushed the bug Tucker had planted on it.

He turned on his heel. It was possible the book was still in the hotel. As he hurried back, he took out his Secure Mobile Environment Portable Electronic Device—an SME-PED handheld computer. With it he could send classified e-mail, access classified networks, and make top-secret phone calls. Created under guidelines from the National Security Agency, it appeared ordinary, like a BlackBerry; and while either on or off secure mode, could be operated like any smart phone with Internet access.

Keeping it in secure mode, he speed-dialed Tucker Andersen's direct line at Catapult headquarters.

"I've been waiting to hear from you, Judd," Tucker said. "What have you learned?"

He crossed Piccadilly Street to where he could watch the hotel's entrance. He settled back into the shadows. "I've got a shocker for you. Charles Sherback didn't die in that car crash. He's still very much alive." He described what had happened in the museum, following Eva Blake from the police station, and witnessing Sherback's attempt to run her down. "The bottom line is planting *The Book of Spies* worked—we got a bite. But what it means that Sherback is alive I sure as hell don't know yet. There's another big wrinkle—*The Book of Spies* has been stolen, and the thieves dumped the bug."

Tucker's voice rose. "You don't know where the book is?"

"It may be in the Méridien hotel. The bug was there until a few minutes ago. Sherback was taking photos or making a video of the book in the museum, and the way things are going, it seems likely to me he and the book are together or he knows where it is. According to Blake, he's had cosmetic surgery. As soon as I hang up, I'll e-mail you the video I made at the Rosenwald show. I've keyed it on him. See if his new face is in any of our data banks. And find out who's buried in his grave in L.A. That could lead us to whoever helped him disappear."

"I'll make both priorities."

"You also need to know I had to tell Blake I'm working for you and the connection to Dad and the Library of Gold."

There was a pause. "I understand. What do you think of her?"

"She seems as functional as you or me. She's smart and tough."

"She's also beautiful and athletic. And vulnerable. Just your type. Don't like her too much, Judd."

Ryder said nothing. Tucker had researched him more than he realized.

When Ryder continued, his voice was brusque. "Blake is going to a hotel for the night. Whether I do anything more with her depends on what I find out next."

"With luck you can send her home," Tucker decided. "She did a good job, but I don't like employing amateurs."

Ryder wanted to see her again, but Tucker was right. It would be better for her if he did not. He had a lousy track record for keeping those he cared about alive. As he thought about it, he checked the other bug his reader was tracking—it was moving, too, but not toward Chelsea. It was headed north . . . toward him?

CHAPTER 16

DRESSED IN THEIR BLACK trench coats, Robin and Charles took the elevator down to the hotel's garage. From there they walked up a driveway and out into a shadowy cobblestone alley. Pulling their big roll-aboard suitcase, Robin glanced at Charles, who was looking handsome and intense. He wore the backpack in which *The Book of Spies* was secured, his hands gripping the pack's straps possessively.

They emerged onto the boulevard, away from the vast hotel and its bright lights. Side by side they continued on, at last stopping where Preston had told them to wait.

"I'd hoped Preston would be here by now." Charles stared at the traffic. "Maybe it's taken him longer to find Peggy than he thought."

"Are you all right?"

He took her hand and kissed it. "I'm fine. How are you?"

"Oddly, I'm fine, too." And she meant it.

A sense of inevitability had settled inside her. It was

not simply that Preston had taken on the job of getting rid of Eva, or that she had high hopes Preston would not tell the director, but that some old resource—courage, perhaps, touched with foolhardiness—had risen to return her confidence. Whatever happened, she would figure out a way to handle it.

Charles focused on her. "Does Preston strike you as an *abnormis sapiens crassaque Minerva*?" An unorthodox sage of rough genius.

"He does. But then he's also a *helluo librorum*." A bookworm, a devourer of books. "Do you think we can trust him?"

"We don't have a choice."

They straightened like Roman tribunes, alert for Preston's Renault. Horns honked. Vehicles rumbled along the boulevard. A few people strode on the sidewalk, swinging closed umbrellas under the cloudy night sky.

For a few moments the sidewalk was empty. When a taxi stopped down the block, Robin only glanced at the red-haired woman who stepped out and leaned over to pay the driver.

"Merda." Charles tensed as the woman turned toward them.

"What is it? What's happened?"

"That's Eva. Take care of *The Book of Spies*." He slung off the backpack and laid it at her feet. He slid out his Glock.

"Are you insane? You already tried to kill her once and failed. Someone could see your gun." As she spoke, she watched Eva stare at Charles. "She sees you."

Charles's face was flushed. He nodded and hid the weapon again. "I'll follow her and call Preston. Hail a taxi and take *The Book of Spies* to the jet."

As Charles finished talking, his wife turned on her

heel and rushed away, toward Piccadilly Circus. He hurried after her.

AS CHARLES MOVED PAST other pedestrians, he put on his headset and called Preston, telling him about Eva.

"I'll be there in twenty-five minutes," the security chief said. "How did she know to be at the hotel?"

"I have no idea. Unless . . . but it doesn't seem possible. Our scanner found a tracking bug on the cover of the book."

"Jesus Christ. What did you do with the bug?"

"I flushed it. But it makes no sense that Eva would've planted it."

"Don't lose her, dammit. Keep the line open."

He saw Eva had joined a crowd at the corner with Piccadilly Circus, waiting for the light to change. But before he could reach her, she crossed with them to the plaza and merged with the crowd there.

He craned and ran. Where was she?

CHAPTER 17

THE NOISE AND CHAOS of Piccadilly Circus reverberated inside Eva's head as she sped onward, her cell phone dug into her ear, talking to Judd Ryder.

"It's Charles. He's following me. I'm in Piccadilly Circus, heading toward the Criterion. Are you close? He's got a gun."

"I'm already moving. Leave your cell on."

Five streets flowed into the speeding roundabout encircling the busy plaza. Gaudy neon and LED lights advertising Coca-Cola, Sanyo, and McDonald's cast the area in manic red and yellow light. She watched for a bobby. Now that Charles was near, she wanted a policeman.

"I'm passing Lillywhites," she reported to Ryder. When she saw her reflected face in the glass of the sporting goods store, the strain on it, she looked away. Six of the tourists with whom she had crossed the street peeled off toward the Shaftesbury Fountain and statue. She went with them, peering around their shoulders.

"Charles is still behind me. He's wearing a phone head-set, and he's talking to someone on it."

"So now we know he's got a friend. Is there anyone with him?"

She checked. "Not that I can see. My group is climbing the steps to the fountain, and I'm going with them. I'll move to the other side. The fountain will be good cover to block me from him."

"I'm at the crosswalk with Piccadilly Street. Can you circle back to meet me?"

"He'll spot me."

"Okay. Go to the Trocadero Center. I'll be there."

The bronze Shaftesbury Fountain shone nickle gray in the night's lights. A scattering of people sat on the steps. At the top, Eva rushed around to the far side and looked down on the plaza, congested and rimmed by a waist-high iron fence interrupted by the crosswalk she needed. There was no sign of Charles or a policeman. But across the teeming traffic stood the London Trocadero Center, a huge building where people thronged for food, alcohol, theater, and video games. That was where she would meet Ryder.

She joined a young couple as they sauntered down the fountain's steps, holding hands. At the base, they headed right, and she moved straight ahead.

Suddenly something hard and sharp pressed into her left side. "That's a gun you feel, Eva." Charles's voice. "You're caught, old darling. It was logical you'd come this way. *Sic eunt fata hominum*." Thus goes the destiny of man.

"Bad grammar, Charles. *Homina*. The feminine in my case, you bastard." As they continued along the street, she looked down and saw his trench coat pocket bulged with his hand aiming his weapon.

In her ear, Ryder ordered, "Hide your cell. Leave it on."

But as she slid the cell phone inside her jacket, the gun's muzzle jammed her side again.

"No," Charles snapped. "Give it to me."

She froze, then looked back at him, saw the frosty expression, the hard black eyes. The anger and frustration that had been building in her burst out in a torrent. "I loved you. I thought you loved me. I want to be glad you're alive, but you're making it really hard. What in hell do you think you're doing?"

"Keep walking, and lower your voice. Hand over the phone. Now." A few people were glancing at them. "If you think I won't shoot, you're going to find yourself dead on the pavement."

Her heart was pounding, and a cold sweat bathed her. She handed him the cell. "Don't call me old darling again. I never liked that, you son of a bitch."

He turned off her cell and spoke triumphantly into his headset. "I've got her, Preston. I'll hold her so you can take care of her. Where do you want to pick us up?"

CHAPTER 18

AS CHARLES WALKED BESIDE HER, the gun held against her side, Eva repressed a shiver. She tried to mute the outrage and hurt in her voice: "Why did you fake your death and disappear? I thought we were happy. But because of you I spent two years in prison—and now you want to kill me. After all those years together, don't I mean anything to you?"

"You meant a lot . . . once," he said impatiently. "You'll never understand. You were always too much in the world."

"And you weren't enough in it. Is this about the Library of Gold?"

"Of course it's about the library. I was invited to become the chief librarian," he said reverently. Then he announced into his headset, "It doesn't matter, Preston. She's not going to tell anyone now."

"I don't recognize you. What have you become?"

He waved his free hand, dismissing her. "Some things are worth any cost."

"The Library of Gold was more important than the

friends and colleagues you left behind to grieve? More important than me?" She ached for the love she had lost.

"You've got a petty mind, Eva. Thank God a few people over the centuries were bigger. They kept the library alive, and not just physically but completely in spirit."

She was silent, working hard to control her emotions. She needed to find out as much as she could while she looked for a way to escape.

"Where is the library?" she asked.

"I don't know."

"You must be kidding."

He shook his head. "You'll never understand," he said again.

Charles had always enjoyed the sound of his own voice, the brilliance of his logic, the forceful power of his personality.

"Who kept the library alive?" she asked, hoping to trigger his passion for holding forth.

His face broke into a smile. "When Ivan the Terrible lost the last war with Poland, he gave the library secretly to King Stephen Báthory as war tribute. The next ruler passed it on to Cardinal Mazarin of France, who had a famous library of his own. Eventually it went to Friedrich Wilhelm of Brandenburg, the Great Elector. Peter the Great had it, too, and so did George II of England. Later it was in the care of Napoléon Bonaparte, Thomas Jefferson, and Andrew Carnegie—all selflessly devoted to the library. That sort of commitment has never wavered through the years, and the secret of the Library of Gold's existence has always been sacrosanct."

Nervously aware of his gun, Eva glanced over her shoulder, hoping to see Judd Ryder—but he had been heading toward the Trocadero, a completely different direction. To make matters worse, Charles now took her around the corner and onto Haymarket Street. Was this where the man named Preston was going to meet them—and "take care of her"?

She looked back. Still no police. A man in a ragged gray raincoat buttoned up to his chin and a black watch cap pulled low over his forehead and ears was shambling along, head bent down.

Charles pushed her around onto another street. Now it would be harder for Ryder to find her. Maybe impossible.

She rallied. "So what you're saying is you've finally gotten half your wish. You're in charge of the library, but you're still screwed, because you don't have the other half—international acclaim for discovering it. You ached for that, but you're never going to have it, because you can't or won't tell anyone where the library is."

Charles gave a smug smile. He reached a hand up to his headset. He hesitated, then turned it off. Preston could no longer hear what he said to her.

"There's a chance someone someday will figure out where it is," he told her.

"You *do* know. Why wait?" She put sincerity into her voice. "You could be famous now. Tell me. I'll help you."

"To get the job, I had to agree to stay with the library until I died. All of us are lifers."

"You mean captives. Tell me now. If we expose the library, you'll be free."

"No, Eva. It's not safe. You don't know Preston. Besides, I don't want to leave the library." Staying close to her, he changed the subject. "Remember the old board games we used to play? The simplest ones in all countries are based on three ancient pursuits—the hunt, the race, and the battle. Their equivalents today are fox and geese, backgammon, and chess."

"Of course I remember. The Greeks and Romans had them, and so did the early Egyptians. Scripta and Latrunculi come to mind."

"Very good. You haven't forgotten everything I taught you."

"You taught me a lot, but some of it I never wanted to learn, especially from someone I loved—like lying and betrayal. I still don't understand why you let me go to prison."

"Because you are Diana, the relentless huntress. I had to vanish completely. Assuming you believed I died accidentally in a car crash while you were asleep at home, you still would've been in our little world. If there was ever a hint about me and the library, you would've jumped on it. That was a threat far too dangerous."

"You drugged me! Someone else is in your grave!"

His face torqued with outrage, as if she were the disloyal one. "I had to work like hell to convince the director not to let you burn up in the car. Sending you to prison was my idea. I saved your life."

"And you think that makes what you did right? My God, Charles, you have the morality of a stick of wood. *Stat fortuna domus virtute.* Without virtue nothing can be truly successful. You may be the chief librarian— but you're a failure."

As Charles bristled, at his side appeared an outstretched hand, palm up and open. "Can you spare a few quid, mate?"

Eva peered around. It was the man in the ragged trench coat and watch cap. The corners of his mouth were pulled down in a permanent grimace, and he radiated self-pity. Then she caught a flicker in his gray eyes and noted his square face. Stunned, she gazed off. He was Judd Ryder.

"Get the hell away." Charles hurried her onward.

Ryder was instantly back at Charles's side, matching

their pace. "Come on, be a good bloke. Help a feller out. See, me hand's empty. Fill it with a nice coin, and I'll be gone quick as a stink in the wind."

From bad grammar to imagery, she knew it would be too much for Charles.

Furious, he turned on Ryder. "Fuck off."

And Eva acted. Watching Charles's hand still in his pocket but now pointed away, she took one quick step back, kicked the inside of his knee, and slammed the side of her hand in a *shutō-uchi* strike into his neck. He grunted and staggered.

Ryder's gun appeared in his hand. "Pony up your weapon, Sherback." He ripped the headset off Charles's head.

His equilibrium regained, Charles's heavy jaw jutted with anger.

"Do it now," Ryder snapped. "I won't be nice and ask again."

Fear in his eyes, Charles silently passed the pistol to him.

Eva took a deep breath. "How did you find us, Ryder?"

There was a small smile on his lips. "The ankle bracelet Tucker gave you."

He hustled Charles down the quiet sidewalk, and she moved to Ryder's other side, away from Charles. Pointing both guns at him, Ryder directed him around the corner to one of the silent single-block avenues in this part of London. Lined with tall buildings, it was so narrow there was no sidewalk and no place to park. No cars cruised past.

"Where are we going?" Charles demanded.

"In here."

Ryder directed him into a dead-end alley where trash bins and cardboard boxes stood along the sides. It was deserted. The few doors were closed. The place reeked of garlic and old food. The buildings surrounding them were steep monoliths, showing only a slice of the night sky.

"Let's call the police," Eva said. "I want Charles arrested so I can clear my name. I want my life back."

Ryder shook his head. "First we need to find out about the Library of Gold."

Saying nothing, his posture ramrod straight, Charles kept walking. Ryder was still between them, holding both his and Charles's guns.

"Charles is the head of the Library of Gold," she tried. "From what he told me, it's been in private hands and secret since near the end of Ivan the Terrible's life."

"But where is it? Who controls it?"

"He wouldn't say. The police will question him. That's their job. Then we can turn over all the information to Tucker."

Ryder gave a firm shake of his head. "This is CIA business."

"I'm going to call the bobbies." She leaned around Ryder. "I want my cell phone, Charles."

Charles gave a strange smile and slid a hand toward the pocket where he had put it.

"Stop," Ryder ordered.

"Better the police than you." Charles said, but his words and gesture were a feint. Abruptly his weight shifted, and with lightning speed he threw himself at Ryder, reaching to get back his gun.

Ryder slammed a fist into Charles's midsection just as Charles's hand closed on the muzzle of the weapon. As he yanked the gun, Charles's momentum carried the pair backward. Elbows shot out from their sides, and their torsos twisted. Before Eva could move, there was a loud explosion, and the stench of cordite ballooned into the alley's dark air.

Charles dropped to his knees.

"Oh, my God." Eva covered her mouth with her hands. Bile rushed up her throat.

Blood bubbled on Charles's lips as he knelt motionless on the alley floor. A pool of blood on his black trench coat turned the fabric glossy.

Charles raised his gaze to look at her. "Herodotus and Aristagoras," he said. Then he pitched forward, landing hard, his arms straight along his sides, his cheek pressed into the pavement.

CHAPTER 19

RYDER DROPPED TO HIS HEELS beside the downed man and felt the carotid artery. No pulse. He swore. He had just lost his best chance of finding the library and answers to who was behind his father's death.

"I'm sorry, Ryder," Eva said. "Is he dead?"

He nodded. Getting to his feet, he peered at the doors lining the narrow alleyway and then down the length to where it opened onto the street. There was no sign the gunshots had attracted attention. He seized Sherback's armpits and dragged him behind a row of trash bins, where they would be out of sight and the dim light was adequate for what he needed to do.

Crouching beside the slack body, he rifled through the trench coat pockets.

Eva joined him, sitting on her heels. "What are you doing?"

"Interrogating him." He took Sherback's phone. "It's a disposable cell." Then he found her cell phone.

She grabbed it.

He stared at her. "Go ahead and call the cops—if you

want to end up arrested as an accessory to your husband's murder."

She stiffened. Her shoulders slumped. She turned off the cell and pocketed it.

Ryder checked Sherback's jacket, discovering a billfold and a small leather-bound notebook. He continued to search.

Eva opened the billfold and stood up to get better light. "He's got a Brit driver's license with his picture on it. The name says Christopher Heath, but that shouldn't matter. His body can still be identified by his DNA."

"Maybe not right away, not if the DNA of the man who was in the car crash was identified against what was supposed to be your husband's DNA. That'll take the cops a long time to sort out—if they even bother to check into such a long shot. Is there anything else in there? Notes to himself?"

She crouched again. "Nothing. No credit cards or anything. Just cash."

The last item Ryder found was in Sherback's pants pocket—a Swiss Army Champion Plus pocketknife, loaded with miniature tools. He stood up, took off the old gray trench coat he was wearing, and put it in a trash bin. Then he shoved everything, including Sherback's Glock, into his peacoat pockets. He would go through Sherback's notebook when he had time.

"I've got to get out of here," he said to Eva. "You coming?" He watched emotions play across her face. The skin was tight, and the eyes bruised. God help him, working with an amateur was tough, but he needed her. She was his last living link to Sherback and the library.

"Yes."

As they hurried down the alley, he told her, "*The Book of Spies* was stolen tonight from the British Museum. My guess is your husband was in London as part of the operation. His people must've left a duplicate book in the museum. A duplicate would explain why he was photographing the original, and it'd buy them time. The real one was in the Méridien hotel at some point."

"Someone named Preston must be part of it. He was supposed to pick up Charles and me and then kill me."

"Swell. Anyone else you can think of who wants to get rid of you?"

"My popularity ends there."

As they hurried on, the sound of their footsteps seemed to echo in the alley.

"What did Charles mean by 'Herodotus and Aristagoras'?" he asked.

"He told me there was a chance someone could figure out where the library was. Thinking about it, my guess is he left a clue or clues to its whereabouts. So Herodotus and Aristagoras might be it. But I don't recall anything about them together."

He felt a thread of excitement. "Let's look at what it might mean from another angle. Who were Herodotus and Aristagoras individually?"

"Herodotus was a Greek—a researcher and storyteller in the fifth century B.C. He's considered the world's first historian."

"So he could've written about Aristagoras."

She paused. "You're right. He did. The story happened twenty-five hundred years ago, when Darius the Great was conquering most of the ancient world. When he captured a major Ionian city called Miletus, Darius gave it to a Greek named Histiaeus to rule. But as time passed, he got nervous, because Histiaeus was growing too powerful. So he 'invited' Histiaeus to live with him in Persia, and he gave Miletus away again—this time to Histiaeus's son-in-law Aristagoras. Histiaeus was furious. He wanted his city back and decided to start a war in hopes Darius would crush it and reinstate him.

He shaved the head of his most faithful slave and tattooed a secret message on the man's skin. As soon as the hair grew back, he sent the slave off to Aristagoras, who had the hair shaved and read the command to revolt. The result was the Ionian War, and Herodotus wrote about it at length."

"You said Charles used to have light brown hair. That he'd dyed it black."

She stared at him.

They turned on their heels and raced back along the alley. They crouched beside the corpse.

He handed her his small flashlight. "Point it at his head." She did, and he pulled out Charles's pocketknife, opened a long blade, grabbed hair, and started sawing.

Almost immediately a police siren sang out in the distance.

"I think they're coming this way."

He nodded. "Someone probably reported the gunshot." There was a mound of black hair on the oily concrete beside him. He slid small scissors out from the Swiss Army knife and quickly clipped close to Charles's scalp.

She leaned close. "I see something."

Letters showed in the flashlight's stark illumination, indigo blue against pasty white skin.

"LAW," she read. "All capital letters. There are numbers, too."

He clipped faster.

"031308," she said.

"What does LAW 031308 mean?" he asked.

"'LAW' indicates it could be a code for a law library. Some codes are universal, others not. I don't recognize this one. It could be special to a particular library—like the Library of Gold. But I don't see how it'd lead us there."

The siren screamed from the street, approaching the alley.

He jumped up. "Try the doors on this side. I'll take the other side."

They ran, grabbing doorknobs. All were locked. They were trapped in a dead-end alley with a corpse. If they ran out to the street, the police would see them. Rotating red slashes of light appeared at the alley's mouth, flicking into the darkness, bouncing off the walls.

"There's a ladder," he told her, nodding.

They sprinted. The beacons had illuminated a fire escape ladder down the side of a building, almost unnoticeable because its black iron blended into the black granite of the wall. It was a good ten feet above them. He leaped. Wrapping both hands around the bottom rung, he hauled himself up and did a quick inspection. There was no way to lower the ladder.

Grasping the side rail, he leaned down and extended his hand. "Jump."

As the grille of the police car came into view, Eva ran ten feet back and then dashed toward him, propelling herself high. He grabbed her hand. Straining, he held tight to the railing and pulled. Sweat beaded his forehead as he dragged her up to the first rung.

They climbed quickly. By the time the police car rolled into the alley, they were far above, with Ryder leading the way. At the top, he crawled over a low wall. The gigantic London Eye was a silver wheel of light on the horizon. Quickly he surveyed the flat roof—utility boxes, vent hoods, and a small shed that should contain a stairwell down into the building.

Eva's face emerged above the rooftop's rim, looking grim. She clambered over, turned, dropped to her knees, and leaned forward, staring down. He joined her. The police car had stopped about forty feet inside the alley,

almost beneath them. Flashlights in hands, two bobbies were patrolling, kicking cardboard boxes, examin-
ing trash cans.

"They'll find Charles," she said in a low voice. "What
will they do when they see what's written on his head?"

"God knows. But he's got no identification, so they're
going to have a nifty time trying to figure it out." He
paused. "I have a proposition. It's likely *The Book of
Spies* is headed back to the Library of Gold. You know
a hell of a lot more about the library and Charles, the
head librarian, than we do. I'd like to stash you someplace safe in London, and then I'll phone or e-mail
when I need to consult."

There was a steely expression on her face. "I'm not
the kind of woman who gets stashed someplace. I'm
going with you."

"No way. It's too dangerous."

Just then there was a shout below.

They peered over the side of the building and to their
right. One of the bobbies was staring down behind the
garbage bins where they had left Charles's body. His
flashlight moved slowly, indicating he was taking in the
full length of the corpse. The second policeman rushed
to join him, his free hand pressed against the gear dangling from his belt to keep it from flopping.

As the bobbies crouched, Ryder nodded at the alley's mouth. "We have another visitor."

A car had stopped on the street, blocking the alley. It
was a Renault. The driver got out. Dressed in jeans and
an open black leather jacket, he was tall and moved
gracefully as he walked toward the police.

Ryder studied him, noting the loose joints, the open
hands that appeared relaxed but were far from it, the
head that moved fractionally from side to side, showing
he was doing a far more thorough scan of the area than

most people would realize. Everything about him announced a well-trained professional in tradecraft.

Eva looked at Ryder. "Preston?"

He kept his focus on the stranger, memorizing his features. "Yeah, I think so."

CHAPTER 20

THE TWO BOBBIES TURNED and closed ranks, blocking the garbage bins as Preston approached. Preston said something to them, but his words were lost over the distance. After listening, the policemen relaxed a bit. One nodded and gestured.

Preston walked over and leaned low to peer at Charles Sherback's corpse. Ryder noted a slight tensing in his shoulders.

And then it happened. In concise, swift movements, he was suddenly upright, a sound-suppressed pistol in his hand as he turned back toward the bobbies. His face showed no emotion.

Ryder yanked out his gun. Too late. Preston fired under his arm point-blank into the heart of the nearest bobby, then immediately into the heart of the second. He had shot them without completely facing them, so certain was he of their positions and his ability to kill.

Eva stiffened. Ryder put a hand on her arm.

The two policemen stood motionless, stunned into bleeding statues. When they went down, one sat cross-legged, and the other knelt on one knee. Then they toppled, the first landing on his belly, the second on his side. As blood oozed out, their limbs made jerky movements.

Preston holstered his weapon and dragged Charles's body out from behind the bins. The scuffing noise of Charles's heels on the pavement drifted upward. Preston hefted the body over his shoulder and loped off. Ryder noted he still showed no emotion.

"He doesn't want anyone to see the tattoo," Eva decided.

Ryder studied the moving killer. Charles's body was draped over one side. Part of Preston's torso was covered by it, but Preston's head and legs were even more chancy targets at this distance. Soon he would pass beneath them, heading out toward the Renault. Ryder had to act quickly. The torso was his best target.

"Call 999 and describe where the alley is," he told her. "Go over to the shed to do it. Your voice shouldn't reach the alley from there. Don't tell them about us."

Without a word she grabbed Charles's cell and ran.

Balancing himself, he aimed carefully, inhaled, exhaled, and fired twice in quick succession, targeting Preston's right side to avoid his heart. The explosions were loud. Preston suddenly staggered.

But as Charles's body fell to the alley floor, Preston recovered, dropped beside it, and rolled. His weapon appeared in both hands, pointing upward, looking for the shooter. The man was damn good.

Ryder aimed and fired twice again.

Preston jerked back, and then Ryder got lucky—Preston's head thudded against the pavement. The additional blow did it. Preston froze a moment. His eyes closed. One hand released his pistol, and the other flopped to the ground.

Smiling grimly to himself, Ryder hurried to the stairwell shed.

Eva was standing near the door. "I called them. Two dead bobbies got their attention. They're on their way. Did you kill Preston?"

"I hope not. I want him to face some intense questioning. Move away from the door."

It was padlocked. Using the handle of his Beretta, he broke the lock and swung open the door. A dank odor blew out. Lit only by thin starlight, concrete steps descended into a black abyss. He turned on his miniature flashlight, and they walked down quickly side by side.

He kept his voice even. "Are you up to talking about Charles's tattoo?" Although she seemed to be coping well, he had no idea how much of what had happened had affected her.

"Are you kidding? You bet I am."

"It seems to me since Charles wanted the library to be found, he intended the tattoo to be decipherable. My guess is he told us about Aristagoras and Herodotus because he thought you'd not only figure out he'd left a tattoo but you'd understand the message. So let's go back to the beginning. What does LAW 031308 mean?"

She said nothing. They descended two more flights. The doors were numbered, indicating they had reached the sixth floor.

Finally she decided, "I suppose LAW might have nothing to do with the law or something legal. Or the letters could be initials, an acronym. But it's not an acronym I recognize. 'Loyal Association of the West.' 'Legislative Agency for War,'" she free-associated. "None of that makes a darn bit of sense. The number's too short to be a telephone number. It might not be just a string of individual numbers either, but a whole number—if one skips the zero, then it's 31,308. Or it could have a decimal. But where does the decimal point go?"

"Okay, let's think in terms of codes. Bar codes. Postal codes. Some kind of shipping code."

"Doesn't ring a bell."

Silently they continued downward.

"Maybe it *does* involve the law," he said. "Were you ever in a lawsuit?"

"That bullet I've dodged."

When they arrived at the ground floor, he cracked open the heavy metal fire door and gazed out. He closed the door gently.

"We've got company," he said. "There's a guard behind a reception desk, and he looks disgustingly alert. I'm not in the mood to take any more chances. We'll go to the basement."

Again they descended.

He had an idea. "Maybe the code is something personal. You know, personal to you and Charles."

At the bottom, the stairway door opened onto an empty parking garage lit by a scattering of overhead fluorescent lights. A hundred feet away a driveway rose toward the entrance. It was sealed at the end by a heavy garage door, but there was a side door next to it. They rushed toward it. It was locked, but this time there was no padlock for Ryder to knock open. Surveying around, he screwed the sound suppressor onto his Beretta.

"Step back," he ordered.

She did, and he directed the muzzle downward so the bullet would go into the ground on the other side. He fired. *Pop.* Metal dust spewed.

Putting the weapon away, he turned the knob and peered out. They were on a busy street, but he did not know which one.

"Looks safe," he told her.

They stepped outside into the stink of exhaust. There were plenty of people on the sidewalk, entering and leaving watering holes. A pub door opened, and loud techno music blared out. But above that was the screaming noise of more police sirens. Two, he guessed.

He glanced at her, saw the alarm in her face. "With luck, they're on their way to the alley," he told her. "They'll find Preston, and the rounds in the policemen's bodies will match his pistol."

"Yes, but they could have a description of us from the call that brought the two bobbies to the alley in the first place. The caller might've seen us."

He was worried about it, too. There had been enough unpredictable events tonight that he was taking nothing for granted.

As they walked, she continued: "I've been thinking about what you said, Judd—that the code could be personal to Charles and me."

It was the first time she had called him by his first name. "Go on."

"The numbers could be a date. Charles and I were married on March the thirteenth in 2000. So '03' could be March, '13' could mean the thirteenth day, and '08' is 2008."

"That was just a month before he disappeared. So what happened on your anniversary in 2008?"

Suddenly two police cars were racing down the street toward them. Their rotating blue and red lights lashed through the night like sabers.

He smoothed his features. "We need to slow down and blend in. Hold my arm."

Instead, she slipped her hand inside his, and he felt a strange sensation so pleasant he forced it from his mind before it could turn to grief. They continued on through the lamplight—and the police cars rushed past.

Dropping her hand, he busied himself by taking out his palm mirror and checking it. "They've turned the corner."

He felt her relax. When she spoke again, her voice

was businesslike. "If I tell you what I've figured out, you've got to promise to take me with you. I'll bet everything that's happened tonight will only make the people with the Library of Gold want to get rid of me more. I want to see them captured. I want to be *there*."

"You're blackmailing me."

She gave a wry smile. "It appears I've learned something from you."

He found himself smiling, too. "All right, it's a deal." Then he stared at her sternly. "But if I do, you've got to do exactly what I say—when I say it. I'm serious about this, Eva."

"You're the pro. Whatever you say, as long as you're reasonable."

"No. This isn't negotiable. Look at it this way—if you come along, you'll be putting me in danger, too. There may not be time to ask questions or argue."

She sighed. "All right. So this is what I think . . . In 2008, Charles and I celebrated our anniversary by flying to Rome. We visited an old friend of his, Yitzhak *Law*. He's a professor, well-known in the field. He and Charles often talked late into the night. They had a shared passion: finding the Library of Gold. Maybe the reason Charles left the tattoo was to say Yitzhak knows where the library is."

He inhaled deeply. "Then we go to Rome."

PART TWO
THE RACE

Hannibal's troops were closing in on Rome when one of his spies reported the city was filled with rumors its dictator, Fabius, was in his pay. With that news, the great military chief went on a rampage across the countryside, destroying and burning everything in his path—except Fabius's properties. As soon as the news reached Rome, Fabius issued proclamations he was no traitor. But his people did not believe him, and Hannibal gained valuable time and psychological advantage.

—*translated from* The Book of Spies

Spying is a pursuit as old as civilization and a craft long practiced by the most skilled and treacherous of strategists.

—U.S. News & World Report
January 19, 2003

CHAPTER 21

IN PAIN, DOUG PRESTON jerked awake. The alley. He was still in the alley, lying on the pavement near Charles Sherback's corpse. With effort he turned his head and saw the two policemen's bodies. Then he looked on the other side of him, past the police car and to his Renault. The alley was still deserted.

He stared at Charles's bald skull, gray as an old bone in the light. What in hell did the tattoo mean?

Suddenly the loud noise of police sirens penetrated his brain. That was what had awakened him. He struggled to his feet. His head throbbed. He rubbed the bump on the back of it—the size of an eagle's egg. The right side of his chest hurt like boiling fire. He was badly bruised but not wounded, because he was wearing one of the new Kevlar tactical body-armor vests, thin and light, under his jacket and shirt, and the rounds had not penetrated.

Feeling weak, he bent over and propped his hands on his thighs, willing the pain away. At last he picked up Sherback's corpse and maneuvered it over his shoulder and staggered toward his car. When he reached the mouth of the alley, he checked the narrow street, then opened the Renault's rear door and heaved Charles inside.

As he got behind the steering wheel and turned on the ignition, he knew from the noise of the sirens he was within seconds of being discovered. Gunning the motor, he laid rubber, fishtailed around the corner, then cut back on his speed. He entered the traffic smoothly.

With a shaky hand he wiped sweat from his forehead and swore loudly. Who in hell had the shooter been? Probably whoever had killed Charles.

He thought about the man he had spotted peering down over the top of the building, gun in hand. But by then he was already injured, and the man had shot twice more before he could return fire. At no time had the man been more than a black silhouette. If a shooter that good was helping Eva Blake, she was going to be more difficult to catch.

Another unpleasant thought occurred to him. He had convinced the bobbies to let him see the corpse not just because he had described Charles and told them his old friend was drunk and lost, but because the bobbies had found nothing in Charles's pockets and had no way to identify him. That meant the shooter probably had Charles's things, including his cell phone. It would contain Robin's and his numbers, and if the shooter were connected, he could track the numbers through the location chips embedded in their phones.

Preston grabbed his cell, rolled down the window, and tossed it into the next lane of traffic. Watching his side-view mirror, he saw the tires of a pickup truck roll over it. Satisfied, he took a new disposable cell from his glove compartment and dialed Robin Miller.

"Are you in the jet?" he asked

"Yes. We're waiting for you and Charles." She sounded sleepy.

"Listen carefully, and follow my directions exactly. As soon as I hang up, open up your cell and take out the battery. Under no circumstances put the battery back in. I don't care where you are or what you think you need it for, do *not* make your cell operable again. Do you understand?"

"Of course. When will you get here?" She sounded testy, insulted he had asked whether she understood. She did not like her intelligence questioned.

"Soon," he said. "Tell me what the jet's satellite phone number is."

There were the sounds of the phone being removed from its plastic case. She read him the number. Then he gave her his new cell number.

"When you saw Charles last, was his head shaved?" he asked.

"No. Why would he do that?"

"I thought you'd know."

Her voice was suspicious. "Is Charles with you?"

"Yes, but he's dead," he said bluntly.

He heard a loud gasp.

Before she could erupt into tears, he added, "He was shot, and probably Eva Blake was involved. The last time I talked with him, he'd caught her. I'm sending his body back with you to the library. Take out that cell phone battery. Tell the pilot to warm up the jet." He hung up.

By telling Robin now about Charles's death he hoped he would find her under control when he arrived. The director encouraged romances among the small Library of Gold staff, since the members were more easily managed if they had some sort of home life. It caused occasional problems when affairs erupted or couples broke apart, but even that kept the staff involved in the community.

As he laid his new cell on the seat beside him, a river of pain swept through him. His eyelids felt heavy. After the first adrenaline rush of making arrangements with Robin, his mind was turning to mush. He could go three days without sleep and still remain alert, but now he was injured, which was dumping his stamina into the toilet.

Opening the glove compartment, he grabbed a large bottle of water and a small bottle of aspirin. He poured a half-dozen tablets into his mouth and gulped water. Blinking, he turned the car west toward Heathrow and continued to drink.

At last he sighed. He was feeling stronger. As he drove, he laid the water bottle beside him and pictured the place to which he went at times when he needed to heal and find himself again. He saw the golden light, the rows of gleaming books, the polished antique tables and chairs. He could hear the soft rhythmic sounds of the air-purification system.

In his imagination he locked the door, chose an illuminated manuscript, and carried it to his favorite reading chair. He sat with the book on his lap and savored the hammered gold and glistening gems. Then he opened it and turned pages, absorbing the brilliantly colored drawings and exquisite lettering. He could read none of the foreign languages in the library, but he did not need to. Just seeing the books, being able to touch them, recalling the sacrifices and care throughout the library's history helped to banish his ugly childhood, the hardscrabble life, the missing father, the angry mother. The sense of loss he felt as he had witnessed Langley spiraling downward in a wash of political bullshit.

The Library of Gold was proof the future could be as cherished and glorious as the past. That the work he did was crucial. That he was crucial.

After a while he could feel his heartbeat slow. The

sweat dried on his skin. The pain eased. A sense of certainty infused him.

Girding himself, he picked up his cell and dialed again. When the director answered, he told him, "There have been some developments, sir. You need to know what's going on. First, someone planted a bug on *The Book of Spies*. It was inside a fake jewel on the cover. It's been flushed down a toilet."

"Jesus Christ. Who would've had the connections to duplicate one of the gems and put a bug inside it?"

"I keep going back to the chief librarian before Charles. We thought he'd stolen the book and sold it to a collector so he'd have cash to try to leave. But if the collector were the anonymous donor to the Rosenwald collection and the one who planted the bug, then the National Library would've found it before it got to the British Museum."

"Unless the donor had real clout. Someone with the money and resources to locate a person in the National Library who could be bought to cover for the bug."

Preston nodded to himself. "I made some calls and found out Asa Baghurst, California's governor, signed a special order releasing Eva Blake from prison—just three days ago. I successfully eliminated Peggy Doty, then Charles called to say he'd found Eva Blake. I was on my way to pick them up and scrub her, too, but they weren't at the rendezvous." He described spotting the police car that had led him to finding Charles shot dead in the alley.

"So we lost Charles in the end. It's just as well. The way he was screwing up, we were going to have to erase him anyway." The director sighed. "Did his wife kill him?"

"There was a man there. He could've done it. He took some shots at me, but I never saw his face. The accuracy of his aim and the way he positioned himself said a lot. He's trained. It looks like a total setup—the bug, Eva Blake, and a shooter. Someone wanted to follow *The Book of Spies*."

"Is there any way Blake could've found out Charles was our chief librarian before the opening at the British Museum?"

"I don't see how. This was the first time Charles was away from the library. And of course after his predecessor smuggled out *The Book of Spies,* we doubled security, so Charles had no outside contact at all. Still, he was up to something. When I found his body, his head was shaved, and there was a tattoo on it—LAW 031308."

"What in hell is that all about?"

"I don't know, sir. You said yourself Charles was a romantic. But he was ambitious, too. He thought a lot of himself."

"Did Charles shave his head, or did someone else?"

"I'd say someone else. Maybe Blake and the shooter. I'll have my staff do a thorough search of Charles's cottage and office. There could be something there that'll tell us what the tattoo means."

"What about the rest of the operation?"

"On track. Robin and *The Book of Spies* are on the jet. I'll stow Charles's corpse on board, then they'll fly home, but without me. I'm going to stay in London to keep looking for Blake. I have a way to find her—I got her cell number off Peggy Doty's phone. I have a NSA source I can use to track her through the cell's location, assuming the phone's turned on."

"Good," the director said with relief. "Do it."

CHAPTER 22

Brentwood, California

ATTORNEY BRIAN COLLUM WAS sound asleep in his large Tudor home when his telephone rang. His eyes snapped open. The master suite was cool and bathed in shadows. He checked the glowing digital numbers on his bedside clock—two A.M.—and snatched the phone.

His wife rolled over to gaze anxiously at him. The days of panicked clients calling at all hours were long past, so something must have happened to one of their children. They had three, all studying at various universities.

"Yes?" he said into the telephone.

"Hello, Brian." The voice was familiar. "Sorry to disturb you. This is Steve Gandy. I've got an unusual situation here. It involves one of your clients, Eva Blake. I need a favor."

Steve Gandy was the longtime coroner for the County of Los Angeles, a straight shooter who could be relied on for a no-holds-barred game of racquetball. Brian made it a practice to cultivate people in government, and since this concerned Eva, he was even more willing to listen.

"Hold on." He turned to his wife. "This isn't about the children. Go back to sleep. I'll take it in my office."

As she nodded, he carried the phone out of the bedroom. "Is Eva all right?"

"I assume so, but I don't have any way to get in touch with her. She's been released from prison. No one seems to know where she went. Do you still have authorization to sign documents for her?"

"I do." He was shocked. Eva was out of prison? "Tell me what's going on." He sat behind his desk in a patch of pale moonlight. Not only had he represented Eva at her trial, he now handled her legal affairs.

Steve's voice was tense. "I need signed permission to exhume her husband's body."

"Why?" Brian's lungs tightened. "Who wants it exhumed?"

There was a sigh on the other end of the line. "The CIA. The term *national security* came up in the conversation several times. They're telling us nothing except it's critical we make damn sure we identify accurately who's buried in Sherback's grave and how he died, and we're to contain who knows about the exhumation. But there's hell to pay these days when anyone gets caught up in a CIA publicity disaster. Maybe this is legitimate, but I sure don't have that kind of crystal ball. And I damn well don't want my office to face repercussions. The problem is, they want us to exhume the body without a signed order. That's why I'm bringing you in."

"Jesus."

"Precisely."

"This is insane. You know Charles Sherback is in that grave. Your office matched the dental records."

"That's not conclusive enough for them. They want another autopsy—and for us to check the DNA."

He swore silently. "Do you have a name at the CIA?"

"Gloria Feit made the call. She's with the Clandestine Service."

"Her bona fides are good?"

"Yes. I don't want a duel with the CIA, but at the same time I've got to protect myself and my people," Steve said. "I want you to sign the order, Brian. I'll drive over there now. That way we can start digging at daylight, and I can get the CIA off my back with some answers."

Brian thought quickly. "Here's another idea. I've got a key to Eva's storage locker. I'm sure she must still have some of Charles's things. I'll swing by there early in the morning and see what I can find to give you a head start on the DNA. Then I'll drive to your office and sign the order."

Steve sounded relieved. "That's not perfect, but you're right. A DNA sample will speed the process. Be here by eight A.M. And thanks."

They hung up, but Brian stayed in his chair, staring at the shadows in his office. The room was full of books, the titles unseeable in the darkness. Still, he was comforted by them and their enduring counsel, handed down through the ages. Smiling wryly to himself, he remembered some earthy advice from Trajan, Rome's long-ago warrior emperor: "Never stand between a dog and where he's pissing."

Fortunately, he did not have to risk interfering with Steve's investigation. The man who was buried in Charles's grave was a salesman from South Dakota, a loner whom Preston had chosen in an L.A. bar and eliminated later with a snap of the neck, which was consistent with an injury received in a car wreck. Then Preston had arranged a late-night break-in at the office of Charles Sherback's dentist, so records of the dead man's teeth could be substituted for Charles's. Brian had kept the dead man's gloves and a few other things locked away in his office safe.

Although the DNA match from inside the gloves and the clean autopsy would make the CIA's curiosity evaporate, Brian was left with a much larger and potentially more dangerous question: Who or what had provoked the intelligence agency's interest?

He picked up the phone and dialed the Library of Gold's director. "Marty, this is Brian Collum. We've got a situation." He described the coroner's call. "The CIA order for exhumation came from someone named Gloria Feit in the Clandestine Service."

Martin Chapman exploded a stream of oaths. "How did you leave it with the coroner?"

"I'm going to provide him with the corpse's gloves for a DNA match. That should resolve things. Can you think of a reason they'd want the identity rechecked?"

"No reason, except now Charles Sherback really is dead."

Brian felt a moment of shock. "That's a blow to the library. He was damn good at the job. What happened?"

Brian had begun cultivating Charles a dozen years ago, admiring his knowledge about the Library of Gold and appreciating his obsession to find it. When they had needed a new chief librarian, he had recommended Charles, and the book club had authorized him to secretly offer him the position. Now the club would have to find a replacement.

"He died in London," the director said. "Shot to death."

"Did Preston retrieve *The Book of Spies* successfully?"

"Yes. It's on its way home."

"That's a relief." He remembered what Steve had said. "The coroner told me Eva's out of prison. Does she have anything to do with this?"

"She's just the beginning of the problem."

Astonished, then increasingly concerned, Brian listened as Martin Chapman described Eva's spotting Charles in the museum, his attempt to kill her, the bug on *The Book of Spies,* and Preston's search for Eva, ending with the discovery of Charles's corpse.

"Preston thinks a trained man is helping Eva," the director said. "Obviously someone was intent on trying to track *The Book of Spies*—maybe back to the library. I'm concerned about who had the ability to plant the bug. Now that the CIA is involved, I'm wondering whether it's them."

"Shit."

"Besides that, Charles had a tattoo on his head— LAW 031308. Does it mean anything to you?"

"Not a damn thing."

"It could be a message," the director said. "But to whom? And why?"

"Think about Charles's predecessor. None of us ever guessed he had the balls not only to want to leave, but also to smuggle out *The Book of Spies*. One of the reasons we chose Charles was because the library was the most important thing in his life. But the downside was his ambition and arrogance. God knows what the message means. Whatever it is, it could be dangerous to us."

"If Eva saw the tattoo—and we have no reason to think she didn't—she may be able to understand it."

"You're right."

"Preston has a way to track her through her cell phone. You take care of the coroner." There was a thoughtful pause. When the director spoke again, his voice had its usual brisk, businesslike tone: "I have a way to handle the CIA."

CHAPTER 23

Washington, D.C.

THE MAN PARKED HIS CAR on a dark residential street in the gently rolling hills north of downtown Washington. In the distance, the tall dome of the Capitol shone like ivory. He opened the car door, and Frodo, his little terrier, leaped out, wagging his tail.

With the terrier leading, they walked down the sidewalk, all part of the man's cover, and turned onto Ed Casey's block. The man noted another early dog stroller heading toward him through the still shadows. As he always did, he assumed an indulgent dog-owner's smile and nodded in greeting. Then he pulled Frodo off the curb to give the pair a wide berth.

As soon as the other walker was out of sight, the man stopped beside a Eugenia bush whose low branches brushed the ground. He slid Frodo's leash underneath, and Frodo followed, crawling in and circling around. His little black eyes peered out.

"Stay." He gave the hand command.

Frodo immediately settled back into the foliage, invisible to anyone who passed. They had done this many times. Frodo would not move nor make a sound.

After a careful look around, the man sprinted across the lawn to Ed Casey's clapboard house and examined the doors and windows on the first floor. All were locked, including French doors overlooking a goldfish pond in the rear yard. He returned to the French doors. No dead bolt. Slide locks had been installed, but no one had bothered to engage them. He loved the way people were lulled into complacency by the passage of uneventful time. His profession depended on it.

With a small tool, he popped open the French doors and stepped into a shadowy family room. He liked to have house plans, but there had been no time to get them. When he hired him for the job, Doug Preston had been able to pass on only Ed Casey's address.

Cautiously he padded across thick carpet into a central hall. A grandfather clock ticked rhythmically. There was no other noise. He listened at the foot of the stairs, then ducked his head into open doorways— a living room, a dining room, and a kitchen. All deserted. He opened the only closed door. Bingo—an office.

Keeping his ears tuned for movement upstairs, he headed straight to the desk, where a computer sat. He went to work, installing tiny wireless transmitting devices inside the hard drive and keyboard.

Finished, he listened to the house again. Silence. He slipped out of the office and let himself out the French doors. The early-morning sky was still black. Tomorrow night he would return and remove the bugs, lessening the chance anyone would ever know his business tonight.

Pausing near the street, he surveyed the area. At last

he strolled to the Eugenia bush and gestured. Frodo scooted out, and the man gave him a dog biscuit. Whistling to himself, he walked his pet back to the car.

Johannesburg, South Africa

IT WAS HALF PAST NOON in Johannesburg when Thomas Randklev received a call from the Library of Gold director. As soon as he hung up, Randklev phoned Donna Leggate, the junior U.S. senator from Colorado. It was only 5:30 A.M. in Washington, and it was quickly apparent she had been asleep.

As soon as he said his name, the tone of her voice modulated from gruff to welcoming. "This is an odd time to be calling, Thom, but it's always good to hear from you."

He knew it was a lie. "I appreciate that. I'd like a bit of information. Nothing unseemly, of course."

"What can I help you with?"

"This is about a woman named Gloria Feit, who's with your Clandestine Service. We'd like to know for whom she works and what she does."

"Why are you interested?"

"I'm not at liberty to say, except it involves someone special like you, someone we like to give good service to—one of our investors. Certainly nothing about your national security. It's just business."

She hesitated. "I'd rather not—"

He interrupted. "I hope your shares in the Parsifal Group are making you smile."

A widow, Leggate had been appointed to the Senate to succeed her husband when he died four years earlier. Her husband's debts had left her in a precarious financial position, but because of Parsifal, she was earning far more than her husband had. She was also far more ambitious, but in Washington ambition unsupported by money was just another social affectation.

Her tone was guarded. "Yes, very much so."

"And of course there are the dividends," he reminded her.

"Even better," she admitted. "But still . . ."

Although unsurprising, her reluctance was annoying. They needed her to move on this, and fast—but he was not ready to tell her that yet.

"You're on the Senate intelligence committee," he pointed out. "You've brought a CIA employee, Ed Casey, into Parsifal. Tell him to e-mail someone at Langley for the information. If you feel you can't, you'll have to drop out of our special club for investors, and I'll transfer your shares to another of our groups. You can count on the returns being decent—but they won't support you in your old age." He let that sink in. "On the other hand, if you can do us this favor, you can stay in the club, continue to recruit selected others, and receive a sizeable contribution to your reelection campaign."

"How sizeable?" she asked instantly.

"One hundred thousand dollars."

"Five hundred thousand would make the sun shine a lot brighter."

"That's a great deal of money, Donna."

"You're asking a huge favor."

He was silent. Then: "Oh, hell. All right, I agree—but only if you call Ed Casey immediately."

"If I'm awake, he can damn well get his butt out of bed, too."

"You always could charm me, Donna." He smiled to himself. She had quit negotiating too soon. He had the director's approval to go to $800,000.

"And you're a delightful rogue, Thom," she said.

"Love that about you. Tell me, will you be needing any other favors?"

"Perhaps. And remember, you can ask occasionally, too. If it's in my power, I'll be delighted to help. After all, we're friends. All part of the same club."

CHAPTER 24

Washington, D.C.

SENATOR LEGGATE PUT ON her bathrobe, lit a cigarette, and waved smoke from her eyes. Washington was a town where favors were exchanged like poker chips. To survive, one learned to be helpful while being careful with whom one played. If you wanted to be a serious contender in the nation's fast, treacherous political waters, you had to be an Olympian at the game.

While she had a sense of ominousness about Thom Randklev's naked laying out of her options if she refused to help, she also felt a sense of exhilaration. He had agreed to her high number easily. That told her he had access to even more cash. What frightened her was whether she could handle him—or herself—if she ever had to refuse.

But that was the future. Maybe years from now. With luck, never. She marched into her office, turned on her desk lamp, spun open her Rolodex, and dialed.

"A good early morning to you, Ed. This is Donna Leggate."

"Good Lord, Donna, do you know what time it is?" Ed Casey was a top gun in Langley's Support to Mission team, which built and operated CIA facilities, created and maintained secure communications, managed the CIA phone company, and hired, trained, and assigned officers to every directorate. His department also handled payroll, which meant he had access to the records of everyone the CIA employed—as long as they were on the books.

"I've been up for hours reading classified reports," she told him, fabricating a lie he would believe. "Sorry to bother you, but I'd like your help with something before I go into the office. One of the reports mentions an officer named Gloria Feit, in the Clandestine Service, but there's nothing about to whom she reports. I'd like to know that as well as what she and her boss do."

"You'll need to go through the D/CIA's office."

"If I'm asking questions about this, others on the subcommittee will be, too. Going through the D/CIA opens up the possibility of a leak, and then the press dogs will drool for everything they can claw up. The reason I'm calling is because I know you and I are on the same page about protecting Langley whenever possible."

"There's a chain of command. I don't buck it."

"As I was dialing," she continued thoughtfully, "I was remembering when you told me you needed a college nest egg for your kids. How old are they now?"

There was a change in Ed's voice. Perhaps a hint of guilt. "I appreciate your paving the way so I could buy shares in the Parsifal Group."

She rammed the point home: "Has it been a good investment for them?"

"Yes," he admitted.

"I'm delighted. I think all of us like to help each other whenever we can. What I'm asking I can get anyway. The only difference is I want it now, while it's fresh in my mind."

"What's the report about?"

"It's M-classified. Sorry." "M" indicated an extraordinarily sensitive covert operation. Among the highest the United States bestowed, single-letter security clearances meant the information was so secret it could be referred to only by initials, and there was no way Ed would be privy to it. "You can e-mail your office for the information about Gloria Feit."

"Hold on," he grumbled.

Senator Leggate smiled to herself. She had watched her husband cajole and threaten to get what he wanted, and now she was the one in the power seat.

Johannesburg, South Africa

THOM RANDKLEV STOOD before the floor-to-ceiling window in his office, hands clasped comfortably behind, and stared out at the rocks and shales of the Witwatersrand—"White Water's Ridge" in Afrikaans. As clouds drifted past and the sun blazed through, pockets of quartz glittered, attracting his gaze. For a moment he felt a fierce sense of pride.

The Witwatersrand was the source of 40 percent of the gold ever mined on the planet, and it had provided his family's first small fortune. Then his lazy father had lost everything in drink, divorces, and wild spending. But now Thom had all of it back and more, including homes in San Moritz, Paris, and New York City, which was where he had met Senator Leggate and begun cultivating her. As he had assured the director, she was the one who could handle the first step in resolving the problem of why the CIA wanted to exhume "Charles Sherback."

As his mind roamed over his accomplishments, he turned to stare at the books stretching across two long walls of his office. He had been disturbed by the director's information, but at the same time he had complete confidence the situation—whatever it was—could be resolved.

What mattered was the Library of Gold had remained secret for centuries because of careful attention to detail, and that secrecy was the hallmark of those who had inherited the library. In today's world, the biggest wars were fought inside boardrooms behind closed doors, and the book club knew exactly how to train, fight, and win every skirmish. And that was what this was—a mere skirmish. As he ruminated about that, he remembered what Plato had written: "Thinking is the talking of the soul with itself." How true, he decided as he poured himself a drink.

When the phone rang, he snapped it up.

As he had hoped, it was Donna Leggate. "Gloria Feit is chief of staff for Catherine Doyle. Doyle has some special assignment, but there's no record of what it is. Since I know something about these matters, I believe Doyle has a team—and it's deep black. And that means there may be no official record of employees or missions. Ed wouldn't tell me more. Frankly, I doubt he knows more, because it's above his security grade. Doyle appears to me to be a NOC." Nonofficial cover officers, NOCs, were those highly talented and daring officers who operated without the official cover of their CIA identification. If arrested in a foreign country, they could be tried and executed as spies.

"Thank you, Donna. I appreciate it. I'll put my people to work filtering in the money to your reelection campaign. We want good friends like you to stay in office."

As soon as he got rid of her, he phoned the director and relayed the information.

Stockholm, Sweden

IT WAS NOON IN STOCKHOLM, and Carl Lindström was sitting in the leather recliner chair in his office, reading financial reports, when the director called. Once he understood what the director wanted, Carl went to his desk, checked his e-mail, and found the note forwarded to him that contained the information the Washington break-in artist had uncovered from Ed Casey's secure e-mail to Langley.

Now he had a record not only of the routing, the message, and the address to which it was sent, but also the clandestine codes used.

With that, he phoned his chief of computer security, Jan Mardis. A former black-hat hacker herself, Jan was in charge of uncovering and stopping attacks on their worldwide network. She also kept her staff's expertise honed with regularly simulated assaults on their systems, designed hacking tools, and drafted network-infiltration tactics.

Upon occasion, she did special jobs for him. Through him, the Library of Gold's director had used her several times over the past few months.

"I have a challenge for you, Jan," Lindström told her. "And when you accomplish it, you can count on a generous bonus. I need you to crack into the CIA's computer system. There's a particular team I want you to find. It's run by Catherine Doyle. One office employee is Gloria Feit. The unit is probably black, which means they're going to appear to be unlisted, but we both know there's a record somewhere. I've sent you an e-mail with the information you'll need."

"Interesting." Jan Mardis's voice was usually bored, but not now. "Okay, I've read your e-mail. Barring complications, this should be fun, a dip in Lake Mälaren on a hot summer day, as it were. I'll route my signals through multiple countries—China and Russia, for sure. That'll stop the digital cops cold. I'll get back to you."

Carl Lindström stood and stretched. Cyber crime was the fastest growing criminal enterprise of the twenty-first century, and his software corporation, Lindström Strategies, was one of the fastest rising in the world. It had been attacked time and again. But because of Jan Mardis, no one had ever breached the firewalls. He had complete confidence in her not only because of her skill, but also because of human factors: He had saved her from a jail term by pulling strings in the judicial system, which included his promise to hire her. The occasional side job he secretly gave her allowed her to exercise her love of taking on some of the most highly secure organizations on the planet. And he paid her excessively well. As Machiavelli wrote, to succeed, it was critical to understand what motivated an individual—and use it.

As he waited to hear back from her, he walked to his bookcase, which was filled with leather-bound and embossed volumes. He pulled out a collection by August Strindberg, one of his favorite modern authors. He opened the book, and his gaze fell upon a passage: "A writer is only a reporter for what he has lived."

He thought about that, then he applied it to himself. His entire life's work, rising from the slums of Stockholm to create and head Lindström Strategies, was a reflection of what he had learned about the need to go to any length to armor against the indignities of poverty.

With pride, he decided his corporation was his book, the book *he* had written.

An hour later, he was reading financial reports in his recliner again when the phone rang. He reached for it.

"It's me, boss," Jan Mardis said. "I've got a bonus for you. I've got access to Catherine Doyle's office computer. Is there anything you want me to look for?"

He sat up straight, and his pulse sped with excitement. "Send me a copy of all Doyle's e-mails for the last twenty-four hours. Then get the hell out of there."

CHAPTER 25

Aloft over Europe

THE GULFSTREAM V TURBOJET soared through the night, its powerful Rolls-Royce engines humming quietly. Above the aircraft stretched an endless canopy of sparkling stars, while far below spread gray storm clouds punctuated by jagged bolts of lightning. From his window Judd Ryder studied the skyscape, feeling a sense of suspension between two worlds, uncertain and somehow dangerous. He wondered what his father had been involved in, and how much he was his father's son.

Shaking off his emotions, he sat back and focused. The Gulfstream had been waiting at Gatwick Airport at a private hangar, one of the aircraft Langley regularly rented for transporting federal employees and high-value prisoners. He and Eva were the only passengers, sitting together near the middle of the cabin. Each armrest contained a laptop and hookups for electronic devices. On their tables stood steaming cups of coffee brewed in the galley. The rich aroma scented the air.

He peered at Eva's tired face, the rounded chin, the light California tan. Her red hair lay in a wreath of long curls around her head where it rested back against the seat. The lids of her blue eyes were at half-mast. At the moment she showed none of the fire and combativeness that had aggravated him, instead looking soft and vulnerable. He was still unsure what he really thought of her. In any case, it was irrelevant. What mattered was he needed her for the operation. He hoped to be able to ship her back to California soon.

Her eyes opened. "I should try to reach Peggy."

"You can't turn on your cell while we're flying, but you can borrow mine." He plugged his mobile's connecting cord into the armrest, tapping into the plane's wireless communications system. He explained about its secure mode, then showed her how to make what would appear to others to be a normal call.

She dialed Peggy's cell phone number. Listening to the voice on the other end, she looked at him and frowned. "May I speak to Peggy, please?" There was a pause. "I'm not going to tell you who I am until you tell me who you are." Another pause. Abruptly she cut the connection.

"What happened?" he asked instantly.

"A man answered. He kept asking questions." As she dialed again, she told him, "I'm calling information for the Chelsea Arms's number." Once she had it, she phoned out again. "Peggy Doty's room, please." She listened. "I know she has a room there. We were going to share it. . . . What? She *what*?" Her face stricken, she hung up and stared at him. "Peggy's dead. The clerk says the police think she shot herself, but there's no way she'd take her own life. Someone had to have killed her." She shook her head, stunned. "I can't believe she's dead." Tears slid down her cheeks.

Watching her, he felt again the awful loss of his father,

his conflicted emotions. He went to the galley and returned with a box of tissues and handed it to her. As she wiped her eyes and blew her nose, he said, "My guess is Charles told Preston that Peggy was your friend, and Preston went to her in hopes of finding you. He's her killer. I'm sorry, Eva. This is horrible for you."

He had a sudden vision of his father when he was about his age, towering over him as he rode the carousel at Glen Echo Park. The full head of blond hair, the strong nose and chin, the happy expression on his face as the music filled the air and he stood beside his son protectively. About five years old, Judd had been riding a palomino horse with a flowing silver mane. As the horse rose and fell and the carousel circled, he felt himself slipping. His mother waved, her face beaming with pride. As he raised a hand to wave back, he fell, his legs too short to reach the floor to steady himself. He dangled half off the horse.

"Hold on tight and pull yourself up," his father had said calmly. "You can do it."

He had grabbed the pole hard, his little arms aching as he slowly righted himself.

"You can do anything, Judd. Anything. Someday you won't need me to stand beside you anymore."

Suddenly he realized Eva was talking.

"Those people are unspeakably evil." She was staring at him, her expression cold. "Those bastards. We've got to find them."

"We will." He grabbed his peacoat from the seat across from them. "Ready to do some work?"

"Absolutely."

He removed the items he had taken from her husband—disposable cell, small leather-bound notebook, billfold, and Swiss Army knife. Leaving the Glock pistol in his pocket, he heaved the peacoat across the next seat. Then he took off his corduroy jacket and tossed it on top. He sat back and adjusted his shoulder holster.

She had the notebook in her hand, turning pages. He thought about it, then decided to let her have a go at the notebook first.

He checked Sherback's cell, looking for phone numbers. "He's coded his address book. What would he use for a password?"

"Probably something classical. A Greek or Roman name. Try Seneca, Sophocles, Pythagoras, Cicero, Augustus, Archimedes—"

"Okay, I get the idea." He tapped in one after another.

"This is interesting," she said at last. "I've looked at all the pages, but there aren't any lists of names with or without phone numbers or addresses. There seem to be only his thoughts and various quotations. Each entry's dated, going back six years. That means he had it while we were living together, but I never saw it."

"He kept it hidden from you, so there was already a pattern of secrecy."

She nodded. "Listen to this—it's the first entry, and it'll give you a taste: 'In ancient times, worshiping a god occurred in some beautiful grove, holy place, or temple. It's no accident almost all libraries were in pagan places of worship, just as in later Muslim, Jewish, and Christian times they were in mosques, tabernacles, and churches. The written word has always had a magical, divine power, unifying people. Naturally religion wanted to control that. But then books are another name for God.'"

"See whether he mentions the Library of Gold or Yitzhak Law somewhere."

"I've been looking. Here's another one: 'There are books I will never be able to find, let alone read.'"

"Poignant."

She nodded and resumed reading silently.

Judd was running out of names to break Charles's cell phone code. He stopped, his fingers poised above the keypad.

She gazed up. "I've just found one of Charles's favorite quotes. It's from Aristotle. 'All people by nature desire to know.' That seems appropriate. Try 'Aristotle.'"

He typed the letters of the Greek philosopher's name, and the screen revealed the address book. "I'm in. The bad news is that it's empty. He must've memorized the numbers he called. Okay, time to check the ingoing and outgoing calls." The list was coded, but 'Aristotle' worked again. "There are only two. Both are London numbers. Do you recognize either?" He read them to her.

She shook her head. "Try them."

He dialed. The first number rang four times, and an automated voice invited him to leave a message. He considered, then ended the connection. She was watching him.

"A machine answered," he reported. He tried the next number and got the same response. "Nothing again."

"When I spotted Charles on the street outside the hotel, he was with a blond woman. Those two cell numbers could belong to Preston and her. I didn't recognize her, but Charles and she were obviously together."

"Describe her."

"Long blond hair and bangs. Pretty. Early to mid thirties, I'd say. Maybe five foot six. She had a large rolling suitcase. He was carrying a backpack and left it at her feet just before he started chasing me. The backpack was fat and solid-looking, so it could've contained *The Book of Spies*."

"That'd account for the book's being in the hotel."

"Yes." She turned back to the first page of Charles's notebook.

Ryder examined the Swiss Army knife. There was nothing to indicate it was Charles's or anyone else's. Opening the billfold, he took out the driver's license and cash and spread them onto the tray table.

"I may have found something." Eva patted the notebook. "As I told you, everything's dated in here. I've been looking for patterns. With one exception, Charles would write something occasionally, once a week at most. But then there's a three-month period before we went to Rome in which he made a lot of entries, sometimes several a day. That's when he was on sabbatical, supposedly visiting some of the world's great libraries. I never got a real itinerary out of him, and he didn't talk much about the trip when he returned."

"Does he mention which libraries?"

"No, but what he wrote is almost entirely about libraries."

"What do you think the change in pattern means?"

"First, he had enough time he could write his thoughts more frequently and the value of libraries was on his mind. But, second, he wouldn't have wanted me or anyone at the library to know he'd tattooed something onto his scalp. So this is the sequence I see: He tattooed himself, spent three months hiding out, and came home to me with hair long and thick enough for it to look normal. Then we celebrated our anniversary with Yitzhak in Rome. Two weeks later we were back in L.A., and then two weeks after that was the car crash."

"Makes sense."

They drank their coffee and continued to work. He found nothing written on any of Charles's cash. He put the driver's license and money back into the billfold and returned everything to his peacoat's pockets. Next he checked the clip to Charles's Glock. The gun was clean and in pristine condition. No rounds were missing.

Eva handed him the notebook. "I can't see anything else that's useful in here. Your turn."

He took it. "You look tired. Why don't you get some sleep?"

"I think I will." She set her coffee cup on his table and stored her table inside her armrest. Then she reached down and pulled up her pants leg. "I'm going to take off this ankle device."

"No. If something happens to separate us again, I can always find you with my reader."

She thought about it and nodded. Reclining her seat, she closed her eyes.

He e-mailed Tucker, asking him to trace the two phone numbers on Sherback's cell and to investigate whether Sherback and perhaps a woman had stayed at the Méridien hotel, adding the false name on Sherback's driver's license, the woman's description, and that *The Book of Spies* might have been in her backpack. When he had phoned Tucker to arrange the jet, he had filled him in on the events of the night and given him Professor Yitzhak Law's address in Rome and asked him to check with the London police about Preston and Charles Sherback's body.

He studied the notebook, finding nothing new. Then he looked at Eva a long time. Finally he rested his head back, hoping he would not dream about the past. At last he fell into an uneasy sleep.

CHAPTER 26

London, England

DOUG PRESTON SAT IN his rental car in a public parking lot near the River Thames, arms crossed, head resting back, drifting in and out of sleep. He had delivered Charles's body to the Library of Gold jet, and it was safely gone. He had also phoned his NSA contact, who had gotten back to him with the bad news that Eva Blake's cell phone was turned off, which meant it could not be tracked yet. Then he had handled a new assignment for Martin Chapman, hiring a specialist in Washington to break into Ed Casey's house.

Now he was waiting for a call from NSA that Blake's cell phone was activated and her location pinpointed, or from the director that he had learned through Ed Casey's intel where Blake was going. Either would do.

Restless, he adjusted his aching body behind the steering wheel. Springtime shadows dappled the parking lot. Somewhere on the river a boat's horn sounded.

He checked his watch. It was a little past one P.M. He closed his eyes, ignoring the pain in his ribs. He was starting to sink back into sleep when his cell finally rang.

Martin Chapman's tone was full of outrage: "Tucker Andersen is CIA."

"So State was his cover. Tell me everything." Preston shook off the chilling news.

"Judd Ryder e-mailed Tucker Andersen. The reason we know is because Andersen sent a copy of the e-mail to Catherine Doyle, also CIA. They're part of some kind of black program. Doyle is chief." The director's voice was tense. "Ryder is a private contractor for CIA now."

"Jonathan Ryder's son?"

"Yes. He's the gunman, and he's been helping Eva Blake. Everything in the British Museum *was* a setup. The CIA's the one that planted the bug on the book and got Blake's sentence commuted. They intend to find the Library of Gold. We're going up against your old employer, Preston. You were loyal." The voice had grown harder, the question unspoken.

"That was a long time ago. Another life. I was glad to walk away. Even gladder you wanted me." Then he said the words he knew the director needed to hear, and he meant them: "My loyalty is only to you, the book club, and the Library of Gold."

There was a pause. "The e-mail said Ryder and Blake were heading to Rome to see Yitzhak Law. You can't get there in time. How do you suggest this be handled?"

Preston stared out the car's window, considering. A plan formed in his mind, and he laid it out for the director.

"Good. I like it," the director said. "Since we're

dealing with a black unit, it's contained. That's the only advantage we have. I have an idea to take care of Tucker Andersen and Catherine Doyle. I'll get back to you when I need you."

CHAPTER 27

Rome, Italy

IT WAS THREE O'CLOCK in the afternoon, the sun bright, almost overwhelming after the cold gray rain of London, when Eva walked through the centuries-old Monti section of Rome. Just south of Via Nazionale, Monti was an oasis of artists, writers, and the monied, and was seldom listed in tourist guides. Tall ivy-covered houses lined the street, interrupted only by cobblestone alleyways not much wider than a Roman chariot. Pedestrians strolled along the streets.

Clasping her shoulder satchel to her side, Eva risked a glance back. As expected, Judd was still several houses behind, looking Mediterranean in his sunglasses, swarthy face, and arched nose. They had stopped to buy new clothes so they would fit in with the warmer weather and locals' tastes. He wore a loose brown sports jacket, an open-necked blue shirt, and Italian jeans. She wore Italian jeans, too, with a green shirt and jacket.

As Fiats and scooters rushed by, she passed a leafy

piazza filled with preschool children romping under the doting gazes of nannies. At last she crossed onto the busy street where Yitzhak Law lived.

AS HE FOLLOWED EVA, Judd covertly scrutinized the bustling area, picking out the three-person team Tucker Andersen had sent to watch over Professor Law's home.

Across the street was one: a man with a cloth shopping sack, dressed in a worn business suit and sitting on a bench. A quarter block away was another—what appeared to be an elderly woman, sunk into a beach chair beneath a pepper tree outside a trattoria while she read the Italian daily *La Repubblica*. The third was a youthful skateboarder in sunglasses and a backpack. He slalomed lazily past, wearing earphones as his hips gyrated to music.

Judd used his mobile to call the skateboarder—the team leader. "Anything new, Bash?"

The unit had been in place an hour, not as long as he would have liked, but they'd had to be assembled from Catapult's undercover officers already on operations in and near Rome.

"Everything's cool, man. No one's gone in or left," Bash Badawi reported. He sailed his skateboard off the curb.

"Let me know if the situation changes."

Judd watched Eva moving ahead, her stride long and confident, her red hair blazing in the shimmering sunlight. He picked up his pace.

As he passed her, he said without moving his lips, "It's safe. Go in."

YITZHAK LAW'S HOUSE WAS a three-story building of aged yellow stone with large windows and white shutters. Eva ran up the worn steps and touched the bell. Chimes rang inside.

When the door opened, she smiled widely. "*Buon giorno,* Roberto." Roberto Cavaletti was Yitzhak's long-time partner.

"Do not just stand there, Eva. Come in, come in. I am delighted." He kissed her on both cheeks, his close-cropped brown beard prickling. Short and lean, he gave the appearance of a sleek fox, with a long, intelligent face and bright brown eyes.

"I've brought a friend," she warned.

She turned and nodded in Judd's direction. Glancing around, Judd was soon at her side, and they stepped into an entryway of antiques and paintings. The fragrant scents of a spicy tomato sauce lingered in the air. In Rome, lunch was traditionally the largest meal of the day and eaten between noon and three o'clock at home, which was why she had high hopes of finding Yitzhak here.

She introduced Judd as her traveling friend from America.

"*Benvenuto,* Judd. Welcome." Roberto shook his hand enthusiastically. "You are not jet-lagged? You do not look jet-lagged." It was an ongoing concern of Roberto's, who never traveled beyond the borders of Rome's time zone, despite Yitzhak's frequent invitations to accompany him.

"Not a speck of jet lag," Judd assured him.

Relieved, Roberto turned to Eva, put his hands on his hips, and scolded, "You have not kept in touch." With a single short sentence, he had covered the car crash, her guilty plea, and her imprisonment, at the same time letting her know as far as he was concerned they were still friends.

"You're right, and it's my fault. I loved the letter from you and Yitzhak." She had not trusted the compassion in the men's note, and so she had never answered it. With sudden clarity she saw how she had isolated herself.

"You are completely forgiven. Like the Pope, I am stern but magnanimous. Are you hungry? Would you like *un caffè*? It is dripping even now." In Rome, coffee was as important as wine.

"Coffee would be great," she said. "The way you always make it, *molto caldo*."

He smiled, acknowledging the compliment, and turned to Judd. "And you, Eva's friend?"

"Absolutely. Let us help you."

Roberto raised his brows at Eva. "He has good manners. I approve." Then he whispered in her ear, "And he's gorgeous." He pointed in the Italian way with an outstretched hand, palm down, toward the hallway, then he followed them.

As they passed open doors showing a sitting room and a small, elegant dining room, she asked, "Is Yitzhak home? We'd love to see him, too."

"Of course. And he will want to see you. You will take coffee to him. He is in his *rifugio*."

They went into the modern kitchen, which gleamed with enameled white walls and a stainless-steel refrigerator and gas stove. The aroma of fresh coffee infused the airy room. Roberto poured coffee into a carafe, then arranged cups, a cream pitcher, a sugar bowl, and spoons on a tray.

He indicated the tray. "It is your responsibility, Judd."

Judd picked it up. "Lead on."

Roberto took them out into the hall again and toward the back of the house, where a broad staircase rose two floors. But he opened the door beneath, the stairs showing simple wood steps going down. Cool air drifted up. They ducked their heads and descended into the cellar, which reflected the house's period in its rough brick walls and uneven brick floor.

In the center of the floor was the area's dominant feature—a ragged hole with wood steps, built only ten years before, going down into what seemed an abyss. Beside it lay a trapdoor of old bricks built on top of a plywood platform. The trapdoor was the exact dimensions of the hole, and when it was put into place, Eva knew, the bricks fit neatly into one another, hiding the hole.

Judd stared down and deadpanned, "Where are the flames? The screams of suffering souls?"

Roberto laughed. "This is not Dante's *Inferno,* my new friend. You are about to see a glorious sight few others have. But then, this is Rome, once the *caput mundi,* the capital of the world, teeming with more than a million souls while Paris and London were mere outposts of mud huts. No wonder we Romans are so proud. Here is where I leave you." He called down, "We have two more visitors, *amore mio.* Prepare yourself for a pleasant surprise."

"More visitors?" Judd's expression was curious, revealing nothing. The presence of outsiders would complicate their ability to find out quickly from Yitzhak what Charles's message meant.

Roberto nodded and said mysteriously, "Eva will be happy about it." He returned upstairs.

Eva had learned about the steep steps in previous visits. She turned and went down backwards, gripping the rail. Balancing the tray, Judd followed, and they entered the professor's private preserve.

It was a vast area, illuminated by torchère lamps and encompassing the width of the house. The length stretched from the rear garden to the street, where there appeared to be a small tunnel at the edge of a long pile of rubble. The flooring was glowing purple Phrygian marble. Placed here and there on it were statues of nudes uncovered during the excavation. Pink marble columns partially exposed—they were still mostly embedded in raw brown earth—shone palely. One wall was revealed; it was smooth, flat brickwork displaying the meticulous craftsmanship of builders two thousand years ago. Its centerpiece, which always made Eva's heart beat a little faster, was a stunning mosaic displaying Jupiter and Juno, king and queen of the Roman gods, reclining on thrones. Few had seen it since it was buried in antiquity.

She sensed Judd's awe, and then an instant return to acute awareness. His gaze swept the room, where Yitzhak sat with a man and a woman in wood chairs around an unvarnished wood table on which lay his notes and reading glasses. An American, the professor was a world-renowned scholar of medieval Greek and Roman history, with an emphasis on Judaism. He had published a dozen books on the subject.

Eva put a smile on her face, and all three stood up. The professor hurried toward her, arms outstretched. He was a small, slope-shouldered man who exuded the energetic optimism of a Rome native. His face and belly were round, his gaze sharp, and his head completely bald, shining in the light. In his early sixties, he was fifteen years older than Roberto.

"My dear, it's been far too long." He enveloped her in his arms.

"Much too long." She hugged him.

When he released her, she introduced him to Judd.

"You like my little sanctum sanctorum, Judd?" Yitzhak asked curiously. "It was once the domain of wealthy families in the Augustan era. Roberto saw some pottery shards beneath the cellar's bricks when we had to do some repair work, and that's how we discovered it."

Eva explained, "Ancient Rome is a buried city, lying

under layers of history forty-five feet deep in places. What you're seeing is unusual—more than eighty percent is still uncovered."

Yitzhak said in a mock whisper, "Please don't tell on us, Judd. We private homeowners do our digging like thieves in the night because we don't want the Beni Culturali knocking on our doors to evict us. And they have a habit of doing just that, so they can make our little finds public." He gazed around, his eyes glowing. "The silence and seclusion make the distant past seem eerily tangible, don't they?"

"They do," Judd agreed as he set the coffee tray on the table. Then he said just what Yitzhak wanted to hear: "Your place is very beautiful."

The professor smiled broadly, his round face crinkling. "You must meet my other guests. This is Odile and Angelo Charbonier, in from Paris by way of Sardinia. We've had a delightful lunch. But then, why not? We're old friends. Such good old friends that Angelo's been buying and reading my books for years, emphasis on 'buying.'" He winked at Judd. "Who can ask more than that? Eva, I believe you already know the Charboniers."

Angelo pumped Judd's hand. "Delighted." His French accent was light.

A little more than six feet tall and in his late forties, Angelo looked fresh-faced and vigorous in his open-necked white shirt, beige jacket, and slacks. His face was chiseled in the way of European men who spent long hours in the gyms of their exclusive athletic clubs. Although he was a rich investment banker, Eva had always found him to be a down-to-earth and charming companion at the openings and dinner parties where they had met.

Eva could read nothing on Judd's smiling face as he responded, "It's good to meet you."

Always more reticent, Odile shook Judd's hand and said simply, "A pleasure."

"For me as well," Judd said.

A little younger than Angelo, Odile was quieter, with refined features and perfectly coiffed platinum-blond hair. She made a graceful athletic figure in her highly expensive velour jacket and trousers. At the same time, there was a steely quality about her that no doubt had been useful as Angelo and she had climbed high in Paris society through his business connections and her philanthropic work.

After exchanging pleasantries with Judd, Angelo turned to Eva. "I am sorry about Charles. Of course his death was a tragedy. Will you forgive me for saying whatever happened, it was also an accident and surely not your fault? Charles was a great man, and you are a great lady. Odile and I have always been fond of you."

He glanced at Odile, who gave a firm nod of agreement.

Odile shook Eva's hand. "Oh, *chérie,* we are simply too sorry for words."

Immediately, Angelo extended his hand, too. Touched, Eva took it. He pressed his lips against the back. When he looked up, he smiled into her eyes. "I'm glad you weren't badly injured in the car accident."

"Thank you, Angelo. Thank you, Odile. You're both very kind."

"Why didn't I know you were coming, Eva?" Yitzhak complained, appraising her. "We've heard nothing from you in a very long time."

"It's all my fault," she admitted. "I wasn't sure—"

"That we still adored you?" Yitzhak finished for her. "Silly girl. Of course we do."

"You will be interested to know Yitzhak and I were just talking about the Library of Gold," Angelo told her. "We missed the opening at the British Museum."

"Ah, *The Book of Spies*. What a find." Yitzhak bent over the table and picked up the carafe. "Who wants coffee?"

"Enjoy yourselves. I am going upstairs to ask Roberto for my usual aperitif," Odile said.

As she climbed the steps, Yitzhak added cream and sugar as requested, then handed the cups around. As the four stood together, Eva glanced at Judd, who had been covertly studying the Charboniers. He smiled at her over his cup as he drank. She could read nothing in his gray eyes.

"If only Charles were still alive so he could have attended the opening," the Frenchman said. "I am certain he would have given us another theory about the library's location. His theories were always very clever." He peered at Eva. "Were you able to go?"

"Yes. It was interesting, and *The Book of Spies* is fabulous."

"I'm envious." The professor sipped his coffee.

"What do you think Charles would have said?" Angelo asked curiously.

Before she could answer, Judd interrupted. "As a matter of fact, Charles did say something—in a way."

Surprised, Eva stared at him.

"Eva," he told her, "I think this is a good time to fill in the professor. No need to bore him with a long explanation. Just give him Charles's message."

Judd seemed to have decided it was safe to do so. Angelo Charbonier was a bibliophile, too, and perhaps he might be helpful—or was Judd testing the Frenchman in some way?

"It's something I discovered recently." Eva paused. "It was just your name, 'Law,' and the date of Charles's and my wedding anniversary in 2008—the one we spent with you and Roberto. Do you know why Charles would leave a message for me like that?"

The professor frowned, trying to remember. He rubbed his chin. At last he chuckled. "Of course. My old brain had nearly forgotten. Charles left a secret gift for you, Eva—or for an emissary if you sent one—but you had to ask for it and mention the anniversary date." He walked toward the ladder.

"It's here?" Eva asked, excited.

He turned, his eyes dancing. "Yes. Come with me. I'm eager to know what it is, too."

CHAPTER 28

EVA FOLLOWED YITZHAK, and they climbed upstairs, first into the cellar and then back into the house. Angelo and Judd brought up the rear. In the hallway Eva could hear Odile's and Roberto's voices floating back from the sitting room.

The professor led them through the airy kitchen and into a large storage room lined with metal shelves stacked with cardboard boxes. They stood beside the professor, the air electric with suspense as he peered around.

"Now, where did I put it?" Lips pursed, he headed into the back and pushed aside some cartons. When he emerged, he was carrying a small box taped tightly shut. He rotated it to show the top. "See? Here's your name, Eva." He handed it to her.

She stared at the handwriting. It was Charles's.

"Perhaps it is some fabulous necklace from ancient Persia, or jeweled earrings from Mesopotamia." Angelo's chiseled features were alight with excitement.

"Open it," Yitzhak ordered.

She tore off the tape and lifted the lid. On top of

Styrofoam bubbles lay two pieces of protective paper boards about eight inches wide by twelve inches long, held together with clips. She separated them, revealing a fragment of parchment. One side showed cramped, faded Arabic lettering, while the other side was blank. There was nothing written on the protective boards.

"What's that?" Judd asked.

"It looks like something from an ancient document." Eva handed the yellowed piece to Yitzhak. It was much smaller than the boards, about three by four inches.

"Let's go into the kitchen, where I can see better." Yitzhak led them back into the room, where he carefully put the fragment on a high butcher-block table.

She watched as he scrubbed his hands at the sink. Many professional archivists wore white cotton gloves when handling manuscripts and other artworks to protect them from skin oils and acids. At the same time, others claimed gloves were dangerous, since they not only could contain unseen dirt and particles, but they also minimized the wearer's sensitivity when handling the article. For them, thorough hand-washing was the better choice. Yitzhak belonged to the hand-washing school, as did she. Charles had been a white-glove archivist.

When Yitzhak finished, she washed her hands, and he ordered Judd and Angelo to do the same.

She joined Yitzhak on one side of the high table as he positioned his reading glasses on his nose. Judd joined Angelo on the other side, two men of the same height with similar body builds, she noticed.

As Yitzhak muttered to himself, translating the fragment, Eva dug through the Styrofoam packing in the box. "There's something else in here."

She pulled out a tapered cylinder of glistening gold, about eight inches long and, judging by its heft, hollow. At the narrowest end it was two inches in diameter; at the other, about four inches. Perfectly round ivory knobs shone on each terminus.

Yitzhak stared at the baton. "Simple, but spectacular."

"Gorgeous," Angelo said. "But what is it? Is there any writing on it?"

"Does it open?" Judd asked.

Eva rotated the cylinder, and everyone leaned close.

"There are small engravings of arrows, shields, and helmets. Decorations, no writing. I can't find a way to open it. You try, Judd." She could see nothing that related to the Library of Gold. She handed it to him.

"It looks very old," Angelo observed.

"It is," Eva told him. "And it's not only a work of art; it had a real purpose. You can tell from the deep patina—the small abrasions and scratches that come from being used. It didn't just sit on some mantel in a throne room."

"If it opens," Judd reported, "I don't see how."

"I will attempt." The Frenchman took the conical baton, cupped it in both hands, and studied it.

Yitzhak peered up at them over his reading glasses. "The fragment is Arabic Judaica. Military poetry. It mentions the Spartans and secret letters."

"That's it," Eva said, understanding. "The fragment gives us the clues—the Spartans, secret letters, and the military. The cylinder is a *scytale*." She pronounced the word *SIT-ally*, rhyming with *Italy*. "The Spartans invented the *scytale* around 400 B.C. for secret communication between military commanders. It's the first use of cryptography for correspondence that we know about, but *scytali* are usually uniform in diameter—not tapered like this one. When I curated an exhibit of ancient Greek artifacts at the Getty, I got lucky and found one to display, but it was plain laurel wood."

"How does it work?" Judd asked.

"A narrow strip of parchment or leather is wrapped

around the baton from one end to the other without overlapping itself. Then the message is written length-wise along the *scytale*. When the strip's unwrapped, the writing looks like scrambled letters, gibberish. At that point a messenger takes it to the recipient, who winds the ribbon around his own *scytale*—which obviously must have the same dimensions. Then he can read it."

"So *scytali* were used for transposition ciphers," Judd said. "Let me see it again, Angelo."

Reluctantly, Angelo handed it over. "It warms the hands. Gold does that."

Yitzhak smiled at Eva. "Charles left you a lovely gift. It's probably worth a great deal of money."

"It would be my honor to buy it from you," Angelo said instantly.

"Thanks, Angelo. But I want to keep it."

He pursed his lips, disappointed. "Is there anything more in the box? I'm still waiting for that necklace from Persia."

She took the *scytale* from Judd, laid it on the table, and dug through the carton.

"I'm wondering whether Angelo's right," Judd said. "Whether there shouldn't be something else—for instance, a strip of paper with another message from Charles that fits around the *scytale* for you to read."

Eva stared at him, then abruptly turned over the carton, spilling out the Styrofoam bubbles. As the others spread them out, she inspected the inside of the box.

"There are tiny words written on the bottom," she said, surprised. "I need something to cut open the sides."

Judd grabbed a bread knife from a magnetic holder above the counter and handed it to her. She sliced open the cardboard, and he returned the knife.

"It's Charles's writing." She read aloud:

" 'Think about the Cairo *geniza*. But the *geniza* of the world's desire has the answer.' "

"What's a *geniza*?" Judd asked.

"It's the Hebrew word for a container or hiding place," Yitzhak explained. "All the tattered books and pages—from old Haggadahs and dictionaries to business invoices and children's readers—are put in some safe place in a synagogue, perhaps inside a wall or in an attic, until they can be given a proper burial."

"Veneration of the written word is common in religion," Angelo said. "For instance, Muslims believe the Koran is too holy simply to be discarded."

"But the Jewish *geniza* is different," Yitzhak explained. "It recognizes that not a single book but the written word in general is sacred. In the rabbinical tradition, a *geniza* is a grave of written things."

"Where does Cairo fit in?" Judd asked.

Yitzhak stood back and closed his eyes, reverie on his face. "It's long, long ago—the end of the ninth century—and the Jews of what became Cairo are renovating a destroyed Coptic church to be their synagogue. They carve an opening near the top of a tall tower. Children and adults climb the ladder every day to drop inside all the books and pieces of paper we'd throw away now. Can you hear the rustle as they fall through the air? The contributions pile up for a thousand years—a thousand years!—and the desert preserves everything. Then a little more than a century ago, the rabbis finally allow investigation."

His eyes snapped open. "Voilà! The *geniza* yields up its treasures. One priceless fragment belonged to *The Wisdom of Ben Sira*—Ecclesiasticus. The earliest version we'd had until then was Greek, although the original was written long before that, in Hebrew in 200 B.C. Because of Cairo's tomb in the air, we know far more about how people from India to Russia and Spain lived, what they thought about, what they ate and bought and fought over. Scores of scholarly books resulted."

"But what does that have to do with anything?" Angelo asked. "This is another mystery. Charles had an annoying habit of being oblique." He eyed the *scytale* shining on the table.

Judd kept them on point. "How does Charles's *scytale* relate to 'the *geniza* of the world's desire'?"

"His note indicates he didn't mean the Cairo *geniza*," Eva said. "So it's not Cairo."

"Of course you're right." Judd smiled. "But Istanbul is. That's what it's called—the City of the World's Desire."

"Every synagogue there would have a *geniza*," the professor said. "But that's a lot of *genizot* to have to dig through."

Judd looked across the table to the professor. "Charles may have left the package with you not only because he trusted you to hold it for Eva, but because you might understand what he meant for her to do next."

"My friend, you have a point," Yitzhak agreed. "Let me think. . . . Istanbul. *Geniza.* . . ." He frowned and ran a hand over his bald head. At last he smiled. "Charles could be such a tease. I think he must've meant Andrew Yakimovich. Yakimovich has the largest private collection of documents from the Cairo *geniza* in Istanbul. Actually the largest in the region."

"I remember him," Eva said. "He's an antiquities dealer."

She had been concentrating on Yitzhak, but now she glanced at Judd in time to see his gaze focus on Angelo, whose hand had just slipped into and out of his jacket pocket. Judd turned casually away.

"Does this Yakimovich person live in Istanbul?" The fine lines on Angelo's chiseled face deepened with curiosity.

"He's notoriously secretive and moves around a lot," she told him. "I don't remember his address there, and even if I did, it'd be no help."

"He's advised Charles and me in the past." Yitzhak took off his reading glasses and addressed Eva: "I wouldn't be a bit surprised that since Charles left the *scytale* with me, he also left what Judd calls a transposition cipher with Andrew." He added cheerfully, "Another gift, Eva. I wonder what message Charles wrote on it."

"Finding Yakimovich will be a trick—" Eva froze.

Angelo had pulled a pistol from inside the back of his waistband and quickly whipped it around to aim at them. But Judd was already moving. As Angelo's mouth opened to warn him off, Judd lowered his head, his feet flew over the floor, and his shoulder rammed into the Frenchman's chest. They landed with a thud against the kitchen wall.

"What are you doing!" Yitzhak bellowed. "Stop this!"

Eva grabbed the professor's arm and yanked him down behind the butcher-block table just as the gun exploded. The noise shook the room. A bullet blasted into the ceiling, and plaster sprayed down in a snowstorm.

Angelo slammed the pistol at Judd's head. Judd dodged, ripped the gun away, and pinned Angelo's throat with his forearm. He pointed the weapon at his temple.

Angelo's face was red and furious. He swore in French.

"A man who doesn't want anyone to know he's a threat shouldn't have a bulge at the back of his jacket." Judd's voice was calm. "I saw it when I followed you up the ladder. What do you have to do with the Library of Gold?"

"You will never know," Odile said from the kitchen doorway.

Eva spun around. Roberto was walking shakily in, with Odile behind him, her hand steady as she held a pistol to the back of his head.

The room turned silent.

"Judd, give the gun back to Angelo," Odile commanded. "Or I will kill Roberto."

CHAPTER 29

RIDING HIS SKATEBOARD, Bash Badawi cruised along the street opposite Yitzhak Law's home. He appeared casual in his baggy shorts, zippered hoodie jacket, and small backpack. His straight jet-black hair framed a dusky-colored face and almond-shaped brown eyes. Although he wore earphones as part of his disguise, the only sound he heard was the constant rumble of traffic and the talk of the pedestrians he passed.

As he slalomed across the intersection and turned back to retrace his route on the other side, he checked Quinn, who still sat stoically on the bench with his cloth shopping sack, and then Martina, who remained in her beach chair under the pepper tree, apparently reading the newspaper, chin tilted high. Everything was under control.

Still, he slowed his skateboard to study the area, wondering about a man who was pushing a baby carriage. Dressed in gray sweatpants and sweatshirt, he had passed by a half hour ago, returned, and was now heading off around the corner again. The man was big and bulky, with sharp features and thick black eyebrows. He could simply be taking the baby out for fresh air, circling the block.

Bash also noted a man with long brown hair and a thin face, riding a blue Vespa motor scooter. He had driven past fifteen minutes ago and perhaps earlier, too. Motor scooters were ubiquitous in Rome, and many Vespas rushed along the street. The man might be a messenger of some kind.

Passing beneath a branching maple tree, Bash again neared Yitzhak Law's old house. He could see no one through the windows. But then as he cruised past, there was a faint explosion from deep inside, the noise muffled by the stone walls. A gunshot. His chest tightened. He did an immediate one-eighty and dug his foot into the pavement, speeding back on his skateboard toward the steps.

IN THE KITCHEN, JUDD HELD his pistol steadily against Angelo Charbonier's temple, his arm braced against his throat. With a single hard thrust, he could crush Angelo's windpipe if he tried to retake his weapon.

But now that Odile had arrived, Angelo smiled triumphantly. His eyes were as hard and black as anthracite. "Return my pistol, Judd," he ordered. "You do not want anything to happen to Roberto."

Roberto's face was pale with fear. Sweat glistened on his forehead. "I do not understand . . ." He stared helplessly at Yitzhak.

The professor had risen from his hiding place behind the table. His eyes blinked too fast as he demanded, "Put your guns away. All of you. What is this insanity?"

Odile asked her husband in French, "Have you summoned the men?"

Eva started to translate for Judd.

Judd interrupted her. "I know what Odile said. And my guess is their men are either here or soon will be. I saw Angelo reach into his pocket when he heard about Yakimovich." He said to Angelo, "You figured you'd learned all you were going to, so you signaled them, right?"

Angelo's smile widened, but he did not answer the question. "We now have, as you Yankees say, a stand-off. If you do not return my weapon, Odile will shoot Roberto. And she will, believe me."

"I'm tempted to fire anyway," Judd said. "Wipe you, and by the time Odile pulls her trigger, I'll get off a clean shot at her. Then you'll both be dead."

Odile stepped farther behind Roberto so his body was a better shield against the threat of Judd. "There is another solution," she said. "You and I can put down our weapons. We can talk."

"Lower your gun, Odile," Judd said, "and I'll lower mine."

She nodded. As their gazes locked, they let their gun hands descend.

AS HE NEARED THE HOUSE'S STEPS, Bash Badawi slowed his skateboard, watching again. Something besides the gunshot was wrong, but he could not quite identify it. The afternoon sunlight beat down harshly, turning the street scene with its growling cars and low scooters and bobbing pedestrians into waves of streaming color. As his mind quickly sorted through what his eyes saw, he realized six men in shorts and T-shirts in wide bands of green, white, and red—the colors of Italy's flag—had rounded the corner in a bunch, feet light and forearms raised, hands loose, in the usual way of joggers. All apparently normal.

But it was not. The pack broke up and scattered, still

jogging. Four moved across the street toward Carl and Martina, while two headed in his direction. They were janitors, hired killers, and they had targeted him and his team, which meant someone—perhaps the Vespa rider or the man in the sweatsuit, pushing the baby carriage—had already cased the area for them.

His gaze on the pair who were jogging toward him, Bash slid his hand inside his jacket, unhooked his shoulder holster, and gripped the handle of his Browning.

AS JUDD KEPT HIS GAZE on Odile, he and she lowered their pistols to their sides. No one moved or spoke, suspended in a tableau of tension. The only sound was Roberto's short, frightened breaths, which seemed to shudder against the hard surfaces of the kitchen. He ran to Yitzhak, who put his arm around him.

Appearing to give Roberto room, Eva moved closer to Odile and stopped when she was about four feet away. Judd exchanged a glance with her, remembering her expertise in karate. She narrowed her eyes and gave a slight nod.

Judd stepped back from Angelo. "Tell me about the Library of Gold."

But it was Odile who answered: "There is nothing to say. All of us have been curious about it for years, of course."

"Bullshit," Judd said. "The library's why you're here. Why Angelo pulled his gun. Why you have men outside. You want to stop us from finding it."

Angelo Charbonier straightened against the wall, smoothing his sports jacket. "What I want to know is whom you have informed about what you have learned."

"I'll tell you that," Judd lied, "if you tell me what your relationship is to the library."

"Hypothetically, let us assume you are correct that

we have some knowledge," Angelo said slowly. "Perhaps even that I am a member of the small book club that supports the library."

"Was my father a member, too?" Judd asked immediately.

Angelo looked surprised a moment, then shook his head firmly. "Your turn."

It was a beginning, but Judd did not trust Angelo. "Suppose we give you the *scytale*, and you tell us more. Then all of us can walk away alive and forget this ever happened."

"That has possibilities," Angelo agreed.

Judd checked Eva again, and she stared back.

He gestured at the table. "There's the *scytale*. It's all yours, Odile. Take it."

"No!" Angelo shouted.

But he was too late. Odile was already striding toward it.

BASH MADE A FAST DECISION. His assignment was to protect Judd Ryder and Eva Blake. His fellow team members, Martine and Quinn, would fend for themselves. He had to break into the professor's house, and quickly.

Neither of the two janitors jogging toward him had showed a weapon yet, and they likely planned not to until they were beside him and could liquidate him quietly. He focused on them, propelling himself faster and faster on his skateboard.

The pair was only twenty feet away. Still jogging, they tensed as they saw his increasing speed. They lifted their shirts a few inches and drew out small-caliber pistols with sound suppressors screwed on.

Bash snatched out his Browning. The air felt hot and slick as he raced through it. The two killers aimed. He bent his knees, slid his left foot forward to the nose of his skateboard, and used the other foot to stomp down on the tail. Instantly the board ollied, flying into the air.

Surprised, the men jerked their gazes up. Bash shifted his weight, and the skateboard crashed into the chest of one. He fell hard on his back, and his gun spun away.

Bash landed and rolled, shaking off the impact. A bullet bit into the pavement next to him, but he continued to roll. Pieces of concrete cut into his skin. The downed janitor was swiftly reaching for his gun and rising into a crouch as a second bullet blasted into the pavement near Bash's head.

Bash fired twice, once into the chest of the standing man and then into the chest of the other. Blood exploded from their T-shirts. Pedestrians who had been walking toward them from both directions rushed away, screaming and shouting. At the same time a gunshot sounded from across the street.

Jumping to his feet, Bash checked across the traffic. Martine was slumped in her chair, her head dangling over her chest, while Quinn lay on his side on the bench. Bash took a deep breath. Both were down. Then he saw their killers were jogging back to the curb, preparing to cross over and come after him.

He snatched up his skateboard and sprinted up the steps to Yitzhak Law's door.

CHAPTER 30

THE SOUND OF ANGELO'S loud "No!" reverberated in Judd's ears as Odile lunged for the gold *scytale* glittering on the kitchen table. Eva slashed out a fist in a *kentsui-uchi* hammer strike into Odile's side, pivoted, and, keeping her hips horizontal and her torso perpendicular, rammed up her elbow in a *tate hiji-ate* blow to the underside of Odile's chin.

Odile's head snapped back, and her pistol fired. There was a moan, and Roberto crashed against the table and slid down to the floor, blood oozing from the top of his shoulder, where his shirt was torn by the bullet.

"Roberto! Roberto!" Yitzhak knelt over him.

Despite the attack, Odile had kept her grip firmly on her gun. As the two women struggled for it, Angelo dove at Judd.

Judd moved quickly out of reach, training his weapon on Angelo. "Stop, dammit."

Angry furrows creased Angelo's forehead. He cursed loudly but froze, staring at the pistol.

Judd glanced over at the women just as Eva prepared

to smash the side of her hand at Odile's gun. But Odile slammed a *shutō-uchi* sword-hand strike to Eva's arm, then balanced and lashed out in a brutal *mae-geri* front snap kick to her leg.

Eva toppled, and Odile pressed the pistol's muzzle into her belly. Odile's platinum hair was wild, and her eyes naked with fury. Judd fired, his bullet going into the top of the Frenchwoman's head as she suddenly lowered it. Blood sprayed, and she dropped hard onto Eva, still clasping her weapon.

"Get her gun, Eva," Judd ordered as he turned back to cover Angelo.

But Angelo had yanked a sharp fileting knife from the magnetic holder above the counter. *"Bâtard."* He closed in.

Two more gunshots sounded from the kitchen doorway. Freezing in midstride, Angelo reeled, then fell, blood blossoming scarlet across his beige jacket where the rounds had entered.

As the stink of cordite spread through the room, Bash Badawi walked in, his gun still raised in one muscled hand while his skateboard dangled from the other.

"Lucky shots." Judd grinned at him.

"Lucky shots, my ass. Glad I got here in time for the party. How you doing, Eva?"

"Never better." Holding Odile's pistol, Eva crouched beside Roberto and Yitzhak. Her face and green jacket were splattered with blood.

Bash peered across at Angelo's motionless body, then down at Odile's. "They must've arrived before I did. There was no sign they were here."

Judd nodded. "How many janitors outside?"

"Four still in action, dressed like joggers. Two others down." He gave a brief smile, his young face suddenly amused. "I had a bit of a dustup with them." Then he added soberly, "We lost Martine and Quinn."

"That's bad. I'm sorry. How did you get in?"

"I picked the lock. The Polizia di Stato are on the way. I heard sirens, very close. Their focus is going to be on the two janitors in the street and Martine and Carl. The good thing is the sirens and witnesses have probably scared away the last four in the wet squad."

"But they could still come in the back door." Judd slammed the dead bolt, then peered out the kitchen's large window, which overlooked a small rear yard of lilacs and grass. A brick pathway led to the end of a high brick wall, which enclosed the property. There was a cobblestone alleyway on the far side, showing through a wrought-iron gate. No one was in sight.

"We've got to get the hell out of here," Judd told them. "Check the woman, Bash. I'll take the man." He went to Angelo.

"Roberto needs a doctor," Eva reminded them. "How do you feel, Roberto?"

"It is over?" Roberto whispered. He was sitting up, leaning against a table leg. His bearded face was pasty, his lips dry.

"Everything's fine," she assured him.

"Hold this down for me." Yitzhak indicated to Eva the bloody handkerchief he had clamped onto Roberto's shoulder wound. "I'll call an ambulance."

"This one's a dead rat," Bash reported from where he stooped over Odile. "How's yours?"

"Dead, too." Judd wiped the handle of Angelo's pistol and pressed it into his flaccid hand. He searched Angelo's pockets, leaving the billfold. There was nothing useful inside, not even a cell phone. "Is your gun traceable, Bash?"

"No way. That dumb I'm not."

"Good. Put the woman's prints on it and leave it next to her. They'll look as if they shot each other. Take Odile's gun from Eva. You need to be armed."

"No." Reaching for the kitchen telephone, Yitzhak turned to glare at them. His face was an angry red, and drops of sweat dotted his bald head. "We have to give the police the whole truth."

Feeling the pressure of time, Judd ignored the professor and told Bash, "As soon as you're done here, go to the front of the house and check the windows. I want to know what's happening outside." Then he focused on Yitzhak. "Hang up the phone, professor. Roberto's got a flesh wound. We'll get him medical attention, but not just yet. Sticking around here could be your death warrant. Roberto's, too. These people have been trying to terminate Eva."

Yitzhak frowned at her. "That's true?"

"Yes," she told him. "Remember Ivan the Terrible's Oprichniki? That's what they're like—utterly ruthless."

"They're going to want to find out what you know about us and where we're going," Judd said. "They'll track you down, and as soon as you tell them, they'll kill you. All of us need to leave—and fast. Can you walk, Roberto?"

"I think so." His voice was weak. He had been listening, his brown eyes round and frightened. "Yes, it is obvious we must go."

Yitzhak put the telephone back into its cradle. "Eva, you take one side of Roberto, and I'll take the other."

As they supported him, Roberto rose to his feet, and Bash ran back into the room.

"The police are blocking off the street," he said. "I found the dead woman's purse in the sitting room. She didn't have a cell, either."

"I'd rather not risk going out the back door," Judd told him. "Yitzhak, I saw what looks like the beginning of a tunnel at the end of your refuge downstairs. Can we get out that way?"

"I think so, but it may not be easy." Yitzhak's voice was strong. With Roberto's uninjured arm draped over his shoulder, he had returned to his normal self.

Eva took the gold *scytale* and fragment of Arabic Judaica, and she and the others went ahead. Judd tore up the top and bottom of the cardboard box with Charles's writing and Eva's name. Stuffing the pieces into the garbage disposal, he turned it on, then threw the Styrofoam bubbles and the rest of the box into the trash. He peered around the kitchen to make certain they had left nothing behind. Last, he checked the window—and dropped below the counter. He rose up slowly, just enough to see out again.

Men were at the rear gate. One wore a gray sweatshirt and sweatpants; the others were dressed in jogging shorts and T-shirts. The big man in the sweatsuit tried to open the gate, but it was locked. Muttering to himself, he took out picklocks.

Judd raced to the stairs under the broad staircase and descended into the brick-lined cellar. Voices sounded, floating up from the ragged hole in the floor. He started down it, stopping to drag the brick trapdoor over the opening. It was heavy, but he leveraged it up and settled it into place. With luck, none of the killers would discover Yitzhak's secret domain.

He hurried down to the bottom, where Jupiter and Juno gazed regally from their thrones. The silence was luminous in the ancient room, a stillness that seemed to wrap around him and promise safety. But there was no safety yet.

Everyone was gathered at the street-side end of the long room, where rubble was strewn and a brown wall of dirt rose to the ceiling. Bash and Eva were throwing rocks out of the way. What had been a small tunnel was now much larger.

Eva saw him. "Are Angelo's men in the house?"

"Not yet, but they will be in minutes." Judd hurried toward them.

The tunnel was about four feet high and three feet wide. There was darkness on the other side, and he could hear the sound of distant running water. Five flashlights lay in a row on the marble floor.

"You must lead," Roberto told the professor, who was still supporting him. "I can walk by myself. Judd is right. I am fine—just messy looking." He glanced at the bloody handkerchief he was holding to his wound.

The professor nodded. "We're going under the street. Take your flashlights." He handed one to Roberto and picked up one for himself. Hunching over, he moved into the darkness.

"I'll go last," Judd told the others, thinking about the janitors who might be smarter than he hoped.

Bash grabbed his skateboard, and Eva slung her satchel onto her back. They disappeared into the burrow. Judd paused. When he heard nothing from above, he crouched and hurried into the darkness, his flashlight shooting a cone of light. The air began to smell of moss and damp.

The small group was waiting for him at the end.

"You need to see this," Eva told him.

He squeezed past to look out at a natural underground tunnel, black and seemingly endless, a crude dirt bore through ancient Rome. It was more than six feet high and twelve feet wide, carved out over the millennia by a freshwater stream that rushed past at high velocity. As he beamed his flashlight over it, it sparkled like mercury.

He moved his flashlight again. There were dirt banks on either side of the stream, not far above the fast-moving water. The banks were dangerously narrow, only a foot wide in places. Walking would be treacherous. They would have to go single file.

"The stream follows the street?" he asked.

"Yes, at least part of the way," the professor answered. "I believe it feeds into the Cloaca Maxima—the Great Drain—west of here. That's an ancient sewer that runs beneath the Roman Forum. Several of the city's underground streams feed into it."

"How do we get out of the tunnel?"

"We should find a place to exit somewhere along the way. We can't be the only homeowners who've discovered the stream. Roberto and I explored once, but we didn't go far. It didn't matter before . . ."

Judd nodded. "Sounds like better odds than what's waiting for us in the house. Yitzhak, you lead again. You know the signs that'll tell us we've got a way to escape. Then Eva and Roberto. Bash and I go last, in case we're followed. Let's move out."

CHAPTER 31

Dubai, United Arab Emirates

THE SWANK COCKTAIL PARTY was on the thirtieth floor of the stunning Burj al-Arab—the Tower of the Arabs, the world's tallest and arguably grandest hotel. The suite soared two full stories, boasting a spiral marble staircase, miles of twenty-four–carat gold detailing, and expansive windows showcasing panoramic views of the oil-rich Persian Gulf. Two Saudi princes in flowing white *kanduras* had just arrived via the twenty-eighth-floor helipad below, flying in from St. Tropez with full entourages.

Martin Chapman, the director of the Library of Gold, turned his attention from the flurry around them to watch a Russian exporter and his mistress take calls on ten-thousand-dollar cell phones encrusted with diamonds. Chapman smiled, amused. Still, he would never allow such gaudy affectation in his employees.

Dressed conservatively in a three-piece, side-vented suit, Chapman excused himself from a group of international bankers and walked off. He wore his vast personal fortune with the natural ease of Old Money, although he damn well had earned every penny himself.

Winding through the partygoers, he savored the undercurrent of excitement and raw avarice. But then, this was Dubai, epicenter of a storm of commerce, with free-trade zones, speed-dial corporate licensing, no taxes, no elections, and almost no crime. It was said the city's bird was the building crane—skyscrapers seemed to sprout from the desert sands overnight, most apartments and offices presold. Eager and filthy rich, Dubai was perfect for Chapman, who was here to raise money.

"Appetizer, sir?" Dressed in a money-green tuxedo, the server kept his gaze lowered.

Chapman chose Beluga caviar piled on a triangle of toast and continued on. From religion to crime and terrorism, everything in Dubai took a backseat to profit, and the profit was enormous. Even before Haliburton decided to move its world headquarters from Houston to Dubai, Chapman knew it was time to pay attention. So he had added to his string of homes, buying a villa in exclusive Palm Jumeirah—and had begun making friends.

It was time to go to work. He headed for Sheik Ahmad bin Rashid al-Shariff.

The sheik's black mustache curved upward as he dismissed a bevy of bronzed blond celebutantes and smiled at Chapman. He lifted his bourbon glass in greeting. *"Assalaam alaykom."* Peace be upon you.

"Alaykom assalaam." And peace upon you. Chapman did not speak Arabic, but long ago he had memorized the correct response. "I'm enjoying your party."

Sheik Ahmad was a dark wisp of a man in his mid forties, elegant in a gray pinstriped suit. A cousin of the emirate's ruler, he had been partially educated in the

United States, with an MBA from Stanford. Earlier that day he had personally taken the wheel of a white Cadillac limousine to escort Chapman around several of his building sites. But then Chapman was no ordinary visitor. He headed Chapman & Associates, once the richest private equity firm in the United States. It had dropped from some $98 billion in assets under management to a mere $35 billion in the economic crash, but all U.S. equity funds had been eviscerated, although his perhaps more than others. Chapman was counting on his Khost project to put him back at number one, where he belonged. Even more important, it would please his wife.

"Yes, the usual financiers and industrialists," the sheik said. "A sprinkling of the idle rich. They're like saffron—zesty and attractive, entertaining for working stiffs like you and me. There are several of you private-equity people here, too."

Private equity was the sanitized term for leveraged-buyout firms. In the first four months of the year, Chapman & Associates had spent and borrowed far fewer billions of dollars than in its heyday, as he had searched out underperforming or undervalued companies to buy. With every deal, a new war chest had to be raised, so he was constantly on the money circuit, charming, cajoling, rattling off figures as he seduced those he targeted with his strong handshake and visions of a glorious future. Since he retained a larger interest in the company than anyone, he took a hefty percentage from every new transaction.

He ate his caviar, dusted his fingers on the cocktail napkin, and dropped it onto the tray of a passing waiter. "I was speaking with some of them earlier. They're eager to go on personal tours of Dubai with you, too."

The sheik laughed. "That's what I like about you, Martin. You're happy to give away my wealth, even to your competitors. As usual, they'll be too small for me, as you already know. By the way, I've made my decision about your proposition."

He paused to increase the drama and hint his answer might not be what Chapman wanted.

Without hesitation, Chapman gave an understanding nod and countered, "Yes, I've been thinking about the buy-in, too. Perhaps it's not right for you. I think I should withdraw the invitation and save us both embarrassment."

Sheik Ahmad blinked slowly, his hooded eyelids closing and opening like those of a hawk perched in a banyan tree, awaiting prey. But his prey was Martin Chapman.

He smiled. "Martin, you are too much. Playing my game, are you? I'll come to the point. I want in. It's five hundred million dollars, yes?"

"Three hundred and twenty million. No more. Still, that will give you twenty percent."

Chapman's rule was always to leave investors hungering for more, and if the deal went sour, which he knew it would not, the sheik would have fewer reasons to lash back. Chapman was confident the $16 billion leveraged buyout of a mass-market retail company would return profits of at least 60 percent. Management had been unable to keep up with the changing times, but the structure was sound for a turnaround, financed by selling off ancillary holdings and taking loans. Only five thousand employees would have to be fired.

"Then it will be three hundred and twenty million," Sheik Ahmad agreed good-naturedly. "I like investments where I don't have to lift a finger. Do you have anything else I can give you money for?"

"Soon. The deal isn't ready yet—but soon."

"What is it? A retail chain, a distribution company, steel, timber, utilities?"

Chapman said nothing and smiled, thinking about his highly secret Khost project.

The sheik nodded. "Ah, I see. I'll wait until you're ready to reveal all. Your glass is empty. You must have another drink so we can celebrate." He raised a hand and signaled. Within seconds, a waiter stood before them.

It would be impolite to refuse, so Chapman accepted another bourbon and talked longer, resisting the urge to check his watch. Finally the sheik invited him to attend a *majlis*, his royal council, which was convening upstairs, and Chapman was able to exit gracefully.

On the sweeping steps of the palatial hotel, Chapman dialed his wife as he luxuriated in the outdoor air-conditioning. He looked out over the gulf to the collection of man-made islands called the World, one of Dubai, Inc.'s recent Las Vegas–style fantasies come to life. He had heard Rod Stewart had bought "Britain" for £19 million. Perhaps the next time he came, after the Khost project was certain, he would see about buying a continent, too.

When there was no answer, he left a message on the machine. "I'm flying out, darling. I just wanted to let you know I love you." She was still in San Moritz but was scheduled to leave for Athens soon.

As he watched the blazing red sun sink toward the gulf's purple waters, his limo pulled up. The chauffeur opened the door, and Chapmen climbed into the rear, where his briefcase was waiting. Soon they were on the Sheikh Zayed Road, cruising east beneath the city's Manhattan-style skyline while the darkening desert and gulf spread flat and austere on either side.

He called his assistant at the Library of Gold. The Khost project was so secret that Chapman was running the operation from there.

"Where are we?" he demanded.

"The army uniforms and equipment have arrived in Karachi." The port on the Arabian sea was notorious for being porous. "Preston has handled everything impeccably. Your meeting with the warlord is scheduled for tomorrow in Peshawar."

"And security?"

"I'm working with Preston. It will be complete."

After he hung up, Chapman made several more phone calls, bringing himself up-to-date on other pieces of business and of course issuing orders. No matter how high the quality of the people one employed, they still needed guidance.

When the limo reached the private section of Dubai International Airport, the chauffeur drove out to the Learjet. Its engines were humming. He stopped the limo and ran around to open the rear door.

Chapman climbed out, carrying his briefcase. Handing over his passport to the waiting customs agent, he expected no trouble and got none—the agent simply stamped it. As the chauffeur unloaded his suitcase, Chapman marched toward the aircraft.

Two more men were waiting at the foot of the stairs. One was the pilot; the other was the armed man Preston had arranged. He was carrying a small bag.

"Good to see you, sir." The pilot touched the brim of his cap.

"Any problems?"

"No. We've followed your instructions and haven't spoken to her."

Chapman nodded and climbed into the opulent aircraft. It had wide leather seats, custom colors, and high-tech accessories. Sitting in the last row was Robin Miller, the only passenger.

"Hello, Mr. Chapman." She stared at him down the length of the aisle, her green eyes red-rimmed, her face flushed from weeping. She was a mess. Her long blond hair was disheveled, her bangs pushed to the sides, her white sweater rumpled over her chest.

He ignored her and gazed at the black backpack strapped into the seat across the aisle from her. Pleasure coursed through him. Then he remembered the CIA was intent on finding the Library of Gold. With a brusque gesture, he told the armed guard to sit in the bulkhead.

As the pilot closed and locked the door, Chapman marched down the aisle and rotated the seat in front of Robin to face her. He locked the seat into place, sat, and snapped on his safety belt. Still saying nothing, he folded his hands into his lap. Now he needed to find out how deeply she was involved in Charles Sherback's deceptions.

AS THE JET'S ENGINES revved up, Robin glanced nervously at the director. His unlined face was stern, his thin lips set in a straight line, and his long fingers entwined over his suit coat as if in his hands he controlled the universe. And he did control her universe—the Library of Gold.

The silence was frightening. She had seen the director do this before—saying nothing—which encouraged the other person to blurt into the vacuum, often with revelations that were later regretted. She forced herself to wait.

The jet took off, rising smoothly into Dubai's starry night. She looked out her window. Below them the city's lights extended along the coastline in sparkling colors.

Then she heard her voice filling the unbearable silence: "Are we still going to Athens?" That seemed neutral enough. The plan had been that from there they would helicopter *The Book of Spies* home to the library.

"Of course. Why didn't you phone to tell me immediately Eva Blake recognized Charles at the British

Museum?" The question was posed curiously, an uncle interested in a favored niece's reply.

"Preston was going to take care of her." She thought about Charles's poor dead body, wrapped in canvas and hefted into the jet's baggage compartment like someone's castoff belongings.

The director gave a slight frown. It came and went quickly, but she knew her answer was wrong. Preston must have told him Charles and she had kept the information from him.

"What's important is we got *The Book of Spies*." She nodded at the backpack across the aisle. "It's fabulous, more even than our records show. Wouldn't you like to see it?" Once he cradled the illuminated manuscript, he might forget she had not reported Charles immediately.

"Later. Tell me what happened."

Girding herself, she described everything in London carefully, making certain she was accurate. She had a sense he was comparing every word to what Preston had said.

When she finished, he asked, "You saw the tattoo on Charles's head?"

"Yes."

"What does it mean?"

"I don't know. I didn't even know he had it."

He nodded. "Why do you think he wanted a secret tattoo?"

"I don't know."

"If your head were shaved, would I find one there, too?"

She felt a shiver of fear. "Absolutely not."

"Then you don't mind if I check."

"You can't mean you want me to cut off my hair?"

"No, Magus will do it." The director called over his shoulder to the front of the jet, "I'm ready for you."

The guard picked up his small bag and walked down the aisle.

She peered up at him helplessly.

Magus took shears from his bag, grabbed hair, and cut. Long blond curls floated to the floor. He grabbed more hair and cut. And more and more. The hair fell around her. Robin felt tears heat her eyes. Furious with herself, she blinked them away.

The only sound in the jet was of the clipping scissors and the distant thrum of the engines. As she used shaky fingers to wipe hair from her face, Magus put away the shears and took out a battery-powered electric razor. The steel was cold as it ran over her scalp. Her skin vibrated and itched. Little hairs flew. Her head was too light. She felt naked, ashamed.

"Do you see anything, Magus?" the director asked. "Any words, numbers, or symbols?"

"No, sir." He turned off the razor and dropped it into his bag.

"Go back to your seat." The director fixed his gaze on her. "Did Charles ever talk to you about where the library's located?" His eyes were blue frost.

Looking into them, she suddenly saw her father's eyes, black but just as icy. She remembered the moment she knew she must leave and never return to Scotland. She had walked away from everything, got rid of her accent, and put herself through the Sorbonne, then Cambridge, studying classical art and library science. She had made a life of her own, first working in rare books and manuscripts at the Houghton Library in Boston then at the Bibliothèque Nationale de France in Paris, where she had heard about the Library of Gold and steeped herself in its mythic history. The more she learned, the more she had hungered to know, until the exhilarating moment Angelo Charbonier had recruited her to join the elite staff, where she had met Charles and thought finally, after a decade of wandering, she had found a home.

"Charles never mentioned the library's location," she told him coolly.

"Does Charles's tattoo reveal it?" the director asked.

"I already told you I don't know what the tattoo means."

"Do you know where the Library of Gold is?"

"No. I never asked Charles, but I don't think he knew anyway. I never tried to find out from anyone. It's against the rules."

He nodded again, seeming to like that answer. "Remember the old Latin proverb 'What was sour to endure is sweet to recall.' You've proved your point, and your hair will grow back. Now I have business to conduct. Go to the front of the plane and sit near Magus."

Despite his words, dread filled her. She had a sense she was doomed, and doomed ironically by Charles's tattoo. If the director had been unable to trust Charles, who had seemed to love the library more than life itself, how could he ever really trust her when she so obviously had been in love with Charles?

She had made a huge error—not loving Charles, but associating with the library at all. Her mouth went dry as she realized what she had to do. She must walk away again, just as she had from her father. When the Learjet landed in Athens, she must find a way to escape.

CHAPTER 32

Rome, Italy

IN THE DARK DIRT TUNNEL, Judd followed Yitzhak, Eva, Roberto, and Bash. Their shoes stuck and sank, slipped and slid on the narrow muddy ledge a foot above the stream. Time passed, and the enclosure grew claustrophobic, the noise of rushing water oppressive. Their flashlights did little to ward off the bleakness.

Commanding everyone to stop and be silent while he listened, Judd checked behind again. It had been a half hour, and there was still no sign of pursuit. They resumed their slow pace. Roberto's breathing was labored.

"How are you doing, Roberto?" he called over the shoulders ahead of him.

"I am trembly but well."

"Let us know when you want to take a break."

Roberto nodded, then asked worriedly, "How deep do you think the water is, Yitzhak?"

"No way to know." The professor paused. "Eva, it's time you explained what's going on."

"If I did, I'd only put you in more danger."

"When we get out of here," Judd assured him, "Bash will take you and Roberto to a private doctor who'll keep his mouth shut. Then when Roberto is treated, he'll find you a place to hide out. Don't go home until you get word from him that it's safe. He has his own work to do, so say nothing about him—or us—to anyone."

The professor thought about it. "Who *are* you, Judd? You and Bash?"

"All you need to know is we're helping Eva. I brought Bash and a couple of other people in to back us up."

Yitzhak's voice toughened. "In the kitchen, Angelo said he might be a 'supporter' of the Library of Gold. In the book club. What does that mean?"

"That's something else you should forget about," Eva told him.

The professor hesitated. "You're asking a lot, but I'll do as you say."

As they continued on, their flashlights revealed ancient Rome embedded in the dirt walls—fragments of pottery, spearheads, pieces of marble tiles, and chunks of brick. They stopped for Roberto to rest, then resumed their treacherous journey.

When they heard the scurrying of rats, Bash said, "Someone told me the rats under Rome were as big as cats." His skateboard was clamped low on his chest, one arm wrapped around it.

Yitzhak chuckled. "You've been drinking with unsavory people."

"I don't like rats," Bash admitted. "Does anyone other than crazy lab people like rats?"

"I'm more concerned about the albino creatures," the professor said, baiting him.

"Albino rats?" Roberto steadied himself by pressing his hand against the wall. Then he stared at his muddy palm.

"Yes, but they're not here—they're in the Cloaca Maxima," Yitzhak said. "In any case, we don't want to go that far. For those of you who don't know, the Cloaca isn't an ordinary sewage conduit—it's a huge, fast-moving river of crap. It was built twenty-five hundred years ago, but Rome is still using it. No one's safe going into it without covering every inch of themselves with boots, gloves, hooded suits, and masks."

"I wish I'd known," Eva said. "I would've brought my wet suit."

"Reminds me of a root canal I once had," Bash said. "Bad outcome."

"The stink is memorable," Yitzhak went on. "A bouquet of mud, diesel, feces, and rotting carcasses. *Rat* carcasses."

Bash groaned.

Judd laughed. "You get an A-plus for tormenting students, Professor."

The professor glanced over his shoulder, his round face grinning.

They fell silent as the underground passage descended steeply, and the air grew cold and clammy. Ghostly stalactites hung from overhead rocks, caused by the seep of calcium-rich groundwater. Then as the tunnel made a sharp bend, the noise of racing water quadrupled—and a stench of rot wafted toward them. Dizzying in its intensity, it carried all the horrific odors Yitzhak had described.

Judd's nose burned. "The Cloaca can't be far ahead."

"We cannot go into the Cloaca," Roberto said nervously. "Let us turn back."

"Not just yet—"

But before he could finish his sentence, the professor screamed. His arms lashed up over his head, and his feet flew out from under him. He twisted, his hands scrambling against the rough dirt wall, seeking purchase as his feet dropped into the water. If the stream were fast and deep enough, it would carry him into the big sewer.

Before Judd could jump in to help, Eva grabbed the professor's arm. "I've got you."

The current caught the professor's legs. He was being pulled away.

"Face the bank, Yitzhak," Judd ordered. He leaned out to peer around Bash and Roberto. "See if your knees can find a slope."

"You can do it!" Eva's hands were white from tension. Her jaw muscles bunched as she held on to him.

Sweat coated Yitzhak's bald head as he turned slowly away from the current until he faced Eva. His free hand grabbed her arm, and he curved his back and hunched his hips.

"Come on. Come on." She was bent nearly double, her profile strained, as she held on to him with both hands.

Yitzhak grunted and lifted one knee out of the water, then the other. As less water dragged at him, she helped him inch upward. Finally he was out. With a shudder, he planted his feet on the narrow shelf, standing between Eva and Roberto.

"You are in one piece, Yitzhak?" Roberto asked, patting his shoulder and back.

He peered down at his trousers, now laminated to his legs. Water streamed out of his shoes.

"Right as rain." He gave a sober smile. "Thank you, Eva."

"What made you slip, Yitzhak?" Judd said. "Check around your feet. What do you see?"

There was a pause. "You're right. Here's the top of a

skull. I didn't see it before. It must've been hidden under the mud."

"Are there more skulls?" Eva slid her foot along the ledge, moving the muck away.

"I've found another one," the professor announced.

"So have I," Eva said.

The professor shone his flashlight along the cave wall above them, then ran the beam back and forth, lower and lower until he reached the wall's intersection with the bank.

"Here's a small opening." He crouched and aimed his flashlight into it.

"What's in there?" Eva squatted beside him.

"I can't tell. Help me dig, Eva."

"We'll do it," Judd told them. "Come on, Bash."

The others moved ahead, and Bash sat on his heels in front of the hole. He plowed the nose of his skateboard into the wet dirt, scooping piles of it back onto the ledge, where Judd slid the dirt into the stream. They continued a half hour, taking turns until the hole was three feet in diameter and formed a tunnel two feet deep. A scent of musty age wafted toward them.

Judd beamed his flashlight into the small passageway and crawled through. Standing erect, he inhaled sharply as he shot his light around. He had entered a gray world of the dead. Age-bleached skulls pinioned one on top of another blanketed the walls from the floor to the vault ceiling.

He moved into the center of the large crypt and turned, continuing to shoot his flashlight over the eerie scene. It was like a macabre carnival. Skulls arched around nooks, framing stone walls on which faded crosses and religious symbols had been painted. Full skeletons dressed in tattered brown monk robes reclined on stone benches as if awaiting the call to prayer.

"My God." Eva took a deep breath as she walked up to him. "The only time I've seen an ossuary like this was in a history magazine."

"It's impossible to know what Rome's underground has in store." The professor joined them, supporting Roberto. "Buried passageways, latrines, aqueducts, catacombs, firehouses, access tunnels—and that's just the beginning. It looks to me as if this crypt belonged to the Capuchin order. That means some of the bones could date back five centuries."

"There's got to be thousands of them," Bash decided. "But how in hell do we get out of here?" Beneath his shorts, his bare knees were coated in mud—but then, all of them were muddy now.

"I'm hoping that way." Judd aimed his flashlight at the end of the room, where a tall arch of skulls wreathed worn stone steps leading upward. "Roberto, do you want Bash to carry you up?"

Roberto pushed himself away from Yitzhak. "I will do it myself."

Judd nodded, and he led them past mounds of bones and up a stone stairwell, where more crosses and religious symbols were painted. As they turned the corner of a landing, the wall above their heads displayed pelvic bones arranged like angel's wings.

He stopped, listening to Roberto's panting breath behind him. He turned. "Carry him, Bash."

Before Roberto could object, Bash handed his skateboard to Eva and swept the small man up into his arms. "Combat victims get special treatment. Hey, it's a free ride."

Roberto looked up into the muscular young face. "This is not an unpleasant fate. Thank you."

Finally they reached the top, where an ornate iron door blocked their path. Judd peered through the grillwork—there was another stairwell on the far side, this time of modern cement.

"I hear traffic," Eva said, excited.

Judd tried the door. "Locked, of course." They were silent, and he could feel their exhaustion. "I seem to be shooting out a lot of locks these days."

Telling them to stand back, he screwed his sound suppressor onto his Beretta and fired. Metal dust spewed into the still air. The popping noise bounced off the stone walls.

He pushed open the door and gazed up. "Blue sky."

"Hallelujah," Eva said.

They resumed climbing, Judd still leading. As he neared the top, he stopped and rose up to see. They had emerged into a ruins of toppled columns, slabs of travertine, and chunks of granite scattered among dirt and weeds between two ancient buildings. Behind the area was another old building. A commercial chain-link fence blocked the ruins from the sidewalk and street.

He turned back. Their expressions were expectant as they stood beneath him in the stairwell. "I don't know exactly where we are. At least it's an open area. All of us are dirty, but it's the blood that'll draw the kind of attention we don't want. That means you—Eva and Roberto."

In seconds, Eva was out of her jacket. Her green shirt was clean. As she turned the jacket inside out and tied the arms around her waist, Bash lowered Roberto onto his feet. Judd studied him. He was standing erect, but his skin color was slightly pink, perhaps feverish. The handkerchief was gone from his shoulder, lost somewhere along the way. Blood coated his white shirt. Gingerly he unbuttoned it.

"Bash, give Roberto your T-shirt," Judd decided.

Bash took off his jacket and peeled the black T-shirt up over his head.

Judd checked Roberto's gunshot wound, a ragged slash through the top of his shoulder.

"You're going to be fine," he said. "Probably hurts like hell, though."

"The pain is a small matter. We are free." Roberto stood motionless as Yitzhak tugged the T-shirt down over his head.

"Take the professor and Roberto," Judd told Bash. "Eva and I'll wait until you're gone. You'll have to break through a chain-link gate to get out of here."

Bash grinned. "After this . . . a piece of cake."

"So now we leave you." The professor smiled at Eva. He was wet and bedraggled, but his optimistic disposition shone through. "Be well, and even though I don't understand anything that's happened, my heartfelt thanks." He hugged her, then shook hands with Judd. "We've had an adventure. Next time we meet, I hope it'll be boring."

Roberto kissed Eva on both cheeks. "You must stay in touch."

"I will," she promised.

Finally Judd and Bash faced each other. "There's no way the Charboniers should've known we were going to Yitzhak's house," Judd told him, choosing his words carefully. "I'll call our mutual friend and fill him in. We have a leak somewhere."

The young spy nodded soberly, and they shook hands. Then he led Roberto and Yitzhak up the steps into the ruins.

Eva joined Judd, and they climbed so they could watch the trio approach the fence. Bash looked around. When there was no one on the sidewalk, he used his skateboard to smash open the padlock. Soon they were out the gate and walking away, the tall young man and his two older charges.

"We have to assume the Library of Gold people have figured out who you are now, too," she told him. "So we can't use your credit cards, and obviously we can't use mine. It's a long hitchhike to Istanbul."

"I have an extra set of ID on me. I'll buy the tickets. What's worrying me is whether they'll follow us to Istanbul."

CHAPTER 33

AS VEHICLES SPED PAST, red taillights streaming red, Preston waited impatiently outside the terminal of Ciampino International Airport, Rome's second-largest. He had chosen it because it was closer to the city's heart and therefore more efficient. Efficiency mattered particularly now—the report from his man in Rome had been bad. Angelo and Odile Charbonier had been shot to death, while Judd Ryder, Eva Blake, Yitzhak Law, and Roberto Cavaletti had vanished. In a foul mood, he checked his watch—eight P.M.

When a long black van pulled up, he slid open the side door and stepped inside. The car entered the airport traffic, and he crouched in the rear beside the corpses. He lifted the blanket: Angelo Charbonier's face was angry in death. Odile's head was coated with dried blood and splintered bone.

He crawled forward to the half-seat behind the driver. "Took you long enough to get here."

Nico Bustamante, still dressed in his gray sweat suit, was behind the wheel. A big barrel of a man, he swore in Italian, then spoke in English. "What did you expect? I told you we had a rotten mess to clean up."

In the seat next to him, Vittorio nodded. Slender, with a wiry build, he had changed out of his tricolor jogging clothes into jeans and a denim shirt.

"Tell me again exactly what you found," Preston ordered.

"Signore and Signora Charbonier, both murdered in the kitchen," Nico said. "We searched the house. No one was there, and we did not find any hidden exits. The targets did not leave through the front door. I know this because I posted men at both ends of the street. And they did not leave through the rear—we were there."

"It was as if they evaporated into the world of souls." Vittorio crossed himself.

As they stopped at a traffic light, Preston said, "What about when you cleaned up the kitchen?"

"There was just the usual junk in the trash—I say this because I know you will ask. The only piece that was strange was blood splatters too far away from the *signore* and *signora* to be theirs."

"So someone else was injured. Tell your people to check the neighbors, the hospitals, and the police."

Taking out his cell phone, Nico drove the van onto the congested Via Appia Nuova.

As Nico made the call, Preston said to Vittorio, "What about the Charboniers?"

"It is all arranged. A yacht rented in their name is waiting at Ostia Antica."

Ostia Antica was Rome's ancient seaport, where the Tiber River flowed into the Tyrrhenian Sea. Today the town was little more than a bookshop, a café, a tiny museum, and mosaic-filled ruins, but it was appropriate for the Charboniers: Ovid's play *Medea* had premiered in its amphitheater some two thousand years ago and was now lost—except to the Library of Gold.

"And then?" Preston prompted.

"We will put the *signore* and *signora* onto the yacht, sail it far out into the Mediterranean, steal everything—and abandon it. It will seem as if pirates attacked and robbed them."

"You have their suitcases?"

"Of course. We got them from the hotel, and paid the bill, too."

Preston nodded, satisfied. Now he had a larger problem: Where had Blake, Ryder, Law, and Cavaletti gone?

As the van headed toward Ostia Antica, he considered everything he knew. It seemed as if at least one of the four was wounded, but not so badly he or she could not escape. He needed the Rome operatives to find all of them. He thought about Charles's tattoo—the security staff had torn apart his and Robin Miller's offices and the cottage they shared, but had found nothing about it or any records of the library's location. The tattoo reminded him of the director—by now he was on the jet with Robin Miller. If the director learned anything from her, he would phone.

As he thought that, his cell rang. "Yes?"

It was his NSA contact. "Your person of interest has turned on her cell and made three calls from Rome."

"From where exactly?" Preston felt a burst of hope. It was Eva Blake's cell phone—he had found the number on Peggy Doty's cell after he had wiped her in London.

"Fiumicino airport."

He cursed. It was the other airport, and too far away to reach quickly. "Whom was she calling?"

"Adem Abdullah, Direnc Pastor, and Andrew Yakimovich. I can give you the phone numbers she dialed. All were to Istanbul. Two have accompanying addresses."

"Did you listen to the conversations?"

"You know better than that, Preston. That far I can't go—even for you."

"Whom did she dial first?"

"Yakimovich. It was short, less than a minute—a disconnected number. The two other calls were five and eight minutes."

"What are their numbers and addresses?" He wrote the information in the small pocket notebook he always carried. When he no longer needed a note, he tore it out and destroyed it. There were few pages left. "Thanks, Irene. She'll have to turn off her cell phone while she's in the air. When she activates it again, whether she phones out or not, tell me. I need to know exactly where she is." NSA could pinpoint locations within inches, depending on which satellite was in orbit. He ended the connection and looked at Nico. "Turn the van around. Take me back to Ciampino." He would charter another jet and beat them to Istanbul.

CHAPTER 34

Washington, D.C.

IT WAS LATE AFTERNOON, the shadows long across Capitol Hill, as Tucker Andersen stood at the front door to Catapult headquarters and gazed out longingly. He was tired of being cooped up. A young officer from OTS at Langley was standing on the porch, holding a small package wrapped in brown paper. His expression was one of being properly impressed at meeting the storied spymaster.

Tucker took the package, tucked it under his arm, and signed for it. Then he went to Gloria's desk. She was nowhere in sight, still on coffee break. He dropped the parcel next to her computer and walked down the hall to his office. Sitting behind his desk, he pushed aside the report he had been reading and checked his e-mail.

One had been forwarded by Gloria from the L.A. coroner's office. It said the body in Charles Sherback's grave had been exhumed and they were rushing the autopsy and DNA match, but it would take a couple of days. A second e-mail confirmed a room in the Méridien hotel in London had been registered to Christopher Heath, the name on Sherback's driver's license. One of the desk clerks remembered him with a blond woman, but there were no details.

Restless, Tucker was just about to leave when a new e-mail arrived from MI-5. He read it quickly: No adult male corpse with a shaved, tattooed head had been found in London the previous night. Consequently, there were no arrests connected with it. He stared at the message, then leaned back in his chair, trying to understand what it meant. Judd had told him he had shot carefully so Preston would survive. Finally he decided Preston had likely awakened before the police arrived and taken Sherback's body away with him. Tucker sent an encrypted e-mail to Judd, warning him.

Disturbed, he stretched, stood, and headed down the hall to Catapult's small communications center, which included data research and IT—information technology. At the door he was greeted by a rumble of voices, clicking keyboards, and a sense of urgency. Worktables arranged in neat rows housed a dozen secure computers and phones. High on the walls hung big-screen TVs tuned to CNN, MSNBC, FOX, BBC, and Al Jazeera, but the monitors could also view classified images. The usual cans of soda, crumpled take-out bags, and empty pizza boxes littered the area, impregnating everything with the salt-and-grease odor of fast food.

Tucker paused, surveying the staff, most of whom were bent over their keyboards. All were under the age of thirty. Since 9/11 the number of applicants to Langley had soared, and now half of all personnel were new hires. He worried about the loss of experience and institutional memory, but that was what happened when good longtime operatives and analysts quit or were fired, which had occurred in the 1990s and again in the next decade, during the tenure of a morale-killing D/CIA. Still, this young new group was dedicated and enthusiastic.

Walking through the room, he joined Brandon Ohr and Michael Hawthorne, who were standing with Debi Watson at her worktable. She was the head of IT. The trio looked as if their average age was twenty-five, although they were around thirty. They were eager, talented, and smart.

"Working hard, I see," Tucker deadpanned. Not original, but it would get the job done.

Michael and Brandon were home after long tours overseas, waiting for reassignment. Technically neither belonged in here, but then Debi was single, a pretty brunette with large brown eyes and a Southern accent. Tucker was interested in their excuses.

"I'm on break," Brandon said quickly. He had a square, handsome face with a hint of a movie-star beard.

"I had a question I hoped Debi could help me with," Michael explained. He was tall and rangy, his black face dimpled.

"It's all true, suh," Debi assured Tucker, her Southern belle accent in full flower.

He stared soberly at the men and said nothing. "The glare," as Gloria called it.

Brandon took the hint first. "Guess I'd better get back to the stack of papers on my desk." He sauntered off, swiping a can of Diet Pepsi from a six-pack near the rear of the room.

"Thanks, Debi," Michael told her. "I'll check in with you tomorrow about the Tripoli refugee I've got my eye on." He followed Brandon.

Tucker liked that neither was completely intimidated

by him. It showed the sort of inner fortitude necessary for the job.

Debi sat down behind her worktable and tugged on her short skirt. "I was just about to send you an e-mail."

"You've got answers for me?" He had assigned her to track down Charles Sherback's altered face and the two anonymous phone numbers in his cell.

"It's not what you want to hear. Nothing in any of the federal databases matches the face of your man. Nothing in the state databases, either. And no positive match with Interpol or any of our foreign friends. Since he's an American, you'd think he'd have a driver's license photo at least. It's almost as if he doesn't exist."

"What about the two phone numbers?"

"They're to disposable cell phones, but you suspected that already. There's been no activity on them yet. NSA will let me know immediately."

Disappointed, Tucker returned to his office. As he went inside, the phone on his desk rang. It was Judd Ryder. He fell into his chair and listened.

Judd related what he and Eva had learned at Yitzhak Law's house and described the attack by the Charboniers. "There's no way the Charboniers should've known we were going there," he finished worriedly. "You've got to have a leak."

Stunned, Tucker thought quickly. "Only one person at Catapult besides me has any details—the chief, Cathy Doyle. What about on your end?"

"It's just Eva and me, and she's been with me the whole time. Whenever I get in touch with you, I use my secure mobile. Both phone and e-mail." The mobile's coding technology not only encrypted voice and data but also scrambled the wavelengths on which the messages traveled, making it impossible for anyone to decipher them.

Tucker swore. "Somehow we've been breached. I'll talk to Cathy."

"See what you can dig up about the Charboniers, too, and their relationship with the Library of Gold, and whether they've been up to anything hinky that might be terrorist related. Angelo said he was a member of the book club. When I asked whether Dad was, he wouldn't answer."

Judd's tone was flat, professional, but Tucker sensed conflicted emotion when he spoke about his father and the book club. "Of course. You're going to Istanbul?"

"Yes. We're taking a commercial flight. It seems safest under the circumstances. Eva called ahead, but Yakimovich's phone is disconnected. He's probably moved again. She was able to reach two of his longtime friends in Istanbul, but they don't know where he is now. If you can track him down, it'd be a big help. It'll take us a few hours to get there."

"I'll see what I can do." As soon as Tucker hung up, he dialed a colleague with whom he had worked during the cold war: Faisal Tarig, who was now with Istanbul police.

"I know Andy Yakimovich," Faisal said. "A sly fellow, that one. But then, he's half Russian and half Turk. Perhaps I can locate him. You still smoking those manly Marlboros?"

"No, gave them up for bottled water."

"I hope you have not become boring, old friend. But if you are asking questions like this, perhaps not. I will be in touch."

"Don't tell anyone I called, or the intel I need."

There was silence. "I see."

After he hung up, Tucker sat a moment, thinking, then he left, heading to Cathy's office. It was a large one, directly behind the receptionist's desk. As chief, she got the best one. Fronting the street, it had special glass in the windows so no one could see inside or use a demodulator to listen in on conversations.

The door was open. He peered in. Family photos hung on the wall alongside CIA commendations. More photos stood on her desk. Some kind of green ivy was growing in a pot. Cathy was typing, staring at her computer screen, her short, blond-streaked hair awry.

"I know you're there, Tucker. What's on your mind?" She had not looked at him.

He walked inside and closed the door. "Who's heard about my Library of Gold operation?"

As he sat, she glanced around at him and frowned. "Why do you ask?"

He explained about the leak. "There's no way the Charboniers should've been at Yitzhak Law's place, waiting for my people."

She spun around to her desk, facing him. "I've told only one person about Yitzhak Law—the assistant director, in my regular report, about fifteen minutes ago. That's too late for the leak to have come from us."

"I'll talk to our IT people. I suppose it's possible someone's broken into our system. But if so, it didn't set off any alarms. I'll make my reports to you verbally from now on."

They were silent. Every day thousands of amateur and professional hackers tried to breach U.S. government computers. So far Langley had lost no important data, and like other small specialized units, Catapult used the same highly secure system.

She nodded. "Anything new about the Library of Gold?"

"Ryder and Blake are on their way to Istanbul, following a good lead. As for me, I'll be glad when I can go home." At least he was getting a lot of work done on the missions he was overseeing.

She nodded again. Then she gave him an understanding smile. "We all have to sacrifice sometimes."

He said good-bye and returned to the communications center. Debi was still at her computer console. He told her what he needed.

"No one's gotten into our system that I know of, suh." Her brows knitted. "I'll get right on it."

Concerned, he returned to his office.

CHAPTER 35

Athens, Greece

THE LIBRARY OF GOLD LEARJET circled down slowly, the lights of Greece's ancient capital gleaming beneath. Nervously making plans, Robin turned away from the panorama and stared back down the length of the cabin to Martin Chapman, his tall figure upright in his seat. He was on his cell phone, his jaw working angrily.

As the jet touched down at Athens International Airport, she studied her cell phone and battery, remembering Preston's awful call to her while she was waiting on the jet in London for Charles and him to arrive. He had ordered her to take the cell apart, and then he told her Charles was dead. Grief swelled her throat. She forced herself to repress it.

Preston had never told her why she was to not activate it again. It did not matter; she was going to need a phone. Sliding the pieces into her pocket, she stood and walked to the rear of the plane.

Chapman peered up as she slung on the backpack

that contained *The Book of Spies*. She did not like the look in his eyes.

Still, he spoke neutrally. "The helicopter is ready."

She nodded. "Good." But she knew it was not good. Once she was in the helicopter, she would be on her way to the hidden Library of Gold, where security was so intense no one could escape—but people occasionally disappeared. People like her. "Will you be going with us, Mr. Chapman?" she asked, although he had made no move to rise.

"I have other business. Magus will take care of you."

From the front, Magus nodded knowing agreement. "Yes, sir, Mr. Chapman."

She followed Magus out of the Learjet and into the black hours of night. The cool air made her shaved head feel even more exposed. She forced herself to stay calm. The airport extended around them, a wide sweep of tarmac with jets coming and going from the long arms of the terminal. It seemed far away, an impossible distance.

A small luggage truck had pulled up to the tail of the jet, and the driver was unloading bags and other items. He was a small man and elderly, with stringy arms showing beneath the short sleeves of his airport shirt. She felt a moment of hope; she might be able to handle him. As he humped Charles's canvas-wrapped body into the back of the truck, she turned away.

"Let's go." Magus's face was a mask. "I'll bet you're ready to get home and settle in."

"You're right," Robin lied. "It will be good to be home."

They walked toward the waiting vehicle, which would take them to the helicopter. It was only about seven feet long and narrow, with space in front for just two people— the driver and a passenger. The rear was an open bed, packed with her large roll-aboard slammed against the cab, Charles's corpse, and several wood boxes Preston had picked up in London.

"I'll help you in." Magus stopped at the rear, where, as the junior member, she would ordinarily sit.

She stared at him, allowing a sense of helplessness to sound in her voice. "I'm so tired. And I'm supposed to keep this backpack with me all the time. Mr. Chapman's orders. Would you mind if I sat in front with the driver?"

They looked at the bed of the truck. There was no gate or upper flap at the end, while the sides had short walls about a foot tall. The floor was hard steel.

"Sure," he said. "Why not." But he touched his hip, where she suspected he kept his gun inside his jacket. The gesture might have been automatic, but it felt like a threat.

Robin gave him a bright smile. "Thanks."

He walked her around to the passenger side. There were no doors on the cab. She took off the backpack and climbed in. Then he walked around to the driver's side, which was also open. He ordered the elderly man out from behind the steering wheel, and her heart sank. Now it would be Magus sitting next to her, armed, young, and strong.

As soon as the driver crawled into the back, Magus studied the automatic transmission, then put the light truck into gear. They rolled away.

She held the backpack on her lap, cradling it in her arms, realizing she had one lucky break—he was an unsure driver, glancing at the steering wheel, the small rearview mirror, the gear shift. That might help—that, and if she surprised him.

She turned around and watched the Learjet taxi away. Returning to face the front, she asked innocently, "Wouldn't you like to see what's in the backpack, Magus?"

"No." He was focused on his driving.

But she started to unzip it, the sound jagged and sharp.

He glanced at her. "Close that up." He reached a hand toward it.

She bit the hand and tasted blood. Swearing, he jerked his hand back, and she slammed the heavy backpack against the side of his head. Reeling, he lashed out with an arm, connecting only with the pack. With the sharp toe of her boot, she kicked the calf of the leg that had a foot on the accelerator and immediately crashed the backpack against his head again.

His foot bounced off the accelerator, the small truck careened, and there was a shout from the back as the driver slid out.

Magus hit the brakes and reached inside his jacket for his gun. In a flurry of motion, Robin slammed her foot down on the accelerator and bit his ear. The truck shot ahead. As his gun appeared in his hand, she slashed her fingernails down his face and eyes, ripping skin.

He yelled and lashed the gun toward her. But he was off-balance now, and the truck was lurching forward, alternating between braking and accelerating. His gun was aimed at her.

In a fury, she smashed the backpack into his face again and rotated her hips toward him. Bracing one hand on the back of her seat and gripping the handhold on the dashboard with the other, she rammed her boots into his hip, inching him across the vinyl seat.

His gun went off, the shot deafening as the bullet exploded through the cab's roof. Blood dripped into his eyes as he tried to see. He shot wildly again, and she shoved him out the door and floored the gas feed. The truck hurtled forward.

Her heart pounded like a kettledrum as she slid

behind the wheel and began to steer. More bullets sliced through the cab, barely missing *The Book of Spies* on the seat beside her. Driving, she crouched low, eyes just above the dash, thankful for the vast open space of the tarmac. A shot flew over her head, a lethal whisper. And then there was no more gunfire.

She rose up and peered into the rearview mirror. Magus was running after her, more and more distant, a hand angrily wiping his face of blood. Behind him lay a trail of capsized wood crates and Charles's corpse. For a long moment she was furious with Charles, furious he had put her in this position, and then the emotion vanished. She was on her own now, as she had been in years past. *You know how to do this,* she told herself.

Determined, she spun the steering wheel, heading toward a chain-link fence. At last she saw a gate beside a dark airport outbuilding. It was quite a bit away, which was good. More distance between her and Magus. The night air cooled her face as she kept the gas feed pressed to the floor.

At the wire gate, she screeched the truck to a stop and jumped out. Putting on the backpack, she looked back. Magus was very far away and had slowed to a jog. His hand was at his ear, no doubt calling for help. But as long as she had *The Book of Spies,* she had a bargaining chip. Martin Chapman would stop at nothing to get her back, hunt her to the far reaches of the planet if he had to, but with the illuminated manuscript she could perhaps negotiate permanent freedom.

She wrestled her roll-aboard out of the truck's bed. It had been crammed against the cab and had missed the fate of the rest of the luggage. Pulling it, she hurried through the gate and into a big parking lot.

She moved quickly among the cars, vans, and SUVs, peering inside. At last she found an old Peugeot, battered and rusted, with a key in the ignition. Scanning around, she took her purse from the roll-aboard. She still had pounds from England; she would exchange them for euros. Last, she found the straw hat she had bought in London. She slammed it down on her bald head and tied the ribbon under her chin.

She loaded the roll-aboard and the backpack into the car. Fighting fear, she drove off through the moonlight toward the exit, her gaze constantly going to her rear-view mirror.

CHAPTER 36

The Sultanate of Oman

MUSCAT INTERNATIONAL AIRPORT lay on flat sands above the Gulf of Oman. In the distance, clusters of oil rigs stood glittering with lights, their toothpick legs sunk deep into the gulf's black waters. The night smelled of the desert as Martin Chapman descended from his Learjet. He was breathing hard with anger: Robin Miller had stolen *The Book of Spies* and escaped. Magus and a team were searching for her in Athens, but it was one more problem, and right now he did not need it.

The danger that worried him most was Judd Ryder, who was CIA, and in that one word lay all the worry in the world: Langley had the resources, the knowledge, the expertise, the guts, to accomplish far more than the public would ever know. One did not cross the Agency lightly, but once done, one had no choice but to end it quickly, which was why Chapman was in Oman now.

The Oman Air section of the ultramodern passenger terminal was quietly busy. He passed tiles, potted palms, and Old Arabia wall decorations without a glance. Turning down a wide arrival and departure corridor, he followed memorized instructions toward a duty-free shop. Near the bathroom door an airport employee in a desert-tan janitorial uniform and a checkered Bedouin headdress was bent over, swabbing the floor.

As Chapman passed, he heard a voice float up toward him: "There's a supply room four doors to your left. Wait inside. Don't turn on the light."

Chapman almost broke his stride. Quickly he regrouped and went to the supply room door. Inside, he flicked on the light. The little room was lined with shelves of cleaning products, paper towels, and toilet paper. He turned off the light and stood in the dark against the rear, a small penlight in one hand, the other hand inside his jacket on the hilt of his pistol.

The door opened and closed like a whisper.

"Jack said you needed help." The voice was low. The man seemed to be standing just inside the door. "I'm expensive, and I have rules. You know about both. Jack says you've agreed to my terms. Before we go further, I need to hear that from you."

"You're Alex Bosa?" Chapman assumed it was a pseudonym.

"Some call me that."

"The Carnivore."

No expression in the voice. "I'm known by that, too."

Chapman inhaled. He was in the presence of a legendary independent assassin, a man who had worked for all sides during the cold war. Now he worked only occasionally, but always at astronomical prices. There were no photos of him; no one knew where he lived, what his real name was, or even in which country he was born. He also never failed, and no one ever uncovered who hired him.

The assassin's voice was calm. "Do you agree to my terms?"

Chapman felt his hackles rise. He was the boss, not this shadowy man who had to live hidden behind pseudonyms. "I have a cashier's check with me." There were to be two payments—half now, half on completion, for a total of $2 million. Ridding himself of the CIA problem was worth every cent. "Do you want the job or not?"

Silence. Then: "I work alone when it's time to do the hit. That means your people must be gone. You must never reveal our association. You must never try to find out what I look like or who I am. If you make any attempts, I will come after you. I'll do you the favor of making it a clean kill, out of respect for our business relationship and the money you will have paid me. After tonight, you will not try to meet me again. When the job is finished, I'll be in touch to let you know how I want to receive the last payment. If you don't pay me, I will come after you for that, too. I do wet work only on people who shouldn't be breathing anyway. I'm the one who makes that decision—not you. I'll give you a new phone number through which you can reach me when you have the additional information about the targets' whereabouts. Do you agree?"

The menacing power in the quiet voice was breathtaking. Chapman found himself nodding even though there was no way the man could see him in the dark.

He spoke up, "I agree." The Carnivore specialized in making hits look like accidents, which was the point—Chapman wanted Langley to have nothing to trace back to him or the Library of Gold.

"Tell me why Judd Ryder and Eva Blake need to be terminated," the Carnivore demanded.

When Chapman had decided to bring in outside talent, he had gone to a source outside the book club, a middleman named only Jack. Through encrypted e-mails, he and Jack had arranged the deal. Now he repeated the story for the Carnivore: "Ryder is former military intelligence and highly skilled. Blake is a criminal—she killed her husband when she was driving drunk. I'm sure you've checked both facts. They've learned about a new secret business transaction I'm working on, and they want it for themselves. I tried to reason with them, but I got nowhere. If they steal this, it'll cost me billions. More important, now they're trying to kill me. They're on their way to Istanbul. I should have information soon about exactly where."

"I understand. I'll leave now. Put the envelope on the shelf next to you. Open the door and go immediately back to your jet." He gave Chapman his new cell number.

There was a movement of air, the door opened and closed quickly, and darkness surrounded Chapman again. He realized he was sweating. He put the envelope with the cashier's check for $1 million on the shelf next to him and left.

As he walked down the corridor, he looked everywhere for the cleaning man in the brown uniform and Bedouin headdress. He had vanished.

CHAPTER 37

Istanbul, Turkey

JUDD STARED DOWN from his window on the jet at the twinkling lights of fabled Instanbul. He drank in the sight of what had once been mighty Constantinople, the crown of the Byzantine Empire—and the birthplace of the Library of Gold.

Eva awoke. "What time is it?" She looked nervous.

"Midnight."

As the jet touched down and taxied toward the terminal of Ataturk International Airport, he checked his mobile.

"Anything from Tucker about where Yakimovich is?" she asked.

He shook his head. "No e-mail. No phone message."

"If Tucker can't find him, it could take us days."

Although there seemed to be no way they could have been followed, they had stopped in Rome on their way to the airport not only to buy supplies but also to disguise themselves. Now as they deplaned, Judd helped

Eva into a wheelchair. She curled up low, her head hanging forward as if asleep. A blanket covered her body, and a scarf hid her hair. He put her shoulder satchel and a large new duffel bag containing other purchases on her lap. He was dressed like a private nurse, in white slacks, a white blast jacket, and a white cap. Tucked inside his lower lip was a tight roll of cotton, making the lip protrude and his jaw look smaller.

Keeping his cheeks soft and his gaze lazy, he adjusted his internal monitor until he was comfortably projecting a not-too-bright attendant to the nice lady in the wheelchair. Watching surreptitiously around, he pushed her into the international terminal and showed his fake passport and her real one at the visa window. They acquired visa stamps and passed through customs. Although the terminal was less congested than at high-traffic hours, there were still plenty of people. Beyond the security kiosk waited even more, many holding up signs with passengers' names.

Rolling the wheelchair down the long corridor toward the exit doors, Judd stayed on high alert. Which was when he spotted the one person he did not want to see—Preston. How in hell had he known to come to Istanbul? His chest tight, Judd studied him from the corners of his eyes. Tall and square-shouldered, the killer was leaning against the exterior wall of a news store, apparently reading the *International Herald Tribune*. He was dressed as he had been in London, in jeans, a black leather jacket, and probably a pistol.

Because he did not have ID to carry a weapon onto a commercial flight, Judd had left his Beretta in Rome. He considered. It seemed unlikely Preston had been able to see his face in London from the floor of the alley. On the other hand, it was possible the killer had somehow figured out who he was and had acquired a photo.

"Preston." The worried whisper floated up from Eva.

"I see him," Judd said quietly. "You're asleep, remember?"

She returned to silence as he continued to push the wheelchair at a sedate pace.

Above the newspaper, Preston was studying the throngs. His eyes moved while his body gave the appearance of disinterested relaxation. He paused at the faces of not only women but men the right age, the right hair color, the right height—which told Judd that Preston had somehow learned what he looked like. Watching couples and singles, Preston missed no one, took no one for granted. He pulled a radio from his belt, listening and speaking into it. That meant he had a least one janitor nearby.

As Preston hooked the radio back on to his belt, he noticed Judd and Eva. And focused.

His gaze felt like a burning poker. Judd did not look at him, and he did not speed the wheelchair. Either action would make Preston even more curious. Then he saw a tall woman sweeping along, pulling a small suitcase. Despite the late hour, she wore large diva sunglasses—and her hair was long and red, like Eva's.

Seeing an opportunity, Judd moved the wheelchair alongside her and slumped his shoulders to make himself appear even more boring in his attendant's uniform. Preston's eyes moved, attracted to the woman. He stepped away from the news store, following as the woman hurried in front of Judd and Eva to a car rental stand.

Judd exhaled. He pushed Eva out the glass doors and to the line of waiting taxis.

AS SOON AS THE YELLOW CAB left the terminal, Judd closed the privacy window between the front and rear seats. It was an old vehicle, the upholstery threadbare, but the glass was thick, and the driver would not be able to hear their conversation.

"How could Preston have found us?" Eva asked again. "The Charboniers knew about Yakimovich and Istanbul, but they died before they could tell anyone."

"It's hard to believe Tucker has another leak. IT will be covering headquarters like a mushroom cloud. Maybe it's us. Could Charles have planted a bug on you in London?" As they talked, he watched the rear for any sign of Preston.

"If he did, those clothes are gone. But why would he bother? He thought he had me. Did you see anyone following us at any time?"

He shook his head. They were silent.

"Okay, let's take it from the top," he finally said. "It's not a bug, and it's not a cyberbreach at Catapult."

"If Charles were alive," she decided, "he would know we'd be heading to Andy Yakimovich."

"Peggy Doty's the only loose end I can think of. But she didn't know about Yakimovich or Istanbul, so there's no way Preston could've gotten the information from her."

Eva suddenly swore. "Of course—Peggy's cell phone. Whoever killed Peggy could've found my number on it." She pulled her cell from her satchel. "The only time I dialed out was in the Athens airport, when I called around looking for Andy. I was calling Istanbul."

"Give it to me." He turned on the phone, then watched the screen to make certain it was connected to the network. Rolling down his window, he tossed it into the open bed of a passing pickup.

Eva smiled. "That'll give Preston something to chase."

He smiled back. In the small rear seat of the taxi they inadvertently gazed deeply into each other's eyes. For a long moment warm intimacy passed between them. Judd's heart rate accelerated.

Saying nothing, Eva looked away, and he turned to stare out the side window. That was the problem with shared danger. Inevitably it led to bonding of one sort or another, and one of the "sorts" could be sexual. He sensed her discomfort, her sudden aloofness, but he was not going to go there and explain what had just happened. Or that he had liked it.

Mentally he shook himself. They were on the outskirts of the city. Choosing a busy intersection, he told the driver to stop. There was a chance Preston had gotten their taxi's plate number.

After helping Eva into her wheelchair, he paid the driver. The taillights disappeared into traffic, and he wheeled her around, heading in the opposite direction. He scanned cautiously.

"There's an alley ahead," Eva prompted.

"I see it." He pushed her inside.

She got up and discarded her blanket and scarf, piling them into the wheelchair's seat. From the duffel bag she took out a midnight-blue jacket. As he removed the cotton from his lower lip, stripped off his attendant's jacket, and unbuckled his white trousers, she pulled on her jacket and, without looking at him, took her shoulder satchel and hurried off to keep watch.

He slid into jeans, a brown polo shirt, and a brown sports jacket. Folding the wheelchair and their discarded belongings against the wall, he turned to gaze at her, a slender figure dwarfed by the alley's tall opening, somehow jaunty and more unafraid than he would have thought.

Carrying the duffel, he joined her. "See anything?"

"No sign of Preston. Which way?"

They walked six blocks, went around a corner, and Judd hailed another cab. Within twenty minutes they were in the Sultanahmet district in the heart of historic Old Town, not far from Topkapi Palace, the Hagia Sophia, and the Hippodrome. The taxi stopped, and they got out.

They walked another ten minutes, at last crossing onto a narrow street, at best a lane and a half wide. There were no cars, but trolley tracks ran down the middle. Tall stone buildings from centuries past abutted one another, shops and stores on the ground and second floors. He inhaled. The exotic scents of cumin and apple-flavored tobacco drifted through the night air.

"This is Istiklal Caddesi," he told her. "*Caddesi* means avenue. Our hotel's four blocks farther."

As they continued on, she commented, "You seem to know a lot about Istanbul. Have you been here before?"

"No. I Googled it."

The hotel was a stuccoed structure with a simple wood entry door and two shuttered windows on the right. The street was quiet, businesses closed, with no restaurants, cafés, or bars to attract customers.

He slowed. "We have a small problem. All you've got is your real passport, which means you'll have to give the hotel your name. So I'm going to go in alone and register myself under one of my covers. Then I'll come out for you."

He gestured, and she stepped up into the recessed entry of a trinket store. Her dark jacket and jeans blended into the shadow.

She's learning, he thought to himself as he left her and went into the hotel. The interior was narrow and deep, with old unvarnished woods and faded upholstery. As expected, the clerk handed over a plain cardboard box with the correct cover name printed on it. Mentally Judd thanked Tucker. He placed an order with room service, walked toward the elevator at the rear, and continued on, exiting out the rear door.

When he appeared in the mouth of the alley, he

could not see Eva, so well was she hidden in the doorway.

She hurried out, a question in her eyes.

"We're fine," he told her as they retraced his path
down the alley. "I told them my brother would be joining me in a couple of days."

"I thought you had only cousins."

He grinned. "I have a brother now."

They climbed the rear stairs to the sixth floor. She
had agreed with him it was safer for them to stay together. Their room had two small beds and was sparsely
furnished with florid furniture in the Old Turkish style.

While she went into the bathroom, he dropped the
duffel onto the bed nearest the door and opened the box.
Inside was another subcompact semiautomatic Beretta
pistol just like the one he'd had to leave behind in Rome.
He checked it, loaded it from the box of ammo, and
tried on the canvas shoulder holster, adjusting it. Satisfied, he went to the window. The lights of the city spread
out before him in a glittering vista, beckoning.

"Come look at this." He pushed open the two vertical panes and leaned out.

She emerged from the bathroom, her striking features
smoothed at last. She was beginning to feel safe again,
he decided. She smelled fresh, of soap and rose water.

She leaned out the window, too. "What a magnificent
view."

"Istanbul is the only major city in the world to strad-
dle two continents," he said. "It's built on seven hills,
just as Rome is. Where we are—the Sultanahmet district—is on top of the first hill, on the south side. It's
the historic core of the city. See that?" A series of fire-
works in calico colors sprayed above the dark waters of
the Marmara. "That's from a wedding boat. Look at
the lighted mosques. The domes and minarets. The
temples and churches. The maze of winding streets."

The night gave a spectacular quality to the ancient city, as if it were secretly reinvigorating itself while its inhabitants slept. "It must've looked something like this during the Byzantine period, when the emperors were conquering the world and collecting the best books."

"It's beautiful. Did you learn all of that from Google?"

"From my father. Visiting ancient Constantinople was something we'd always planned to do together. That's how I knew Istanbul was called the City of the World's Desire. He particularly liked this hotel. There's a lot of history connected to it." His chest tight, he turned to her. "If my father were a member of the book club when your husband joined the library, he could've been responsible in one way or another for the dead man in your husband's grave and for sending you to prison. I just want you to know I'm sorry."

"Charles told me they wanted to have me killed, but he talked them out of it." She sighed heavily, and he felt a gap open between them. "I know you loved your father. Whatever he did or didn't do has nothing to do with who you are. It's not your fault."

But he sensed that somehow, in her mind, he was tainted by it. He turned back into the room, remembering. When he was growing up, his father was gone for longer and longer periods of time. He had moved them around Washington from one house to another, always larger, more expensive. His mother's loneliness. The beautiful gifts brought back from each trip. Artworks, jewelry, furnishings, books. His father had grown not only richer but leaner and stronger. As his hair grayed, their conversations more often focused on lessons he wanted to pass on: Think for yourself. You can never learn enough. No one can protect you but yourself. Money solves almost every problem.

"You said you're a CIA contract employee," Eva said. "What did you do before?"

"Military intelligence. The army. I retired about a month before Dad was killed."

"You're a rich kid with every opportunity in the world. I'll bet your father would've loved for you to jump on the fast track to the executive suite at Bucknell."

"True." It was his father's dream.

"But you ended up in the army. Why?"

"It seemed like the right thing to do. And no, it was before 9/11."

"So you rebelled by being a stand-up guy. But that's not all, is it? Who are you really, Judd Ryder?"

For that he had no answer. He was saved by a knock on the door. Sliding out his weapon, he padded toward it and peered through the peephole. Dinner had arrived.

They ate at a small table in the corner—lamb meatballs with lemon sauce, tangy roasted eggplant salad, and a spread of ground walnuts and sweet red peppers. They talked quietly, and when they finished, he poured raki, a milky aperitif flavored with anise, a Turkish drink he had enjoyed with his father at home. As he handed her a glass, his encrypted mobile rang.

She looked across the room to his bed, where the mobile lay. "Tucker with good news, I hope."

He was already picking it up. As he punched the Talk button, he confirmed by saying, "Hello, Tucker."

Setting down her glass, she listened as he put the mobile on speakerphone.

"You've arrived?" Tucker wanted to know.

"Yes, we're at the hotel," Judd said. "Your package was waiting. Thanks. You should know Preston was at the airport. We got past him. This time it wasn't a leak; they tracked us through Eva's cell phone."

"Christ." The spymaster sounded frustrated.

"Did you find out anything about Yakimovich?" Judd asked.

"Yes, a good lead from an Istanbul source. There's a merchant of old calligraphy in the Grand Bazaar who's supposed to know where Yakimovich is. His name is Okan Biçer, and he shows up for work around three P.M. I'll e-mail you his photo and give you directions to his shop."

When they had memorized the directions and examined the photo, Judd ended the connection and tossed the mobile back onto his bed. Then he raised his glass, and Eva raised hers. They touched the rims with a soft clink. Drinking, they avoided the intimacy of each other's eyes, the pain of their shared past, and the worry about what tomorrow would bring.

CHAPTER 38

Fairfax County, Virginia

CATHY DOYLE WAS EXHAUSTED. It was nearly one A.M., and the day had been filled with work and the usual pressures to succeed at the various missions on which Catapult was working. As she drove across the Potomac River into Virginia, heading home, she turned on the radio. But it was a report of new terrorist attacks in eastern Afghanistan, and she already had enough facts about it; the last thing she needed was the somber news repeated. She punched off the radio.

Virginia was a land of urban congestion amid broad swathes of woods and farmland. She loved it—it always made her think of Ohio, where she had grown up. She turned off onto a two-lane road washed with moonlight. It ran along the river north of the District. At this hour, traffic was light, the widely spaced houses mostly dark.

She thought longingly of her twin daughters, home from spring break at Columbia, and her husband, a lawyer at the Department of Labor, who had just returned from a conference in Chicago. All would be sleeping, which she would be soon, too.

Humming to herself, she checked the road. There was almost no traffic, and she felt herself relax. She was thinking about home and bed again when she realized there was another car behind her now. She glanced at her speedometer. She was locked in at forty miles an hour, just where she wanted to be, and so was the other guy. Someone else heading home for a good night's sleep.

To her right, the forest opened up, and she could see the river with its rippling surface painted a silky silver by the moonlight. She liked that, too. Nature in all its beauty. She cracked her window. The air whistled in, the cool night air tasting moist, of the river. She turned on the radio again, this time found a blues station. Ah, yes.

Settling back into her seat, she glanced into her rearview mirror. And stared. The other vehicle's headlights were closing in, bombarding her car with light. She hit the accelerator, pushing out. As she passed sixty miles an hour, she checked her rearview mirror again. Her follower was even closer. There was still no other traffic as she started up the long, high hill that would eventually dip down into the valley where her house was, only a couple of miles farther.

Again she looked into her rearview mirror. The other car had moved out of their lane and into the oncoming lane. It was a big pickup. He had not signaled, and he had not slowed, either.

She slammed her foot on the accelerator, speeding toward seventy miles an hour. The pickup dropped back behind, in their lane again. But then the headlights loomed abruptly closer. As she floored the accelerator, he swung into the other lane, overtaking her. Her mouth went dry as they raced up the hill together

She braked to drop behind. Too late. The pickup crashed sideways into her car. Furious, she fought to control the steering wheel. The pickup slammed into her again, holding, pushing her toward the cliff over the river. This time the wheel ripped from her grasp.

Terror filling her, she gripped the steering wheel as the car hurtled through the guardrail, shot over the cliff, and crashed down through young pines, smashing against boulders. One collision after another hurled her back and forth. As the sedan flew over a final precipice and dived toward the shadowy river, she felt a moment of blinding impact, and then nothing.

Washington, D.C.

AT EIGHT A.M. THE HEADQUARTERS of Catapult was solemn and quiet, although all of the morning staff had arrived. A sense of shocked grief infused the building. The news of Catherine Doyle's fatal accident had spread. Tucker had heard hours before, awakened by his old friend Matthew Kelley, the director of the Clandestine Service. When she had not returned home, Cathy's husband had called. Then the Virginia State Police found her car submerged in the river, only a patch of the top visible. The vehicle was badly banged up, which was consistent with the terrain it had crashed down through, and she had apparently drowned. There would be a coroner's report and the results of forensics in a few days.

Tucker wandered the old brick building, chatting with their people, comforting them, and by doing so comforting himself. Cathy had been a good boss, tough and fair, and they had liked her. He urged them to get back to work. Their operators abroad were counting on them. Besides, it was what Cathy would have wanted, and they knew it.

By the afternoon, the pace had quickened, voices talked business, telephones rang, computer keys clicked. He returned to his office and tried to concentrate. Finally the habits of a lifetime returned, and he bent over his work.

"Hello, Tucker." Hudson Canon stood in the doorway, looking concerned. He was an assistant director in the Clandestine Service, a longtime field officer who had been brought home to Langley to oversee a slew of people who in turn created and managed missions. Short, dignified, and heavily muscled, he gave the impression of a high-class American Kennel Club bulldog, with his pug nose and round black eyes and thick cheeks. "How are you doing?" Canon asked.

"It's terrible news, of course. Cathy will be greatly missed."

"Gloria says everyone is working hard, but I must say the place feels a bit like a mausoleum. Damn. I liked Cathy a lot. A fine woman."

"Have a chair." Tucker motioned to one. "What can I do for you?"

Canon gave a quick smile and sat in front of the desk. "Matt Kelley sent me over to take Cathy's place until a new chief is named. You interested in the job?"

"That's fast."

"Don't I know it. Are you interested?"

Tucker's soul felt heavy. "Let me think about it." The position had been offered to him before Cathy was appointed, but he had turned it down.

"I haven't been to Cathy's office yet," Canon went on. "I told Gloria to pack up all of her private things before I moved in. Meanwhile, I'd like you to bring me up-to-date. Start with the hottest missions."

Canon crossed his legs, and they talked. Tucker filled him in on Berlin, Bratislava, Kiev, Tehran, and others. Canon knew the basics about all from Cathy's weekly reports.

"I hear you might've had a breach in your e-mail or Internet system."

"Debi is honchoing it," Tucker told him. "Someone did get in and was able to access Cathy's e-mail for about three minutes."

Canon grimaced. "Long enough to steal more than any of us would want."

"Agreed. Still, we're not sure what they took. Maybe they got nothing. In any case, that pathway is now a dead end, and Debi's team is on high alert, looking for even the smallest signs of attempt to trespass. There's been no other successful cybersleuthing since. The problem was, the breach occurred during the night shift, when we had fewer bodies. They missed the invader—he was damn good at it obviously."

"I see. What else do you have for me?"

Tucker launched into a description of the Library of Gold operation.

When he had finished, Canon sat back, thinking. "Is this a wise use of Catapult's resources? You still have no evidence of involvement in terrorism. Who in hell cares about the Library of Gold? So what if it's some marvelous old relic. That's the bailiwick of historians and anthropologists. This is a waste of time better spent on more critical missions."

Tucker stiffened. "I understand your point, but we're deep into it now. I've got a contract employee and a civilian on the run, being hunted. And a dead man who turned up alive who said he was the chief librarian. He's dead now, too, and it's real this time. There are other corpses—people like Jonathan Ryder and the Charboniers."

"Have you learned anything about the library's location through Ryder or the Charboniers?"

"Nothing yet. Jonathan's life is far easier to probe. We have his travel records, but he was an international businessman and flew around the globe. A lot of cities and towns. As for the Charboniers, we have to work with the French to get information, and that's difficult. You know how secretive they can be."

"It'll be another dead end."

"Maybe. But my two people in Istanbul have a good lead. We need to follow up on that."

"A good lead? What is it?"

"The man's name is Okan Biçer. He sells calligraphy in the Grand Bazaar." Tucker checked his watch. "He's supposed to know where an old acquaintance of Eva Blake's husband is, an antiquities merchant named Andrew Yakimovich. They're hoping Yakimovich may be holding something for Blake that'll tell them where the library is."

Hudson Canon seemed to think about it. At last he nodded. "I'd already expressed my reservations to Cathy about whether this operation was worth it, but she convinced me to give it some time. Your argument for more time is good, too. However, I've also taken it to my boss. Especially now that Cathy's gone and we'll need to rethink Catapult, we're going to have to pull in our horns. You have thirty-six hours to find the library. If you don't know where it is by then, the boss says to pull the plug and end the operation."

CHAPTER 39

Peshawar, Pakistan

THICK STORM CLOUDS ROLLED black and angry overhead, and the temperature dropped five degrees as Martin Chapman rode into the polluted and paranoid city of Peshawar. He was dressed in a traditional *shalwar kameez*—the long shirt and baggy trousers worn by most Pakistani and Afghani men—so he could pass for an Uzbek, Chechen, or light-skinned Pashtun.

A hotbed of Taliban and al-Qaeda, the city was where he was to meet the warlord who had promised him safe passage. Still, Chapman did not believe in relying on promises. His pistol was on his belt, the holster latch unfastened, and his hand on the weapon's grip. Beside him lay the truck driver's fully loaded AK-47.

Peshawar was an armed garrison. Men and boys as young as five years old wore, cradled, or shouldered an array of weapons. But then, it was the capital of the politically unstable North-West Frontier Province and just six miles from the lawless Federally Administered

Tribal Areas. Jihadists poured into the city to regroup, to fight, to buy and trade weapons and supplies, and to partake of civilization. It had always been a smugglers' haven and a center for indigenous arms manufacture, but now more so than ever. Private homes were functioning gun factories. Using the crudest of tools, entire families fabricated quality copies of major small and medium arms.

As the truck drove through the city, Chapman was taken aback by the poverty and destruction. Empty shells of buildings, some towering precariously several stories high, dotted streets, the result of suicide bombings, personal disputes, police assaults, and the occasional drone attack from across the mountains in Afghanistan.

Despite it all, people strove for normalcy. Women draped in ghostly burkas drifted like shadows among the stores, carrying string shopping bags. Men in tribal headdresses or *pakul* hats—traditional flat round wool caps—sat for portraits in front of old box cameras screwed into rickety wood tripods.

"We there soon," the driver told Chapman. An Afghan Pashtun, he worked directly for the warlord. Thankfully he understood English far better than he spoke it.

The driver turned the big truck onto Lahore Road. Bouncing over potholes, he turned again and slammed on the brakes. Dust spewed a choking cloud around them. They had stopped in front of a gun shop.

"This is it?" Chapman asked.

The driver nodded enthusiastically.

"Wait here," Chapman ordered.

Nodding again, the man turned off the ignition and peered up through the windshield, eying the stormy twilight sky. He shook his head in despair, then climbed out and lit a brown cigarette.

Chapman got out, too, silently cursing Syed Ullah

for insisting they meet in Peshawar. But that was Ullah for you. He was one of a long line of Pashtun tribal chiefs from the border province of Khost in Afghanistan. The warlord was his own man, regarding Kabul's commands with indifference.

As Chapman walked toward the store, Ullah appeared in the doorway, filling it. Gigantic, powerfully built, he had hands that looked as if they could palm bowling balls. His cheekbones were high, the coldly intelligent brown eyes widely spaced, the thick mustache above his wide mouth neatly trimmed. He wore a brown wool sweater, a *shalwar kameez,* and sturdy black boots. Twin pearl-handled pistols were holstered on his hips.

He looked comfortable and pleased with himself. "You are here, Chapman. Come in. *Pe kher ragle.*" Welcome.

Chapman walked inside and stopped, keeping his manner casual. Weapons ranging from small two-shot pistols to juiced-up rocket launchers were for sale, stacked four and five deep against the walls, lying on shelves up to the ceiling, and bunched and leaning together like haystacks in the corners. The place smelled like cheap grease. In the back of the store, silently blocking a door, stood six of Ullah's soldiers. They carried rifles, while flowers were tucked into their belts in the Pashtun style. Two bandoliers crossed each of their chests, displaying not only bullets but dangling grenades.

Smiling proudly, the warlord looked around the store, then peered down at Chapman.

"Impressive," Chapman admitted.

With a nod from Ullah, his men headed for the open front door. "They will bring in the crates. You have what we agreed on in the back of the truck?"

"Everything."

"Good, good." Ullah gestured grandly at the two low stools beside a desk.

They sat. A white silk cloth edged with lace had been spread out, and a white porcelain teapot decorated with red poppies waited in the middle of it. The warlord poured tea into two glasses rimmed in gold and set into decorative golden bases with golden handles.

Offering no milk or sugar, he handed a cup to Chapman. "This is a fine black Indian tea, flavored with cardamon and honey. I serve it on only the most important occasions, to my most important guests. According to our Pashtunwali code, it is my duty to host you, treasure you, and protect you." Ullah lifted his cup in salute.

Chapman lifted his cup, too, and gave a nod of appreciation. They drank, and Chapman said nothing about the code, knowing full well the warlord's hospitality would evaporate and Chapman's life would be in danger if he did not fulfill his end of their agreement. Pashtuns were bound by fierce cultural, emotional, and social ties—the Pashtunwali code. At the same time, if they breathed, they fought. An old Pashtun saying was "Me against my brother, me and my brother against our cousins, and we and our cousins against the enemy, any enemy." In that way they confirmed their honor, and it did not seem to matter whether they ended up successful—or dead.

The first crate came in, one of Ullah's men rolling it on a dolly, followed by another, and another, all disappearing into the back. From Karachi, the crates had been shipped to Islamabad, then trucked into Madari, where Chapman had jetted in from Oman and met Ullah's driver.

Thunder rumbled somewhere in the distant hills.

"My boys will hurry now," Ullah commented, amused.

He barked an order in Pashto to a soldier who had picked up speed and was rushing past with another crate. The man wheeled it around, brought it to Ullah, and ripped off the top with a crowbar.

Ullah and Chapman stood and looked down. Ullah lowered his great height to finger a new U.S. Army camouflage uniform. "Good, good."

"The other boxes contain more uniforms," Chapman told him. "Kevlar helmets with night-vision scopes, grenade belts, GPS units, encrypted cell phones, flares, M4 carbine rifles with telescopic sights, and body armor. Everything we agreed upon and more, all regulation army and authentic."

"I will check each crate before you leave." The warlord settled back down onto his stool, his dainty teacup disappearing into his big hand as he sipped.

For a moment Ullah was not a ruthless brawler, not the Mike Tyson of the tribal lands, but a gentleman of good taste. Driven into exile in Pakistan by the Taliban in the 1990s, he had returned to Afghanistan after 9/11 to lead anti-Taliban soldiers, moving in and out of alliances, keeping his distance from the national government and coalition forces. Today his home base was a vast area of eastern Khost province that was largely rural and backward. His photograph hung in every office, shop, and school, and he maintained firm control with a personal army of more than five thousand.

What mattered most to Chapman was he owned ten square miles of land he needed.

Lightning split through the dark clouds, illuminating the shop in a moment of startling white light. Thunder boomed, and the heavens opened. Rain poured down in a brutal torrent as the last of the crates rushed through.

Ullah peered over his teacup. "About my money. I am eager to have it back."

"And you will. Soon."

"Now."

When Chapman had discovered Ullah owned the land, he had ordered a complete investigation of the man. Through book club member Carl Lindström's chief of security—an accomplished black-hatter—a hidden overseas account containing some $20 million in profits from drugs and gun-running was uncovered. If Chapman told the Kabul government about it, the minister of finance would confiscate it, and the president would find unpleasant ways to punish Ullah.

Instead, Chapman had led his equity firm in a leveraged buyout of the bank—and frozen the account. With that incentive, Ullah had agreed to meet him at a Caspian Sea resort, where Chapman had offered to release the money and give him a small percentage in a deal the greedy bastard could not refuse. He would earn enormous profits for decades to come in an honest business venture through which he could launder his heroin and opium profits. But it hinged on Chapman's being able to buy the land, which the warlord could not sell because he was renting it to the United States for a secret forward base.

"When you finish the job, you'll get your money," Chapman told him.

Ullah stared hard.

"As we agreed," Chapman reminded him, thinking of the Pashtunwali code.

There was a pause. Then Ullah chuckled and changed the subject. "Why do you want my land?" He had asked the question several times before.

"You'll find out as soon as you sign it over to me."

Ullah nodded. "It is good you arrived on schedule. We will be able to truck the crates into Khost by tomorrow."

"And then?" Chapman prompted.

"The next night two hundred fifty of my men will

put on your uniforms and use your weapons to take out about a hundred villagers. A lot of gunfire and dead bodies. Much blood. I will have a Pakistani reporter and cameraman there. They will make many videos. It will be a splendid show that all the world will see of 'American' soldiers slaughtering innocent civilians." He laughed loudly, his solid white teeth gleaming.

Because of the changed—and charged—political atmosphere in Afghanistan, the Kabul national government insisted its complicity in the U.S. forward base be kept secret. But with the harsh light of international outrage shining on the massacre, Kabul would have no choice but to close the base. Of course before then Ullah would have made all of the American uniforms and equipment vanish, and those who knew what actually had happened would be bound to silence by the Pashtunwali code. The result would be the warlord would at last be able to sell the land to Chapman.

As the rain drummed down, Ullah boasted of his past successes in battle, hair-singeing tales to remind Chapman of his power. But Chapman had something Ullah did not—the knowledge of what lay in the land, and the technical expertise to exploit it. Afghanistan had many natural riches, but the war-torn country was unstable, illiterate, untrained, and in no position to make use of them and would not be for decades to come.

As soon as they finished their tea, the warlord announced, "We will inspect the crates now."

"Go ahead. I need to make a phone call. I'll join you when I finish."

As Ullah left for the back room, Chapman walked to the front of the shop and stood alone at the window. The thunderstorm had stopped as suddenly as it had started, and the sky was clearing. With that good omen, he dialed his wife's iPhone. It had been days since they last talked, a month since he last saw her. He longed to hear her voice.

But it was her assistant, Mahaira. "She is showering. I am so sorry."

He kept his voice calm. "Where are you?"

"In Athens, as you requested."

He sighed with relief. He would see his wife in just a few hours. "How was the party in San Moritz?" It was supposed to have been a gala affair—jet-set society in all its ravenous glory.

"She wore the diamond necklace, earrings, and tiara to the ball," Mahaira said proudly. "She looked gorgeous. Glowing, like a star."

The necklace and earrings had been her mother's and grandmother's. He had bought them two decades before, when her family had lost its money. The tiara was new—purchased just last year. He remembered the excitement in her eyes, how she had clapped her hands and danced around the room wearing it, naked, beautiful.

"Does she miss me?"

Mahaira answered too quickly. "Of course. Terribly."

When he hung up, he took out the photo from his wallet and stared at it, reliving the past, the happiness, the hopes and dreams of youth. It was a copy of the picture that always stood on his desk at his Arabian horse spread in Maryland, his home base. There she was—a glorious young Gemma in her tight long formal gown, the family diamonds sparkling at her ears and around her throat—and he in his rented tuxedo. A long time ago now, when they were in their early twenties and deeply in love.

His cell phone rang. Putting the photo away, he answered.

It was Preston, sounding jubilant. "Catherine Doyle is dead, and I have the information about where Ryder and Blake are going in Istanbul."

"Give me the details."

"The contact is Okan Biçer, a calligraphy seller in the Grand Bazaar. I've hired local men, and I'm on my way."

"Good. Let me know."

As soon as he hung up, Chapman phoned the Carnivore and repeated the information. There could be no loose ends to interfere with the warlord's attack in Khost, especially no further CIA interest.

"Preston will merely set up the hit, as we agreed," he finished.

The Carnivore's voice was neutral. "That is acceptable. I'm in Istanbul. Your two targets are as good as scrubbed."

CHAPTER 40

Istanbul, Turkey

A WORLD ATLAS OF LANGUAGES filled the air as crowds poured in to the Grand Bazaar through the Light of the Ottomans Gate. Eva peered around as she and Judd moved with the throngs. While many women wore shoulder-baring sundresses ending above the knee, others concealed their hair beneath traditional *khimar* scarves and their bodies under long coats. Some men sported fezzes and large mustaches, and some were clean-shaved and dressed in business suits or skin-exposing tank tops and walking shorts.

They had been watching for Preston or a sign they were being followed. To lessen the chances of discovery they had changed their appearances in the hotel before checking out. Now her hair was black, pulled severely back into a bun at the nape of her neck, while Judd's chestnut brown hair was bleached blond and cut very short. He wore glasses with plain lenses and looked very much like a tanned Viking tourist.

She'd had a restless night, wondering how she could have so badly misjudged Charles and whether Judd was somehow also going to betray her. Truthfully, she did not hold him responsible for his father's actions. But still, there was something about it all that made her uneasy. She hoped she could continue to trust him.

Inside, the marketplace was teeming. Completely roofed and domed, with thick exterior walls, gates, and doors, it boasted some four thousand shops, miles and miles of avenues and lanes, and hidden nooks known only to locals.

Judd was giving her a tour. "It's the largest covered mall in the world and the most famous souk. This street is Kalpakçilarbaşi Caddesi, the main one. Look at all the gold stores. That's what it's known for."

Kalpakçilarbaşi was a tunnel of light, with a tall arched ceiling, high windows, and pale walls adorned with exquisite blue tiles. Seeming to extend endlessly, it emanated taste and wealth, with gold jewelry, gold plates, and decorative gold items shining from the glass display windows.

Judd directed them into a giant labyrinth of tiny streets and alleyways, all swarming with shoppers. The view changed time and again. They passed mosques, banks, coffee shops, and restaurants. From the doors of *hans*—stores—merchants called out their wares in a variety of languages—the strongest Turkish Viagra, the best pottery, the finest watches, the most lovely antiques, the most religious icons.

Suddenly there was a scream. A woman turned, her hands gripping her face in distress. "My purse! He stole my purse!" she yelled in German.

A bag-slasher raced off, his long hair flying as he rounded a corner and vanished. It had happened so quickly no one had time to react. As someone gave the woman directions to a police station, Eva and Judd went onto another street, finally reaching their destination.

A picturesque relic of Old Istanbul, it was a small, dead-end shopping area surrounding a tiled patio. Photos of whirling dervishes in their ecstatic dances decorated walls. Goods spilled from *hans*. Games of backgammon were in progress at wood tables in the patio, where the players drank from tulip-shaped tea glasses. Eva spotted a cabal of pickpockets, a mother with three children, but no actual dipping.

"I see the shop," she told Judd.

The windows of the *han* showcased aged pages of calligraphy. As they walked inside, a sturdy middle-aged man in an embroidered caftan grinned at them.

"Merhaba." Welcome. He quickly took in their appearances and switched to English. "British and Swedish, yes? You are obviously interested in our gorgeous old script. You must take home many pages. Hang them on your walls. Impress all your family."

Eva remembered the photo of Okan Biçer that Tucker had e-mailed. This merchant was not he.

"We're looking for Mr. Biçer, Okan Biçer," she said. "A friend told us about him."

"Ah, you have mutual friends. No doubt he sent you to buy calligraphy. We have the best in Istanbul. In all Europe and Asia."

"My name is Eva Blake," she tried again. "Andrew Yakimovich is a personal friend. We were told Mr. Biçer would know where Andy is."

His small black eyes examined her shrewdly, then Judd. "No calligraphy? How sad. You will leave your phone number and address, and I will see."

The beaded curtain separating the store from the back rustled, as if someone had been starting to come through and then changed his mind—or had been listening. When the shopkeeper glanced back nervously, Judd strode past him.

He hurried after Judd. *"Hayir, hayir."* No, no. "Okan is not here. He is not here."

Checking the other shoppers who were watching curiously, Eva followed as Judd pushed the merchant aside, brushed through the curtain, and opened a wood door. A sweet, cloying odor filled the narrow hall.

They strode down it, the shopkeeper on their heels, wringing his hands and lamenting. When they finally passed through an arched stone opening, Eva and Judd stopped and stared.

"I'll be damned," she said.

Their shirts off, men lay on faded lounges against stone walls, eyes half closed, fezzes crowning their heads at drunken angles. Some propped themselves up on elbows, holding long pipes, the bowls heating over oil lamps. In the bowls were waxy brown "pills"—opium. It was an old-fashioned opium den. In the light of the small lamps, the men turned toward their visitors, their gazes dreamy, their cheeks puffing as they continued to inhale the intoxicating vapors.

Okan Biçer was standing in the middle of them, rubbing his elbows, distraught. His long thin face was sweaty, and his eyes darted nervously around. He gave a quick nod to the shopkeeper, who shrugged and marched back toward the store.

Collecting himself, Biçer walked forward and bowed. "This is no place for you. We must leave. You can tell me everything I can do for you then. That way." He gestured toward the shopkeeper's retreating figure.

But Eva was already moving toward a man asleep on his side on a lounge. His large fez lay over his ear, and one chubby hand dangled to the floor. Fifty-plus years old, he had a large head, thick gray hair, heavy round cheeks, and oddly sensitive lips. The bags under his eyes were huge and dark, almost bruised—but that was opium for you. Dressed only in loose trousers and tennis shoes without laces, he was snoring lightly.

She shook his shoulder. "Andy, wake up. Andy Yakimovich. Wake up."

Yakimovich, the antiquities dealer, rolled over onto his back, his large white belly spreading. He snored louder.

Judd grabbed Yakimovich and propped him up against the stone wall. "Wake up, Yakimovich. *Polis.*" Police.

His eyes snapped open, and the room emptied—Biçer raced away through a different door, off to the side, and the other men staggered to their feet and stumbled after him. Opium poppies were one of Turkey's largest crops, and through international agreement, the United States annually bought a large percentage of their legal opium. But just as it was in the United States, the narcotic was illegal for self-entertainment in Turkey.

"Polis?" Yakimovich muttered worriedly. He looked at Judd. "You are police? You do not look like police. What kind of police are you?"

Eva tapped Judd's arm, and he moved aside. "Hello, Andy. I'm Eva Blake, Charles Sherback's widow. I believe Charles left something with you for me."

His eyes wandered. "You are not police. Go away."

She grabbed his stubbled chin. "Look at me, Andy." When he focused, she repeated, "My name is Eva Blake. I'm Charles Sherback's widow. I want what he left for me. Judd, get out the *scytale.*"

Judd took the tapered gold cylinder from the duffel bag and handed it to her. Even in the dim light it glowed, engraved and beautiful. She held it up for Yakimovich to see.

A tender look entered his eyes. He snatched the baton from her. Holding it in both hands, he pressed it against his heart. "I have missed you," he murmured.

"I believe Charles left a message for me that fits around the *scytale*. I need it—now."

His eyes narrowed. *"Absque argento omnia vana."* Then he gave what he seemed to think was a winning smile.

"What does he want?" Judd asked.

"It's a Latin phrase: 'Without money all efforts are useless.' He expects to be paid." She yanked away the *scytale* from Yakimovich.

His gaze followed it hungrily.

"Do you want it back?" she asked.

He nodded. "Yes. Please."

"Give us Charles's message, and you can keep the *scytale*."

Yakimovich's eyes adjusted. For the first time he seemed really to see Judd and her. His body shuddered with a sigh. "All right. It is in my office."

CHAPTER 41

ANDREW YAKIMOVICH DROPPED a white cotton shirt over his head and led them out through the side door and into a meandering stone passageway. The air smelled of dust, and the walls were rough. Naked light-bulbs flickered overhead. Positioning his fez carefully onto his gray hair, he walked slowly, a wounded lion, aged but proud.

"The foundation is Byzantine, the floor plan Ottoman," he told them. "This is one of the hidden worlds of the Grand Bazaar. Along here are rooms that have been workshops for centuries."

As Eva watched, he gestured at doors. Few displayed signs. Most were open, showing antiques being repaired, stones being set in silver and gold, and tourist T-shirts being sewn. The mother with three children whom Eva had spotted earlier stood inside one room with a half dozen other people. She pulled billfolds from her purse and handed them over to a man sitting behind a desk.

"How far does this go on?" Judd wanted to know.

Yakimovich waved a hand. "It winds. A quarter mile perhaps."

He took out a large old key and stopped. Unlocking a door, he stepped inside and rotated a switch. Electrical conduit ran up the wall and across the ceiling. Low-wattage lightbulbs beamed into life.

Eva and Judd followed him inside. Once a prominent antiquities dealer, Yakimovich seemed to have packed his entire life into this cavernous room. Crates rose to the ceiling, most unlabeled, fading into the dark recesses. Pieces of beautiful but dusty old furniture were stacked in a corner. Tall rolls of handmade carpets leaned against walls.

With a proprietary glance around, he moved to a marble-topped table and sat. "The *scytale*, if you please." His tone was businesslike.

Eva laid it on the table, which was empty. There were no record books, no accounts, no letters from buyers eager to purchase one of Yakimovich's treasures. No chairs in which customers could sit.

She tried to figure out how to phrase the question without insulting him: "You've retired, Andy?"

He let out a loud hoot, his face animated in the way she remembered. "You are too kind. I have no illusions about what I have become." He peered at her, his gaze sharp for a moment. "Once I was great, like Charles. He could be a bastard, but I understood that. We have our own code, we bastards. Especially when we share a passion."

He opened a small drawer and took out a long strip of tan leather on which letters in black ink were visible on one side. Eva inhaled, excitement coursing through her. At long last perhaps they would learn where the library was. As he started to lay down the strip, Eva snatched it up. The leather was stiff but pliable. She grabbed the *scytale*.

"Wrap from the large end first," Yakimovich advised.

She did as he said, working slowly. It was an awkward process, the leather's stiffness making it even more difficult. She could feel Judd's intensity beside her. Finished, she gripped the *scytale* by both ends, holding the strip in place with her thumbs, then turned the cylinder horizontal to read the words.

Disappointment filled her. "All I see is gibberish."

"I will do it," Yakimovich said. "One must help the letters to grow into words."

With a flourish, the antiquities dealer pulled the dry leather slightly and used a thumb to press it flat against the *scytale* as he rotated it and rewrapped the strip. It was slow work. Finished at last, he gave a nod of satisfaction. Holding the baton at the ends as Eva had so the strip would not slip, he turned the *scytale* and studied the script.

"It is Latin, and it is from Charles, but perhaps that is to be expected, since he is the one who left it here with me." For a moment he continued to read silently to himself. Then his head jerked up, and his eyes flashed with excitement. "My God, Charles did it. He *did* it! He tracked the *library*! Listen to this: 'You can find the location of the Library of Gold hidden inside *The Book of Spies*.'"

THE CALLIGRAPHY SHOP was silent. The customers had been banished, and the door locked. A large bruise was appearing on the shopkeeper's cheek where Preston had hit him with his fist. He cringed as Preston grabbed his arm roughly.

"Show me exactly where they went," Preston ordered and shoved him through the beaded curtain into the back.

The man ran down the dim hall toward an arched

opening. Following, Preston took out his S&W pistol and screwed on the sound suppressor. Behind him were his two men, weapons in hand. A third man soon joined them.

JUDD LEANED FORWARD. "Keep reading, Andy," he ordered.

"Hurry!" Eva said, thrilled.

"It says here Charles's predecessor wrote it inside the book, then smuggled the book out of the library—" Yakimovich stopped, the *scytale* frozen in midair.

Pounding feet in the corridor echoed loudly against the stone walls. The feet were coming toward them.

Judd pulled out his Beretta and ran toward the door, the only door to the storeroom.

Eva snatched the *scytale* from Yakimovich's hands.

"No!" he yelled, reaching for it.

"I'll send it back to you." Eva sprinted.

Judd had flattened himself behind the open door. He motioned Eva to stand back beside him.

At his desk, the antiquities dealer seemed unable to move.

"Hide!" Judd commanded.

Yakimovich's face blanched. He scuttled back among the crates and disappeared.

Suddenly the shopkeeper from the calligraphy store burst through the door as if he had been thrown. His eyes were wild, and sweat poured down his bruised face.

"Help me! Help me!" He ran in among the old furniture.

Light noises of a struggle reverberated from the stone corridor. Feet scuffed and snapped against the floor. There was a loud grunt, then another. The dull sound of something hitting flesh. A swift *crack*, then another. From the floor?

It was if they were listening to a radio, with the only clue being that some kind of fight was going on. Eva peered at Judd, who had a distant, cold look that sent chills over her skin. Finally there was a horrible quiet.

Judd raised a hand, silently telling her to wait as he stepped to the edge of the doorway. Pistol up, he peered out cautiously. Then he vanished into the hall.

Ignoring his order, Eva followed.

Four men were down. Two were about twenty feet away, bloody exit wounds showing on their foreheads. The other two—Preston and another man—lay close together near Yakimovich's door. There were no obvious wounds on either.

Instantly Judd kicked Preston's pistol from his limp hand, then swept it up.

"Dammit, Preston found us again," she whispered.

He nodded. "We'll talk about it later." Looking up and down the winding hallway, he crouched beside the killer. "Check the other guy's pockets, Eva. Do it fast. We can't stay here long."

She knelt. The man had gray hair and a long gray mustache. His face was the color of a roasted almond, the lines deep, the nose prominent. His fez lay upside down beside him. She rustled through the caftan and found only a wallet. Inside was an Istanbul driver's license for Salih Serin, a credit card in the same name, and a few Turkish lira. The photo on the driver's license matched the face of the man lying beside her.

"No weapon," she said. "His name is Salih Serin. He lives in Istanbul."

"Preston has a pistol and cash, no ID, and a small notebook. He's pulled out most of the pages, but there's one left. He wrote, 'Robin Miller. *Book of Spies*. All we know is Athens—so far.'"

Eva felt a surge of excitement. "Then we have to go to Athens."

"Yes." He gave her Preston's weapon. "If he so much as moves, shoot him. We don't know about Serin yet, so be careful of him, too." He tucked the note and money inside his jacket and hurried back into Yakimovich's room.

Serin moaned and murmured something in Turkish. Opening his eyes, he jerked his head from side to side, panicking, until he saw Preston was lying unconscious.

He looked up at her and smiled. "You are pretty."

Judd returned, carrying rope and their duffel bag. "The shopkeeper was no help. He's blithering, scared to death." As he tied Preston's hands tightly behind him, he peered across at Serin. "What happened?"

The Turk sat up. "I know those two." He pointed a thumb down the hall at the prone men. "They are evil. I was back there in a workroom, visiting a friend, and I saw them run past. A long time ago I was with MIT." He gazed at them and explained. "Our Milli Istihbarat Teskilati, the National Intelligence Organization. So I thought I would see what badness they were planning. By the time I got here, both of them were on the floor with gunshot wounds, and that one"—he gestured at Preston—"had just hurled Mustafa through the door. He and I had a large battle." He gave a conspiratorial grin. "But I am an old street fighter, and he thought he could take me. Still the weasel managed to whack me a good one just before I got him, and I fell and cracked my head." He rubbed the back of his skull. "In the old days . . . ah, in the old days I would've eaten his gizzard." He sighed tiredly.

"Are you all right, Mr. Serin?" Eva took his arm as he struggled to his feet.

Judd was suspicious. "There wasn't any bump on Preston's head. How'd you knock him out?" He finished binding Preston's feet together.

"Pressure." Serin grabbed his own throat, his thumbs pushed deep, then quickly released them. "We learn useful things in the secret service."

Judd nodded. "Thanks for your help. You aren't armed, so who shot the other men?"

"Maybe that one." He gestured at Preston. "I saw no one else. I know those guys. They could have waited until he had no choice and demanded more money—or something else he could not or would not provide." He shrugged, then scrutinized them. "You are in trouble, yes? I think they were planning to kill you. But you look like such nice tourists."

Judd only glanced at him. "Come on, Eva."

"I believe I heard someone mention Athens," Serin continued. "You wish to go? I know a boat rental place where few questions are asked. I can take you in the boat to a small airport south of here where the owner and I are friendly. Perhaps it would be good for you to slip out of Istanbul before this one"—he pointed at Preston lying hogtied on the stone floor—"gets free, or someone else is sent to take his place. I am a poor man now. You could pay me well. Perhaps you are glad for the assistance of someone who knows the terrain."

Worrying how Preston had found them again, Eva looked at Judd. Her inclination was to accept the offer.

Judd made a decision. "You won't mind if I check you for weapons."

Serin threw up his arms, the sleeves of his caftan billowing down past his elbows. "I insist."

Judd patted him from his neck to the soles of his feet, paying particular attention to his armpits, lower back, thighs, calves, and ankles.

Finally Judd said, "All right. Let's go."

Serin rushed ahead, trying doorknobs until he located a closet. Judd found rags inside. Stuffing one into

Preston's mouth and tying another around it, he left the unconscious man bound tightly in his ropes.

"You didn't kill Preston," Eva whispered as they hurried after Serin.

"I thought about it. But he's unarmed, apparently doesn't know where *The Book of Spies* is in Athens, and anyway, he's out of commission long enough for us to get away." He hesitated, then admitted, "And I have enough blood on my hands."

CHAPTER 42

THE APRIL DAYLIGHT WAS FADING, the lavender colors of sunset spreading softly across the indigo-blue Sea of Marmara. In the vast Istanbul marina where Salih Serin had taken Judd and Eva, waves lapped boat hulls and ropes rattled against masts.

Judd took up a position fifty feet away from Eva and Serin, observing as Serin negotiated in Turkish with a stooped youth for the boat they had selected—a sleek Chris-Craft yacht powerful enough to make the journey easily and outrun other small vessels.

Judd was on his mobile with Tucker. It was about eleven A.M. in Washington, six P.M. in Istanbul. He described the events in the Grand Bazaar. "Preston found us again."

"Dammit. What in hell is going on? There's no way anyone could've gotten the intel on my end . . ." There was a pause. Tucker sounded worried as he continued, "I'll think about it. Go on. What else did you learn?"

Judd repeated the information in Preston's notebook. "See if you can track down who Robin Miller is.

I'm wondering whether she might be the blond woman
Eva saw with Sherback in London. Remember, *The
Book of Spies* might've been in the backpack he left
with her."

"NSA is monitoring the two numbers you got off
Sherback's phone. I'll let you know instantly if we get a
hit."

"Good. Eva's going to translate the rest of the message on the leather strip as soon as we're alone. Supposedly it says exactly where the library's location is
hidden inside *The Book of Spies*."

"Langley had that book in storage three years."
Tucker sighed with frustration. "I take it you're leaving
for Athens?"

"Immediately. I'm not going to tell you exactly how
we're planning to get there."

He watched as Serin jabbed a thumb toward the
yacht, the darkening sky, and the boat merchant, at last
extending both palms up in a gesture of attempting to
be reasonable. Serin had told the boat merchant he was
going to insist they receive a large discount, since so
few people wanted to rent at night. His animated face
showed deep enjoyment in the haggling.

"A damn good idea," Tucker said. "Stay safe."

The Sea of Marmara

WITH SERIN AT THE HELM, the yacht cruised through the
night, heading southwest across the Sea of Marmara. A
wind had arisen out of the north through the Bosporus
Strait, whipping the sea and making for a bumpy ride.
They had progressed some ten miles, eaten fish sand-
wiches bought in the marina, and adjusted to the boat's
rough rhythms.

Judd was confident they had not been followed to

the Istanbul marina, but still he found himself peering back to where the city's lights spread across the horizon. He studied the traffic—fishing boats, cargo ships, and behemoth oil tankers and container ships, all blinking with lights. The great inland sea was a busy thoroughfare linking the Black Sea in the north to the Aegean and Mediterranean seas on the south through the Dardanelles Strait. None of the other boats seemed to be pacing them.

"Where exactly are we heading?" Eva raised her voice to be heard over the wind, sea, and motors.

Despite a bench seat directly behind them, Serin stood at the wheel, Eva beside him, where he had invited her. A low windshield partially protected them. Judd stood behind the bench seat, gripping the back with both hands. Eva's midnight-blue jacket was buttoned up to her chin, and tendrils of her long black hair had fallen out of the knot at the nape of her neck. Windblown and rosy-cheeked, she looked quietly happy. As she turned to listen to Serin, Judd was struck by how much he liked her, liked being with her. Then he remembered the role his father had probably played in her imprisonment for manslaughter. He gazed away.

"South of a big city called Tekirdağ," Serin yelled, "and north of a little village called Barbados. We are going to the Thrace part of Turkey, on the Europe side of course."

Serin held the wheel confidently in his brown hands. He was a little shorter than Judd, but broader, with thick muscles. He appeared nonchalant and self-satisfied. At the same time, there were signs of his past—the athletic way he moved on the boat and the flashes of intense acuity in his gaze. If he had not already said he had been a member of the national government's tough MIT, Judd would have suspected some sort of similar background.

"An old comrade of mine has a private airstrip," Serin was continuing. "We will be there in about three hours."

Judd saw they were doing a good thirty-plus knots despite the waves. Speedy, with two powerful inboard engines, the Chris-Craft was a stunner. Belowdecks were fully appointed staterooms, a salon, and a galley.

"You're not taking us through the Dardanelles?" Eva asked. "We'd pass the ruins of Troy if you did, and we'd be much closer to Athens."

"Too dangerous. The strait is narrow and crowded. It twists itself this way and that. Besides, the current is unusually swift."

"What do you do with yourself when you're not ferrying people in rented boats?" Judd asked.

"Ah, that is a long story. To make it short, I am what you call a jack-of-all-trades. I am hired to guide, to guard, and to deliver important items. I have a reputation, you see. I am trustworthy. And you two are very important items and now know I am trustworthy also. What about you, Mr. Ryder? You have not told me anything."

"We're tourists, just as you thought."

"You are trying to fool an old dog, but I know all the tricky tricks. I am curious. What is wrong with curiosity, I ask you?" His loud voice sounded hurt. "At least explain this thing called *The Book of Spies*. Entertain me while I work so hard."

Eva laughed. "It's an illuminated manuscript from the sixteenth century. A one-of-a-kind book and very valuable. It's been lost. We're trying to track it down." She glanced back at Judd. "I'm getting tired of shouting."

"So this book is in Athens, and you wish to find it. It is part of some big business deal?" the Turk coaxed.

"Why would you think we're involved in a business deal?" Judd asked.

"I had hopes it would make you much money, and

then you would come back to Istanbul and hire me again. Is it for this book your lives are in danger?"

"As a matter of fact, yes." It seemed like innocuous enough information, Judd decided.

Serin glanced over his shoulder at him, frowning. And as he turned back, he wiped his face. The wheel spun out of his other hand. Serin grabbed the steering again with both hands—too late. The craft lurched from side to side, the waves pounding, the wind screeching. Banging down hard in the trough of one wave, the yacht lifted sharply on the crest of the next. Water drenched them.

Eva reeled as Serin fought to control the yacht, but it slammed and torqued violently. One of her hands slipped from the safety handle on the console. The boat heaved to the starboard, tossing all of them. But Eva's foot slid, and she fell to her knees.

Instantly Judd snatched her arm, locking his other hand on to the back of the bench seat, trying not to lose his balance, too.

As the boat continued to rotate back and forth, up and down, the wet steering wheel whirled through Serin's grasp.

The boat pitched hard again, banging and yawing. Judd lost his grip. His hand slid uncontrollably across the moist seat back, and he stumbled. Eva fell halfway over the boat's side, pulling him with her because he would not let her go. One more lurch, and both would be hurled into the black churning water.

His heart thundering, Judd looked back, searching for a way to save them. Instead he saw something else: Serin was not panicked, not even worried as he clinically noted their life-threatening situation. The icy intelligence in his gaze told Judd he could easily let them fall overboard and would abandon them. Was that what he had planned all along?

"You bastard!" Judd yelled. "Why are you doing this!"

Serin blinked. He looked off into the distance, then back at them. He seemed to decide something. Giving a small nod, he fitted his hands into the spokes of the steering wheel. His caftan sleeves fell back, showing the cording muscles. Shoulders hunching, he poured strength into dominating the yacht.

Slowly the boat's heaving eased. Judd yanked Eva back onboard and pulled her to his chest. Chilled and furious, he wrapped his arms around her. She resisted only a moment, then held on for dear life. He kissed her hair. She burrowed deeper. Then he slid his hand inside his jacket and yanked out his Beretta.

He released her and rolled free, aiming the pistol up at Serin.

CHAPTER 43

EVA WAS WATCHING, STUNNED. "Judd, stop!" Black hair blowing around her face, she scrambled toward Serin.

"No, Eva. Come here!" Judd ordered as he sat on the seat behind Serin and slid to the side where he had a fuller view of the man's profile and a safer distance. He steadily pointed his Beretta at him.

Her eyes wide, Eva grasped the arm of the seat and pulled herself around the rocking yacht.

"What did I miss?" She fell in beside him.

Serin's fez was gone, and his almond-colored features had shifted, revealing a depth of something Judd could not quite name but felt in himself and did not like. Something predatory. Serin's facial skin seemed different, too, and Judd had a sudden insight the man was in disguise. A hell of a good disguise, with skin dye and some of the new manmade materials that, when smoothed on skin and allowed to dry, puckered the surface and formed deep crevices. The large nose could be fake, too.

"This has been what we in intelligence call a movie," Judd explained to Eva grimly. "It's a setup that looks and feels completely real." He gestured with his pistol at Serin. "Tell her," he ordered.

There was no hesitation. "I have rules," Serin said over the noise of the engines and wind. "They are inviolate. My employer agreed to all of them. One of them is I do wet work only on people who shouldn't be breathing, and I'm the one who makes the decision. My employer was convincing about both of you, so I agreed to the job. He ordered Preston to create a movie in which you'd believe I'd be useful to help you get away. So when Preston realized you were in Yakimovich's storage room, he eliminated two of his people and called me in." He hesitated.

"Go on," Judd said.

"At that point I took over. But when you arrived I began to wonder. The people I wipe aren't solicitous of an old man. They don't inquire about his well-being. You were prepared to scrub Preston if he moved because he'd tried to do the same to you earlier—but you were just as willing to wait to find out whether I was a threat. Evil people murder first and don't bother about questions. All of this meant I needed to find out more. Were you trying to kill my employer and steal some big business deal as he contended? Finally I learned you claimed to be treasure hunters chasing a chimera, some old manuscript called *The Book of Spies*. That did not fit the profile my employer gave me. Then I looked back at you, Judd, and lost control of the wheel. My specialty is in making hits look like accidents, so I'd planned to erase you out here. Losing control of the boat presented an elegant opportunity. They are few."

"Why did you change your mind?" Eva said.

"Because, God help me, I know human nature—in my world it's nasty, corrupt, and mean. You aren't, so in the end I had to believe you. I'll tell you now I'm glad." He looked at Eva. "You remind me of my daughter. You're about the same age, and both very pretty in similar ways. According to the photo I was given, your true hair color is red. Hers is auburn."

The yacht cruised onward, rolling up and down with the sea. The wind howled around them.

"I can't trust you," Judd decided.

"I understand. However, I'll still take you to my friend and his airstrip."

"Who hired you?"

"I won't tell you that."

"Your rules?"

He gave a curt nod. "I've survived many years in a business in which most of my colleagues have been killed off. Seldom do we die of old age. Rules are not for the timid or the careless. They require discipline. King Lear railed against the universe when he was punished for breaking its rules. I don't want the same fate. Besides, the longer I live, the greater my chance of seeing my daughter again."

"What's your name?" Judd asked.

The assassin's black eyes cut into him. "The Carnivore." Then he smiled.

Thrace, Turkey

THE CARNIVORE TURNED OFF the yacht's engines in calm waters near a strip of uninhabited land north of the village of Barbados. Judd dropped the anchor, they found flashlights, and they took off their shoes. The Carnivore pulled off his caftan. Beneath it he wore black jeans and a black T-shirt. His muscle tone was excellent, but his skin elasticity showed advancing age. Judd guessed him to be in his fifties.

They rolled up their jeans and waded ashore. Judd carried the duffel, and Eva wore her satchel, the strap across her chest. The wind was quieter here. They crossed the beach, and the Carnivore led them up ancient stone steps carved into a cliff.

At the top, they paused. The moon had risen, casting an eerie light across acres of grapevines tied neatly to wires running between gnarled wood posts. The vines were just beginning to leaf. The air smelled raw, of freshly tilled soil.

They headed off on a narrow dirt trail through the grapevines.

"Do you want to tell me what this is all about, Judd?" the Carnivore asked.

"Reciprocity is another of your rules?"

"A good one, don't you think."

"I like it," Judd said. "But no, I'll handle this."

The trail widened, and the three moved on side by side.

The Carnivore peered around at Judd and said thoughtfully, "Yes, I believe you will—if it can be handled at all. But as for reciprocity, I consider us even by my giving you a safe route into Athens."

"Is Preston free now?" Eva asked worriedly.

"He must be," the Carnivore said. "He had backup."

"What if I'd decided to kill him back in the Grand Bazaar," Judd said. "Your movie would've been burned."

"That would've worked just as well," the Carnivore instructed. "He would've 'awakened' and attacked you. I would've saved the day by helping you to escape, him to live, and the movie to continue."

Judd changed the subject. "What about his note, the one that mentioned Athens. Was it legitimate or a plant?"

"Legitimate. A note to himself. It added to the authenticity and gave you a significant reason to believe what you saw was real. Perhaps more important, we didn't expect you to live long enough to use it or anything else you might've learned there."

"Do you have any information about *The Book of Spies* and Robin Miller?" Eva asked.

"It was none of my business."

"What about the Library of Gold?"

The Carnivore frowned. "I've heard of it. Is that what this is all about?"

"Yes." But Judd said no more. Venomous snakes like the Carnivore shed their skins occasionally, but their bites remained just as unpredictable—and poisonous. "What will you tell your employer?"

"Nothing."

Judd sensed fury behind the one-word answer. The Carnivore was making his employer pay for lying to him. It also meant the employer would think he and Eva were dead—at least for a while.

"It gives you time," the Carnivore said, "but it's also good business for me. When one deals in death, one must make certain the rules are clear—and there are costs involved when they're broken." He glanced at Judd. "And it means you don't have to contemplate eliminating me, and I don't have to take proactive measures to make certain you don't try."

The words were calm, matter-of-fact, but they sent a chill through Judd.

"You won't be paid," Judd said.

"I have half. I'll keep it."

"Where do you come from?" Eva asked the Carnivore. "Where do you live now? How did you get into this business? You sound almost American."

"I'm sorry, Eva. It's really better you don't know. Once a KGB assassin from the old cold war days went after my daughter, thinking I was dead and he'd get his revenge on me by eliminating her. Fortunately she was able to save herself. If anyone finds out you have information about me, your lives could be threatened, and there's no guarantee you'd be as lucky as she."

At the top of a slight incline they saw a house, large and expansive, built of weathered stone with a blue-tile Ottoman roof. Lights showed inside, and as they approached, exterior lights flashed on, illuminating flower beds, patches of grass, and a stone gazebo. Empty wine barrels were stacked against sheds. There was a large clapboard structure toward the back that was probably where the wine was made and aged.

The door to the house opened, and a man in his late fifties appeared, a shotgun resting across an arm.

"Who goes there?" he shouted in Turkish and English.

"An old friend from long ago, Hugo Shah," the Carnivore replied. "You remember me, Alex Bosa."

"Alex, you've come to taste my wine again. I'm honored." Then as they approached, Shah stared. "Alex? Yes, it is you. What a magnificent disguise. What are you up to now?"

"No good, as always."

Shah laughed. The pair shook hands, and the four trooped into a living area of tasteful wallpaper and thick carpets. Fine old furniture was placed here and there, while a modern sofa and easy chairs faced a handsome fireplace.

"Who are your friends, Alex?" Shah asked.

"It doesn't matter. They need your help, which means I need your help. Is that light plane of yours available?"

"At this hour?" Shah's eyes narrowed as he studied the Carnivore. "I see. It is an emergency. Very well, I will fly them myself. Do you wish to accompany us?"

"I'll wait here with the wine."

Shah smiled broadly. "Excellent. Please give me a moment." He returned soon, wearing a jacket and carrying a small valise.

As all four walked outside, Shah explained about his vineyard, "I grow gamay, cabernet, and *papazkarasi* grapes. I have in mind two fine reds I will open for us, Alex—it will be Alex and Hugo again."

About a half mile from the house, they went into a large garage where a single-engine Cirrus SR20 was waiting. They helped Shah roll out the plane. He gazed at the wind socket and sniffed the air.

"I'll say good-bye now." The Carnivore backed off.

They climbed on board, Judd sitting next to Shah, and Eva behind. As the engine warmed up, Judd gazed out the window. The Carnivore was smiling. He lifted his hand and pressed two fingers against his temple in a smart salute.

Judd found himself smiling back. He snapped off a two-finger salute in return.

"Where are we going?" Shah asked as the propellers started rotating.

Judd glanced back. Eva was looking at him. He heard the strength in his voice—also the urgency. "Athens."

PART THREE
THE BATTLE

When the celebrated Greek general Aristides learned *from one of his assets that a Persian spy had infiltrated his military camp, he ordered every soldier, shield-maker, doctor, and cook to account for another person there. In that way the spy was uncovered. The next month the Greeks defeated the invading Persian army at the Battle of Marathon, in 490 B.C.*

—*translated from* The Book of Spies

Strategic intelligence is the power to know your enemies' intentions.

—The New York Times
May 14, 2006

CHAPTER 44

Washington, D.C.

AS HE ATE A LATE LUNCH at his desk in Catapult head-quarters, Tucker Andersen studied the photo of the blond woman who might be the Robin Miller mentioned in Preston's note.

His people had located thousands of women with the name, ranging from infants to the elderly in the United States and abroad. Narrowing for age and occupation, he had settled on this one as the most likely, thirty-five years old now. Born in Scotland, she had degrees in classical art and library science from the Sorbonne and Cambridge and had worked in rare books and manuscripts in Boston and Paris. A couple of years ago she had quit her job at the Bibliothèque. After that, there was no record of her employment in other libraries or museums. No record of a new address—she had moved out of her apartment when she quit her job. No record of death. No trace at all.

He e-mailed the information and photo to Judd and sat back, thinking.

Then he picked up his phone and called Debi Watson, Catapult's IT chief. "Any word from NSA about those phone numbers I gave you?" She was honchoing the numbers in Charles Sherback's disposable phone, one of which could be Robin Miller's.

"No, suh. I'll call if something turns up. It all depends on where the satellites are, and of course there are millions of data bits to sort through. NSA is watching for us. They know it's important."

"It's crucial," he corrected. "Contact Interpol and the Athens police and tell them we'd be obliged if they'd let us know pronto if they run across a woman named Robin Miller. We believe she may be in Athens. I'll e-mail you the details." He hung up.

There was a knock on his door. When he responded, Gloria Feit, general factotum and receptionist, walked in and closed it behind her.

Her small frame was rigid. "He's back. In her office."

"Hudson Canon, you mean?"

"You asked me to let you know. I'm letting you know he's back."

"You're pissed."

"Me? How can you tell?" Her face broke into a smile, the lines around her eyes crinkling.

"No one's going to take Cathy's place. But we need a new chief. Hudson is temporary."

"Yes, well, temporary as in 'short-timer' suits me just fine."

"You don't like him?"

She fell into a chair and crossed her knees. "Actually, I do like him. I just felt like being petty."

He chuckled. "Then why are you pissed?"

"Because you're not telling me what's going on. You

don't think I've leaked anything about the Library of Gold operation, do you?"

So that was it. "The thought never crossed my mind." Actually it had, but he did not want her to know that. He needed to consider everyone and anyone who could have had access to the information.

"Good," she announced. "So tell me where you are with the mission."

"Gloria."

She sighed and stood up. "Oh, all right. Be that way. But you know you can count on me, Tucker. I mean that. For anything." She walked to the door and turned. "When you're offered the job of heading Catapult—and we both know you will be—take it this time. Please. I've already got you broken in."

He stared as the door closed and shook his head, smiling to himself. Then the smile vanished. He stood up and left. It was time to talk to Canon.

ADJUSTING HIS TIE, HUDSON CANON stared into the mirror in what had been Cathy Doyle's office. He did not like the way he looked. His short nose, round black eyes, and heavy cheeks no longer seemed solid, real to him. There was something otherworldly there, insubstantial, although he knew damn well he was a substantial man in all ways.

He turned back into the office, glad Cathy's photos, plants, and personal things were gone. It had been a shock when he heard the news of her death, and then an even bigger shock when he received a phone call from Reinhardt Gruen, in Berlin, telling him what he had to do—or lose his savings. He had invested all of it in the Parsifal Group at Gruen's invitation, and it had made him far more money than he had ever thought possible.

His cell phone vibrated against his chest. Locking the door, he answered it as he walked around to sit at the desk. Cell phones, PDAs, any sort of personal wireless devices were not allowed in Langley or Catapult, but he was boss here, and no one needed to know he must keep the disposable cell with him at all times now.

"We have a problem with Judd Ryder and Eva Blake. Our man hasn't reported in, and we suspect they're on the loose again. Where are they?" Reinhardt asked in a friendly German accent.

"I don't know."

"You were supposed to stay on top of this."

"I'm not sure I can get the information."

"*Ach*, really?" The tone was less friendly. "You are an important man. You are the head of Catapult. Nothing can be kept from you."

Canon screwed up his resolve, banishing thoughts of losing his house. He was highly leveraged and had planned to take out the next six months of payments from his Parsifal account. He had already sold his beloved Corvette and bought a used Ford. The alimony and child support to his two ex-wives were killing him.

"It's not that," he said. "Look, Reinhardt, this has gone far enough. Obviously it's not an easy fix. Catapult is never going to find your precious Library of Gold anyway. The whole mission has been a disaster."

"Remove Tucker Andersen. Run it yourself."

"I can't take him off it. There's no legitimate reason to do it. I'd be in hot water if I tried, especially now that Cathy's dead. Besides, my boss wants an experienced hand here as number two to back me up."

Gruen swore in German. "We think if Ryder and Blake are free they are heading to Athens. We need to know exactly where in Athens. Have you heard anything about a woman named Robin Miller?"

"No," Canon answered truthfully. "Who's she?"

There was a cold pause. "Let us be clear. Do you really think Catherine Doyle's car crash was an accident?"

Canon felt sweat gather in his armpits.

"We need the information," Gruen told him. "You will get it."

"There's no real need for it," Canon tried. "I can close the operation down in just a few more hours anyway. I have the boss's permission."

"As you know it is far more than a few hours until you can do that, and too much can happen." There was a pause. "You must make Tucker Andersen leave the premises of Catapult. Phone me immediately when he does. Do you understand what will happen to you if you do not?"

TUCKER KNOCKED ON HUDSON Canon's door. Surprised, he heard the lock click open. Why had Hudson locked it? But then, Hudson had once been a highly successful undercover op, and habits of secrecy were hard to break.

The door opened, and the new chief gave him a short smile in greeting. "Come in, Tucker. I was thinking about checking in with you, too."

Tucker entered as Hudson headed for the desk.

"Give me an update on how things are going." Hudson sat and leaned back in the chair, clasping his hands comfortably behind his head.

"There's not much new." Tucker took a chair and recounted the few changes in the various missions. Canon wanted more frequent reports than Cathy had. That was fine—each manager had his own style.

"And the Library of Gold operation?" Canon asked.

"Glad you brought it up. I was wondering whether you happened to mention to anyone that my people were going to the Grand Bazaar in Istanbul?"

The answer was immediate. "Of course not." The expression unchanged.

"They still haven't located the library," Tucker continued, "and the last time we talked, they were on their way out of Istanbul. Preston—he's the janitor who's been dogging them—was left behind alive but tied up in the Grand Bazaar. It'll be a while before he gets free."

"Where are they going now?"

This was the moment Tucker had expected, and it made him sick. After doing a thorough search through his memory, he knew he had written no one, phoned no one, e-mailed no one, made no notes to himself, and told only one person the critical details that Ryder and Blake had gone not only to Istanbul, but to the Grand Bazaar, to find Okan Biçer, and through him Andrew Yakimovich.

And so he lied: "To Thessalonika." It was a large city north of Athens, within logical distance for Robin Miller to reach—if she were in Athens. Continuing the lie, he said, "A woman named Robin Miller got in touch with them. In exchange for helping her, she'll meet them there and tell them where the library is."

"That will solve a lot of problems—if they can pull it off." Canon took a deep breath and stretched. "Thessalonika seems strange, though. Athens would be more likely, don't you think?"

Why did he mention Athens? A sour taste rose in Tucker's throat. "No, I don't agree. This whole operation has been unpredictable. Thessalonika is large and historical. It makes sense to me."

"Who is Robin Miller?"

"She has something to do with the library. I don't have the details yet."

Canon nodded. "Then it's all good news. Your people have another decent lead. How are they getting to Thessalonika?"

"Judd didn't have time to tell me."

"I see. Well, then, you still may pull the proverbial rabbit out of the hat and find the library." Canon studied him, concern on his face. "Do you have any idea how lousy you look? You're pale. Your clothes are a mess. With all of the action in Europe, there's no need to be concerned someone is still after you here. It's a beautiful afternoon. Get out and breathe some fresh air. Take a walk. Use my car if you'd rather drive than walk. If you don't want to go home, at least go shopping and buy some new clothes. This is a direct order, Tucker—get the hell out of Catapult."

CHAPTER 45

TUCKER ANDERSEN STALKED around his office, mulling whether to phone his old friend Matt Kelley, the head of the Clandestine Service. But he had only one piece of evidence that Hudson Canon was the leak. It was possible Judd and Eva had been tracked to the Grand Bazaar through another means. One did not report one's colleagues unless one was damn sure.

He stopped in front of his wall of books. It was not nearly as impressive as Jonathan Ryder's huge library, but he had carefully chosen each one. As his gaze ran over the titles, mostly politics and intelligence and spy thriller fiction, he remembered the journeys he had taken in them, learning and entertaining himself with others' lives, ideas, and knowledge. He thought about what Philip K. Dick had written: "Sometimes the appropriate response to reality is to go insane."

Shaking his head, he poured himself a whiskey. He probably should get out of here. A walk around the block might clear his head. But then, Hudson Canon had been the one who suggested it, which made him want to stay put. Looking out the window, he gulped whiskey and saw that night had fallen. Dammit, he was tired of the cold in-transit room upstairs in which he had been bedding down.

Making a decision, he grabbed his sports jacket and slammed his arms into the sleeves. He went into the communications center. Debi Watson was still there.

She was looking disgustingly alert and young.

"Do you have anything new for me?" he asked.

"No, suh."

"Phone your NSA person," he told her. "Give him my mobile number. I want him to call me directly if either of those numbers for the disposable phones turns up. If you get any word about Robin Miller, call me on my mobile." He wheeled around and left, her voice agreeing behind him.

He stopped at Gloria's desk. "Hand over my mobile. I'm going out."

She peered at him from above her rainbow-rimmed reading glasses. "It's about time. You look like a caged animal."

"Thanks. That cheers me up considerably."

"I aim to please." She handed him the secure mobile.

He had an idea, one he did not like. "Is Hudson still here?"

"You betcha. The man's working away as if he's the head of Catapult."

"Are you supposed to let him know if I leave?"

She blinked. "Yes, he's worried about you, too."

"Don't tell him."

"Why, Tucker?"

"Just damn well do as I say."

Her brows rose. "We're not married—yet. Karen will be jealous."

He sighed. She was right; he was in a huff. "Sorry. Don't tell the boss, please."

"Okay," she said cheerfully.

But as Tucker turned away, he saw a motion—Canon's door must have just opened, because it was closing now. Tucker went back to his office and found his Browning and holster in his locked desk drawer. Taking off his jacket, he put on the holster and slid the Browning inside. Hesitating, at last he took out the wad of cash he kept in the drawer, the two billfolds that contained cover identities, and other supplies.

Again he headed out.

"You haven't left yet?" Gloria said as he passed her desk.

"I forgot my lollipops."

"Silly me. I should've reminded you. If anyone asks, when shall I tell them you'll be back?"

"Oh, a half hour. Maybe never." He paused. "I didn't say that."

Her brows rose again, but she simply nodded.

He left through the side door into Catapult's parking lot. The April night was cool, not a breeze stirring as he forced himself to slow to a normal pace. He passed staff cars and went out to the sidewalk. It was a balmy spring evening. He inhaled the scent of the freshly cut grass on the adjoining property.

Turning down the street, he noted who else was on the sidewalk and kept his head turned slightly so he could watch approaching cars with his peripheral vision. People were walking home from the Metro after work and school, tired, carrying groceries and briefcases and pushing children in strollers. The street was filled with traffic, many vehicles slowing to look for parking spots. In this neighborhood of mostly row houses, there were few garages or carports.

The trained mind was like a computer, and Tucker's was automatically sorting through the array of humanity. At last he settled on a man in a loose gray jacket zipped up halfway, dark jeans, and black tennis shoes, about forty feet behind. In the light of street lamps, he seemed innocuous enough, but there was something about the way he moved, loose, rolling easily off the balls of his feet, alert. He had a destination in mind that had nothing to do with the relaxation of home.

Tucker turned the corner, then another. The man was staying with him, threading among the other pedestrians behind, always keeping several between them. Tucker rounded one more block and headed west onto Massachusetts Avenue. The man was still with him, but closer, probably waiting for the right moment. A weapon could easily be hidden beneath his gray jacket.

Tucker pushed into Capitol Hill market, a favorite in the area, small, crammed, and busy at this hour. Going to the back of the store, he stopped at the cooler to eye the selection of sodas but really to check back around the end cap to where he could sight down the aisle to the front door.

The man walked in, nodding to the kid behind the checkout stand, peering casually around as he continued on toward the butcher. The store was doing some construction. Tucker spotted two-by-four boards leaning at the rear of the back hallway. Cocking his head just enough to make certain the man had spotted him, he strolled into the dim corridor. Before he turned the corner, he glanced back. The man was coming, his expression pleasant.

Grabbing one of the boards, Tucker rushed out through the revolving glass door and into the cool night air. Tall trees cast dark shadows over the small parking lot. Instantly he pressed back against the store's wall, holding the two-by-four. The door slowed its revolutions. As it picked up speed again, he jammed the two-by-four between the moving panes. And slid out his Browning.

As the pane slammed against the board, he stepped out, aiming as he looked inside.

Trapped, with no way to get to the wood, the man was pushing the door, trying to get back into the store. His shoulders were bunched with effort, but the door would not move—it spun only counterclockwise. The man whirled around, his face furious. He was in his late twenties, Tucker guessed. He had beard stubble, short brown hair, an average face. A forgettable face, except for the dimples in his cheeks. When he saw Tucker's weapon through the glass, his hand immediately reached to go inside his jacket.

Tucker gave a shake to his head. "Don't."

The hand moved an inch more.

"We both know you were planning to wipe me," Tucker told him. "My solution is to shoot you first. I'll start with your gut and pinpoint each of your organs." A gut wound was the most painful, and often fatal when organs were involved.

The man's eyes narrowed, but he stopped moving.

"Good," Tucker said. "Take out your gun. Slowly. Put it beside your feet. Don't drop it. We don't want the damn thing to go off."

In slow motion the man removed his weapon and set it down on the floor.

"I'm going to take out the board now. Then you come outside. We'll have a nice chat." Keeping his gun trained on him, Tucker crouched and slid out the wood. The revolving door moved, and he grabbed the man's gun. As soon as the man was outside, Tucker told him, "Over there."

They walked into the black shadow of a tree.

"Give me your billfold," Tucker ordered.

"I'm not carrying one."

He was unsurprised. When a trained janitor went out on a job, he went clean. "Who are you?"

"You don't care about that really, do you, old man?"

"Let's see your pocket litter," Tucker told him. "Carefully."

The man pulled car keys from his jeans.

"Drop them."

He let them fall through his fingers, then extracted the linings of his jeans pockets to show there was nothing more inside. He did the same with his outside jacket pockets. Using only two fingers on each hand, he opened his jacket, showing the lining had no pockets. He was wearing a pocketless polo shirt.

"Where's your money?" Tucker demanded.

"In my car. Parked back where I picked you up."

In other words, parked near Catapult. Tucker considered. "Who hired you?"

"Look, this was just a job. Nothing personal."

"It's personal to me. Who the fuck hired you?"

The dead tone got to the man. His pupils dilated.

"Sonny, I know how to kill without leaving a mark," Tucker told him grimly. "It's been a while. Tonight seems like a good time to take up the sport again. Would you like a demonstration?"

The would-be assassin uneasily shifted his weight. "Preston. He said his name was Preston. He wired money into an account I have."

Tucker nodded. "When did you get the call from him?"

"Today. Late afternoon."

With a sudden move, Tucker took a step and slammed his Browning against the killer's temple. He staggered, and Tucker hit him again. The man dropped to his knees on the pavement, then sat back and keeled over, unconscious.

Tucker dumped the ammo out of the man's weapon and pocketed it—9-mm. It might come in handy later. He pulled out plastic handcuffs and bound the man's hands behind him and his ankles together. He rolled him against the trunk of the tree where the shadows were deepest.

Activating his mobile, Tucker punched in Gloria's number. As soon as she answered, he said, "Don't say my name. Put me on hold and go into my office and close the door. Then pick up again."

There was a surprised pause. "Sure, Ted. I have time for a quick private chat." Ted was her husband.

When she came back on the line, Tucker told her, "I'm outside the rear of Capitol Hill market. I'm leaving a janitor here who tried to wipe me. He's handcuffed, and I've got his ammo. Come and get him."

"What! Oh, hell, what have you been up to now?"

"Hudson Cannon is dirty."

"Is the janitor why Hudson wanted you to leave?"

"Yes."

She swore. "I knew something was wrong. What do you want me to do with the guy when I get there?"

"He should still be unconscious. He's tied up. Drag him into your car and then park him in the basement at Catapult. I don't want Canon to know about any of this, for obvious reasons. Don't tell Matt Kelley, either. There may be another mole inside Langley, and it could leak back to the Library of Gold people. This is a lockdown on security, got it?"

"Got it."

"The kid parked his car somewhere near Catapult. I'll put his keys on the ledge above the back door of the store. Locate the car and toss it. Phone me if you find anything."

"I take it you're not coming back."

"Not until the Library of Gold operation is over. The story is I'm taking a short, well-deserved vacation."

CHAPTER 46

Rome, Italy

THE EFFICIENCY FLAT WAS in a forgotten corner of Rome, tucked away on one of the little streets on Janiculum Hill just south of St. Peter's Basilica. The husky blast of a boat horn sounded from the Tiber River as Yitzhak Law paced to the flat's open window. Running both hands over his bald head, he stared out at the unfamiliar terrain.

"You are distressed, *amore mio*." Roberto Cavaletti's voice sounded behind him.

Yitzhak turned. Roberto was studying him from the table beside the sink, their only table. The flat was one room, so small that opening the oven door blocked entry to the tiny bathroom. It reminded Yitzhak of his student days at the University of Chicago, and that was the only charm to it. That, and it was safe. Bash Badawi had brought them here yesterday, after a doctor had treated Roberto's shoulder wound.

"I have a class to teach this evening," Yitzhak said.

"A meeting later tonight. When I don't show up, they'll worry." It was not an issue yesterday, when he had no other classes or meetings. He was a professor in the Dipartimento di Studi Storico-Religiosi at the Università di Roma–Sapienza, and he took his responsibilities seriously.

Roberto massaged his close-cropped brown beard, thinking. "Perhaps it is worse than that. They will phone the house, leave a message, and when no one returns the call, they will go looking for you."

"I thought of that, too. There'll be an uproar. But it's the students who concern me most—no one will be there to teach them."

"You wish to tell the department? We have the cell phone Bash gave us. He said we must not leave, and no one could know where we are. A cell call is not leaving. And you do not have to say any details." Roberto held up the cell.

"Yes, of course. You're right."

Feeling relieved, Yitzhak marched over and took the device. Calling out, he settled into the chair across from Roberto. He had changed the dressing on Roberto's wound earlier. Thankfully it was healing nicely, and Roberto had had a good night's sleep.

Gina, the department secretary, answered. She recognized his voice immediately. *"Come sta, professore?"*

Speaking Italian, he explained he had to leave in an hour for emergency business. "I'll need a substitute for my lecture, Gina. And please alert Professor Ocie Stafford that I can't attend his meeting, with apologies."

"I will. But what am I to do with your package?"

"Package? . . . I don't understand."

"It looks and feels like a book, but of course I cannot be certain. It is in a padded envelope. This morning a priest from Monsignor Jerry McGahagin at the Vatican Library delivered it. He said it was most important.

The monsignor wants your advice." Monsignor Mc-Gahagin was the director of not only one of the oldest libraries in the world, but one that contained a priceless collection of historical texts, many of them never seen by outsiders.

He thought quickly. "Send someone over with it to Trattoria Sor'eva on Piazza della Rovere. As it happens, I'm near there now." Bash had pointed out the place as a good restaurant serving excellent handmade pasta.

"Yes, I will do that. A half hour, no more."

Yitzhak ended the connection and relayed the conversation.

Roberto shook his head. "You are bad. We are supposed to stay here."

"You stay. That puts half of us in compliance."

Roberto gave an expressive Roman shrug. "What am I to do with you. You are always the dog looking for one more good bone."

"I'll be back soon." Yitzhak patted his hand and left.

Dusk was spreading across the city, the shadows long. Yitzhak had steeled himself not to think about Eva and Judd, but as he walked, passing apartment buildings and shops, he felt strangely vulnerable, which made him worry about them. Not until he heard from Bash that their dangerous situation was settled and they were safe would he feel right.

Twenty minutes later he reached the piazza and stopped across the street from the trattoria. All seemed normal, but then, tumult was normal to Rome—the streets a cyclone of traffic, bustling with shoppers, locals, businesspeople, cars parked two and three abreast. The windows of the trattoria showed customers inside eating and drinking.

Then he saw Leoni Vincenza, one of his advanced students, hurrying toward the restaurant, a padded envelope under his arm. It was bright yellow, a strange color for the Vatican. Perhaps the *monsignore* was using up donated stock.

Yitzhak pushed himself to rush, and he crossed at the intersection. "Leoni! Leoni!"

The youth looked up, his long black hair blowing around his face. "*Professore,* you have been waiting for me?"

Yitzhak said nothing and slowed, catching his breath. When Leoni reached him, he said, "Good to see you, boy. Is that my package?"

"Yes, sir." He handed it to him.

"*Grazie.* My car is around the block. I'll see you back at the university in a few days."

Leoni nodded. "*Ciao.*" He returned the way he had come.

Yitzhak went in the other direction, feeling smart he had thought to misdirect the student. As he climbed Janiculum Hill, he stopped. His heart was thundering. He had been meaning to lose weight for years. Now it was evident he had better hurry on that promise.

He resumed walking, slowly this time, and finally reached the apartment building. He opened the front door and gazed up at the long staircase. He had to mount two flights, and the second was as long as the first. He hefted the package—it felt heavy, the weight of a book. He would rest a moment, and he was curious.

Ripping off the staples, he pulled out the volume. And stared, surprised. It was a thick collection of Sherlock Holmes stories, so battered it looked as if it had come from a used-book store. Definitely not a first edition. Why would the *monsignore* send this? He checked for a note but found none.

Shaking his head, he stuffed it back inside the envelope and climbed. Behind him he heard the front door open and close. When he reached his floor, he could hear footsteps on the stairs, hurrying upward. For some reason he found himself rushing down the corridor. As he slid the key inside the lock, he glanced back and froze.

Two men were running toward him, aiming guns.

"Who are you?" Yitzhak demanded, although even to him his voice sounded weak. "What do you want?"

There was no answer. One man was large, burly, and ferocious looking, the other small and wiry, with a mean face. The shorter man grabbed the key from Yitzhak's hand, unlocked the door, and the big man shoved him inside. The door closed behind them with an ominous *click*.

CHAPTER 47

Athens, Greece

THE CARNIVORE'S FRIEND FLEW Eva and Judd into Athens International, and from there they took the suburban railway Proastiakos northwest through the night, transferring to Metro line three, which would take them into the city. They had been watching carefully for anyone too interested in them. The Metro car was crowded, people sleeping or talking quietly. Eva was eager to check into a hotel so they would be alone and she could rewind the leather strip around the *scytale* and translate the rest of Charles's message.

She peered out the windows as the Metro sped past houses and apartment blocks built in modern Greece's ubiquitous cement-box architecture. Ancient ruins occasionally showed, alight in the night. The juxtaposition of new and old was somehow reassuring, the past meeting today and making the future seem possible. She clung to her hopes for a future as she sat beside

Judd, very aware of him. There was a lot about him she liked—but also something she feared.

She looked down at his hands resting on his thighs, remembering Michelangelo's statue of David, his great masterpiece, in Florence. Michelangelo had said when he cut into the marble it had revealed the hands of a killer. Judd's hands looked like David's, oversize and strong, with prominent veins. But when he had sculpted David's face, Michelangelo had uncovered a subtle sweetness and innocence. She glanced at Judd's weathered face, square and rugged beneath his bleached hair, the arched nose, the good jaw. There was no sweetness or innocence there, only determination.

"How old are you, Judd?" she asked.

His body appeared relaxed, despite his constant watchfulness. There was no way to be certain how long it would take Preston to figure out the Carnivore had not eliminated them. Preston might be chasing them now.

"Thirty-two," he said. "Why?"

"So am I. I'll bet you knew that already."

"It was in the dossier Tucker gave me. Is my age important?"

"No. But I thought you might be older. You've been through a lot, haven't you?"

He stared at her. "Why do you say that?"

"In prison there were women who had a sense about them of . . . it's hard to describe. I guess I'd call it a challenging past. You're something like that."

What she did not mention was the women came from violent backgrounds, many sentenced on murder or manslaughter charges. They seemed to ache to fight, although, win or lose, the consequences for them would be serious. But she had never seen Judd start a fight or even look for one. Then with a chill she recalled his saying he wanted no more blood on his hands.

"I was undercover in Iraq and later in Pakistan," he explained. "Military intelligence. Of course both were 'challenging.' But there were good things, too. In Iraq, I was able to help rebuild several schools. The Iraqis were coming back from the brink, and education was high on their list. Dad put together shipments of books for their libraries."

"That doesn't sound like military intelligence."

"I had some downtime. That's what I did with it, particularly at the end."

She heard something else in his voice. "And before then?"

Smiling, he said, "Do all eggheads ask so many questions?"

"I'm an egghead?"

"A Ph.D. qualifies you."

She scanned the other passengers. "Think what you know about me, including my shady past. I know almost nothing about you."

He chuckled. "At least I'm sure you're not a perpetrator of vehicular manslaughter." He stared at her expression. "Sorry. That was stupid of me." He faced straight ahead again.

Eva said nothing, sitting quietly.

At last he continued: "I uncovered some intel on an 'al-Qaeda in Iraq' operative and finally was able to catch him and take him in for questioning. God knows how he managed to get rope, but he did. He hung himself in his cell. His brother was also al-Qaeda, and when he heard about it, he came after me. It went on for weeks. He was ruining my ability to do the rest of my job, and I wasn't able to track him down. Then there was a shift. It seemed as if he'd lost interest. I couldn't figure it out—until a message was passed to me he was going to punish me by liquidating my fiancée."

His fingers drained color as he knotted his hands.

"She was MI, too. A damn good analyst. I got the intel just as she reached her usual security check. A Muslim woman stumbled and fell beside the checkpoint, and her suitcase slid under my fiancée's Jeep. It looked like an accident, but the guards were instantly on it. The woman managed to shake free and run for it just as the suitcase exploded. It was an IED, of course. 'She' was wearing a burka, but one of the soldiers saw legs in jeans, and big feet in men's combat boots." He took a deep breath. "Four people were killed, including my fiancée. Later I got another message. In English it said, 'Whatsoever a man soweth, that shall he also reap.' The New Testament, of course. Apostle Paul. The son of a bitch was an Islamic jihadist quoting the Bible to me to justify murdering her."

"You haven't told me her name," she said gently.

He cleared his throat. "Amanda. Amanda Waterman."

"I'm so sorry. How horrible. You felt responsible for her death."

"She'd still be alive. Her job wasn't that dangerous."

"I'll bet you wanted to kill him for what he did."

His body tensed. "I could never find him."

"Do you still want to kill him?"

He looked at her sharply. "Would you blame me?"

"When I believed there was a chance I'd been driving and had killed Charles, it took me a long time to come to terms with it." She paused. "No one went to Iraq without knowing the risks. Both of you were very lucky to find love." She heard the sadness in her voice and wiped it away. "A lot of people never have that."

He nodded, his expression granite.

Still, she wondered whether that was the only story behind the chilling looks she had seen on his face. One of his hands moved toward hers, to hold it. She remembered how he had pulled her to him after she had almost pitched off the yacht, how he had wrapped his arms around her and held her tight, how he had kissed her hair . . . the wonderful sound of his pounding heart. His musky, wet smell. He had saved her at the risk of his own life. In that moment she had wanted nothing more than to burrow in and forget the hard times. Pretend his protectiveness was the beginning of love. But the truth was she did not know what she really thought of him, much less what she felt, or whether someone with deep heartache and a violent past could ever be stable enough for enduring love. Could she, even?

She gave his hand a quick squeeze and released him. "Your mobile is chirping."

Judd took it from his pocket. "An e-mail from Tucker. Some good news—he thinks he may have found Robin Miller." He handed the device to her. "What do you think?"

She analyzed the photo of the woman displayed on the mobile's screen—green eyes and thick ash-blond hair, but no bangs. The mouth was lush and round. Included were the woman's age, height, and weight.

"The statistics match Robin Miller," she told him. "But if I didn't know better, I'd still say it's not her. On the other hand, Charles had plastic surgery when he joined the library, so she might've, too. If she did, then her nose could've been shortened and turned up at the end, and an implant inserted in her chin. The eyes, hair color, and the rest of the face are the same."

"With plastic surgery they'd be identical?"

"Absolutely." She was still thinking about his fiancée's death. "It's interesting about the al-Qaeda jihadist and his last message to you. A version is in the Old Testament, too. Job said, 'They that plow iniquity and sow wickedness reap the same.' Then, thousands of years later, Cicero wrote, 'As you have sown, so shall you reap.' Anyway, what strikes me is it's also in the Koran, which came some seven centuries later, after Cicero:

'Have you considered what you have sown?' The jihadist must've been at least somewhat educated. Otherwise he would've fallen back on what he knew—the Koran."

"I thought about that, too. But I'm not going there, and God knows where he is or whether he's even alive. Besides, you and I have a much more urgent problem— how to find Robin Miller and the Library of Gold."

And survive, she thought.

CHAPTER 48

EVA AND JUDD DISEMBARKED at Platia Syntagma—Constitution Square—the center of modern Athens. A grand expanse of white marble, the plaza stretched below the parliament building, glowing serenely in lamplight. At the edges were elegant cafés sporting outdoor tables, where people were eating, drinking, gossiping.

As they walked toward the taxi stand, Eva mulled whether she could stay with the mission. As she glanced around, the Athens traffic seemed unusually thick, the shadows too dark and dangerous. She was troubled, her mind in turmoil.

They stopped as the ruins of the Parthenon temple came into view, towering majestically above the high Acropolis. The glowing white columns and pediments could be seen from all over the city, from between buildings and at the crosswalks of streets.

"The Parthenon is really something," Judd decided. "And before you ask—no, I've never been to Athens. This is my first time."

She forced a smile.

They took a taxi into the Exarchia district near the Athens Polytechnic, a quirkily bohemian neighborhood she had visited before meeting Charles. At the bottom of Stournari Street they got out and climbed into the Platia Exarchia, the nerve center of the area, where Athenians satisfied their love of political debate, and intellectuals came to spout their latest theories. Serious nightlife started in Athens after midnight. Through windows she could see the bars were bustling.

"Let's get some food," Judd said.

They went into a *taverna* named Pan's Revenge. A musician strummed a mandolin-like *bouzouki* and sang a Greek sea song of yearning for a far-off love. Stopping at the bar, Eva translated as Judd chose a bottle of Katogi Averoff estate red, 1999, 90 percent cabernet, 10 percent merlot. She ordered the house speciality—moussaka and zucchini stuffed with wild rice—to go.

Purchases in hand, they walked around the corner. She felt Judd's tension as he continued to watch for tails, and her own tension as she tried to decide what to do.

"You're being awfully quiet," he said.

"I know. Just thinking."

Soon she saw the small hotel she remembered—pink stone with white stone moldings and enameled white shutters—where she had stayed years before.

"Hotel Hecate," Judd read. "A Greek god or goddess?"

"The goddess of magic."

"Maybe it's a good omen." He stared at her a moment, seeming to try to read her mind. "Are you going to be all right?"

Quite a few people were entering and leaving the various establishments. The door to a bar opened, and waves of laughter rolled out. She saw no sign of threat.

"Sure," she said. "I'll just hang out while you register."

"Don't run out on me."

Her brows rose in surprise. Had he guessed she had been considering it? Before she could respond, he hurried into the hotel.

Walking along the block, she studied the other pedestrians as she tried to sort through her thoughts. She had made a lot of mistakes, and now she feared staying with the operation was another. What kind of man was Judd really, to do such violent work? Could he turn off the violence? Would he ever use it against her?

At the corner she paced back toward the hotel. She felt responsible for putting Yitzhak and Roberto in danger and for being the cause of Peggy's murder. But once she had discovered Charles was alive and had left a message for her, she had blindly followed the trail to know more about what he might actually have felt for her. As she was thinking about that, an old man and woman passed, holding hands, talking to each other as if no one else in the world mattered. She felt a stab of heartache.

Judd appeared in the driveway beside the hotel. He scrutinized the area, then gave a casual nod.

"Everything okay?" he asked when she joined him.

Her gaze went to a black shadow that ran along the drive, suddenly aware that in the dark it was hard to tell the difference between a dog and a wolf. She sighed. "Thanks for everything, Judd. I'll translate Charles's message for you tonight, but then I'm going to fly out tomorrow for home."

He did not try to change her mind. "I'm glad you've hung in as long as you have. You've been a great help, Eva."

They went in the hotel's rear entrance and climbed the stairs. The room was larger than the one in Istanbul and again had two beds. This time it overlooked the next-door hotel and the driveway far below. In the distance, the Parthenon shone.

As Judd bolted the door, she set their meal on a table beside the radiator and shrugged off her shoulder satchel to get the *scytale* and leather ribbon.

Watching expectantly, he dropped the duffel bag onto the bed nearest the door and removed his Beretta and the S&W 9-mm pistol and suppressor he had picked up from Preston.

She unlatched the snap that closed the side pocket of the satchel and reached inside. Instantly her hand felt an awful wetness. She pulled out the *scytale* and strip.

"Oh, no," she breathed. "No."

"What?"

"The ink's run." She held up the long piece of leather, soggy, the letters bleeding into one another. "It must've happened in the yacht, when we got drenched."

"Is the message readable?"

"I don't know yet."

She grabbed a box of tissues from the bureau and sat on the other bed, holding the strip beneath the bright light of the lamp. As she dried it, he sat across from her, leaning forward with his forearms on his thighs, watching tensely.

"The letters are a blur," she reported. "I may be able to get something, though."

Remembering how Andy Yakimovich had done it, she carefully wrapped the strip around the *scytale*, pressing and pushing it gently into place, watching to make certain the blurred letters fit in lines. She worked a long time in the silent room. Finally she grasped the *scytale*'s ends, holding the leather in place with her thumbs.

"A few words make sense," she said. "I can partly read where it says the secret is hidden in *Spies,* but I can't read the following sentence." She caught her breath at the next words, the signature at the end: "*Te amo,* Eva, 3-8-08."

"What is it?" Judd leaned forward.

She translated: " 'I love you, Eva.' "

He saw where she was looking. "It's dated the month before Charles disappeared. That answers one of your questions. A critical one, I imagine."

She hesitated as she felt an onslaught of emotions. "I always thought of Charles as my strength, my anchor. When I'd have doubts or get sidetracked, he'd bring me back to center. Now I think that's what he believed to be love. But the truth is it wasn't concern or interest in me. He just couldn't stand that I wasn't as focused, as compulsive as he was." She looked at him. "We still don't know where the library's location is written in *The Book of Spies*."

There was a long silence of deep disappointment.

Judd sat up straight. "I'll just have to find it in *Spies* myself."

But the book was enormous. Trying to uncover the message without a clue or expert help could be impossible. And there was an even larger problem—he did not even know where the book was.

"Don't worry, Eva. You should still go home tomorrow." His gaze was steady. "I really meant it when I said you'd done a good job. In fact, you were invaluable. Without you I likely wouldn't have been successful in Rome or Istanbul."

His mobile rang, and he snatched it up.

She checked her watch. It was past four A.M.

"Yes, Tucker." His jaw clenched as he listened. He told Tucker about the Carnivore's attempt to wipe them and his change of mind, then about their discovery the leather strip was damaged. "We're at the Hotel Hecate. I understand. Be careful."

Eva watched as he punched the Off button.

When he turned to her, his expression was grim. "Cathy Doyle—that's Tucker's boss—has died in a car accident, and the man who took her place appears to be the leak. Another hired gun just tried to erase Tucker."

"Oh, God. How's Tucker?"

"Angry. Worried. The usual. In other words, he's fine. He's at the Baltimore airport. He's flying here to help."

"He didn't have any new information about *Spies* or the Library of Gold?"

"No, but he's given NSA my mobile number, so if one of the numbers on Charles's cell is activated, both he and I will get the news. There's more. Preston hired the guy to take out Tucker *after* we left him hogtied in the Grand Bazaar."

"So Preston is back in action, just as the Carnivore said he'd be. Did Tucker know anything about the Carnivore?"

"He said the Carnivore was one of the underworld's dirty secrets. Too useful to too many sides to kill, and anyway too elusive to find. Apparently back in the cold war, Langley occasionally did business with him. Tucker said he'd heard the Carnivore had ironclad rules, but he'd never had any reason to hunt him."

"Doesn't it seem to you Cathy Doyle's death was more than an accident?"

"Yes. The assholes."

She watched as he slapped his thighs, stood up, and paced the room.

"Why don't you ask me to stay?" she said. "You can use my expertise."

He turned, his muscular face severe. "People either love this work, or they put up with it because they have a sense of mission, of commitment to something larger, something for the common good. In religion it's called faith. In a nation it's patriotism. The risk of death is worth it to them. I can't ask you to stay. You could die."

"Do you love the work?"

"Never have. As soon as this is over, I really am going

back to being a civilian. I figure I've contributed enough. It's someone else's turn."

"Will you be able to live peacefully?"

"If you're asking whether I have flashbacks or I'm a prime candidate to take a sniper rifle up into some tower and wipe anyone who's in sight, the answer is no. Most of us aren't affected that way. We don't even get into fistfights in bars. We're just normal people who've been doing a tough job and have some bad memories."

Relief washed over her. With sudden clarity she realized she had been dwelling on her own personal fears. "Charles and the book club conspired in something that should've been good but turned it into evil and a loss to civilization so large it's incalculable. The Library of Gold belongs to the world. I have the knowledge to help you find it and the awful people behind it. With luck it'll be soon enough to stop from happening whatever your father was so worried about." She took a deep breath. "I want to make my own commitment. Make the mission mine, too, and try to be braver than I ever was able during the years with Charles and in the penitentiary. I've changed my mind. I'll see this through."

He sat on his bed, facing her. "You're sure?" He studied her, his gray eyes grave.

"Absolutely." And she meant it.

"Then I'm glad. I have a feeling you've always been brave. But do me a favor—don't like the work too much."

"Fat chance." Setting aside the *scytale*, she turned to him, sitting cross-legged. She had an idea. "We've got to find another way to go about this. I'll start with Charles's tattoo. It had to have sent shudders through the book club. Even a hint someone might reveal the library's location would be a threat to them. That's my first point. The second is, when I saw Charles and Robin together there was something intimate about them. I don't know whether they were close friends, close colleagues, or maybe lovers. But if I'm right, she's connected to Charles, which means his tattoo may have thrown suspicion on her. I know I'd be suspicious. Read Preston's note again."

He took out the torn notebook page. " 'Robin Miller. *Book of Spies*. All we know is Athens—so far.' "

"The beginning part of the note is like a list. 'Robin Miller. *Book of Spies*.' One. Two. Then we get to the heart of the matter: 'All we know is Athens—so far.' The tone makes me think they don't know where *The Book of Spies*—or Robin Miller—is, except they're in Athens, and they must be found."

"You think she not only has the book but she's on the run with it," he said.

"It's a good possibility."

He grabbed his mobile. "I'll call her." He tapped in one of the numbers from Charles Sherback's cell. "I'm getting a recording," he told her. Then: "Ms. Miller, my name is Judd Ryder. I'm in Athens, and I've got the resources to protect you from Preston. I'd like to buy *The Book of Spies*. Call as soon as you can. I'll leave my mobile on." Then he dialed the other number and left the same message.

"Fingers crossed," she said.

He went into the bathroom and emerged with water glasses. He opened the bottle of wine to let it breathe. "I'm going to take a shower. Then we eat."

He grabbed a clean T-shirt and shorts from the duffel and went into the bathroom. She listened to the music of the running shower and walked around the room, arms crossed, holding herself, feeling relieved she had decided to stay and hoping Robin would call soon. Then she emptied the side pocket of her satchel and laid out everything to dry.

Judd emerged with droplets shining on his short bleached hair, his face wet and relaxed. The T-shirt was damp, clinging to his tapered waist. His stomach muscles were amazing, like rebar, and he had good long legs beneath his shorts, straight, the hair golden brown and curly, lovely. She turned away, busying herself by taking out her shirt and shorts. Then she went into the bathroom without looking at him again.

"Drink your wine," she told him over her shoulder. "Behave yourself."

"I'll save half for you."

The hot water soothed her. She washed her hair, caught by surprise at the black color as it fell over her face. She had never in her life dyed her hair. Toweling off, she fastened on her ankle device, buttoned her shirt, and stepped into the shorts.

When she emerged from the bathroom he was sitting at the table, inspecting Charles's notebook again.

"Find anything?" She slid into the chair across from him.

"Nothing."

"No call from Robin?"

He shook his head. "Tell me about your family."

"Isn't that in my dossier?"

"Just the basics. Mother, father, brother, sister, and you. They moved from Los Angeles to Iowa. You didn't. I'd really like to know."

She hesitated. "There's not much to say, really. Dad worked construction. Mom cleaned houses. Dad drank—a lot. He'd have tirades and slap Mom around when she tried to convince him to quit. Eventually she started drinking, too. They got along a lot better, but it still was miserable. We could never bring our friends home because we never knew what we'd find."

"You were the oldest, weren't you?"

"Yes, and probably the luckiest. In Al-Anon you learn about the family mediator, the peacemaker—that was me. It kept me from falling into the bottle, too, because I was always trying to smooth things over to protect my little brother and sister. Then Dad started losing one job after the other, and his uncle offered him work at a lumber company he owned in Council Bluffs. I'd had my brush with the law by then. They were good about that and stood by me. But when everyone left, I stayed on in L.A., to go to college." Her shoulders were tense. She raised her arms above her head and stretched.

"You didn't want to end up like them."

"No, I didn't, but it didn't stop me from loving them. They came to visit me in prison several times. I don't know how they scraped the money together to do it, but they did." She bit her lip. "Love is a crazy emotion, isn't it?"

He was watching her, kindness glowing in his eyes. "Let's eat."

He poured wine as she got out the food. The moussaka was warm and spicy, the zucchini and wild rice crunchy. It was a simple but fine meal, and for the moment the lamplit hotel room felt cozy and safe.

"What about you and your family?" she asked as she ate.

"You know part of it. Dad was ambitious, but the higher he rose, the more pressure he was under, and the more traveling he had to do. When I started school, Mom went back to work, teaching kindergarten. Then, after a couple of years, she quit so she'd be free when he was home. It was great for me. The door was always open for my friends. She'd make chocolate pudding and oatmeal cookies and let us play outside and get dirty." He studied his wine. "What was rough for both of us was not having him around. But when he was, he filled the house with his personality, and he spent every moment with us. Now that I look back, it's obvious he was trying to make it up to us."

"I'll bet he enjoyed you, too."

"I hope so." He lowered his head. "You should know Dad started telling me stories about the Library of Gold when I was young. He must've known about it then. And that makes me think he was in the book club when the decision was made to bring Charles on board. Knowing how managerial Dad was, I have to believe even if he didn't make the final decisions, he must've at least known about the arrangements."

She felt her breath catch in her throat. Then she shook off her anger. "You're not him. You've made your own choices, and it seems to me they're one hundred eighty degrees different from his. I think you've inherited his best traits."

He poured the last of the garnet-colored wine into their glasses, then he held up his.

"To our partnership." He grinned.

She touched her rim to his and smiled into his eyes. "To finding the Library of Gold."

CHAPTER 49

THE AFTERNOON WAS BRIGHT, sunlight bouncing off the windshields of cars as Martin Chapman's plush limousine rolled up to the Hotel Grande Bretagne on Constitution Square. One of the globe's top establishments, the hotel looked like a palace and had a long history as a seat of power, which Chapman appreciated: The Nazis had made it their headquarters when they occupied Greece during World War II, and later the British Expeditionary Force took it over. Wars had been planned here, and treaties signed. From kings to corporate heads, jet-setters to diplomats, it was the place to stay, the only hotel Chapman ever used when in Athens.

The chauffeur rushed around the limo to open the door. Chapman got out, his mane of wavy white hair gleaming, blue eyes twinkling, tan face composed, carriage erect. Valets scurried. The hotel's massive doors opened, and he marched inside.

The manager waited beside a tall Ionic column in the lobby, perfectly positioned for effect, surrounded by the hotel's nineteenth-century art and antiques. He

bowed and, after appropriate welcoming remarks, led
Chapman across the mosaic marble floor to the private
elevator, bypassing the registration desk.

They rose silently to the fifth-floor Royal Suite.
Opening the door, the manager bowed again, and Chapman strode into a rich world of damasks and silks and
antique furnishings from Sotheby's, eager to see his
wife. But there was no sign of her. Instead, standing in
the middle of the grand triple living room was Doug
Preston, holding a wood box. He inclined his head
slightly, indicating the box contained what Chapman
wanted. Dressed in a three-piece suit tailored to show no
sign of his holstered pistol, the security chief's expression was serious.

Chapman's luggage was wheeled in, and the manager bowed himself out the door.

"Where's my wife?" Chapman asked.

"Shopping, sir. Mahaira is with her."

Chapman nodded and gestured. They went into the
private formal dining room with its elegant table, set for
a business meeting of only eight, since Jonathan Ryder
and Angelo Charbonier were dead. Over the next year
the book club would decide on their replacements. The
centerpiece was a lavish display of orchids. Pads of paper and pricey Mont Blanc fountain pens with the hotel's logo waited at each place.

Preston closed the door. "The butler will serve
drinks. Is there anything else I can order for you?"

Chapman chose a Partagas cigar from the burled-wood humidor. He rolled it between his fingers next to
his ear, hearing the muffled sound of fine tobacco. He
clipped off the end and sniffed. Satisfactory. Lighting it
with the hotel's gold lighter, he went to stand by one of
the tall windows overlooking the city's landmarks.

"How close are you to finding the Carnivore?" Chapman smoked, controlling his fury.

When after four hours the Carnivore had not given Chapman confirmation of the kill, he had phoned the number the Carnivore had given him. It was disconnected. Then he had sent an e-mail to the contact man, Jack. It had bounced back.

Preston joined Chapman at the window and said, "It's a problem. As you said, the Carnivore's security is very tight. The e-mail address was routed through several countries. So far Jan's had no luck tracing it back to its origin, but she's still working on it." Jan Mardis was Carl Lindström's chief of computer security. "As for the disconnected number, there's nothing we can do about it. I checked in with the man who recommended the Carnivore to you, but he claims he has no other way to reach him and you'll never find him now. He doesn't understand what happened, but whatever it was, he figures he's burned, too. When the Carnivore takes a client's money, it's a trust to him. He always delivers. And he never forgets."

Chapman felt a chill, remembering the cold litany of the Carnivore's rules. Then he brushed it off. The bastard owed him the $1 million advance.

"Find him. I want my money, and then I want him terminated."

Preston inclined his head. "Yes, sir. As soon as Jan has anything, it'll be a pleasure to take him out."

"What about Judd Ryder and Eva Blake? According to our Washington asset, they were heading for Thessalonika and had hooked up with Robin Miller."

"It has to be Athens. They took a note I'd written to myself, and the Carnivore knew it was legitimate. I've posted men at the airport, train stations, and docks to look for them. I don't see how they could've reached Robin, but maybe they have. That could work in our favor." He paused. "I know how to find her."

Chapman stopped, his cigar suspended on its way to

his mouth. He studied Preston, who stood calmly beside him, the box still in both hands. He was not rattled, not apologetic. In fact, there was a deadly calm about him. His blue eyes looked like chipped ice. He had been humiliated, and he wanted revenge. Good.

"Tell me."

"I had the pilot check the Learjet," Preston said. "Robin didn't leave her cell behind. If she were planning to escape, she'd take it with her because it was the only one she had. She doesn't know she can be tracked through the cell. My NSA contact is waiting for her to activate it, and as soon as she does, we'll have her. But there's another problem: Tucker Andersen got away, and the man I hired in Washington to scrub him has vanished. So has Andersen. I have people looking for both."

Chapman swore loudly. "Anything else?"

"My men in Rome captured Yitzhak Law and Roberto Cavaletti."

"They're dead?" he asked instantly, pleased.

Preston shook his head. "Not yet. Ryder and Blake have turned out to be far more trouble than any of us envisioned. With Law and Cavaletti, we have something to hold over them if we need it."

Chapman thought about it. "Agreed. We can wipe them whenever we wish."

"There's one more thing. I talked to Yakimovich after I got free in the Grand Bazaar. He said Charles left behind a strip of leather with a message—the location of the Library of Gold is hidden in *The Book of Spies*."

"Jesus. The old librarian smuggled out that book. He knew the location was in it?"

"He's the one who put it there. Charles must have found some message he left. In any case, it's not a problem. We'll retrieve the book. Ryder and Blake will never get close."

Chapman dropped his cigar into an ashtray and rubbed his hands. "Give me the box."

But as Preston handed it to him, there was a tap on the door. With a nod from Chapman, Preston opened it.

Mahaira stood there in a beige linen suit, her graying hair perfectly coiffed in a frame around her soft face. "Madame asked me to tell you she is delayed, sir. Friends found her and insisted she have tea with them. She is most regretful."

Stung by the news, Chapman turned his back on her. As he listened to her pad away, his gaze fell on the box. Quickly he opened it. Sighing with pleasure, he plucked from its velvet lining an illuminated manuscript spectacular not only for its physical beauty but also for what it would mean to his wife and the great new fortune he would have.

CHAPTER 50

THE MEMBERS OF THE BOOK CLUB had been checking into the Hotel Grande Bretagne throughout the morning. The meeting began promptly at two P.M., and their arrival infused the room with electric energy. All stood at least six feet or taller, and despite the nearly thirty-year range in their ages, each moved with the grace of an athlete, their bodies trim and fit.

Chosen in their youth, when they were struggling for money and power and displayed great promise, they had been cultivated, mentored, and financed—as Martin Chapman had. Still, very few who received such attention rose to join the fraternity of the secret book club. Those who did were living examples of the ancient Greek ideal of the perfect man.

Studying them as they stood talking around the table, Chapman felt a sense of pride. He had been director five years. They could be troublesome, but that was understandable. Spirited aggression was necessary to accomplishment, and they were warriors in and out of business—another critical trait of the Greek ideal. But at the same time he was concerned about the unusually high pitch of their energy and the sideways glances in his direction. Something had set them off, and he worried he knew what it was.

He checked the butler, who was serving drinks. They would wait to start the meeting until they were alone.

"You're crazy, Petr," one was saying, amused.

"You spend too damn much time in the library," laughed another.

Petr Klok chose a martini from the butler's silver tray and announced, "This is an organized universe based on numbers. The ancients knew that. The markets—their prices and timings—move in harmonic rhythms." A bearded man with stylishly clipped hair, he was fifty years old and the first Czech billionaire. Taking advantage of his nation's privatization reforms, he had begun small, buying an insurance company with vouchers and loans from Library of Gold funds and then growing it into an empire stretching across Europe and America.

Brian Collum found his glass of barolo on the butler's tray. "You're claiming financial ups and downs aren't random? Clearly you're nuts." Graying, with a long handsome face, the Los Angeleno was the junior member, just forty-eight. He was the library's attorney.

"Study the geometrical codes hidden in Plato's *Timaeus*," Klok insisted. "Then connect them to the architecture of Hindu temples, Pascal's arithmetical triangles, the Egyptian alphabet, the movement of the planets, and the consonant patterns in the stained-glass windows of medieval cathedrals. It will give you an edge in the markets."

"I, for one, am interested. After all, Petr predicted the worldwide crash of 2008," Maurice Dresser reminded them. A Canadian, he had turned regional wildcatting into a trillion-dollar oil kingdom. He had thinning white hair and strong features. At seventy-five vigorous years, he was the oldest.

"Perhaps Petr is ahead of his time. He wouldn't be the first," Chapman said, a challenge in his voice. He paused until he had their full attention. Seeing the opportunity, he hoped to lull them with a small tournament. "Let's see what you know. Here's the subject—in 350 B.C., Heracleides was so far ahead of his time that he discovered the Earth spun on an axis."

Collum instantly held up his cigar, volunteering. "A century later Aristarchus of Samos figured out the Earth orbited the sun. Also far ahead of his time."

"But in the same era, Aristotle insisted we were stationary and the center of the heavens." Dresser shook his head. "Big error, and rare for him."

There was a hesitation, and Chapman stepped into it. "Reinhardt."

Reinhardt Gruen nodded. "In the 1500s most scientists again believed the world was flat. Wrong. Finally Copernicus rediscovered it rotated and went around the sun. That's a hell of a long time for the facts to come out again." From Berlin, Gruen was sixty-eight years old and owned a global media conglomerate.

"But he didn't dare publish his findings," Klok remembered. "It was too controversial and dangerous. Ignorant Christian churches fought the idea for the next three hundred years."

"Carl?" Chapman said.

"They claimed it went against the teachings of the Bible." Regal, his blond hair graying, Carl Lindström was sixty-five, the founder of the powerful software company Lindström Strategies, based in Stockholm.

"Not enough," Collum called out competitively.

As director, Martin Chapman was also referee. He agreed. "We need more, Carl."

"I thought you idiots knew the Bible by now," Lindström said goodnaturedly. "It is in Pslams: 'The world also is established, that it cannot be moved.'"

"Very good. Who's next?" Chapman asked.

Thomas Randklev raised his highball glass. "Here's to Galileo. He figured out Copernicus was right, and then he wrote his own books on the subject. So the Inquisition jailed him for heresy." From Johannesburg, Randklev was sixty-three and led mining enterprises on three continents.

"Grandon. You're the last man," Chapman said.

Fifty-eight and a Londoner, Grandon Holmes headed the telecom giant Holmes International Services. "It wasn't until the Renaissance that the Western world accepted the Earth rotated and orbited the sun—more than a millennium after Heracleides made the original discovery."

Everyone drank, smiling. The tournament had ended with no errors in history, and each had contributed. A sense of friendly warmth and shared purpose infused the room. A full success, Chapman thought with relief.

"Well done," he complimented.

"But just because Copernicus and the others were vindicated doesn't mean Petr is right about all his financial nonsense," Collum insisted.

"Spoken like an attorney," Petr chortled. "You are a Neanderthal, Brian."

"And you think you're a friggin' clairvoyant." Collum grinned and drank.

Everyone had been served, so Chapman told the butler to leave. As the door closed, the group settled around the table. He noted the mood had changed, grown tense.

Uneasily he took the chair at the head, where the wood box was waiting. "Maurice, you called this meeting. Begin."

Maurice Dresser adjusted the pen on the table beside him, then peered up. "As the senior member, it's my job occasionally to bring grievances to your attention. You've been hiding something from us, Marty."

Martin Chapman kept his tone conversational. "Elaborate, please."

Dresser sat forward and folded his hands. "Jonathan Ryder, Angelo Charbonier, and our fine librarian Charles Sherback are dead, murdered. We suspect you had something to do with that. You asked Thom, Carl, and Reinhardt to acquire information. It involved blackmailing a U.S. senator, hacking into a secret CIA unit's computer, and the murder of a CIA officer, one Catherine Doyle. Until we began talking to one another, we didn't realize the extent of your actions. What in hell is going on?"

"Secrecy is based on containment." Reinhardt Gruen drummed his fingers on the table. "This is far larger than I thought."

"You've exposed us to discovery," Carl Lindström accused.

"If the Parsifal Group is investigated, it may lead back to us." Thom Randklev glared.

The room seemed to vibrate with tension.

Chapman looked around at the cold faces. Inwardly he swore again at Jonathan Ryder for starting the domino disasters that had brought him to this precipice.

He cleared his throat. "The Parsifal Group is safe, because it's made too damn much money for too many important people for them to allow anything to be known about it. The exposure would have to be calamitous to change the equation, and this isn't a calamity."

The initial support money for the Library of Gold had been small but adequate, passed down through the centuries to ensure the library was cared for and secure. But in the second half of the twentieth century, when international commerce boomed, and its select group of supporters was formalized into the book club, common sense took over. A process to choose members was created. Opportunities opened through their successes, and investments were made, backed up when necessary by "persuading" Parsifal's members to cooperate.

Today the group's funds of some $6 trillion were registered, regulated, and owned by a series of fronts. They had much to be proud of—the Library of Gold had a permanent home and was maintained to the highest standards, and it would never be threatened as long as it was in their control. Since they saw to that, they were rewarded in kind.

"Doesn't bloody matter," Holmes said. "Risk is never to be taken lightly. You've gambled in grave ways that can impact all of us. We want to know why, and where you are going with it."

Chapman said nothing. Instead he opened the wood box and lifted out a small illuminated manuscript, about six by eight inches, and stood it up so it faced the members of the book club. There was an intake of breath. Diamonds blanketed the cover in a dazzling array, shaped into overlapping circles, triangles, and rectangles, each filled in completely with more diamonds. Of the highest quality, they sparkled like fire.

"I know the book," Randklev, the mining czar, said. He recounted the title in English: "*Gems and Minerals of the World*. Written in the late 1300s. It's from the Library of Gold."

"You're correct," Chapman told him. Then he addressed the group. "I was curious about the diamonds on the cover, so I asked a translator to search through the book, and he found the story behind them. Perhaps you remember that Mahmud, a Persian, invaded Afghanistan at the end of the tenth century. He made

Ghazni his capital and lifted the country to the heights of power with an empire extending into what is modern-day Iran, Pakistan, and India." He nodded at the lavish book. "Diamonds were one of the sources of his wealth—diamonds from a huge mine in what today is Khost province, near Ghazni. Then, some two hundred years later, Genghis Khan tore through Afghanistan, slaughtering the people. He left Ghazni and other cities in rubble. The devastation was so complete even irrigation lines were never repaired. The diamond mine stopped production. When Tamerlane swept through in the early 1380s, he destroyed what was left. The mine was forgotten. In effect, lost."

"Khost province is a dangerous place to do business, Marty," warned Reinhardt Gruen, the media baron. He looked around the group and explained. "The Afghan government has taken over the country's security, but they don't have a big enough army, and local police forces are stretched thin and are frequently corrupt. So province governors are supposed to be doing the job, which is a bad joke. In Khost, as I recall, several warlords have divided up the territory. Those warlords may be in collusion with the Taliban and al-Qaeda."

"Shit, Marty." Grandon Holmes, the telecom kingpin, stared. "No mine can operate in that atmosphere. Worse, you'll be aiding the jihadists."

"The exact opposite is true," Chapman told them calmly. That was the conclusion to which Jonathan Ryder had jumped. "Syed Ullah is the warlord in charge in the area where the mine is, and he hates the Taliban and, by extension, al-Qaeda. When the Taliban were in charge in the 1990s, they crushed the drug trade. Heroin and opium were—and are again today—his biggest source of income. So you see, the Taliban and al-Qaeda are his enemies. He's got an army of more than five thousand. He'd never let the jihadists infiltrate and take over his territory."

Heads slowly nodded around the table.

Thom Randklev's eyes brightened. "You know exactly where the mine is?"

"I do. I was going to bring all of you in," Chapman lied. "This is merely sooner than I expected. And of course, you can have the contract to do the mining in addition to your share, Thom."

Randklev rubbed his hands together. "When do I begin?"

"That's the problem," Chapman told them. "The deal isn't ready to be signed." In calm tones, and putting a positive spin wherever he could, he described the events of the last few weeks from Jonathan Ryder's discovery of Syed Ullah's frozen account in the international bank Chapman had bought, to Robin Miller's escape from the Learjet in Athens. Then he explained what remained to be done in Khost, and that Judd Ryder, Eva Blake, and Robin Miller were still on the loose but would be found soon.

When he finished, there was a long silence.

"Christ, Marty," said one.

"This is a hell of a mess," said another.

"It's not that big a mess," Chapman said, "and think of the fortunes to be made."

"If the mine is as big as you say," decided Holmes, "we'd be bloody fools to interrupt the deal."

"How much do you think it's worth?" asked Klok.

"From what I read, Mahmud's people had barely scratched the surface," Chapman said. "And of course they had the disadvantage of working with primitive equipment. I'd say it'll bring in at least a hundred trillion. Over decades, of course."

They smiled around the table. Then they laughed. The future was good.

Dresser concluded the discussion. "I'd say you have our complete cooperation, Marty." Then he glared. "But make damn certain you contain the situation. Do whatever you have to do. Don't fuck it up. If you do, there'll be consequences." He looked around at the stony expressions. The men nodded agreement. "You won't like them."

CHAPTER 51

Somewhere around the Mediterranean

ABOVE THE TURQUOISE SEA stood a small stone villa about three quarters of the way up a long green valley. It was nearly four hundred years old. Four stone cottages flanked it, two on either side, built more than a century ago for a don's large extended family. Green ivy grew up the aged white walls of the buildings, and red geraniums bloomed from window boxes.

It was a beautiful afternoon, the air scented with the perfume of honeysuckle blossoms. Don Alessandro Firenze was sitting outdoors beneath his leafy grape arbor at the side of the villa. Here was the long wood table and upright wood chairs at which he and his *compadres* gathered to drink wine and tell stories of the old days. A man in his sixties, the don was in his usual chair at the head of the table, a straw hat on the back of his head. He was alone except for his book and 9-mm Walther, which lay on the table beside a tall glass of ice tea.

He lifted his head from Plato's *Republic*. One of the

advantages of semiretirement was he could indulge himself. As a foolish youth, he had neglected his education. For the past dozen years he had spent much of his free time reading, the rest in tending his vegetable garden, grapevines, and honeybees. And of course there was the occasional outside job.

He gazed around, enjoying this piece of earthly heaven that meant so much to him. He noted the vibrant health of the bushes and flowering plants that grew around the grassy front yard. His large vegetable garden showed toward the rear, surrounded by a low white picket fence, and next to it was an enormous satellite dish and a generator in bomb- and fireproof housing. Much farther away was a honeybee colony in white boxes. The hillsides beneath the compound were lined with well-tended grapevines and dotted by gnarled olive trees. The property covered five square miles, so no neighbors disturbed him.

Through the window of one of the cottages he could see Elaine Russell in her kitchen. Her husband, George, had gone into the village for supplies. Next to their cottage was another, where Randi and Doug Kennedy napped outside in hammocks. On the other side of the villa, Jack O'Keefe—once known as Red Jack O'Keefe—was working at his computer, visible through his living room window. The other cottage was home to more of his *compadres*, two brothers. Intelligence work was as integral to all of their systems as veins and tendons, so they were merely semiretired, too. They reveled in his jobs, acting as a moral compass whenever he needed debate.

Just as he was about to return to his book, Jack came at a half-run from his door. The don watched the easy gait, remembering when the older man could run the half mile faster than most people on the planet. About five foot ten inches tall, Jack still had catlike grace. But he looked worried, his corrugated face tense.

The don said nothing.

"Dammit, we've got a problem." Jack dropped onto the chair beside him. "Someone's been trying to trace back the e-mails between Martin Chapman and me. The bastard didn't succeed, but he got damn close. I scrambled the two Internet service providers I created out of Somalia and the Antilles and shut them down. There's no way they'll find us now."

The don felt hot fury explode in his skull. He said nothing, waiting for the storm to subside. His bad temper had caused enough grief for himself and those he loved.

"You told Chapman the rules," the don said. "I told him. He agreed. Now he's broken them twice."

"I did some research on him and Douglas Preston. Preston's ex-CIA, the bastard. You'd think he'd have a better way to earn a living now. Anyway, according to Chapman's equity firm, Chapman is in Athens now. My deduction is Preston is with him, looking for Eva Blake and Judd Ryder. You told me this was about the Library of Gold, so I sent out word to our contacts and got some interesting results."

When searching for the rich and powerful, most people never thought to investigate the less obvious sources—protection services, independent bodyguards, private mercenaries, party planners, chefs, maid and nanny businesses, boat crews, pilots, anyone who served the affluent.

"You have a lead?" the don asked.

"You bet I do. Wasn't going to talk to you until I did. The problem is, it's risky."

As Jack explained the possibilities, the don took off his hat and rubbed his forearm across his gray crew cut. His fingerprints had been burned off years ago, his face altered many times by plastic surgery. He had the body of a man in his forties, although his skin had aged—a regime of hormones, vitamins, and exercise could accomplish only so much. He nodded as he listened. Yes, that would do.

"It won't be easy," Jack warned again.

"I've just been reading Plato." The Carnivore closed the book and set it beside his Walther. He gazed across his tranquil estate, wishing his daughter were here. But she did not approve of him. "It's an insightful book. I don't agree with everything. Still, one thing he wrote seems to apply: 'Only the dead have seen the end of war.'" He stood up. "Summon the *compadres*. We'll go into the villa and make preparations."

CHAPTER 52

Athens, Greece

A GREEK NEWSCAST SOUNDED from down the hotel corridor as Judd set their brunch tray on the floor outside the door. Listening, he peered left and right, then stepped back inside the room. Eva was at the table and looked tense, elbows on the top, a hand cupping her chin as she reread Charles's notebook. Last night he had thought he was going to lose her. He was glad she had decided to stick it out, except now he felt even more responsible for her.

He shot the dead bolt and grabbed Preston's S&W from under his pillow. Sitting, he emptied it of rounds, including the bullet in the chamber.

"Join me." He patted the bed beside him.

Eva looked up and saw the gun. "Are you going to shoot me or teach me?"

"Teach. Then you'll be able to shoot someone—hopefully not me."

"We'll see." She gave a small smile and sat beside him.

"This is the safety. Flick it on and off so you know how it works." When she did, he explained the basic mechanics of the weapon. "Stand up."

"Okay." She stood, long and slender, her dyed black hair falling around her face.

"Balance on both feet."

She assumed a *heikō-dachi* karate stance, her feet at shoulder-width distance and parallel. Her knees were flexed, just the way he wanted them.

He passed her the gun. "Hold it in both hands, choose a point on the wall, stretch your arms a bit, but not so much you strain yourself. Aim. . . . Stop hunching your shoulders. Let your bones relax—your muscles need to do the work." Her grip looked capable but not confident. "Your hands automatically want to coordinate with your eyes—let them do it. Good. Now squeeze the trigger." He watched. "Slow down. Pretend the trigger is a baby's ankle. You don't want to hurt it, but you've got to be firm, or the little guy will skedaddle away."

"You did a lot of babysitting in your youth?"

"I have an active imagination."

"You've raised babies in your imagination?"

"No, but I can act like one."

She laughed, settled herself, and tried the trigger again.

"Much better," he said. "You won't know how true your aim is until you fire, but this is better than nothing. Practice one hundred times—slowly. Then take a break and do another hundred. You'll begin to get the feel of the weapon and what it's like to shoot it. If you actually do have to fire, you'll get a powerful kick. This will help you prepare for that, too."

Listening to the clicks, he took out his mobile, downloaded the phone numbers of all hotels in the Athens metropolitan area, and started dialing. At each place he asked to speak to Robin Miller. There were a few Millers, but no Robin Miller. He talked to the ones he could reach. They knew no one named Robin Miller.

Finally Eva said, "That's another hundred." She did not look bored but seemed definitely fed up. "How do I load this thing?"

They sat on the bed again, and he filed rounds into the S&W's magazine. He took them out and handed the magazine to her. She fumbled for a while, then got better, sliding the bullets inside.

Finally, at around two o'clock, she put the weapon into her satchel. When he finished a call to another hotel, she held up a hand.

"Pame gia kafe," she said. "That means let's go for coffee, which in Athens really means let's go out. Enough already. You haven't heard from NSA. Robin hasn't called. Tucker isn't getting in until late. Preston has never seen our disguises, so we're reasonably safe. And once I have a cell, I can help call hotels, too."

She had a point. In fact several of them. They left.

The day was warm. Athens was having a touch of summer in April. Through a thin layer of brown smog, sunshine glazed the concrete buildings and sidewalks. They took the Metro to Plaka, the city's humming market and popular meeting place.

"We can get lost in the crowd here," she explained.

She was right. Plaka swarmed with tourists and locals, cars banned from most of the streets. They walked through winding avenues and passageways crammed with small stores selling trinkets, souvenirs, religious icons, and Greek fast food. He smelled hot shish kebabs and then the cool scent of fresh flowers. Many of the streets were so narrow, sunlight fought for a place to shine through.

"You should be aware of a couple of things before

you try to do any business in Athens," she told him. "Never raise your hand, palm up and out, when you greet someone. It's a hostile gesture here. Instead, just shake hands. And when a Greek nods up and down— especially if there's a click of the tongue and what looks like a smile—it's an expression of displeasure. In other words, *no*."

"Good to know. Thanks."

He bought her a disposable cell without incident, and they stopped at an open-air café to go back to work. So far he had seen no sign of a tail.

When the waitress came, he started to order Greek coffee, but Eva said, "Two Nescafé frappes, *parakaló*." The waitress gave a knowing smile and went inside.

"Instant coffee?" he asked, worried.

"What. You're a coffee snob?"

"I spent too many years inhaling desert sand not to appreciate a fine cup."

"Sympathies. But you really have to have it at least once. It's a local favorite, and it goes with the climate and the outdoor lifestyle. Besides, it's expensive, which means we can sit here for a couple of hours without ordering anything else."

He was doubtful but said nothing more. As he wrote a list of hotel phone numbers for her, two glasses of water and two tall glasses of a dark-colored beverage topped with foam arrived with drinking straws.

He glanced at the water and stared at the frappes.

She grinned. "I'm beginning to worry you don't have a sense of adventure."

He sighed. "What's in it?"

"Two cubes of ice, two heaping teaspoons of Nescafé powder, sugar, milk, and cold water. I know it sounds dreadful, but it's actually heavenly on a warm afternoon like this. You're supposed to drink the water first, to cleanse your palate."

"I've got to clean my palate? You must be kidding." But he drank the water.

She was sipping her frappe through her straw and laughing at him.

He tried it. It was almost chocolate, the coffee flavor strangely rich and soothing. "You're right. It's good. But next I want real Greek coffee. I like to chew as I drink."

"You have my permission." She glanced around. "I've been thinking about your dad's news clippings. I know you told me the analysts didn't see anything revealing, but I'd like to hear again what was in them."

"International banks were mentioned, and our targeting analysts have been closely monitoring their transactions. Nothing about the Library of Gold. There was a lot about affiliate jihadist groups in Pakistan and Afghanistan and the dangers they pose, but our people are already watching them so closely every one has a skin rash."

"Remember," she said, "I've been off the reservation—in prison a couple of years. Is al-Qaeda as dangerous as it was? Aren't we safer now?"

"Yes and no. It'll help if you understand al-Qaeda's structure. Years ago Osama bin Laden and his people saw what happened to Palestinian jihad groups that let new members join their leadership—intelligence agencies were able to infiltrate, map, and hurt them badly. That made al-Qaeda's leaders reluctant to expand, and after 9/11 they slammed the door entirely, which meant they couldn't even replace losses. They've had a lot—we've captured or killed most of their top planners and expediters. So now they can't compete on the physical battlefield anymore, but they don't need to. Their strength—and an enormous threat to us—is the al-Qaeda movement. It spread like wildfire during Iraq. The new jihadists revere al-Qaeda central and go to them for advice and blessings for operations, because they believe the leaders' bloody theology. It's proved to be an effective recruiting tool and keeps bin Laden and his cronies relevant—and powerful."

As the waitress passed, he ordered real coffee. "What's worrying us about Dad's clippings is the focus on Pakistan and Afghanistan, where the Taliban is strong. The two countries share a border through the mountains, but it's an artificial one the Brits created in the nineteenth century. The people on both sides— mostly Pashtuns—have never accepted it. For them the entire region has always been theirs. As for Pakistan, it's in crisis and has pulled its troops from the North-West Frontier Province. If the province falls to the jihadists, the whole country could crash. At the same time, Afghanistan has taken on its own defenses, so the U.S. and NATO have only a limited presence. Warlords rule the borderlands, and there's concern whether they have the country's best interests at heart, since many have jihadist connections."

Eva sighed worriedly. "And somewhere in there may be where your father thought something awful was being planned."

They worked two more hours without finding Robin Miller. Eva had another frappe, and he ordered another traditional Greek coffee. The sun was below the horizon, sending a violet cloak across the street's paving stones.

"It's discouraging." She put down her cell, leaned back in her chair, and stretched. "Where is that woman?"

"God knows." He leaned back, too. Just when he picked up his mobile again to phone another hotel, it rang. Quickly he touched the On button.

It was the NSA tracker. "One of the disposable cells was turned on briefly. But it's off now. I'll let you know if it's activated again." He relayed an address. Judd jotted it down and turned the paper so Eva could see it.

"It's near," she said excitedly. "South of us but still in Plaka."

CHAPTER 53

WHEN THE BOOK CLUB meeting concluded, Chapman opened the door. Mahaira was sitting in the foyer, hands folded neatly in her lap. As the members of the club trooped past to prepare for an evening on the town, she rose, smiling.

"She's taking a bath," she whispered.

Eagerly he headed across the carpet, removing the long-ago photo of beautiful blond Gemma from his pocket, burning her image into his mind.

Flushed with excitement, he hid it again and opened the bathroom door onto the opulent sanctuary of the bath, with its spacious glass shower, ornate full-length mirror, and marble-clad floor, walls, and ceiling. The air was infused with the fragrance of camellia-scented bath oil. Beneath the softly glowing crystal chandelier was the massive soaking tub set on a pedestal in the center of the enormous room. Bubbles rose above it, and above them was his gorgeous wife.

Her hair was piled on her head, a mass of golden curls, her smooth shoulders fragile and sweet. She turned to look at him, the vibrancy of youth in her violet-colored eyes, aquiline nose, and good chin.

"You're here at last, Martin. How wonderful to see you." Her voice was musical. "Bring me a towel, will you?"

"Later." Stripping off his clothes, he stalked toward her.

Her laughter sang. She balled up a washcloth and threw it, sopping, at him.

He sidestepped and climbed the pedestal naked. He slid into the tub's warm water.

She glided through the water toward him, bubbles cascading away. "I've missed you. Oh, how I've missed you."

"I've missed you, too." He pulled her to him, running his hands hungrily over her breasts, her thighs.

"Umm," she purred. "Umm, umm."

He arched her backward and nipped her shoulders. Kissed the hollow of her throat. She laughed happily, the vibrations sending shudders through him. He felt her hands on his cock, stroking, twisting, pulling.

Fever inflaming his brain, he slid his hands under her bottom and lifted, his fingers digging into muscle. She licked his ears, the tip of his nose, and locked onto his mouth. The taste of her sent a titanic wave through him. Her legs straddling him, he lowered her slowly, then, in a heated rush, pulled her down and made love to her. To Gemma.

THEY DRESSED IN THE MASTER SUITE, Beethoven playing from the tall armoire. The long rays of the setting sun spread across the carpet and touched their naked feet.

Wearing a long white skirt with a tight waist and a red silk strapless top, she sat on a brocaded chair, slipped on high heels studded with diamonds, and buckled the tiny straps around her slim ankles.

"Well, that was a waste." Chuckling, she sat up and gestured at the smoothly made bed. "I'd planned to be lying here undressed for you."

"How's Gemma?" he asked casually as he adjusted his tie in the mirror. He watched her reflection in it. She had put on her makeup, and her lips were like rubies. She looked and sounded so much like Gemma his heart ached.

"Mother's fine. She's in Monte Carlo with her new boyfriend. I do wish she'd settle down. She's costing you a fortune."

Gemma had been married five times, but never to him. The summer they graduated from college, her family had given her a choice—either end the relationship or be disinherited. To spare her the pain of choosing, he left California and hitchhiked across the country to New York City, where he dove into the pirana-infested sea of finance, determined to earn the wealth that would make him acceptable. By the time he had, she had married her second husband, who drank, gambled, and went through all her money. That husband was Shelly's father.

"She looked beautiful at the San Moritz party," Shelly said. "But she never mentioned the family necklace and earrings. Or the new tiara you bought me. I wore all of them, you know."

"Mahaira told me. I'm glad you enjoy them so much."

"Mother loves diamonds, too. She must miss having them a lot. I offered to give the necklace and earrings back to her, but she wouldn't take them. As long as I can remember, I think she's hated you. Why is that? She won't tell me."

"I suspect that's more her parents' attitude than her own." It was what he always said, because he had never understood why Gemma had been so furious at him for leaving California. It was some foolishness about insisting she had a right to be part of such an important decision. Now he breezed past his wife's questions by focusing on what she could understand: "I doubt she's ever really hated me, but now I agree she's quite unhappy about the difference in age between you and me." And, he hoped, jealous.

Shelly shook her head, her golden hair floating across her bare shoulders, and studied her four-carat diamond engagement ring and the diamond-encrusted wedding band. "I thought when you bought the family jewels to help her, she'd get over it."

He said nothing. His tie satisfactory, he turned.

"Will you be here tomorrow?" she asked eagerly.

"I have business," he said kindly.

A cold look crossed her face. "Okay. I'll fly to Cabo, then. Friends invited me."

"Where's your wrap, darling? We'll be late for cocktails." While they were separated, he yearned for her. But when they were together . . . In the end, she was not Gemma.

As they crossed the living room, his cell phone vibrated against his chest.

Looking at her, he took it out. "Sorry, darling."

She nodded, her face frozen. Alabaster.

He went into the dining room and closed the door.

It was Preston, and he sounded jubilant. "I just got a call from my NSA contact. Robin Miller turned on her cell phone, then turned it off. I've flown in men from the library for backup and to bring supplies, and we're in Plaka—that's where she was. We'll find her and *The Book of Spies* very soon now."

CHAPTER 54

ROBIN MILLER HAD HAD a busy two days in Athens, and at last she was beginning to feel prepared as she walked through the twilight and deeper into Plaka. Besides oversize sunglasses, she wore a wig—a simple brown hairdo ending just below her ears. Long bangs brushed her dyed black eyebrows. Brown contact lenses colored her blue eyes, and she wore no eyeliner or mascara, no lipstick.

Her clothes were two sizes too large—baggy cotton pants and a loose button-down cotton shirt. Only her battered tennis shoes fit—bought at the Monastiraki Flea Market. She carried a shopping bag she had found on top of a trash can. It was stuffed with crumpled newspapers, while her billfold and other items were in her pockets. The first time she caught a reflection of herself in a shop window, she had not recognized the dowdy, overweight woman. She had smiled, pleased.

Now she needed money. As usual, Plaka marketplace was bustling. Vendors called from the doors of small shops, promoting their wares. A herd of black-robed

Orthodox monks passed, holding black cell phones to their ears. She entered the little bank she had chosen and went up to a teller. Before disappearing to join the Library of Gold, she had put her life savings into a numbered Swiss account. Just a half hour ago, she had called the phone number she memorized long ago, releasing the funds to this bank.

The teller led her to a desk, where a bank officer had forms waiting. She filled in the account number and other required information and orally gave him her password.

"How do you wish the funds?" he asked.

"Four thousand in euros. A cashier's check for two thousand more. The rest in a second cashier's check. Leave the line to whom the checks are to be made out blank."

"So much money. Would you not like to open an account? It will be safe here."

"Thank you, no."

He nodded and left. Turning in her chair, she watched the people coming and going.

When he returned, he ceremoniously handed her a fat white envelope. "If there is anything more I can do to help with your financial matters, madame, please tell me."

She thanked him again and left. In total, she had about $40,000. It was not enough to ensure her safety from the book club for long. Still, at least she would have immediate cash.

The sun had set, and the shadows were deep across Plaka's crowded streets. She liked the drama of the approaching night, and it would help to hide her. She slid the envelope inside the waistband of her pants. Her feet felt light, and her heart was hopeful as she wound south through the marketplace. She wanted to be as close as possible to where she had left her rolling suitcase and *The Book of Spies*.

As she walked, she took out her cell phone and dialed. Sometimes fortune smiled. Trying to negotiate her freedom with Martin Chapman had frightened her, but now she had an alternative.

When the man's voice answered, she asked, "Is this Judd Ryder?"

"I am. Are you Robin Miller?" He had a strong voice. She liked that.

"Yes," she said. "Who are you?"

"I'm with the U.S. government. Do you know the location of the Library of Gold?"

So that was what he wanted. She ignored the question. "How did you hear about me?"

"I've been hunting for the library. I had a clue that took me to Istanbul, but Preston found me there and tried to eliminate me. There was a note in his pocket with your name, 'Athens,' and *'The Book of Spies'* written on it. Earlier, in London, I'd gotten two phone numbers off Charles Sherback's cell, but I didn't know for sure to whom they belonged. I phoned both with the same message in hopes one of them was yours."

She bit her lip. "You know who killed Charles?"

"We'll talk about that when we meet."

She had been trying to put Charles out of her mind. Whenever she thought about him, a bottomless ache filled her. The loss was so great, so raw, her world so destroyed, she had a hard time thinking. After several deep breaths, she considered her situation. Ryder had escaped Preston, which went a long way toward indicating he might really be able to protect her. And she understood his hunger to find the library.

"I'm sure Preston is searching for me," she told him. "You're lucky to have gotten away."

"Luck had nothing to do with it. Explain why I should be doing business with you." The voice had grown harder.

"I worked at the Library of Gold, but I never learned exactly where we were. I can tell you the library is on an island, but I don't know which island. We're always flown in with hoods over our heads, usually from Athens. There's a helipad, a dock, and three buildings that look as if they're a vacation compound, with a swimming pool and tennis courts. About twenty people are on staff, most of them security. Tomorrow night is the annual banquet, so beginning today Preston has been putting on even more guards."

He seemed to like her answers. "Are there other islands in sight?"

"There's one far away. When the day's particularly clear, you can see the tip of it."

"Do you have *The Book of Spies*?"

"I've hidden it in Athens, and I'm willing to sell it to you."

"All right. Let's meet."

"I want five million dollars for it," she said firmly. "Before you object, the Getty paid five-point-eight million for *The Northumberland Bestiary* just a few years ago." The *Bestiary* was a rare thirteenth-century English Gothic illuminated manuscript. "This is the only copy ever made of *The Book of Spies* and should be worth a lot more, so I'm offering you a bargain."

"You're right; it's a good deal if you look at it from your perspective. On the other hand I'm offering something of even greater value—I'm going to get you safely out of Athens. What's your life worth?"

She felt a chill. "I'll settle for three million."

"Much better. I'll make the phone call to release the funds, but it'll take a few hours for it to be deposited into your account. Or you can have it in a cashier's check or any other financial instrument you like. By tomorrow morning you'll have your money."

"A cashier's check will be fine."

With a flush of excitement, she looked around. She had left Plaka and had entered the Makrigianni district. She was on the Dionysiou Areopagitou, a wide pedestrian boulevard. To her left stood a line of stylish houses in Art Deco and neoclassical styles, and to her right was the massive Acropolis, the city's long-ago spiritual center. With a thrill she stared up the slope. She could see only a white crest of the spotlighted ruins high above. Then she noticed people were streaming past her, toward the entrance to the Acropolis park, which lay below and on which were the remains of what had been ancient Athens's intellectual and cultural center. She could see bright lights in the Theater of Dionysus. There must be a concert or show of some kind, she decided. A crowd could be useful.

She explained where she would wait for him. "What do you look like?"

When he told her, she described her disguise.

"I'll be there in only a few minutes," he assured her.

CONTROLLING HIS FRUSTRATION, Preston stood with his cell phone in his hand as he and two of his men scanned for Robin. They were in an alcove on Adrianou, Plaka's main street, which was packed with tourist shops. She had phoned from the outdoor café across the way. They had searched the area and seen no sign of her, which told him either she had spotted them and was hiding, or she had moved on.

When his cell rang, he snapped it up. The caller was Irene, his NSA contact.

"Your person of interest has been talking on her cell again." Irene sounded nervous. "The call ended about fifteen minutes ago. She was heading south. I can't help you anymore, Preston. Something's happened here. Everyone's being watched. I had to get into my car and drive off the premises to phone you. I'm worried they're going to investigate my NRO queries and searches." The NRO was the National Reconnaissance Office, which designed, built, and operated U.S. recon satellites—and collected the data from them.

Inwardly he swore. "Give me the exact information. Everything you've learned. I'll take it from here."

CHAPTER 55

THE AIR WAS WARM, the stars bright overhead as Judd and Eva hurried up wide marble paving stones to the entrance of the Acropolis architectural park. Carrying their large duffel, he bought tickets, and they passed through an open gate to where a wide path climbed a gentle slope. Tall cypress and olive trees swayed in a light wind, spectral in the night. He could see an ancient amphitheater in an open area, a magnificent sight. Its rows of crumbled white stone benches rose up the hill in a semicircle, and for a moment he imagined what it must have been like two millennia ago, the vast crowds, the excitement in the air.

The theater's base—the stage—was brightly illuminated by klieg lights. A woman in classical Greek dress stood before the large audience, which sat on blankets and cushions on the remains of the terraced rows. As she spoke into a microphone, a cluster of men and women in white robes and tunics cinched with colored braids waited at the side of the stage. A small camera crew was filming.

"Along here beneath the Acropolis," she was telling her listeners, "are the ruins of the world's first complex of buildings dedicated to the performing arts. This noble old theater dates back to before Alexander the Great. On this very stage immortal masterpieces were premiered—and drama and comedy were born."

"Am I right that we're looking at the Theater of Dionysus?" Judd asked Eva as they neared.

"Yes. It's beautiful, isn't it? When it was new, the walls, stone seating, and thrones were covered in marble and carved with satyrs and lions' paws and gods and goddesses."

Without being asked, she clasped her satchel to her side and slipped into the shadow of a tall marble block across the path from the rear of the open stage, and Judd climbed steps on the west side. The speaker continued, alternating her lecture in Greek and English.

Twenty terraces up, a woman was sitting alone at the edge, a shopping bag at her feet. She looked stiff, stressed. A couple with four children and more people sat in the same row, but close to the center. The stage lights did not reach this far, leaving only the illumination of the moon and stars to show the woman's brown hair and dumpy figure. If he had not known she was Robin Miller, he would not have recognized her.

She slid over to make room for him. "Judd Ryder?" Her tone was strained.

He sat. "Hello, Robin. Ready to get out of Athens?"

She was staring down the hillside. "Who came with you?"

Now he knew one thing—Robin was smart. She had placed herself high and in the darkness deliberately to watch unseen anyone who arrived. He had purposefully not told her earlier about Eva, since they did not know how she would react to Charles's wife—or that he had been the one who had killed Charles.

"My partner," he said. "I'll introduce you. She's keeping watch."

She nodded. "That's okay. Let's go."

He led the way back down and then across the pathway to where Eva was waiting, her black hair and dark blue jacket and jeans hidden in the shadow beside the great marble block.

"Is _The Book of Spies_ nearby?" he asked Robin.

"Yes. In a Metro station."

Eva walked out to greet them, a welcoming smile on her face.

But Robin frowned and took a step backward. "You're Eva Blake. Charles's wife. Preston told me you were involved in Charles's murder." She stared angrily at Judd. "You said she was your partner."

"She is," Judd told her. "I'll explain as we walk. Remember, we're going to help you escape. That's what matters."

Robin's face flushed as she glared at them. Then her eyes darted, and her muscles seemed to tense. Suddenly she turned, threw away her shopping bag, and rushed off toward the park's entrance.

"I'll handle this." Eva ran after her.

Judd caught up with them. Robin was marching quickly along, two furious red spots on her cheeks, her chin held high. And he saw she had not dyed her hair but was instead wearing a wig—it had slipped, exposing the back of her shaved skull. He kept pace on the other side of her.

"I'm sorry about Charles, too," Eva was saying soothingly. "No one wanted him to die. Were you in love with him?"

"What happened?" Robin snapped, not breaking her stride. "Did _you_ kill him?"

"It was an accident," Eva explained. "There was a struggle, and his gun went off. I never knew Charles to carry a gun, so that must've started after he left me. But he'd told me something important, something you should hear—he wanted the library to be found if anything happened to him. There was a message tattooed on his head, and it's what sent us to Rome and then to Istanbul. I don't want Charles's legacy to be lost, and I'll bet you don't, either."

Tears rolled down Robin's cheeks. "You killed him." She increased her furious pace.

As they exited through the park gates, Judd said, "They're suspicious of you, aren't they, Robin? Did they make you shave your head to see whether you had a tattoo, too?"

"Magus shaved it," she blurted.

"Who's Magus?" Judd asked instantly.

She shook her head, then tugged the wig back into place.

"Where exactly is *The Book of Spies*?" Judd said. "With the money we pay you, you can disappear. Start a new life. Find happiness again. Tell us where the book is, and we'll get you out of here."

"You lied to me! I've had enough of people lying to me. I was stupid to have believed you have the money or you'd give it to me anyway. Leave me alone. I'm not going to help you. Charles never loved you, Eva. Never!"

Moving at an increasingly fast clip, the three continued on. Robin's body was rigid, her expression intransigent. Judd was beginning to think there was nothing they could say to persuade her to give them *The Book of Spies*.

"You may be right about Charles." Eva moved closer to her as they entered the wide pedestrian boulevard of Dionysiou Areopagitou.

"Of course I'm right. I'll bet you never loved him, either. And then you murdered him. I'm through working with liars and murderers!"

Just then the toe of Eva's tennis shoe caught on a cobblestone. She stumbled into Robin, her hands sliding over her as she tried to stabilize herself.

Robin pushed her away. "I hate you." She ran again.

They watched as she dodged pedestrians and disappeared into the crowd.

"What did you get?" Judd asked, knowing Eva had pulled her pickpocket routine.

"A billfold, a cell phone, and a key. She said *The Book of Spies* was in a Metro station, which means it's probably in a locker. This looks like a locker key." She held it up.

He took the key and read the number. "It does. But which station?"

"You said it was nearby," she explained, "and she didn't object. It's got to be the Acropolis station. It's only a couple of blocks away."

CHAPTER 56

PRESTON RECOGNIZED ROBIN Miller's gait, the one aspect of the body most people forgot to disguise. He had noticed her as she had rushed down Dionysiou Areopagitou a half block from where she had ended her last cell call, but her hair and clothing had almost fooled him. Then as she passed, he had clearly seen her walk, the rhythmic shifts of her body, the short stride, the way she put weight on the outside of her soles.

He signaled Magus and Jerome, and all three ran after her.

Preston grabbed her arm. "We've missed you, Robin."

Terror filled her eyes. "Let me go." She tried to wrench free.

"Magus," Preston said.

Magus took her other arm, and they moved her to the side of the pedestrian boulevard. She started to struggle.

"Stop it," he ordered. "All we want is *The Book of Spies*. That isn't so hard now, is it?"

"And *then* you'll kill me."

"For what reason? There's nothing you can do to hurt us. You don't know where the library is. In fact, you know very little, do you?"

Her eyebrows lifted. She seemed to understand what he really meant. "You're right. I don't know anything about the library. Who works there, who owns it."

"Good girl."

He told Jerome to stand lookout at the beginning of a drive between two apartment buildings.

"Why do we have to go in here?" She gazed worriedly back over her shoulder as they took her down the drive.

Ahead was a parking lot, well lit, but empty of people. There was no one at the windows above.

"You don't want to be seen with us," he said. "That way there'll be no questions by anyone. You're on your own now. No more baggage from the past, right?"

She looked up at him, seemingly confused by his being understanding.

"Where's the book?" He put warmth into his tone. "Tell us, and we'll leave you here. There's only one other thing you have to do—give us a five-minute head start and go that way." He nodded to a walk that skirted the rear of the buildings.

"You're actually not planning to shoot me?"

"I'm sure you've figured out by now I'm a practical man. We're in the middle of Athens. Dead bodies mean police questions. You'll notice I haven't unholstered my weapon."

"You'll try to find me later."

"Why bother if I have the book?"

She peered at him a long time, then nodded agreement. "It's in the Acropolis Metro station. I have the key to the locker." She shook her arm, and he released it. As she slid a hand into her shirt pocket, a look of shock crossed her face.

Controlling his impatience, he said, "Maybe you put it into another pocket."

Magus freed her other arm, and she frantically searched her trousers and then her other shirt pocket.

"It's gone," she said. "My billfold and cell phone are gone, too. I don't see how all of them could've fallen out—"

"What else happened?" he asked instantly.

"Maybe Eva Blake or Judd Ryder took them somehow." She looked away. "I met them. But I didn't tell them anything. They don't know the book is in a locker in the Acropolis station."

With effort, he kept his voice calm, reassuring. "That's good. You made a mistake, and then you corrected it by not giving more information. Where are they staying, and where are they going next?"

"I don't know. I ran away from them."

"That was smart, but then I've always admired your intelligence. I'll bet you remember the locker number."

"Of course." She gave it to him.

"You're certain that's correct?"

"Of course I am."

"As a reward, I have a little gift for you." He smiled as her eyes widened. He took out a small blue bottle, flipped off the lid, and pressed the nozzle, spraying directly into her face.

She gasped and stepped away. Too late. He let her continue to walk, watching as she slowed and her knees buckled. He surveyed the parking lot and then the windows above. No one was in sight.

A fist against her chest, she sank to the ground, her oversize shirt billowing around her. Her legs spasmed. A quiet, unobtrusive death was one of the great advantages of the Rauwolfia serpentina derivative.

Glancing down the drive to Jerome, who nodded that all was well, Preston knelt over her, searching her clothes. He found a thick envelope inside her waistband and handed it up to Magus.

"Tell me what's inside." He continued to hunt but found nothing more.

Magus let out a low whistle. "She's got one pack load of euros in here."

Preston stood and took the envelope. "We've got to move fast. Watch for Judd Ryder and Eva Blake."

THE ACROPOLIS METRO STATION was on Makrigianni Street, across from lively cafés and snack bars and next to the Acropolis Study Center. Scanning everywhere, Preston and his men rushed inside the sleek station and ran down an escalator. At the base, they hurried past casts of the Parthenon friezes and stopped at the electronic ticketing machines. Two more escalators down, and they found the lockers.

As a Metro train whined to a stop, Preston ran along the lockers, alternately studying the boarding passengers and reading locker numbers until he found the correct one. His men converged to stand on either side, blocking anyone from being able to see as he took out his knife and quickly jimmied the tall door open.

And stared inside. There was no black backpack. No *Book of Spies.* On the bottom was Robin's roll-aboard, and on the shelf above lay her cell phone—open and turned on. Furious, he realized Ryder must have figured out they would use the cell to locate them. Ryder had *The Book of Spies* and was taunting him.

Preston grabbed the phone, slammed shut the locker, and turned. A bell rang, signaling the train's doors were about to close.

"Run," he ordered.

He and his men raced to different doors and leaped inside. Since they were underground, he could not call the other men he had brought to Athens and order them to watch the next stops. As the train pulled out, he noted his car was a little more than half full. Quickly he walked down the aisle, but he did not see Ryder or Blake. He spotted two backpacks—one was brown and the other green.

He checked Robin's cell, hoping for Judd Ryder's phone number. And swore. Ryder had wiped it clean. Blood pulsing with anger, he pushed through the door and entered the next car, determined to find them.

CHAPTER 57

FIGHTING TENSION, JUDD SAT across the aisle and four rows back from Eva as the Metro sped north through the underground tunnel. He was alone in his seat, while she was sitting beside a boy of about thirteen, who wore a red-and-white striped Olympiakos soccer shirt.

They had seen Preston arrive at the lockers with two men. One of them, dark-haired and beefy, had walked up and down their car twice, eying passengers as if he knew exactly for whom he was searching. But besides having black hair, Eva's face and hands were also darkened by makeup. Her eyes squinted, and a thin line of cotton slightly fattened her upper lip. Small changes could be transformational, and she now looked little like the sophisticated intellectual Judd had first seen in the British Museum. Besides his bleached hair and glasses, Judd had stuck folded cotton squares above his upper molars and had adopted a hangdog appearance.

At last the beefy man exited the car, but Preston entered, his tall muscular frame looming, his expression inscrutable. He gazed carefully at each passenger, walking slowly.

A stout woman in a black dress, her purse held firmly in both hands on her lap, spoke sharply to him in Greek. Ignoring her, he continued on, pausing at Eva's row.

"Who are you looking for?" the boy asked Preston curiously in Greek-accented English.

Preston did not answer. He peered at the duffel bag under the youth's legs but then turned to study an older couple bundled in trench coats. When he reached Judd, Judd was leaning his head against the cool glass window, his eyes heavy as he stared out into the monotonous tunnel. Finally Preston moved on again.

The men continued to walk through the car, slower each time, but they never seemed to identify Eva or him. Ten minutes later the Metro pulled into the Syntagma Square station, and Judd watched Eva lean toward the boy and whisper. He smiled and nodded. As the train stopped, they stood, and she preceded him out of the car. He was carrying Judd's duffel.

Judd let the older couple and another passenger feed in, and then he left, too, keeping his place in the crowd.

Preston and his two men were standing at the exit, scrutinizing everyone again. As the train left the station, Eva and the boy chatted animatedly in Greek. Preston's eyes flickered over them, then paused to stare a long time at Eva as they walked past. Judd found himself holding his breath.

But again Preston turned, and he checked the older couple in their body-covering trench coats. Finally he settled on Judd. Judd made no eye contact; it was a sure way to attract interest. Expression unchanged, Preston peered behind him, and with relief Judd stepped onto the escalator.

The station was as glossy and modern as the one at the Acropolis stop. It, too, was a museum, with ancient urns, perfume bottles, and bells on display in lighted glass cases. Judd hurried past them, following Eva and the boy up two more escalators and out into the city's cooling night.

At the curb, Eva looked back at Judd through the crowd. Glancing carefully around, he nodded. She spoke again to the youth and then took the duffel bag from him. He walked away.

Watching a moment to make certain the boy was all right, Judd joined her at the taxi stand, and she handed over the bag.

"My God." She beamed. "That was exhilarating."

Her blue eyes were bright, and she chuckled. She looked very alive, as if she had hit the winning home run in the World Series. He suddenly realized how well she had handled events tonight, sliding unasked into the shadow of the marble block across from the Theater of Dionysus, not inflaming Robin further by admitting he had been the one who had shot Charles, and coming up with the idea to ask the Greek boy to help her onto the Metro train with the duffel with the excuse her back ached.

But then Eva had spent two years in a pickpocket gang. She knew what it was to set up and act in a movie, and what it was like to be under the constant threat of discovery. The two years in prison had taught her more—how to go deep inside herself to survive and, despite the circumstances, to take risks. Now she'd had her crisis of conscience and committed herself to the mission. He was not sure he liked what he saw now.

"You're kidding, right?" he asked hopefully.

Her face broke into a smile, and she laughed.

He had been scanning as they stood in line, the rumble of Athens's wild traffic beside them, filling all three lanes. Eva tugged his sleeve just as he spotted Preston and his two men hurrying toward them from the Metro station. There was no hesitation—the men had pinpointed them. They were drawing their pistols.

"Come on." Judd pushed past the two people ahead of them.

A taxi was pulling up. He yanked open the rear door, and Eva threw herself inside. He tossed in the duffel and dropped in next to her as she told the driver in Greek to leave quickly. It was a one-way street, so there was no way they could do a U-turn. They would have to drive past Preston.

"Get down," Judd snapped as the vehicle rushed off.

They fell low. Shots rang out, and rounds slashed through the doors and roof. Metal and plastic sliced through the air. The driver swore loudly, and the car hurtled faster. More bullets cut through the taxi, and then there was no feel of acceleration. Judd looked up just in time to see the driver collapse silently onto his side, sprawling across the front seat.

"Jesus."

"What's happened?" Eva asked quickly.

The vehicle slowed. It wove from side to side. Horns honked, and drivers shouted as they swerved their cars to get out of the way. The cars behind were signaling, trying to pass.

"The driver's been shot. Stay down," Judd ordered.

Preston was racing along the curb after them, his two men on his heels. They would reach the taxi much too soon.

Judd snatched out his Beretta. "Keep my door open until I get to the driver's side."

Her eyes wide, Eva nodded.

He opened his door. Hunching, he sprinted along the still-moving cab. Rounds crashed through the door and bit into the pavement around his feet, exploding needle-sharp shards. Suddenly hot pain sliced across his side and burned up into his brain. He fought dizziness.

As he rounded the hood, he saw through the windshield Preston had jammed his gun into the open passenger window of a tall SUV four cars behind, all rolling slowly, unable to pass in the fast traffic in the other lane.

As the three men took over the big vehicle, Judd jerked open the driver's door, and Eva closed the one in back. Still running, he shoved the downed taximan across the seat, causing a scalding pain to split up from his side. He gave his head a quick shake and dropped inside. There was an open stretch ahead. He floored the gas feed, his door slamming itself shut. He pressed his forearm against the gunshot wound in his side, trying to slow the blood.

"Is he alive?" Eva leaned over the front seat.

"Get down, dammit."

Behind them, one of Preston's men had his pistol out the window of the hijacked SUV, aiming over the roofs of the vehicles between them. There was a vegetable truck in the other lane. Judd accelerated, overtaking it. He signaled. The truck continued its lumbering speed. He spun the steering wheel, forcing the taxi's nose into the lane in front of the truck. The truck's horn blasted. He heard a loud curse, but the truck gave way, and he slid the taxi into the slot just as the traffic light turned red. There were cars between him and it. No way to run the red light, and Preston's SUV was coming up swiftly on the right.

"Grab the duffel. We've got to get out of here. My side of the cab."

With the taxi still rolling, they stepped out and ran through the traffic. Cars swerved. More horns honked. As they reached the sidewalk, Judd tried to take the duffel.

But Eva held on to it, staring at his bloody jacket.

"You're wounded." She looked around quickly. "I know where we are. This way."

He holstered his Beretta, pressed his arm against the wound again, and followed as she moved swiftly among pedestrians. The noise of idling engines filled his head. Stores were alight, shoppers showing through the windows.

"Preston's coming," he told her.

She hurried inside a large store selling casual clothes. Racks and stacks of women's jeans, shirts, and dresses marched back deep into the building. A saleswoman greeted them in English. Eva said hello and kept walking. Judd felt the eyes of the clerks looking after them.

As the store's front door opened and Preston and his men entered, Eva led Judd into a hallway at the rear. They ran past changing rooms. She turned a doorknob, and they were out again in the night, this time in a cobbled alleyway where trash cans and empty packing boxes were stacked against the walls.

Running, they passed doors.

"Open this one," she told him. "I'll do the next." She leaned over and snatched up two pieces of broken cobblestone. "Prop the door."

His door led into some kind a restaurant, the spicy odor of sauteeing garlic wafting out. He dropped the rock, leaving the door ajar. And met her as she nicked her rock into place. Without a word she ran again and opened a third door. They rushed inside to a short corridor where there were bathrooms. The noise of voices and clinking glasses assaulted them. They were in a bar.

Bolting the door, she took a deep breath. "How badly are you hurt?" She looked up at him, her face full of worry.

"I think it's superficial."

"I hope like hell you're right."

As they walked quickly into the long, crowded room, he chuckled. "Where did you learn a distraction technique like that with the doors?"

She smiled at the bartender as they passed. "A long time ago, in a city far, far away, to paraphrase *Star Trek*."

"In other words L.A. We need to make sure one of those killers isn't posted on the sidewalk."

His hand inside his jacket on the hilt of his pistol, he stepped outside first, looking through the pedestrians. She stood behind him in the doorway.

"Looks good." He felt his heart rate decelerate.

"I'll get us a taxi," she told him.

He let her do it.

CHAPTER 58

TUCKER ANDERSEN PACED THE ROOM in the Hotel Hecate. Judd had left an envelope containing the card key at the front desk for him. After checking in to a room for himself, he had come here to theirs. Waiting two hours, he had been reading Charles Sherback's notebook. When he heard the *click* of a card key in the lock, he pulled out his Browning, slipped into the bathroom, and stood behind the door.

Watching through the crack, he saw the door open slowly and the head of a bleached-blond man appear, gray eyes surveying the room.

Tucker stepped out. "Where the hell have you been?"

"Sightseeing." Carrying a paper sack from a pharmacy, Judd walked in, his gait easy. But there was a sea of blood down the side of his brown jacket.

Eva slipped in behind him and closed and bolted the door. "Glad you're here, Tucker. We've had a few problems. Preston shot Judd, but we got *The Book of Spies*. Robin Miller had it stored in a Metro locker."

She set a large black duffel bag on the table, then

took the sack from Judd and dumped out bandages and other supplies. The aspirin and over-the-counter pain-killers had been opened.

"That's very good," Tucker said. "Congratulations. Don't lie down, Judd. Let's have a look at your side."

As Judd removed his jacket and peeled off his polo shirt, Tucker took in Eva's black hair and darkened skin and peered from one to the other and back again, as-sessing the atmosphere. They radiated tired urgency—and they had become a close team.

As soon as Judd's torso was exposed, Tucker and Eva converged. The injury was a raw red gash through the fleshy part of his waist—long, a good half inch deep, and weeping blood.

"You got lucky, Judd." Tucker saw Eva head for the medical supplies on the table. "Have you ever cleaned and sewn a wound?" he asked her.

She turned. "No."

"Okay. Judd, take off your jeans and come into the bathroom. Let's get started." He wondered whether Eva would turn out to be squeamish.

He grabbed sterile latex gloves, sterile cotton, anes-thetic spray, and antibiotic soap. In the bathroom, he told Judd to sit straddling the edge of the tub. As Eva watched, he put on the gloves, sprayed on the anes-thetic, waited, then squirted the soap inside and around the gash, patting and rubbing gently. Judd made no sound, although Tucker knew it must hurt like hell. He poured glasses of water over the injury, washing it for three minutes. Then he dried Judd's side with cotton and his leg with a towel. He glanced up at Eva. She was following intently.

When they returned to the room, Judd sat on a chair and swallowed more painkillers. His face was pale. Tucker sprayed on more anesthetic, found the right size needle from the supplies, and held it over the flame of a match. After threading fishing line into it, he ran the antibiotic cream over it and laid a thick line of cream inside the wound.

"Time for more pain," he warned.

Judd nodded. "Do your worst."

"The idea is to sew as far away from the cut as the injury is deep," he told Eva. "Then you cut the line and tie a knot every quarter inch."

He heard small noises in Judd's throat as he worked, but Judd did not move. When he finished, the younger spy's face dripped sweat.

Judd sighed deeply and looked up at Eva. She smiled at him.

Tucker taped on a thick sterile bandage. "Go lie down," he ordered.

Judd did, stretching out and propping up his head on pillows. Eva took the quilt off her bed and covered him.

"You look comfortable," she said.

"I'm enjoying myself." He grinned, but his sweaty skin was pasty.

"Good," Tucker said. "Let's get to business. Report."

Going to the duffel bag, Eva described Robin's phone call, Judd's meeting her at the Theater of Dionysus, and Robin's running off.

"Eva got the key to the Metro locker from Robin." Judd gave Eva a proud glance. "She pickpocketed her, did it so well Robin didn't have a clue."

"What happened to Robin?"

"We don't know." Eva opened the duffel. "She wasn't with Preston when he arrived at the Metro with three men."

"I suspect once he got the information from her about where she'd stashed *Spies,* he killed her," Judd said.

They were silent a moment.

"A nice Greek boy was helping me with the duffel on the Metro," Eva said. "Judd and I were split up, and the ride turned out to be safe. After that the men followed us out. We were escaping when Judd was shot. I'm not sure how they identified us."

"I doubt it was electronically," Judd said.

"He's right. My cell phone's gone, and there's no way Preston could've bugged either of us. He was never close enough."

"Training of some kind," Tucker decided.

Eva opened the bag and with both hands lifted out a foam-covered bundle. "This is *The Book of Spies*." She carried it to her bed and removed layers of foam. "Robin told us the library was on a private island, only one other island visible in the far distance. Three buildings, tennis courts, a swimming pool, and a helipad. She was flown from Athens with a hood on, but at least that gives us a radius. The problem is it's a big radius. The island could be anywhere from the Black Sea to the Aegean, Ionian, or Mediterranean seas. And there's a vast number of islands; Greece has more than two thousand, and many are private. The other piece of information you should know is tomorrow night is the library's annual banquet, so there'll be a lot of security on the island, wherever it is."

She went into the bathroom and washed her hands.

Moving slowly, Judd sat up on the edge of the bed to watch as she unwrapped transparent polyethylene sheeting. His color was returning to normal, and a sense of hope infused the room. Tucker joined him, leaning forward, hands clasped between his knees. At last only the archival polyester film remained. The golden cover of the illuminated manuscript shone through.

Eva peeled back the film. "Ah," she breathed.

They stared, silenced by the dramatic artistry of the softly glowing gold, the pearl dagger, the ruby drop of blood, the emerald border. The first time Tucker had seen the book, he had been bowled over. He was still awed.

"I can't believe you took off one of the emeralds so you could bug the book, Tucker," Eva scolded.

"I've still got it. We can glue it back on."

"It's a desecration. If the bug hadn't helped us find the book, I'd really be mad." But she smiled.

He found himself smiling back. "Being a heathen goes with the job."

Eva sat cross-legged on the floor in front of the men, her back to them, facing the book. "Tell me, oh *Book of Spies*, where inside you is the secret to the Library of Gold?" She turned the pages slowly.

They studied the progression of extravagant pictures, beautiful Cyrillic letters, stunning borders. As time passed, Tucker stood up and stretched, then sat again to focus. More pages turned until at last they reached the end of the book—four hundred parchment pages. There was nothing unusual, no contemporary writing, no sign the book had been tampered with at all.

Tucker paced. "I was reading Charles's notebook before you got here, hoping he'd left the answer there."

"I know. Both of us have studied it, too." Eva stood up and went to Judd's jeans, fishing out a billfold. "This is Robin's. Maybe she was lying to us about not knowing where the library is."

"I'm going to call NSA," Judd announced. "Hand me my mobile please, Eva."

Eva reached into his jacket pocket and carried it and the billfold to the bed. As Judd phoned and gave a description of the island, she spread out the billfold's contents—euros, a photo of Charles, and a photo of Edinburgh. Tucker and she inspected everything closely but found nothing useful.

Judd ended the call. "They'll get back to me as soon as they have some information."

"How are you feeling, Judd?" she asked.

"Better. Definitely better," Judd said. "How about another hit of pain pills?"

Shaking his head at Judd's lie, Tucker got them for him. "I'm going to order food. We need to eat. It'll help us to think."

"I'm hungry, too," Eva said. "I'd love a bottle of retsina with dinner. I'll take my shower now." She studied Judd a moment then went into the bathroom and closed the door.

Tucker picked up the phone. "What do you want to eat?"

"Anything. Just order."

As Tucker did, Judd closed the book and examined the binding and spine. At last he shook his head and set it back down. Then he lay on the bed again, pulling the quilt over him.

"Good thing Eva's with us," he said. "She knows what to look for."

"How's everything going between you two?"

"Fine."

"You like Eva."

"Not the way you mean. Don't worry. No fraternizing."

Tucker thought about how he had met his own wife. "That's not what I mean."

"I won't let it interfere with the job." His expression toughened. "They killed Dad."

"I remember. I also know you lost a woman who was very important to you in Iraq. You almost got busted out of the army for going after her killer."

Judd gazed evenly at him. "That was a long time ago."

"Was it?"

The bathroom door opened, and Eva walked out,

so clean she glistened. Her cobalt blue eyes seemed brighter, and her lanky frame more curvaceous. She exuded sexuality but seemed unaware of it.

"Is dinner here yet? I'm starving." She gazed happily at both men.

Judd looked away.

LATER, AT THE TABLE BESIDE the radiator, they ate braised cuttlefish fresh from the docks at Piraeus, the city's seaport a few miles away, accompanied by mushroom pilaf, grilled red and green peppers, and fiery *kopanistopita,* filo triangles stuffed with spicy cheese. The wine was retsina, as Eva had requested.

"Tastes like pine resin." Tucker rotated the glass in his hand, inspecting the deep red color.

"It's the wine of Greece," she said. "I haven't had any this good in years. The reason for the name and the taste is the ancient Greeks knew air was the enemy of wine, so they used pine resin to seal the tops of the amphorae and even added it to the wine itself."

"I like it, too." But Judd had hardly touched his. He turned to Tucker. "What's the situation in Washington?"

Tucker put down his fork. "I talked to Gloria before I took off from Baltimore. The fellow who tried to wipe me is in Catapult's basement. She managed to get him downstairs without anyone's seeing. She's the only one who knows what's going on."

"Thank God for Gloria," Judd said. "Eva, let's talk about Charles, about what he told you in London. Maybe he gave you another clue to where the Library of Gold is, but you just didn't recognize it at the time."

She repeated their conversation, and the two men listened closely. At last they sat back.

Tucker shook his head. "Nothing."

Continuing to analyze, they finished dinner. Afterward, Eva sat on her bed, again going through *The Book of Spies*. NSA called Judd and gave him a list of four islands in the Ionian, Aegean, and Mediterranean seas that met or were close to Robin's description. But which of the four?

As they were puzzling over the list, Judd's mobile rang. They watched as he snapped it up.

"Hello, Bash. What's happened?" Judd's square face grew grim as he listened to the Catapult man in Rome. Then: "Stay on it. Let me know as soon as you learn anything."

Tucker and Eva were silent. It was obvious the news was bad.

When he ended the connection, Judd told them, "Yitzhak and Roberto are missing. Bash called every morning in case they needed anything, but they didn't answer today. He went over to their flat. It'd been torn apart, searched. At least there wasn't any blood. He talked to the neighbors. One saw Yitzhak and Roberto walking away with two men who fit the description of two of the janitors who were outside Yitzhak's house when the Charboniers attacked us. Then Bash checked with the university where Yitzhak is a professor. The department secretary told him he had phoned yesterday for her to find a teaching replacement because he was going out of town. She had a package for him from the Vatican Library, so she sent it with a student. Yitzhak met him outside a trattoria. That's the last time anyone from the university saw him."

"No," Eva said.

"Jesus." Tucker sat back in his chair. "The Library of Gold people have them."

CHAPTER 59

THE EVENING WAS JUST BEGINNING. It was only ten o'clock, but Alexander's was already packed with patrons. The leather bar stools were filled, and people stood behind, drinking. Voted by *Forbes* magazine the best hotel bar in the world, Alexander's boasted marble-topped tables, beach-umbrella palms, and an eighteenth-century tapestry of victorious Alexander the Great, hanging across the wall behind the long bar. Of course the clientele was the best in the city and from abroad. The aroma of rich liquors and designer perfumes scented the air

Martin Chapman was drinking Loch Dhu, the only black whiskey with a mellow charcoal aftertaste. He savored the rich flavor, felt the heat. After dinner in Churchill's with his wife and Keith and Cecilia Dunbar—investors in shopping malls Chapman & Associates was building in Moscow—the four had moved to a central spot in the bar where they could be seen. Chapman estimated some $30 billion was sitting around their table alone.

"Ah, no," Keith was saying. "The Grand Caymans are perhaps fine for the untutored. But I far prefer Liechtenstein for my money."

"What about Britain's Channel Islands?" Shelly asked with a glance at Chapman, showing him she knew a thing or two herself.

But as Keith launched into an explanation, Chapman's cell phone vibrated. He looked at the screen and saw Preston was calling. Excusing himself, he wound off through the crowd, feeling Shelly's dark look on his back.

"Yes?" he answered, hoping for good news.

"I'm outside the hotel, sir. I'll be waiting."

The connection went dead. Chapman's lungs tightened, and he marched through the lobby. The massive front doors opened, and he hurried out and down the steps. The dark night air enveloped him. Preston was across the street, in the plaza.

"How bad is it?" Chapman asked as he joined him.

Preston showed no signs of a fight—his clothes neat, his hair combed, his face and hands clean—but he radiated disgust as he stood between pools of lamplight. They walked off together.

"It's not an entire disaster," Preston said. "I terminated Robin Miller with the Rauwolfia spray. I thought you'd enjoy that."

The drug was a derivative of Rauwolfia serpentina, developed at Bucknell Technologies under Jonathan Ryder. It depressed the central nervous system and killed in seconds. Vanishing from the body in minutes, it was named for Leonhard Rauwolf, a sixteenth-century German botanist whose notes Jonathan had discovered in one of the Library of Gold's illuminated manuscripts on trees, plants, and herbs. Preston was right. It was appropriate one of Jonathan's creations had been the instrument of a successful step in a business deal he had tried to stop.

"The problem is we didn't get *The Book of Spies*." Preston's lips thinned as he described what had happened. "I managed to wound Judd Ryder."

"How did you identify Eva Blake?" Chapman asked.

"At first I didn't. Then when the Metro stopped, she passed me at the exit, and I thought I recognized her walk from when I studied her in L.A. I watched from the window as she went outside. She took a duffel bag big enough to hold *The Book of Spies* from the kid who'd been sitting next to her, and then a man met her—he was the right size and age to be Ryder." He filled in more details.

Chapman's mind worked furiously. "In Istanbul you found out from Yakimovich that the old librarian wrote the library's location in the book. As long as the book's in circulation, we could have serious trouble. And God knows whether there are other clues out there somewhere. We can't take the chance Ryder, Blake, or someone else will find the library. Phone Carolyn Magura to get ready. How long will it take to move the library?"

Ten years ago the book club had decided that electronic monitoring and international communications were advancing so rapidly that discovery of the island could become a problem. It was time to find a backup home. A remote area in the Swiss Alps on a glacier-fed lake north of Gimmelwald had been perfect. The place had been ready for years, managed by a skeleton crew.

"Yes, sir. I'll get everything ready," Preston said. "Figure a day and a half."

"Tomorrow night's banquet will be our last on the island. A fitting end to a good long run. Plan to move out the next morning." For a moment nostalgia swept through him. Then worry returned. "What about the Carnivore. Have you found him?"

"Mr. Lindström's computer chief hasn't been able to track him."

"Christ. Has your man in Washington eliminated Tucker Andersen yet?"

Preston paused. "Both have vanished. We're looking for them."

Chapman controlled his temper. "You do that. I'm going to move against Catapult. We can't afford to let the situation in Washington get any worse than it is."

CHAPTER 60

Washington, D.C.

IT HAD BEEN A LONG DAY at Catapult, and Gloria Feit was clearing her desk to leave. The usual office chatter sounded from the corridors. As she folded her reading glasses, she noticed a soft sound as the door behind her opened. She turned.

"I need to see you, Gloria." Hudson Canon's bulldog face vanished back inside his office.

With a quiver of uneasiness, she walked after him.

"Close the door and sit down." He was already settled behind his desk, his big hands splayed on top.

She thought for a moment about the man in the basement who had tried to erase Tucker, but she had taken the spare keys to the door from the lockbox and they were safely in her purse. There was no way Canon or anyone else knew the man was down there. He would not talk, but he was eating like an elephant.

She settled herself into one of the chairs facing the

desk, crossed her legs casually, and put a pleasant smile on her face.

"What can I do for you, boss?"

"Where's Tucker?" The question was abrupt, the tone full of authority.

She gave a little frown. "He hasn't returned. That's all I know."

"When he called in, what did he say?"

That took her aback. How did Canon know Tucker had phoned from the grocery store to have her pick up his attacker, and later from the Baltimore airport? Then she realized he could have checked Catapult's automated phone logs.

"He asked whether I wanted a sandwich from Capitol City market," she lied. "I told him no. He called a second time, but I don't know from where. He asked if there were any important messages for him. There weren't. That was the last I heard. Are you worried something's happened to him? I don't think you need to be. He would've told me if he was in trouble and needed backup."

He leaned forward. "What's he up to?"

"I haven't a clue."

"Is it more of this nonsense about the Library of Gold?"

"Well," she said carefully, "it is the operation he's focused on. But it's not the only one he's managing, of course."

"That operation is over. You and I both know that that's what he's working on. He's disobeying a direct order."

The force of his intensity shook her. "I haven't heard anything about any of that."

"So Tucker didn't tell you he had a deadline. Now you're informed. It's your duty to help find him. The Senate subcommittee on intelligence is investigating waste in the CIA. They're meeting tomorrow. I had to tell Matt about Tucker. It's minor in some ways, but it's the sort of thing they're looking into. It won't be good for Tucker. He needs to report in."

Matt Kelley, head of the Clandestine Service, was an old friend of Tucker's. It seemed impossible he would report or reprimand Tucker for something so small.

"It's less than minor," Gloria insisted. "My God, if we held our breath over every incident like this with one of our officers, we'd all die of asphyxiation. We have to rely on their being self-starters, entrepreneurial."

Canon shook his big head. "One of the senators knows about it. She sits on the subcommittee. She's got a bone between her teeth, and she's not letting go. She wants Tucker."

"How did she hear?" she asked, shocked.

"God knows," he snapped back. "But that's the situation. We don't want Tucker to be burned. Where is he? What's he doing?"

She was silent, remembering her long history with the spymaster. She had always trusted him, and he had always trusted her. And all the evidence pointed to Hudson Canon's being dirty. Still, he did not sound dirty.

She took a deep breath. "I'm sorry, Hudson. If I knew where Tucker was, I'd say so."

He stared. "You'd damn well better tell me if you hear anything. Go home and think. Think hard. We've got to find Tucker."

HUDSON CANON STOOD IN front of the mirror in his office, adjusting his tie. His face seemed pale. He slapped both cheeks. When the color returned, he cracked open his door. Gloria was gone. Good. He marched down the corridor, stopping in offices, asking whether anyone had had contact with Tucker or knew where he was. All claimed ignorance. Finally he went into Tucker's office and closed the door. He searched the desk and the file cabinets. In the bottom drawer, he found a bottle of whiskey. He opened it and drank deeply. At least he had uncovered something useful.

Wiping his mouth, he went down the corridor again, repeating his questions and again getting nothing. Then he stepped inside the communications center and stopped at every desk until he reached Debi Watson.

"Where's Tucker?" he asked her.

She peered up, her large eyes wide. "I don't know, suh."

"When's the last time you talked with him?"

"Yesterday. It was just the usual instructions."

He fought impatience. "What were they?"

"To track a cell phone number. I turned it over to NSA."

"Call NSA."

Quickly she picked up her phone and dialed.

"I'll take that." He snapped the phone from her hands. "This is Hudson Canon. Tell me exactly what you've been doing for Tucker Andersen."

"Just a minute. Let me get into that file." The man on the other end of the line paused. "All right, here it is. We traced a cell phone number for him. It was last turned on in the Acropolis Metro station in Athens. I reported the information to Judd Ryder. Then I got a call to locate an island for them. I found four."

An island? That was something Canon knew nothing about. Still, he felt a moment of relief. At least he had something to tell Reinhardt Gruen: Judd Ryder was in Athens and had received information directly from NSA. "You obviously have Tucker Andersen's and Judd Ryder's mobile numbers. I need to know exactly where both are."

"I'll have to get back to you. I've got to go through NRO, you know, and if Ryder and Andersen are using secure mobiles, it'll take some time."

Canon gave him his number. "As soon as you get the information, call me immediately. And I mean *immediately*."

CHAPTER 61

Athens, Greece

DAZZLING MORNING SUNLIGHT illuminated the quiet hotel room. As Judd slept, Eva lay back down on her bed, dressed again in her jeans and green shirt. Tense, she threw her arms above her head and stared out the window as a redtail hawk circled lazily against the blue sky. She'd had a restless night, awaking and drowsing, then awaking again, haunted by a sense she already knew where in *The Book of Spies* the librarian had likely written the Library of Gold's location—if she could just figure it out.

"How long have you been awake?"

She turned her head. Judd was staring at her, gray eyes sleepy, bleached hair messy. She studied him for any signs of fever.

"Not sure. An hour maybe. How are feeling?" She handed him aspirin, painkillers, and a glass of water.

"Much better. You've been thinking." He propped himself up on an elbow and took the medication.

"Yes. About where in *Spies* the librarian would've left a message. I've been going over everything Charles told me again and again, and what I remembered from his notebook. I know I'm close to the answer."

He was silent. "Too bad Charles didn't leave a different clue."

She frowned. "Say that again."

"Too bad Charles didn't leave a—"

"*Different* clue. That's it." She sat up excitedly. "I was looking for what we hadn't used before. Big mistake." She hurried to the big *Book of Spies,* which lay closed on the table.

"What are you talking about?" In his T-shirt and shorts, Judd pulled up a chair and sat beside her.

"The reason we shaved Charles's head was the story about Histiaeus and the slave messenger. So maybe it wasn't a clue just to check Charles's scalp; maybe it's where we're supposed to look inside *Spies*, too. I know I saw the story here somewhere."

She turned pages quickly. Finally, in the middle of the big book, she found the tale on a single page as ornate as the others, decorated with Persian and Greek soldiers along the outside margin. Black Cyrillic letters filled the rest of the space, the text block recounting the ancient narrative.

"I don't see anything unusual." Judd stared.

"Me neither. I'm going to translate the story quickly to myself." As she read, it was soon clear the recounting was much as Herodotus had chronicled it centuries before. Finished, she sat back.

"Nothing?"

She shook her head, then picked up the book. "I need light."

They sat on the side of her bed, where sunlight streamed through the window. Holding the book open on her lap, she leaned close. In her life as a curator she had learned an old adage was true—the devil was in the details. Now that she had an overview, she studied the spaces between the letters and words and the brush-strokes. When nothing struck her, she moved on to the paintings of soldiers.

She sat up straight. "I think I've found it. Look at these, Judd." She pointed to tiny letters beneath some of the colors.

He leaned close. "They're almost invisible."

"They're meant not to be noticed. They stand for the Latin words the artist who painted them was instructed to use to fill in the line drawings. This *v* means *viridis*, or green. So the robe on the slave is painted various shades of green. The *r* is for *ruber*, or red—the apples on that tree behind him. And of course the sky is *a*, *azure*, for blue."

He frowned, puzzled. "Then what do *lat* and *long* and the numbers with each mean?"

She grinned. "That's the same question I asked my-self. In the first place, I've never known anything like three or four letters strung together to indicate a color on a manuscript page. In the second place, neither is a Latin word."

He grinned back. "Since we're looking for the loca-tion of the island, I'm guessing they're abbreviations. Add in the fact there are numbers—*latitude* and *longi-tude*."

"As Archimedes said, eureka!"

He grabbed his mobile and activated it. "This is where being online gets really useful. Read what you have to me, and we'll see whether we're right."

He lowered the mobile so she could watch the screen. As he tapped the keyboard, Google's world map ap-peared, shifted, then shifted again, shrinking to the south Aegean Sea.

His forehead knitted. "Nothing. No island. No atoll. Not even a pile of rocks."

She felt a chill. "Try again." She gave him the digits, one at a time.

He entered each carefully. Again the map zeroed in on empty sea. Her shoulders slumped. He tried other public domain maps. The only sound in the room was the clicking of the keyboard. But each map showed the same disheartening results.

They were silent.

"It doesn't make sense," she insisted. "The easiest, most direct explanation for the abbreviations and numbers in the book is they're meridian points. Even if those are old maps, they should show an island."

He stared at her. "Not true. By God, if I'm right, it's a real display of the power of the book club." Again he tapped the keyboard. "Because of terrorism, the government mandated Google and other online map services not show certain places in the world. Sometimes it was a government facility. Other times it was an 'area of interest' that was clandestine for one reason or another. Private companies doing defense work could ask the government to make spots off-limits, too."

"How could the book club get the government to hide their island?"

"An inside source, or maybe someone they bribed. Let's check this."

He called up the text message he had received yesterday from NSA, and they read the list of islands that had come close to fitting Robin's description.

"My God," Eva breathed as they stared. "One of the islands has the same coordinates as the book has."

Relieved excitement rushed through her. She flung her arms around Judd's neck, and he hugged her tight.

Feeling the steady beat of his heart, his breath spicy against her ear, she lingered for a moment.

Then pushed away. "You'd better call Tucker."

The spymaster arrived in minutes, wearing the same rumpled chinos, button-down blue shirt, and sports jacket from the day before. Eva saw the lines on his face were deeper, and the large eyes behind his tortoiseshell glasses were red-rimmed from lack of sleep. But his light brown mustache and gray beard were neat, and he radiated hyper alertness.

"You've found it?" he said as he bolted the door behind him.

"Damn right she did." Judd pointed at Eva.

She smiled, pleased. "Took me a while, though."

They sat around the table, and she explained how they had discovered the answer.

"I'll get back in touch with NSA for the latest satellite photos and data about the island," Judd said brusquely. "Eva, is your laptop still working, or did it get doused when we were on the yacht?"

"It was in the main pocket of my satchel, so it's fine."

"Good. I'll forward what NSA sends to it."

"Does the island have a name?" Tucker asked.

"Just a number," Judd told him.

"Do it," Tucker ordered. "Now."

CHAPTER 62

Khost Province, Afghanistan

AFTER A LARGE BREAKFAST, Syed Ullah walked out to the front porch of the redbrick villa where he, his wife, and remaining children and grandchildren lived with the wives and children of his four brothers, all of whom had died fighting the Soviets, the Taliban, al-Qaeda, or local clans and tribes.

Restored from rubble on land his family had long owned, the sprawling villa stood two stories above the hard-packed earth. A satellite uplink dish was behind it next to a rusty Soviet T-55 tank. There was a vegetable garden to one side, with apple, peach, and mulberry trees just as there had been when he was a child. He had planted everything in the last few years. The young trees were like the future, he had told his youngest and last remaining son—strong, but they must be protected.

Wearing turbans and wraparound sunglasses, his gunmen prowled around the rebuilt stone wall that surrounded the expansive property. A dozen tribal elders—striking old men with high-bridged noses and the beards of patriarchs—were lining up in front of the porch to pay their respects. At fifty-four, Ullah had fought off and killed his rivals for this position, but that was the way it had been for decades. Men had little food for their bellies but plenty of rounds for their guns. He could hardly remember when it was otherwise.

The warlord sat down on his tall-backed wood chair on his brick front porch. Adjusting his girth, he nibbled sugared almonds as he greeted the elders courteously, accepted their respectful sentiments, adjudicated neighbor disputes, and assured them of his protection. These were men with large families and sons and grandsons and great grandsons whom he needed.

"It is tomorrow night?" the last elder said. There was impatience on his leathery face, indicating he had expected someone to have asked earlier.

"Tonight," Ullah corrected him, then he addressed the others. "Stay in your houses with your wives. Your sons know what to do."

And then they were gone, scattering the chickens and marching off into the mountains and down toward the town of some three thousand. In the hills he could see a small U.S. army patrol driving along a dirt road in two armored HMMWVs—Humvees—painted in camouflage colors. A donkey with a high bundle was being led down a treacherous path.

The warlord stood up, a giant of a man, burly and strong, with a fierce face that could easily break into a smile. But that was the strength of the Pashtun—resilience. He took great pride in his heritage of warriors, poets, heroes, jokesters, and warm-hearted hosts. They loved the land and their families. Centuries of being conquered and occupied had changed nothing, only hardening their devotion. His devotion.

His family must survive, after that his clan, and then his tribe.

He studied the vast sweep of rugged mountains, where snow glistened on the high slopes. Serpentine ribbons of smoke curled up from houses in the distance, mostly made of mud bricks with thatched roofs. A maze of smoke tendrils rose over the town, where many of the buildings had been pulverized by fighting and raids. Khost province was a crossroads of trade and smuggling, and in the crosshairs of the Taliban and al-Qaeda, who sneaked in from North Waziristan directly across the border in Pakistan. They came under the cover of night to recruit, do business, and murder collaborators, often local police.

On the far side of the town was America's secret and highly secure forward base, painted in camouflage colors and draped with camouflage netting to make it invisible from above and difficult to see from the land. No smoke trailed upward, since a huge generator gave them all the power they needed.

Lifting his head, Ullah sniffed. He could smell mutton, hearty and sweet, cooking in the villa's kitchen. A good lunch. Since he had taken control in this war-ravaged area, he and his family ate well, and if it were not for Martin Chapman, he would have even more funds at his disposal—the overseas account Chapman had frozen. Until the poppy harvests in the autumn, he had little income from opium and heroin. He needed Chapman to release his money, and that meant tonight his men would put on the U.S. Army uniforms Chapman had supplied and eliminate about a hundred locals from the town and nearby villages, chosen because of their opposition to him, and recorded by the cameras of friendly tribal newsmen from Pakistan. Finally he would have his money plus Chapman's payment for buying the land.

Just then the two army Humvees veered toward his

villa. His guards turned and lifted their heads, watching, too.

The warlord called into the house for tea and paced along the porch. As the tea arrived on an enameled tray, he sat in his chair.

The Humvees roared into the compound and stopped in a cloud of white dust. Soldiers sat behind the machine guns mounted on each vehicle, their helmets low against the morning sun, their eyes hidden behind black sunglasses.

The forward base's commander, Capt. Samuel Daradar, jumped down from the passenger seat of the lead vehicle and strode toward him, taking off his cap and running his arm across his forehead.

"Pe kher ragle." Ullah did not stand, but he welcomed him.

"Mr. Ullah, good to see you," Captain Daradar answered in Pashto as he climbed the steps. "You are well?" In his early thirties, he had golden skin, clear black eyes, and a sober expression.

"Yes, thanks to Allah's blessings. You will honor me by joining me for tea?"

"Of course. I appreciate your hospitality."

AS HIS MEN WAITED in the Humvees, Sam Daradar took the other chair, the seat and back lower than the warlord's. It was as if he were sitting next to a king on a throne. He would have found Ullah's little reminders of power amusing, except each was a deadly signal of the complex weave of loyalties and vendettas among Pashtun tribes, and that Afghans in general were often far more antiforeign than the West was capable of understanding.

"You are patrolling," the warlord said, showing benign interest. "Have you found anything?" He poured tea into cups on the wood table between them.

"Nothing but the wind, the sky, and the earth." Sam gave a short smile.

"Spoken like a true Pashtun. I will never understand why your family moved to the United States."

"We have our wide-open spaces, too. Visit me in Arizona sometime. I'll show you the Grand Canyon." The captain sipped tea. "I got an update today I thought you'd like to hear. Since you helped us oust the Taliban and al-Qaeda, there are two thousand new clinics and schools across the country, jobs are being created constantly, and the bazaar in Khost is completely rebuilt. Nearly seven million children have been educated through primary school, the new central bank is solid, and the currency is stable."

"It is all good," Ullah said. "I am pleased." He smiled, showing a row of thick white teeth. "Still, there are many problems. Look around you. Such poverty. My people go hungry. It is the corruption in Kabul. No one can solve that."

It was also Ullah's corruption, but Sam was not about to say that. Developing countries tended to have relatively effective central banks and armies but corrupt and despised police forces, and Afghanistan was no exception. Corruption was also why it was easier to build roads than to create law and order, easier to build a school than a state. No amount of education could help a judge faced with drug kingpins prepared to murder his family. It was almost impossible for outsiders to reform this kind of system, and although Ullah liked to think of himself as operating independently from Kabul, he was part of a very broken system.

"I'm concerned about rumors there are Taliban here today," Sam told him.

"Ah, so that is why I have been honored."

"And that some sort of action is in the works, with or without the Taliban."

The Taliban were mostly Pashtuns, and both, like al-Qaeda, were Sunni Muslims. In a country where men with guns reinvented themselves in loyalty to every new power that came along, it was inevitable former Taliban and al-Qaeda fighters were in their ranks. Even Ullah had once pronounced himself Taliban—until the Taliban had outlawed the drug trade when they took over the country. After that, they were his enemy.

"It is Pakistan' fault," the warlord announced. "They should keep the Taliban from crossing the border. They invented them."

"I agree, but neither Pakistan or Afghanistan is succeeding," Sam said mildly. "I know you want nothing but the best for your people. Tell me what's going on."

Ullah's heavy black brows lifted, and his broad mustache twitched. A look of complete innocence crossed his face.

"I have heard nothing," the warlord said. "You can be certain I will call if I receive even a rumor. Would you like more tea?"

THE MEN IN THE TOWN MOSQUE stood and bowed and stood again, finishing noon prayers. A sense of reverence filled the hall, making Ullah proud. It was his mosque—he had paid for every block and tile.

But then the mullah in his white turban and young face with the neatly trimmed beard commanded all to be seated. They settled themselves on their prayer rugs. Ullah sighed and lowered himself, crossing his legs.

Holding a Koran between his hands, the mullah stood before them, his long black robe flowing. "When the Prophet and his companions went to jihad, they carried black flags because war is not a good thing. When we go to jihad today, it should not be because we want to fight, but because we are compelled to fight for the sake of Islam, and for the freedom of Afghanistan. Still, that is the role of the army and the police—not of private citizens."

Ullah adjusted his backside, inwardly groaning.

"There is only one Allah, and our life on Earth is to serve Him alone," the mullah continued. He stared at Ullah. "But the human is weak, and unwise mullahs with wrong ideas have disobeyed the Koran's laws and sent people onto dangerous paths. This fighting among Muslims and against the West is about power, not about Allah. He does not want our people to be killing. Long ago the Muslim world was under attack in a crusade by Christians who wanted to make all of Islam vanish from the planet. Jihad was about survival then, a last resort. Allah teaches us the greatest jihad is the struggle within each of us for the soul, the jihad of the heart. The heart is a holy place, and we must always take care never to hurt one another."

When the sermon finished, Ullah pointedly ignored the mullah, picked up his AK-47, and strode toward the door, his two guards close behind. The mullah was new and very young, he told himself with disgust. He had a lot to learn about what the Koran really said.

Ahead of him, the forward base's commander, Sam Daradar, was leaving, too. The military man must have arrived late and stayed in the back. Ullah slowed, waiting for him to get far ahead. Then he went out to the doorstep and watched Daradar climb into a Humvee. They exchanged nods and smiled.

Ullah waited impatiently as one of his men ran for the car. But when the silver Toyota Land Cruiser arrived, he noticed a strange expression on his driver's face.

414   Gayle Lynds

Frowning, he climbed into the passenger seat, and the remaining guard got into the rear, immediately making a small sound deep in his throat. Quickly Ullah turned. Lying on the floor was Sher Chandar, his black Taliban turban beside him, his *shalwar kameez* and vest spread around him like the wings of the angel of death.

"Drive," the Taliban leader ordered.

"I should have killed you a long time ago," Ullah rumbled.

As the vehicle sped down the street, bouncing over potholes, Chandar laughed and gave directions. The street became a dirt road and then a trail that took them up the slopes away from Ullah's villa. When they dropped over the other side, out of sight of the town and the military base and the villa, Chandar sat up, looked around at the bare foothills, and gave more directions.

They circled back around to the rear of Ullah's property and at last lurched down into a deep canyon where a small stream fed a big stand of cypress and pine trees. Uneasiness swept through the warlord—here in this woods was where his men were to gather tonight.

Chandar ordered them to drive into the trees and stop the Toyota beside the American crates, covered with dark tarps. A half-dozen men in black turbans seemed to melt out from among the greenery, pointing assault rifles. Chandar's men.

"Kill the engine." When silence enveloped them, Chandar gestured at the mound of crates. "A gift for the Taliban?"

Ullah said nothing.

"There is a change in plans," Chandar told him. "I know what you were going to do tonight. You will not kill the villagers—some of them are Taliban. Instead your men will put on the American uniforms and arm themselves with the American weapons as they expect to do. Once they are disguised they will be able to get inside the military base. And then they will kill all of the infidels."

Ullah's throat went dry. "It cannot be done."

Chandar chuckled. "You have a greater imagination than that. Your Pakistani journalists will record it from a distance. They will think the Americans are at war with each other in a tribal blood feud as we have here. With that you will have the publicity you need to get the base closed down. That is what you want, is it not?"

Ullah silently cursed.

"These American infidels do not have Allah's blessing," Chandar continued. "We have worked with you these past few years. You have made accommodations. We have made accommodations. If word were to reach Kabul of our arrangement . . ."

He left the sentence unfinished, but Ullah immediately understood the threat. As weak as the Kabul government was, it still had teeth. If enough troops were dispatched here, he and his family could be erased from the earth.

"The Americans will investigate," Ullah argued. "Instead, I offer a compromise. I will leave unharmed any villagers you wish."

"Not good enough. We want the American soldiers dead. The order comes straight from South Waziristan." In other words, al-Qaeda.

Ullah glanced over his shoulder at Chandar's stony face. Then his gaze swept the six armed men whose rifles pointed unwaveringly at him.

The problem was, if he had killed Chandar when he'd had the chance, another would have taken his place and come to murder him. There was no way he could win this fight. Having decided that, he felt a moment of relief. Chandar's plan could actually work.

"I will do as you wish if you agree to help me later," he decided. "Americans are going to buy the military base property from me and start a business. I do not know exactly what yet. I will need you to agree to their safety."

"At a good price."

Ullah smiled. "Of course. A good price."

Their business concluded, the Taliban leader got out and joined his men in the grove. And then they vanished.

"Home," Ullah commanded.

In his mind he could smell again the sweet aroma of mutton roasting in the kitchen. He was beginning to like the new plan, which meant he would be able to enjoy a good lunch.

As they circled back toward the villa, his satellite phone rang. He answered and heard Martin Chapman's voice. He greeted him in Pashto.

"Are you on schedule?" Chapman asked.

"Of course," the warlord assured him easily, thinking of the infidels who would die. "It will be a fine night, all to Allah's glory."

CHAPTER 63

Athens, Greece

AS A FRESH BREEZE BLEW in through the window, Judd sat with Eva and Tucker at the table in the hotel room, her laptop open before them. They were studying NSA's photos and geographical information about the un-named island that might house the Library of Gold.

There were rocky outcroppings, wide valleys, and rolling hills. The island was ten square miles of beautiful wilderness, except for orchards and a flat-topped mesa on the south side on which stood the three buildings Robin had described.

"The library could be in the big building," Eva said. "But if there are twenty people living there year-round, where are they housed? It doesn't seem large enough."

Judd ran through the small photos on the screen until he found three pictures showing the mesa at a slant. Working quickly, he grew the images, choosing the best. The resolution was excellent, zeroing down to six inches. All had been taken just an hour earlier.

"Four stories underground," Tucker announced. "That answers one question. Too bad the glass is darkened. No way to see inside."

"Now it makes sense. I'll bet the library is down there somewhere," Eva said. "That would be optimum for keeping out sunlight and controlling for humidity, temperature, and so forth."

They had already seen armed guards patrolling in Jeeps—thirty men, two in each vehicle—on the dirt roads that ribbonned the island and gave access to remote areas. Judd focused on one pair.

"M4 assault rifles. They're not there to play games. Do you recognize anyone, Tucker?" He showed him photo after photo.

"No, all strangers," Tucker said. "Check one of the beaches. Let's see what other kinds of security the island has."

Judd clicked a photo, making it bigger and bigger. "There are your security cameras, Tucker. And look— movement- and heat-sensing monitors."

"Swell."

"We saw squirrels and birds. Wouldn't they set off the monitors' alarms?" Eva asked.

"The system can be programmed to ignore wildlife," Judd explained.

They analyzed the other beaches and the cliffs around the island, finding the same tight protection everywhere.

"It's a fortress." Eva's voice was discouraged.

Judd focused on the wharf, where a cargo ship was docked. Men were carrying boxes onto it.

"They're loading something." Eva stared. "I wonder what that means."

"Did either of you see any guard dogs?" Judd adjusted himself in his chair, pushing from his mind the aching gunshot wound in his side.

Both shook their heads.

"At least we have that. Okay, so let's focus on the cliff beneath the compound."

They studied the photos.

"Very steep," Tucker said. "At least five hundred feet high, I'd say. It'd be impossible to dodge the cameras and monitors if we tried to climb it."

"You're right. Let's check the top of the mesa."

Judd enlarged more photos, showing the swimming pool, a picnic area, and a satellite dish. A gardener was watering plants on an outdoor patio, and a woman was setting out buckets of balls on the tennis courts. Two dirt roads coming from the east and west converged north of the complex and became a two-car cement driveway that ran south, passing the satellite dish and descending under the east side of the main house. There on the flat area beside the house stood a mountain of boxes and crates. Men were loading them into a van. Following the drive east, Judd saw it curved not only north but south, to the wharf.

"I don't like this," he muttered. He chose photos of the buildings' exteriors.

"No monitors," Tucker said. "They probably figured no one was ever going to get close enough to be a threat. Zero in on the ground-floor windows of the big house."

Judd did. The windows extended across and around the building, showcasing the ocean view. Tall glass panels were open to the air. They could see two middle-age women in white skirts and blouses walking across the main room inside, carrying drinks on trays.

"No sign of Preston," Judd said. "Or Yitzhak and Roberto." Then he noticed more boxes against the back.

He enlarged the photos, homing in. The stack was so tall and wide it looked like a wall. Beside it, pieces of furniture waited, covered with sheets.

Tucker leaned close. "My God, they're packing up and moving out. Crap."

"They could be gone tomorrow," Judd agreed. "We could lose the Library of Gold."

A worried hush filled the room.

"This isn't going to be easy," Eva observed. "There are a lot more guards than Robin told us. We saw thirty in the Jeeps alone."

"She said tonight was the annual banquet," Judd reminded her. "She expected more security, but you're right—this is getting increasingly dangerous. Yitzhak and Roberto may be hostages, so we've got to save them as well as figure out who's behind Dad's murder and what the Library of Gold has to do with terrorism. Whatever it is, Dad must've felt it was imminent. And now we've got the pressure of the library's being moved. If we don't go in soon, we might never find it again."

"Can we call in Catapult for help?" Eva asked Tucker. "How about Langley?"

The spymaster drummed his fingers on the tabletop. "Hudson Canon is likely working for the other side, so we don't want him to discover where we are and what we're up to. It's safest to tell no one. But I have a partial solution: There's a small U.S. naval base at Souda Bay, on Crete. It's not far from the island. If we don't have any of our paramilitary teams stationed there now, Gloria should be able to stay out of Hudson's way long enough to pull some strings to get a couple sent over for short-term duty."

Judd nodded. "I like that. We can use some help."

Tucker took out his mobile and turned it on. Then he dialed. "Gloria isn't answering," he told them. Then into the phone: "This is Tucker. Call me as soon as you get my message."

Judd stared at his watch and frowned. "Gloria knows the operation's gone hot. Shouldn't she answer no matter what? For Chrissakes, she must be home in bed. It's the middle of the night there. Surely the call would've awakened her."

"Not if she's deactivated her mobile," Tucker reminded him. "I'm going to check my e-mail."

Judd looked for e-mail on his mobile, too. Then he checked for messages. "Nothing."

"Take a gander at this," Tucker said grimly and turned the screen so Judd and Eva could read.

Canon is hunting you. I talked to Debi, who told me he has NSA tracking Judd's and your mobiles. I'm sending this from a new BlackBerry. No encoding. I'm going to toss it. You're on your own. Get rid of those mobiles! Sorry.

Shock filled the room.

"We've got to get out of here." Judd jumped to his feet.

Eva opened the duffel and threw things inside.

"I'll be back with my stuff." Tucker ran out the door.

In minutes they were packed. As Judd opened the window and peered down, Tucker stuck his head inside the door.

"Give me your mobile."

Judd tossed it. "What are you—"

But Tucker had vanished.

Judd zipped the duffel. "I'll go first," he told Eva.

Slinging it over his shoulder, he crawled out onto the ledge. A warm wind whistled past. They were five stories above a driveway that resembled a narrow alley. On the other side stood another hotel, brick and as tall as theirs. Sunlight filtered down between, leaving half the drive in shadow.

"Come on, Eva." He reached a hand inside the window and felt her firm grip.

Her shoulder satchel hanging across her back, she gingerly crawled out onto the ledge beside him.

She looked around. "Thank God there's a fire escape. After London, I can now claim to have experience."

"I'm here," Tucker announced from inside, behind their legs.

They moved aside, and he pulled himself out onto the ledge. "My room faces the hotel's rear, and there was a bus with luggage on top getting ready to leave. It was too good an opportunity to pass up. I threw the mobiles onto it. Now they'll have a moving target to follow. Canon's probably having NSA live-tracking our mobiles."

"That could buy us some time," Judd agreed.

He swung a foot onto the metal rung and started down. He felt the fire escape wobble as Eva, then Tucker, followed him. He looked back up to check on them.

"So how are we going to get on the island?" Eva asked.

"Can you parachute?" Tucker replied.

"Who, me?"

"I thought not. The safest way is to go in at night with black parachutes and gear. I have a former colleague in town who can help with that. I'm hoping the Library of Gold banquet will be a good distraction to cover us, since it looks as if we're going into the serpent's mouth without hope of backup."

Judd felt a chill. "We can't take you with us," he told Eva. "You're not trained. Too damn dangerous."

"You're not leaving me behind." Her eyes glinted. "I'll parachute in with one of you. You may need what I know about the library."

Tucker made a decision. "She's right. This is too important to fuck up."

Judd did not like it. A wave of worry shot through him as he reached the third story. Then he froze. The

two men who had been with Preston on the Metro were
striding from the rear of the building, their heads swiveling, their hands against their ears, clasping cell phones
as they listened. Their other hands were inside their
jackets. They had still not looked up.

"Shit," Eva muttered behind him.

Judd gave himself a shake to loosen his muscles.
The noise of a large engine sounded, and a long white-
and-gray tourist bus entered the drive behind the men,
cruising toward the street. A short toot of the horn
sounded, causing the pair of killers to scramble to the
side—to their hotel's side—so the bus could pass. They
were less than thirty feet away.

Judd whispered over his shoulder, "We're going to
join our mobiles."

Tucker sighed and nodded. Eva stared at him, then
gave a short nod.

Going as quietly as he could, Judd continued down
as the bus neared. But then the fire escape creaked behind him. At the noise, Preston's men gazed up in unison. Their pistols appeared in their hands as the tourist
bus rolled beneath the fire escape.

"Let's go!" Judd leaped, landing hard on two flat
canvas suitcases.

Eva and Tucker dropped near the rear of the bus. All
of them burrowed down among the piles of luggage.
Shouts followed the bus as it turned onto the street.

"Are you all right?" Judd asked immediately.

They nodded and turned, studying the hotel. Preston
ran out the front door and gestured. A van squealed to
the curb, and he jumped inside. The lumbering bus was
no race car, and Preston would soon catch up.

"Is that who I think it is?" Tucker had been staring
at the jeans and black jacket.

"Himself," Judd said. "That asshole Preston."

"Oh, hell," Eva said. "What do we do now?"

"Improvise. Come on." Judd scrambled to the side-walk side of the bus.

Traffic noises filled the air. They were going downhill, passing Platia Exarchia. Shops, restaurants, hotels, and office buildings lined the avenue. From their elevated vantage point, they watched it all.

"I know this section." Eva was looking ahead. "See that big building in the next block? That's where we want to go. It's a parking garage."

They peered back. There was only one car between them and Preston's van.

"You know," Tucker decided. "I'm tired of this. You handle the parking garage. I'll take care of Preston. Then I'll catch up." He slid out his Browning.

"Are you sure?" Judd asked.

"I'm not *that* old, Judson."

The bus rumbled on. As they neared the garage, Tucker hunched up enough so he would be visible to the van. He scuttled across the bus to the street side. Over the luggage, Judd watched the van pull into the other lane to be closer to Tucker.

"But he *is* old," Eva worried.

"If only a tenth of everything I've heard about him is true, he can more than handle himself."

As Tucker aimed his pistol, they turned to watch again for the parking garage. They were only one building away. Grasping the guardrails atop the bus, they slid over, their legs dangling, and dropped and staggered. At the same time, a rain of gunfire sounded from above and from the van on the other side. The bus wobbled. Judd had a brief glimpse of passengers' faces, stunned, then horrified, by the sight of him and Eva. They whipped their heads around to peer across the bus toward the noise of gunshots.

Judd pulled out his Beretta and ran toward the driver's side of a car that had just pulled into the garage.

"Give me your keys," he demanded of the driver as he emerged.

The driver's face was white. His clenched fist opened, and the keys started to slide off.

Judd snatched them, and Eva slid into the car's passenger seat. Hearing the loud noise of a car crash, from his peripheral vision Judd saw Preston's van had hit a car in the oncoming lane of traffic. Tucker slid off the back of the bus, stumbled, and ran onto the sidewalk toward them. His corrugated face showed a grim smile.

Judd opened the rear door of the car, then dropped in behind the steering wheel. He gunned the motor. Breathing heavily, Tucker fell into the backseat and slammed the door.

"Did you erase Preston?" Judd said.

"Don't know," Tucker rumbled. "But there are enough holes in the top of that van, it looks like a fine Swiss cheese."

"Drive straight ahead," Eva ordered. "This parking garage has an exit onto the next street. They'll never find us."

Until the next time, Judd thought but did not say. He slammed the accelerator.

CHAPTER 64

The Isle of Pericles

AT FOUR O'CLOCK IN the afternoon the eight members of the book club flew toward the Isle of Pericles in a comfortable Bell helicopter. Although the rotors chopped noisily, and the craft vibrated, Martin Chapman was enjoying himself. He had spoken with Syed Ullah before taking off and had received a good report. The news of the warlord's success in Khost should reach him during the banquet.

As the helicopter circled, Chapman stared down at the lush thyme-covered hills, the stately olive and palm trees, the wild native herbs. Acres of blooming citrus groves swept over the hills. Glistening waterfalls spilled at the ends of ravines. Smiling to himself, he took in the white pebbled beaches, the deserted coves, and the dramatic seaside cliffs, savoring the fact this secret Shangri-la had belonged only to him and few others.

The craft swept low over the south beach, passing the wharf where the cargo ship was being packed, and then up the valley toward the mesa, lower than surrounding hills. On it stood the Library of Gold compound, built a half century ago. Just beneath were four long stories of darkened glass, set into the steep slope and largely invisible from above and difficult to spot from the beach. Most of what went on at the compound was beneath the surface.

The craft landed on the helipad, and Chapman climbed out, the other book club members following. Their heads and shoulders low to avoid the whirling blades, they hurried off. At the same time, Preston gave a signal, and an equal number of bodyguards rushed toward it. Each grabbed one member's bag and briefcase.

A sense of anticipation was in the salty sea air as the eight walked toward the buildings, Preston and the guards following.

"Damn disappointing we won't have a librarian tonight," Brian Collum said as he adjusted his sunglasses.

"It is most unfortunate we will not have a tournament," Petr Klok agreed. "I will miss that a great deal. I spent two days preparing with the translators."

"Think of something, Marty," ordered Maurice Dresser, the eldest member. The bossy Canadian oil man strode out ahead, the hot sun turning the skin on his skull pink beneath his thin white hair. "That's an assignment."

The others glanced at Martin Chapman good-naturedly. But with Charles Sherback and Robin Miller eliminated—their only librarians—there was no way the tournament could go on.

"Yes, Marty. It's your problem." Reinhardt Gruen deadpanned.

"Absolutely," Martin Chapman said, continuing the conviviality. Then he had an idea. "The impossible is nothing to me. That's why you voted me director."

"I need a drink—and I want to see the menu so I can start salivating," Dresser said over his shoulder. "Then who wants a round of tennis?"

They entered the grassy compound with its rows of roses. Glazed in sunlight, the three simple white buildings with their Doric columns stood like Grecian tributes to the past. The Olympic-size swimming pool shimmered. The tennis court was empty, but obviously not for long. Behind the complex rose a huge satellite dish, the island's link to the outside world. Once a village had covered the mesa and surrounding hills, its main source of income high-quality salt mines. But the mines had worn out, and now the island's only inhabitants besides the regular staff were rodents, seagulls, flamingos, and other birds.

"Damn, I'm going to miss this place," Collum said.

"Won't we all," Grandon Holmes agreed. "Pity to have to move the library. Still, I've always liked the Alps."

"We knew this day would come," Chapman reminded them.

Silently they passed two cottages. Charles Sherback had lived in one; the other was Preston's. They entered the big main house, which encircled a palm-shaded reflecting pool. Chapman paused to enjoy the view one last time. All was as it had been on his last visit. Decorated with Greek furniture, the walls full of museum-quality paintings from across Europe. Chandeliers of Venetian glass glittered, hanging on wrought-iron chains from the high ceiling. Ancient Greek statues and vases stood here and there on the glowing white marble floor, quarried on Mount Penteli, near Athens. A walk-in fireplace of the same marble stretched across the end of the long room. The air was cool, thanks to the giant temperature-control system buried belowground. Men were moving furniture from other rooms toward the elevator and down to where it would be loaded onto trucks to be taken to the cargo ship.

The guest rooms were on this floor, in three of the arms around the reflecting pool. The book club split into two groups, each heading into a different wing to go to their usual rooms.

Chapman entered his suite, his bodyguard a respectful six feet behind. "You're new." He turned to study the man, who had a tanned face. It was one Chapman did not recognize.

"Yes, sir. You're Martin Chapman. I read about you in an article in *Vanity Fair,* the one about your big equity deal to buy Sheffield-Riggs. The financing was a thing of beauty. My name is Harold Kardasian. Preston brought me in this morning from Majorca with two others."

Majorca was known as a home for wealthy independent mercenaries. The guard was sturdy, obviously athletic from the way he moved, with thick brown hair that had streaks of gray at the temples. A pistol was on his hip. He was in his early fifties, Chapman judged, and had a touch of class—refined features, erect posture, deferential without being obsequious. Chapman liked that.

"You're a short-timer?" he asked.

"Just here for the two days you'll be here. I'd heard about Preston for years, so of course I signed up so I could work with him. Didn't know I'd have the privilege of working for you, too, Mr. Chapman."

Preston appeared in the doorway. "I'll take those." As Kardasian left, he laid the suitcase on the butler's stand and the briefcase on the desk.

Chapman went to the window. He looked out, drinking in the panorama of the sky, the wind-carved island, and the impossibly blue sea. When Preston handed him the menu, he ran his gaze down the seven-course feast.

"Excellent," he said. "You've made arrangements to blow up the buildings as soon as we've moved out?"

"Yes. I estimate tomorrow afternoon. By the time we're finished, all evidence the library or we were ever here will be scrubbed."

Chapman nodded. "Any problems on the island?"

"None. The chefs and food are here. They've been in the kitchen all day. A few loud arguments but no serious fights so far—maybe I'll get off easy this year. The silver is polished. The crystal is shined. The wine is standing up. The library never looked better. I've ordered more than the usual extra security men. A total of fifty in all. Everyone's oriented and knows their assignments."

"Good. Send the translators to my office and tell them to wait. I need to talk with them after I finish some phone calls." He turned to study Preston, noticing a faint red streak down his cheek. "Any news about Judd Ryder and Eva Blake?"

"I almost caught them in Athens again. A very close call."

Chapman gestured. "Is that what happened to your face?"

Preston's hand went to his cheek, and he grimaced. "As I said, it was close. Now I know why we couldn't find Tucker Andersen—he's with them. Hudson Cannon learned they've been searching for the island, using our coordinates."

"Christ! Then we have to count on them coming here." Chapman thought a moment. "On the other hand, one's a rank amateur, and another is past his prime. You have fifty highly trained men on security. In the end, taking care of them on the island may be our best solution. They'll simply disappear, and Langley will never know what happened to them, or where."

CHAPTER 65

Langley, Virginia

AT NINE O'CLOCK IN THE MORNING the storied seventh floor in the CIA's old headquarters building bustled with activity. Behind the closed doors were the offices of the director of Central Intelligence and the other top espionage executives, plus conference rooms and special operations and support centers. Gloria Feit hurried along the corridor, passing staff carrying briefcases, plastic clipboards, and color-coded folders. The air exuded a sense of urgency. Usually she felt a thrill being here, but right now her mind was on failed operations— and their costs.

Hudson Canon had told her to spend the night thinking about Tucker Andersen and the Library of Gold mission, but she would have anyway. She had tossed and turned and stalked the floor until daybreak.

Worried, she stepped into the suite of Matthew Kelley, chief of the Clandestine Service.

His secretary looked up from her desk. "He's expecting you."

When Gloria tapped on the door, a strong voice answered, "Come in."

As she walked into his spacious room of books, family photographs, and framed CIA awards, Matt rose from behind his expansive desk, smiling. A tall man with a warm, lined face, he had looked like the perfect spy in his day, nondescript, dowdy, almost invisible. Now slightly more public, he was able to show his taste. Today he was dressed in a sleek tailored suit and a cuffed white shirt. With his angular face and the hint of predatoriness he once relied upon, he looked as if he had just stepped off the fashion page of a men's magazine.

They shook hands. "Good to see you, Gloria. It's been a while. How's Ted?"

He gestured, and they sat at the coffee table in the distant end of his office. He chose a leather armchair, and she took the sofa.

They exchanged family information for only a minute, then Matt got down to business. "You've got a situation. What is it?"

"Did you close down the Library of Gold operation?" she asked.

"Yes. Tucker's got a burr under his saddle, that's all."

"Would Hudson ordinarily have brought you in on the decision?"

"Of course not. But it was a pet project of Cathy's, and he wanted to make certain I'd be on board." He frowned. "Your point?"

"What would you say if I told you I'm beginning to think Cathy's car accident was no accident?"

Matt went rigid. "Fill me in."

For the next half hour Gloria described the events she knew about or had learned earlier this morning by going through Tucker's and Cathy's e-mails and notes.

"After Tucker left Catapult, I got a call from him. He'd just captured a janitor at Capitol City market. While I collected the janitor, Tucker left to join Ryder and Blake in Athens."

"You believe Hudson alerted someone. That's why the janitor was there to do a wet job on Tucker."

"Yes."

Matt thought about it. "It's flimsy evidence against Hudson at best. Janitors could've been taking turns, waiting outside Catapult for days for Tucker to appear."

"But how did the book club people find Ryder and Blake in Istanbul? Tucker believed the only explanation was someone inside Catapult told them. The one person who knew was Hudson Canon."

"That damns Hudson—but only if Tucker is right." Matt changed the subject. "That's a hell of a thing to do, Gloria. Christ. Sticking the janitor down in the basement on your own authority."

She lifted her chin. "We've got a mole inside Catapult. The operation has to be protected. The guy's fine. I've got his hands and legs cuffed to a heavy chair. He gets three squares a day, better than a lot of people in the world."

"A desk job hasn't changed you a damn bit." He sighed. "All right, I want the janitor." He picked up the phone on the coffee table, then glanced at her. "I'm going to have to tell Hudson. He could still be innocent."

Her throat tightened. " 'Flimsy evidence.' I understand."

He dialed. "Hello, Hudson. This is Matt. Gloria's sitting with me in my office. She tells me she's got a two-legged source secured in Catapult's cellar." He moved the phone from his ear, and Gloria heard a stream of loud oaths. Then he continued. "We'll worry about disciplining her later. The man's a janitor. Tucker was his target. We need to question him. Have two of your people bring him to Langley. I want him here immediately."

"Tell him I left the keys to the basement on my desk," Gloria said.

Matt sighed and said into the phone, "The keys are on her desk. We should talk. I want you to come with them. I'll be in my office."

"We need to help Tucker," Gloria said as soon as he had ended the connection. "I checked with Catapult's com center and found out Blake, Ryder, and he have been looking into a privately owned Aegean island. My guess is that that's where the Library of Gold is hidden, which means they're going to be heading for it soon. Maybe they're already on their way. Judging by all the deaths so far, it's going to be a very dangerous insertion. But we've got a naval base on Crete. We could send fast-rope teams from there." She peered at her watch. It was nearly six P.M. in Greece.

But Matt was not going to be hurried. "You could be right. Still, first things first—Hudson and the janitor. If Hudson is the mole, then he's got a handler. The handler could have the information we need. Look at it this way: Maybe Tucker isn't planning to go to the island. Maybe it's the wrong island, or something might've happened to change his mind altogether. Do you have a way to reach him?"

She shook her head anxiously. "I'm hoping the janitor or Hudson knows more than I do. If not, unless Tucker decides to risk phoning or e-mailing me, he and the others are hanging in the wind."

"I'm sorry about that. But there's no way I'm invading a private island in Greece's territory unless I've got something concrete to go on. The last thing Langley needs is an international incident. We'll just have to trust Tucker's good sense—and his luck."

Washington, D.C.

HUDSON CANON COULD HARDLY breathe. He turned away from his desk, leaned over, and pounded a fist into his palm. Gritting his teeth, he threw his head back and kept pounding. Eventually the fear eased. Sitting upright, he took long, deep breaths.

Then he phoned Reinhardt Gruen. "We've got a problem." He described the phone call from Matt Kelley at Langley. "What does your janitor know?" Then, demanding: "Does he know about *me*?"

There was a long pause. With relief he heard a soothing calmness in Gruen's voice: "It is not the end of the world, my friend," the German told him. "The assassin was hired anonymously. He has no way to track either us or you. Do as your chief says. Go with the janitor and your people to Langley and act like the great spy chief you are. You are safe."

Isle of Pericles

FURIOUS ABOUT THE BOTCHED handling of the situation in Washington, Reinhardt Gruen snapped out a hand with his cell phone. The Isle of Pericles attendant instantly took it and replaced it with a thick towel. Drying himself, Gruen stalked away from the swimming pool.

"Giving up so soon?" Brian Collum challenged from behind. "One more race. What do you say, Reinhardt? Come on, man. Come on!"

Damn Americans, Gruen muttered under his breath. "Hold onto your trunks. I will return."

He found Martin Chapman sitting behind his desk in his office, surrounded by pedestals on which stood classic marble statues he had collected in Greece. Lined up before him were the library's four translators, two men and two women, dressed in tuxedos to help serve at the banquet. All scholars, they were graying and had the hunched shoulders of those who spent long hours poring over books. Their expertise was critical to the book club's ability to use and enjoy the library, and as such, each was treated with a certain amount of deference. That was even more true of the librarians—unless their loyalty was in question.

Gruen put a smile on his face. "I see you are plotting with our great translators, Martin. Are you by any chance finished? I would like to have a word with you."

Chapman laid two sheets of paper on his desk, then placed a hand possessively on them. "Yes, they've just finished a job for me, and they've given me a good report. The library's records are already on the boat. As soon as the banquet is over, they'll pack their personal things. They'll be ready to go at daybreak."

"Good, good." Gruen stepped aside to let the translators leave. When the door closed, he scowled. "I just received a call from Hudson Canon in Washington." He fell into a leather chair. "The janitor Preston sent is locked up at Catapult and will soon be on his way to Langley. Canon has been ordered to go with them. I told him he had no exposure and calmed him down. What is the truth?"

Chapman grimaced. "The janitor knows Preston hired him. Goddammit all to hell. When will this end!" He ran his fingers through his hair. "We'll handle Andersen, Ryder, and Blake if they manage to reach the island. But we can't let either the janitor or Canon get to Langley." He snatched the phone from his desk and punched in numbers. "Preston, I need you. Now!"

Washington, D.C.

THE MORNING TRAFFIC WAS THICK as Michael Hawthorne drove Catapult's only armored van out of the city and onto the bridge across the Potomac. Hudson Canon sat beside him, arms crossed, fighting nerves as he planned what he would say to Matt. In the rear seat was the shackled janitor, while next to him Brandon Ohr kept guard with an assault rifle. The two young covert officers had been happy to get away from their desks at Catapult even for such a small assignment.

"I heard Debi has a new boyfriend," Michael was saying.

"She ever level that killer gaze on you?" Brandon said. "My God, that woman has balls."

"Agreed. What a turn-on—" He stopped. "Do you see what I see?" He stared into his rearview mirror.

"I've been watching it. A black Volvo, heavy as a tank. It's just closed in. Pull out." Ohr spoke in the usual neutral tones of the professional spy when facing potential trouble.

Canon's head spun around and he peered through the back window. The Volvo was right behind, its front bumper only ten feet distant. On one side of them was speeding traffic, while on the other the guardrail rushed past—and far below was the fast-moving Potomac River.

Without activating his turn signal, Hawthorne gave a sharp yank to the steering wheel, driving the van away and into the safety of the inner lane.

But suddenly a loud horn gave a long blast. A behemoth truck was rushing up on them, preparing to pass, its big cab high above. Instantly, Hawthorne accelerated, pushing their van into the open space ahead, catching up with the red pickup that had preceded them onto the bridge. Canon saw if they could get clear, Hawthorne could move the van into the inner lane and outrun the big truck.

But almost instantly red taillights flashed and held. The pickup was slowing. And the truck was keeping pace, while the Volvo was locked on their tail.

As Ohr lowered his window and raised his assault rifle, Canon snapped to Hawthorne: "They've got us trapped. I don't care what you do, but get us out of here!"

Before Hawthorne could respond, the big cab of the truck slammed into the van's side. The van yawed. Canon was thrown against his seat belt, then deep into the hard seat. Gripping his windowsill with one hand, Ohr let out a long blast from the assault rifle, ripping through the passenger door of the towering truck cab. Immediately Hawthorne floored the gas pedal and rammed the rear of the pickup.

Too late. The cab smashed again into their van and held. Hawthorne fought the steering wheel, trying to push back. But by inches, then by feet, the van was pushed to the side. Canon's throat went dry as he peered over into the water.

There was the screech of metal against metal as the van crashed along the guardrail. Sparks exploded past his window. The truck nudged the van one last time, and suddenly they smashed through the rail and sailed off into the air. Canon's heart thundered. He screamed, and the van dove headfirst into the Potomac.

CHAPTER 66

The Isle of Pericles

DRENCHED IN MOONLIGHT, the Library of Gold's private island rose suddenly from the dark sea, its high craggy ridges pale, its deep valleys eerily shadowed. Judd was studying it from the window of the Cessna Super Cargomaster piloted by Tucker's friend Haris Naxos. Night lights off, the craft was circling and would soon climb to jump altitude: ten thousand feet.

Time had run out, and they were going in without backup. All were hyper alert and not talking about the danger.

"There's the orange grove and the landing spot we picked," Eva said.

Eva and Judd were sitting together in seats that stretched along the cargo bin's side walls. Like Tucker, who was in the copilot's seat, they wore black jumpsuits and helmets. Infrared goggles dangled from their necks, and black grease covered their faces. They had come prepared not only with their pistols, which were holstered to their waists, but Judd and Tucker had grenades and mini Uzis lashed to their legs. Tucker wore a parachute pack on his back, while Judd had a larger one, holding a bigger canopy that would support both his and Eva's weight. The two men had additional packs containing supplies. Eva carried nothing on her back, since she would be strapped to Judd.

Judd nodded. "Yes, it should work well." He was loaded with painkillers and feeling only a dull ache in his side.

They had been observing the headlights of Jeeps roaming over the island, looking for patterns. One had driven past the orange grove. Now, a half hour later, another passed.

"How's the air clarity seem to you, Haris?" Tucker asked as the plane climbed.

"It is no change. Looks good for you to land." Haris Naxos was gray-haired, angular, and tough-looking; he still did occasional contract work. "You are no spring rooster, Tucker. Night jumping is dangerous. Be careful."

"I know. There are old jumpers and bold jumpers, but there are no old, bold jumpers."

Haris laughed, but no one else did. As usual Judd was planning what he would do if the chutes did not deploy, the lines became tangled, all the myriad events that could go wrong.

After a while, Haris asked, "You remember everything I told you, Eva?" He had given her a half hour of instructions and walked her through a video of tandem skydiving, at his hangar in the Athens airport. He owned a parachuting and plane rental business.

"There's no way I'm going to forget anything." A fleck of nervousness was in her voice.

"Excellent. Then I make the announcement—we are at jump altitude, and we are approaching the drop zone."

Judd and Eva stood up in the plane. She turned around, and he snapped their straps together and tightened his, then hers until her back was secure against his chest. Her body was tense. Her rose-water scent filled his mind. Quickly he dismissed it.

"Okay?" he asked curtly.

"Okay."

As they put on goggles, Tucker crawled into the rear cargo area. "I'll open the door."

He was moving agilely, his expression focused. As Judd and Eva hung onto the ceiling straps, he unlocked the door, swung the handle, and pushed. Cold air blasted in.

Turning on the visual altimeter that was secured inside his helmet, the reader in easy peripheral view, Judd positioned Eva so they were facing the cockpit. Their right sides were inches from the black void.

"Go!" the pilot shouted.

"Try to enjoy it, Eva," Judd whispered.

Before she could speak, he rolled them out of the plane. Abruptly they were in free fall, soaring at speeds in excess of a hundred sixty miles an hour, their arms and legs extended together like wings. The silky air enveloped him, and there was no sense of falling—air resistence gave a feeling of weight and direction. Checking their orientation over the island, he reveled in the exhilaration of complete freedom.

"This is one of those rare moments when you know what it's like to be a bird in flight," he told her. "We can do anything a bird can do—except go back up."

As Tucker jumped out of the plane, Judd repositioned Eva until they were sitting in a ball in the air. He somersaulted her, then straightened her out again, rolling them onto their sides, their backs, and around again, spinning freely. He felt her tense more, and then she gave a joyful laugh.

Returning them to a normal descent, he reached behind and threw out the drogue parachute, lines and small canopy black against the stars. All was well so far. The drogue slowed their free-fall speed from two people to that of a single skydiver. He saw Tucker was nodding, indicating his equipment was working properly, too.

At twenty-five hundred feet, Judd pulled a toggle, and the deployment bag fell out and released the main canopy—a black ram-air parachute. It caught the wind and spread out into the shape of a large cupped wedge. There were a few seconds of intense deceleration, and then they were skydiving at about twelve miles an hour. He studied the area beneath them. Noted the forest of citrus trees, the open space of weeds and boulders awash in shades of green through his infrared goggles, and the long ravine to the south. A Jeep was just passing the trees, so they had about a half hour until the next one arrived. Their biggest immediate risk was broken ankles, assuming they missed the trees and boulders.

As they continued to soar horizontally, lower and lower, he tugged on the lines, directing their flight. So far no more headlights showed near the drop zone.

At one hundred feet, he felt a huge downdraft, and it seemed as if they were heading into a black-green hole. Again Eva tensed. He drew on the lines, controlling their direction and silently gliding, gliding. Satisfied, he used his body to push Eva upright and his knees to angle her knees into a crouch. They swept between tall boulders and landed hard, stumbling to a stop just before they reached the road that skirted the trees. He could feel her heaving for air.

"You did it." He unsnapped the straps that joined them. "Good job. Now let's get the hell out of the way."

He released the drogue and ram-air chutes, and they hurried off. As they gathered the canopies, Tucker slid in low. He yanked his lines, barely missing a shoulder-high boulder. Knees bent, he landed and staggered, finally catching his balance.

Standing stationary, he lifted his head. "Screw you, Haris. This old rooster still has a hell of a lot of life left in him." Then he smiled and collected his chutes.

"Everything went right," Eva said excitedly. "The parachutes opened. No one broke a leg. I could get used to this."

Then a bird called from the trees. There was rustling in the grove—fast movement.

"Shit." Judd pulled out his Beretta. "They were waiting for us. Run!"

Weapons in hands, they tore south across the hard earth toward the ravine. Judd glanced behind and saw six men dressed in black swarming out of the trees, aiming M4 assault rifles. They had night-vision goggles. Shooting as they ran, the men poured out fusillades of rounds. The bullets whined and bit into earth and rocks. Tucker grunted. A round clipped Judd's ear. All three fell flat. Judd pointed, and Eva scuttled into the shelter of a tall rock formation. Judd and Tucker followed.

From the southwest, a Jeep's headlights came to life, and the vehicle rushed along the road toward them. The air reverberated with the noise of feet pounding and the engine's growl.

"Christ," Tucker grumbled. "I hate being ambushed."

"Are you hit?" Judd gazed at Tucker, then checked Eva's blackened face, saw the tightness of her mouth. She seemed all right.

Tucker shook his head. "I'm fine. That's a cute cut on your ear, Judd. Glad they didn't take your brains. The ravine isn't far. Eva, we'll cover you. As soon as we start shooting, stay low and run like hell. Can you do that?"

"Of course." She crouched.

The two men took either side of the rocky mound. Judd peered at Tucker. He nodded. They edged out, firing automatic bursts from their Uzis.

AS THE EAR-BLEEDING GUNFIRE continued behind her, Eva reached the ravine and dropped quickly at the edge, legs dangling over. From the NSA photos, they had calculated it averaged ten feet deep. It led around and down toward the compound. The shadows were a thick green. Only the top of her side of the nearly vertical slope was slightly illuminated, showing raw dirt, weeds, and rocks. Gripping her S&W in both hands the way Judd had showed her, in seconds she was plummeting down on her back into the abyss.

But as she slid deep into the green darkness her gaze was attracted to a boulder across from her at the bottom. Then she saw a small movement there, an arm. A man was squatting to make himself small. Fear started to take over her mind. She repressed it and aimed her pistol. Suddenly there was movement to her right. And she swung the gun, a mistake she realized instantly. A foot slashed through the air. Her pistol flew, and two very strong men were on her.

THE JEEP WAS JUST A THOUSAND FEET away. Judd saw one man in it, driving. For some reason the man stopped the vehicle, engine still running, and leaned across and opened the passenger door.

Eva had deployed safely, so Judd gestured at Tucker. Tucker grimaced and looked as if he were going to argue. Then he leaped up and ran.

Judd leaned out again and shot three bursts. They had managed to take down one man, and the others were lying flat, shooting whenever they thought they had a target and sometimes when they did not.

Before the guards had time to return fire, Judd sprinted, and Tucker vanished down the ravine. Judd did not look, just jumped and let his heels act as inefficient brakes as he slipped and careened down the steep incline into heavy green soup.

Tucker's head was rotating. "Where is she?"

"Eva," Judd called in a low voice.

There was no answer, but there was a yell from above.

"They're coming," Tucker said. "Let's move."

"Not without Eva. Eva!" Judd shouted.

"Dammit, son. They've probably got her. She'd be waiting otherwise. Maybe that's why the Jeep stopped with its door open—to pick up her and whoever captured her. You're not going to do her any good if you get caught or killed. *Move.*"

Judd said nothing. Instead he turned to go down the ravine to the Jeep. To Eva.

But Tucker slammed the back of his helmet. "Dammit, Judson. *The other direction.*"

Judd shook his head to clear it, then ripped off the helmet. They ran southeast, toward the compound. Tucker pulled off his helmet, and both replenished their ammo. The ravine was uneven, filled with rocks slowing their progress.

"This isn't working," Judd said, listening to the noise of the feet running along the top of the ravine, overtaking them. "We need to get rid of the bastards. You go. I'll handle them."

From a trouser loop, he unhooked a frag grenade and held it in his right hand. Tucker saw it and accelerated, while Judd slid low into the deep shadows on the ravine's north side.

He waited motionless as the guards approached.

"They're heading to the house," a confident bass voice said.

Radio or walkie-talkie, Judd thought.

"Sure," the man continued. "No problem. We'll get them."

They were almost above him. Judd inhaled, exhaled, pulled the safety pin with his left hand, rolled the grenade over the crest, and sprinted, his boots hitting rocks so fast his speed kept him upright. White light flashed. The explosion thundered. As dirt rained down, he caught up with Tucker, who had hiked himself up the side and was peering back.

"No one's upright," Tucker reported. "They've got to have some serious injuries. That'll keep them busy."

They jogged off, but Judd saw Tucker was tiring. Judd slowed them to a fast walk and took out the reader that followed the tracker in Eva's ankle bracelet.

"She's in the compound already. Looks as if she's a couple of levels down under the main house." He gazed at Tucker. "Did you see any Jeeps anywhere near us?"

"Nary a one."

"Too bad. I was hoping we could grab one. Okay, Plan B. When we get closer to the compound, I've got an idea how to get us inside."

"It'd better be a damn good one," Tucker said. "They sure as hell are going to be ready for us."

CHAPTER 67

THE BOOK CLUB WAS ABOUT to start the third course. In their tailored tuxedos, with pistols holstered underneath, the men lounged around the great oval table in the spacious Library of Gold, firm in their knowledge the intruders would be killed if not by the guards, then certainly by them.

As they talked, their gazes kept returning to the magnificent illuminated manuscripts that blanketed the walls from marble floor to cove ceiling. Row after row of gold covers faced out, their hand-hammered faces reverberating with light that echoed from wall to wall and across the table like visual music. From dark, rich colors to soft pastels, the jewels and gems glittered and beckoned. The entire room seemed cast in a magical glow. Being here was always a visceral experience, and Martin Chapman sighed with contentment.

"Gentlemen, you have before you two exquisite Montrachet dry white wines," the sommelier explained in a thick French accent. "One is Domaine Leflaive, and the other Domaine de la Romanée-Conti. You will be possessed by their thrill factor—the hallmark of splendor in wine." A muscular man with the usual snooty expression of a top wine steward, he disappeared back against the books near the door, where his bureau of wine bottles stood.

Chapman was enjoying himself, absorbing the library's intoxicating blend of physicality, knowledge, history, and privilege. As the tall candles flickered, he cut into his Maine lobster with grilled portobello mushrooms and fig sauce and chewed slowly, savoring the ambrosial flavors. Taking a mouthful of one of the whites, he held it against his palate. With a rush of pleasure, he swallowed.

"I disagree," Thomas Randklev was saying. "Take Freud—he told his doctor collecting old objects, including books, was for him an addiction second in intensity only to nicotine."

"There's another side to it," Brian Collum said. "We're the only species capable of contemplating our own deaths, so of course we need something larger than ourselves to make the knowledge tolerable. As Freud would say, it's the price for our highly developed frontal lobes—and the glue that holds us together."

"I'm glad it's not just about money." Petr Klok grinned.

Laughter echoed from around the table.

The truth was, Chapman thought to himself, all of them had started as great readers, and if life had been otherwise, each would perhaps have taken a different path. For himself, he had accomplished far more than he had ever dreamed as a boy.

"I have one for you," Carl Lindström challenged. "'When you give someone a book, you don't give him just paper, ink, and glue, you give him the possibility of a whole new life.' Who wrote that?"

"Christopher Morley," Maurice Dresser said instantly. "And John Hill Burton argued that a great library couldn't be constructed; it was the growth of ages. As the Library of Gold is"—the seventy-five-year-old pointed at himself—"and *I* am."

The group chuckled, and Chapman felt his pager vibrate against his chest. He checked—Preston. Annoyed, he excused himself as the conversation moved on to assessing the two ethereal white burgundies. As he left, the sommelier was called over to join the debate.

Chapman entered the first of the two elevators. It rose silently, a solid capsule, but then, all of the underground stories were atomic bomb-hardened bunkers. On the highest belowground floor, he stepped out into the porcelain, steel, and granite of the kitchen. A hallway extended beyond it, where doors opened onto offices and storage. Farther was the enormous garage.

Gazing around, he inhaled the mouthwatering aromas of searing medallions of springbok, gazelle from South Africa. The *chefs de cuisine*, in their tall white hats, were barking orders in French as they prepared the course. The sous-chefs, *chefs de partie*, and waiters chosen from the library staff scurried.

Preston had a harried expression as he turned from the kitchen and met Chapman at the elevator.

"You need to talk to them, sir," Preston said.

"Are they still in my office?"

"Yes. Three men are watching them."

As they rode the elevator down to the third level, he asked, "What's the latest with Ryder and Andersen?" Chapman knew they had killed two of the guards and badly injured four. Preston had sent out additional men on foot to find them.

"I've increased the security around the compound. Everyone's on high alert."

"They'd damn well better be."

The elevator door opened, and they walked out into

the sitting area where the staff gathered for informal meetings. As expected it was deserted, since everyone was working. The doors along the hall were for offices, while the last one enclosed a gym with the latest cardio and Pilates equipment.

Preston pushed open the door to Chapman's office and stepped back.

Chapman marched past toward a frozen tableau of defiance. Motionless and angry, Eva Blake and Yitzhak Law were roped to chairs, their hands tied behind them. Blake was still in her skydiving jumpsuit, her face blackened. Neither seemed to recognize him, but then, it was doubtful they would know his world.

He ignored the guards and pulled up a chair in front of Blake and Law. "I'll make this easy. I've had the translators draw up a list of potential sources for the questions the book club will be asking during our tournament tonight. Since we have texts in the library that have been lost for centuries, there's no way you'd know their contents. Others you'll know already of course. Your job is to try to figure out the correct book for each question. You'll be given a chart showing where all of the illuminated manuscripts are shelved, and a few descriptive sentences about each. If you get all of the book club's questions correct, I'll let you live. That's called incentive."

They glanced at each other, then returned stony gazes to him.

Chapman looked back at Preston. "Bring in Cavaletti." He sank back in his chair, furious about the dinner he was missing.

In seconds Roberto Cavaletti was shoved into the room. "Yitzhak, Eva," he said. The small man was disheveled, his bearded face drawn.

Before anyone could say more, Chapman ordered, "Hit him, Preston."

As Law and Blake shouted and pulled against their ropes, Cavaletti cringed, and Preston rabbit-punched his cheek, connecting with a solid *thump*.

Cavaletti grabbed his face with a trembling hand, staggered, and fell to his knees.

"You bastard!" Blake yelled.

The professor's face paled. "You're monsters."

"Rethink this," Chapman snapped. "There are two of you. Together you have a much better chance of winning tonight than one of you would alone. If you won't do it for yourselves, do it for your friend Roberto here."

A large welt was rising on Cavaletti's left cheek.

Yitzhak Law stared. "All right, but only on condition you leave Roberto alone. No more injuries."

"No, Yitzhak," Roberto said. "No, no. Whatever they want, you will not stop the inevitable."

Blake glared at Chapman. "Very well. I agree, too. Do we have your guarantee you'll let all of us go if we win?"

"Of course," Chapman said easily. "Kardasian, see both are cleaned up and presentable." He stood and walked out.

Preston caught up with him in the sitting room. "I'll keep you apprised of the situation with Ryder and Andersen."

Chapman nodded, his mind already back at the dinner. Just then they heard one of the elevator doors close. They hurried and saw it had stopped at the lowest level, number four—the Library of Gold. Immediately they stepped into the other elevator, and Preston punched the button.

"Who in hell could it be?" Preston's expression was grim.

The elevator door opened onto an elegant anteroom. Straight ahead was an arched portal that led to offices along the windowed exterior corridor. Instead they sprinted left, and Preston opened a carved wood door onto the library and tonight's banquet.

The sommelier was walking toward his bureau, his broad tuxedoed back to them. At the sound of the door, he turned. They saw he was carrying two bottles of red wine—unopened.

Preston made a curt gesture, and the sommelier approached. Although as arrogant appearing as before, the man's eyes hinted at guilt. He held up the bottles as if they were a shield.

"What were you doing on the third floor?" Preston demanded.

"I am very sorry, sir. I found I must go to the kitchen for more wine. You gentlemen are more appreciative than I had expected. I was rushing to return and touched the wrong button in the elevator. Of course, I did not leave the elevator until here."

Chapman felt Preston relax.

"Resume your duties," Chapman said.

The sommelier bowed low and left. Chapman hurried to his dinner.

CHAPTER 68

TUCKER AND JUDD SAT IN THE DEEP shadow of a gnarled olive tree above the compound. As they cleaned their faces and hands and brushed their hair, they studied the buildings and the fifteen men patrolling in the illumination of the compound's security lights. All had M4s and were watching the grounds and hills alertly.

"Wonder how many are in the main house," Tucker said in a low voice.

"With luck, they won't notice us with so many new guards. That'll work to our advantage."

"I like being the new guy. Fewer expectations for you." Tucker inspected his Uzi, then his knife and wire garotte. "The rear door looks good."

"My thought, too. You up for this?"

"Can you still ride a bicycle?"

"Like a son of a bitch," Judd said.

They slung their Uzis onto their backs and slithered on their bellies down among the tall grasses and bushes of the slope. Small rocks cut into Tucker's jumpsuit.

After pausing several heart-stopping times when guards peered out onto the hillside, they reached the edge of the mesa and hid behind a row of manicured shrubs.

Waiting until the closest sentries were looking elsewhere, they ran behind the pool shed and crouched. Judd pointed to himself. Tucker nodded. He hated not being the one out front, but reality was reality—Judd was younger, stronger, and in better condition to take out the guard who would cross in front of the shed soon.

Listening to the sentry's feet pad across the marble path, Tucker crab-walked after Judd to the shed's far side. Judd inched forward, taking out a mirror with an attached bendable arm. He extended the arm, watched the mirror, then tossed both to Tucker and stood, pulling out his garotte.

From his low position, Tucker saw one leg appear and then a second. Immediately Judd stepped close behind the guard and dropped the garotte around his neck, yanking. The man fell back. Strangled noises came from his throat as Judd pulled him around and into the shed's shelter. Tucker ripped the sentry's M4 away and slapped on plastic cuffs. The sentry gasped, seemed to try to yell. Frantically he punched back with elbows and feet, torquing his body.

Tucker used the mirror to check for more guards, then looked back. Judd's grim face was frozen as he avoided the flailing blows. He lowered the man as he went limp.

They stripped him of his gear and clothes. While Judd put on the corpse's black khakis and black microfiber turtleneck, Tucker dressed the dead man in Judd's jumpsuit and smeared black greasepaint on his face and the backs of his hands. Peering carefully around, Tucker dragged him to the edge of the compound and rolled him deep into grasses.

When he returned, Judd was dressed and outfitted with the guard's radio, pistol, flashlight, and M4. He hooked on two grenades and checked the tracker to Eva's ankle bracelet, then slid it into his pants pocket. He pointed toward the house, where another guard would be making rounds. Then he pointed to himself.

Tucker nodded.

Using the mirror, Judd timed his exit, then vanished.

Tucker hurried around the shed. Sitting on his heels, he watched as Judd sauntered up to the next target. Just as the guard frowned, Judd violently bashed his M4 up under his chin, crushing his throat. His head whiplashed, and blood appeared on his lips. As Tucker ran to join them, Judd caught the guard and let his limp body down to the ground silently.

Tucker checked the man's carotid artery.

"Dead?" Judd whispered.

He nodded.

They surveyed around. No more sentries were in sight yet, and none showed on the other side of the rear door's window. After they stripped the dead man, Tucker changed into his black turtleneck and pants, at least one size too big, and cinched the waist tight. Judd added the finishing touches to the dead body and dragged it off to conceal near the other corpse.

As he waited for Judd, Tucker checked the M4 and examined the radio—and sensed more than saw someone through the glass of the door. He put a composed look of greeting on his face and turned.

The door opened. "Why aren't you patrolling?" The sentry was a straight tree trunk of a man, with a brush cut and a heavy jaw. A glimmer of doubt appeared in his eyes. "Who in hell are—"

Tucker slammed the butt of his M4 into the man's gut. It was always a safer debilitating shot than one to the chin. As the man emptied his lungs and started to double over, Tucker crashed the butt back up into his windpipe. Blood erupted from his mouth and nose. Tucker grabbed him, then hauled him toward the slope behind the shed where the other bodies were.

"This is beginning to look like a party with a bad outcome," Judd said.

Tucker rolled the man into the grass, watching as the tall fronds closed over him. "Let's go get Eva."

CHAPTER 69

Khost Province, Afghanistan

IT WAS PAST MIDNIGHT, AND CAPT. Sam Daradar was walking alone, his M4 over his arm. He inhaled, smelling the sweet mountain night air. When he had first arrived here, it had stung his nose, but now he could not get enough of it. Sometimes he dreamed about moving to Afghanistan. Life here was intrinsic to the elements and made sense to him in a way no Western city or rural area ever had.

He looked up. Sparkling stars spread across the night sky. For some reason the sky felt too vast tonight. An unnamed uneasiness filled him. He studied the great expanse of slopes and mountains that hid remote villages difficult to reach with large bodies of conventional forces. He and many of his men had spent the day out there and in town, talking with people.

Tonight he had phoned command, reporting his concerns. But he had been able to point only to restless whisperings in the local marketplace and to the fact that

Syed Ullah had actually appeared at the mosque for noon prayers—midweek—rather than saying them at home or on the trail as he usually did.

Sam turned back under the great tent of special camouflage netting and walked along the secret base's eighteen-inch-thick stone walls. The austere base housed only five hundred soldiers, but they were well trained and experienced. He stopped at the gate. Peering up at the guard tower, he nodded and received a nod in return.

Shaking his head at his unnameable uneasiness, he slid inside the gates and walked onto the base. Two Humvees were still out, watching, patrolling. They were due back in an hour. Perhaps they would have something for him, something that might be meaningless to them but he would understand.

ON HIS BELLY, SYED ULLAH peered down the hillside. The two Humvees were speeding along a dirt road above a valley two ridges away from town. The headlights were bright cones against the night, making the vehicles easy to track. In the pines on the eastern slope above the road were his men, hiding and dressed in the American uniforms, with the American equipment. He and his son Jasim were positioned north, in an open area high enough to have an excellent moonlit view.

"I am not as certain as you that this will work." Twenty-eight years old, Jasim had just returned from Peshawar and was dressed in American gear, too. He had the same large body as his father, and a thick black beard trimmed just enough so that it could bristle. Blessed with his mother's fine features, his face was finally coarsening with age, soldiering, and the weather. He had been a beautiful child, and now he was a real man.

"What concerns you, my son?"

"There are more than twice our number on the military base."

"Ah, but our men have what they do not—surprise. They are dressed like them, and they will wear the American helmets. Except for the ones on duty in the base, the Americans are asleep or playing with their video games. The only doubtful part is getting our people inside. And the answer to that we will know soon." Without moving his gaze from the road, he explained what was about to happen.

As they watched, the armored Humvees entered the attack zone, the sound of their big engines reverberating across the quiet valley. In the turret on top of each sat a gunner in a sling surrounded by steel protective plates, his M240B machine gun stationary in his hands. The guns covered an almost 360-degree swath, but the plates did not fit together. There were four open spaces of several inches at each corner.

Suddenly there were two explosions and fiery conflagrations in recently cut recesses in the trees. One was ahead of the Humvees, the other behind. From the recesses two cars in flames hurtled down toward the road. Smoke billowed out behind them, and sparks flew, igniting dry grasses. The Humvees were between the cars approaching the road, the sturdy pines above, and the cliff beneath.

The monstrous military vehicles slowed. The Americans would initially suspect this to be simple harassment, that the flaming cars would continue across the road and hurtle off the cliff. But Ullah's men had piled walls of rocks on the road's edge.

As the cars stopped, blocking the Humvees, machine-gun fire erupted from both gunners, strafing the trees and the road in hot fusillades. Tree trunks exploded; pine needles disintegrated. And finally there was silence. Slowly the Humvees' doors opened. As the gunners stood watch above, their weapons looking for targets, the infidels jumped out, M4s in hands, heading for the burning vehicle in front of them.

At that moment gunfire from his two hundred Pashtuns erupted from behind the rocky wall and out of holes dug under the pine forest. It was so fast and blistering, the infidels exposed on the road got off only a few shots while the machine gunners in the turrets furiously returned fire. On the road, the infidels fell, yelling, moaning, and six of Ullah's Pashtuns slid along the dirt, crawled up the sides of the Humvees, and rolled stun grenades through the open spaces into the turrets. Two loud *bangs* sounded. And then the only noise was of his converging men putting single gunshots into the heads of the infidels.

As they dragged the bodies into the pines, Ullah stood. They had pulled the unconscious machine-gunners from their cupolas and were killing them.

"Come." He ran.

With a shout of joy, Jasim passed him.

"Praise Allah," Ullah said as he arrived on the battlefield. He caught his breath. "How many of us have been killed or hurt?"

In his U.S. Army uniform, Hamid Qadeer stood straight to report. "Only fourteen."

"Good, good." The warlord walked around the Humvees, studying the vehicles. They were dirty and showed bullet holes, but that was nothing. The guards at the military base would pass them through, which was all he needed.

"I will join our men now." Jasim stood at his side. His excitement had calmed, and he had the severe look of a true Pashtun warrior.

Pride filled Ullah. "Of course, my son."

CHAPTER 70

The Isle of Pericles

THE BANQUET WAS FINISHED, a complete success. As the plates were cleared and the sommelier poured brandy, the men stretched back in their chairs, sated, slightly intoxicated. Chapman related the latest report—Preston's men had not yet found Ryder and Andersen.

"Frankly, I hope those damn people do get into the house and come down here," Grandon Holmes announced. He patted the side of his chest where his pistol was holstered.

At no time in the history of the annual banquet had the members attended armed, but tonight was an unusual night. Despite the good humor, a thread of menace had grown among them. The island had been violated.

"It's been a while since I've done active target practice." Brian Collum gave a cold smile.

"On the other hand," Maurice Dresser grumbled, "why in hell are we paying the guards astronomical sums if they don't handle the job?"

"Maurice is right," Petr Klok said. "Ryder and Andersen will never make it to the library."

"Pity." Carl Lindström sighed.

"I heard from Syed Ullah," Chapman said, changing the subject. "His Pashtuns are uniformed, armed, and eager to go. We should have word in an hour or so."

"Excellent," Reinhardt Gruen said. "I did some checking about the village near the Khost military base. I was correct—the entire area is a hotbed of jihadist activity. Ullah is one hell of a tough warlord to have been able to control it. My thinking is he will use tonight's strike to rid himself of local Taliban enemies—which means our enemies, too. Then the land will be ours. I've been dreaming about those diamonds. All in all, Marty, you're looking very good. It will be a fine night. One for the record books."

ARMS CROSSED TIGHTLY over her chest, Eva paced, inspecting again the closet where they were being held. There was no furniture. The hinges to the heavy door had been installed on the outside, and two dead bolts sealed them in. An overhead fluorescent light was lit all the time, too high for them to reach, and the switch was in the corridor. The walls were solid concrete blocks. If there was a way to break out, she had not found it.

"You must accept it, Eva. We are trapped." Gazing up at her, Roberto huddled in a corner. His eye was swollen shut, and his cheek was distended, a hot red.

"An accurate assessment of our condition," Yitzhak said from where he sat close beside Roberto. "Still, it's not the end of the world."

"Yet." Roberto sighed.

Yitzhak put heartiness into his voice. "For a man who worries about leaving our time zone, look how well you're doing, Roberto."

"I am heroic." He gave a small smile and shook his head. Still, there had been a flash in his eyes that told Eva he had not given up completely.

"We'll figure it out, Roberto," she encouraged. "Do you think we need to go over the list one more time, Yitzhak?" On it were sixteen illuminated manuscripts, twice the number they would need to name. If the circumstances were different, they would have marveled at the many lost books, but their existence only added to their frustration, and the large number to their fears.

"I think not." Yitzhak looked up, his bald head pasty in the overbright fluorescent light. "Together we know nearly half, and we'll just have to make educated guesses about the rest."

"I wish they would take me to the library with you," Roberto said. "But it is obvious they will not."

He was right—she and Yitzhak wore tuxedos Preston had given them, while Roberto was still in the rumpled shirt and pants he'd had on when captured.

"But there's hope, Roberto," she told him. "We're still breathing."

"It is a small hope, and I will treasure it." He sighed.

There was the noise of dead bolts being slid opened, and the guard they had heard called Harold Kardasian appeared, pointing his assault rifle. He was sturdy, with thick brown hair streaked with gray.

"Time to go," he announced.

Eva looked for some sign of help in his eyes, but saw only neutrality.

Both Roberto and Yitzhak stood up.

"Not you," Kardasian ordered. "Only the professor and Dr. Blake."

As Roberto slid back down the wall, they said good-bye to him.

Preston was waiting in the corridor, dressed in his

black leather jacket and jeans, tall and looming, his features stony. He carried two thick bath towels.

"What are those for?" Eva asked instantly.

"That's none of your concern. Move."

They marched Eva and Yitzhak to the stairs beside the elevators and took them down one floor into an anteroom. For a moment Eva felt a frisson of excitement—they were going to see the Library of Gold. She sensed an electric current from Yitzhak and knew he was thinking the same thing.

One guard opened a massive carved door, and golden light appeared. Yitzhak took Eva's arm, and they walked inside and stopped. For a few moments, her fear vanished. It was as if they were in a cocoon of timeless knowledge dressed in the earth's most dazzling elements.

"Bewitching," Yitzhak whispered.

They drank in the four walls of gold-covered books. The embedded gems sparkled in the pure air. For an instant it seemed to Eva that nothing else on the planet mattered.

"Don't give me the cold tomb of a museum but the fire-breathing world of words and ideas," Yitzhak said. "Give me a library. *This* library."

The tall man who had ordered Preston to hit Roberto walked toward them. "Who said that, Professor?"

Yitzhak looked at him sharply. "I did."

The man chuckled. "My name is Martin Chapman. Come with me. It's time you met everyone."

He motioned to the guards to leave. Preston closed the door and stood in front of it. They followed Chapman to a large oval table around which seven men sat, drinking from brandy glasses.

With a shock, Eva recognized Brian Collum—her attorney, her friend. Watching her, he had laughter on his long, handsome face. She glanced away, smoothed her features, and turned back.

"You look wonderful in a tux," he told her.

"You bastard."

"It's good to see you, too. And in such an appropriate setting."

She said nothing, fighting the fury that surged through her as she realized he must have been the one who entangled Charles with the Library of Gold. And he had sent her to prison, knowing she was innocent. As Chapman made formal introductions, she forced herself to be calm. Then she assessed the situation: Besides the eight members of the book club, only the sommelier and Preston were in the room. The bath towels still dangled from his hand. Puzzled, she tried to figure out what they meant.

"Does everyone understand the rules?" Chapman asked. When a chorus of yeses answered, he said, "Then the tournament begins. Petr, you're first this year."

"Socrates, 469 or 470 to 399 B.C.," said a bearded man with stylishly clipped hair. "Of course he is credited as one of the founders of Western philosophy. What most people do not know is his utopian republic ruled by philosopher-kings also included glorification of the benefits of a caste system and a powerful argument for the right of armies to conquer and colonize. Hitler must have loved that. Your challenge is to find the illuminated manuscript in which Socrates is shown as a clown teaching his students to hoodwink their way out of debt."

Eva cleared her throat. "There's no such thing as a real history from Socrates' time that dealt with him or Greece." Hiding her nervousness, she looked at Yitzhak, but he shook his head. He did not know the answer. She had an idea, but it was a long time ago, not since

college, that she had read it. "However, we do have plays
and other writings. What I remember is 'The Clouds,' an
old comedy by Aristophanes."

She gazed at the questioner, hoping to see in his face
whether she was correct. His expression showed nothing.

Yitzhak found the location of the manuscript on the
list, and they walked quickly down one of the long
walls, looking for it. With both hands he lifted out a
gold volume embedded with sapphires and handed it to
Petr Klok.

There was a long pause as they waited for his answer.

With a flourish Klok took the book and stood it up on
the table to admire. "The world has only eleven complete plays by Aristophanes, although he wrote forty.
The Library of Gold has the entire collection."

There was a round of jaunty applause.

Eva and Yitzhak exchanged a look of relief.

Chapman ended it: "Thom, you're next. Try to beat
them, will you?"

JUDD OPENED THE REAR DOOR to the main house and
slid inside, Tucker following. Their M4s ready, they
listened for sounds and checked a wall of glass displaying the reflecting pool and spotlighted palms they had
seen in NSA photos. When they heard nothing, they padded past closed doors and entered an enormous living
room that stretched across the front of the house, glass
windows showcasing the ocean view. The wall of glass
stretched around the corner on the west side, with
heavy glass double doors showing a marble path that
led out toward the tennis courts, pool, and distant helipad.

Two sentries were in sight patrolling, their gazes cast
outward—not toward the house.

"So far so good," Judd murmured. He pulled out his reader.

But just as they hurried toward the stairwell beside the elevators, their radios crackled. They snapped them from their belts and looked outdoors. Both of the sentries were grabbing their radios, too. And now a third sentry was in sight, doing the same.

Tucker swore, and they punched their Receive buttons.

"Three down," the disembodied voice snapped. "Rendezvous behind the pool shed. *Now.*"

"It's just a matter of time until they guess we're inside," Tucker said as he ran past packing crates to the stairwell door and yanked it open.

M4s ready, they raced down one flight of steps, peered through the window on the door and saw a busy kitchen, then ran down another flight. The door window showed an empty hallway of closed doors.

As they tore down a third flight, Judd whispered, "She's on this floor."

At the door, they looked into a sitting area of comfortable sofas and chairs. No one was in sight.

Judd inhaled, exhaled, and slid around the door, crouching, M4 in both hands. In an instant Tucker was beside him. No one was around.

Heart pounding, Judd dashed down the hall, watching the reader, and then stopped. *Eva.* With one hand he slammed open the door's dead bolts and turned the knob.

"Judd, is that you?" Roberto Cavaletti stared up, his battered face breaking into a smile. "You are blond." He scrambled to his feet.

"Where's Eva?"

"In the Library of Gold." He hurried toward them. "She gave me her ankle bracelet so you would find me and I could warn you. We overheard the guards talking—all of them at the big banquet have pistols. Eva and Yitzhak were taken there to be part of some mortal game. If they guess wrong, we will die. But if they guess right, I think they plan to murder us anyway."

"Where's the library?" Judd asked grimly.

CHAPTER 71

Khost Province, Afghanistan

SYED ULLAH MET THE PAKISTANI reporter and cameraman at the mosque and drove them out to the edge of the sleeping town. Parking near the remains of mudbrick huts, the three got out, bundled in long down coats against the night's cold. Ullah sniffed, smelling the strong scent of animal manure.

"Please turn around, General," the reporter said.

The cameraman motioned him into position. The two were from the respected Pakistan Television Corporation, the country's national TV broadcaster, whose news was regularly picked up by wire services and media around the globe.

"This is Asif Badri." The reporter held a mike and looked solemnly into the camera. "Tonight I am in Khost province, Afghanistan. With me is the esteemed general Syed Ullah, a legendary mujahideen hero of the war against the Soviets. Tell us what is in the distance, General."

The camera focused on Ullah. Putting on his gravest expression, he spoke into the reporter's mike and pointed with his AK-47. "That is a secret American military base. About five hundred soldiers." He paused, considering. He did not want to completely insult American listeners, especially since he planned to make a lot of money from Chapman. Phrasing his words carefully, he continued, "They are here to clear out illegal activity and are generally well behaved. Unfortunately, there is a serious problem."

The camera panned over to the military base with its massive lights glowing in and around it, captured beneath the special netting that stretched in a great canopy far beyond the walls. Above the netting was black night; below it, bright daylight. It was a dramatic picture, showing the infidels' technical ingenuity and their awful ability to fool the world.

"Does your national government know about the base?" the reporter asked.

"Kabul is completely ignorant," the warlord lied.

"You mentioned a serious problem. Tell us about it."

"It is a sad story," Ullah intoned, embracing his rifle. "The Americans complain about our tribal differences while they have their own. Sports, politics, religion—and business. Remember, their murder rate is among the highest in the world. One of my people overheard an American soldier talking to another in a town governed by another general. They, too, have a secret base in the mountains. Those soldiers are very angry at our soldiers. I am sorry to tell you all of them are smuggling drugs and exporting heroin. As you know, it is very lucrative." He shook his head sadly. "The other soldiers are planning to murder the soldiers here tonight because they have been poaching their business."

"Have you informed Kabul?"

"What can they do? I am in charge, and another general is in charge of the other town. We are helpless against the Americans' far superior weapons. I am left only with being able to tell the world in hopes this will never happen again." He sighed. "It is a tragedy."

The reporter turned off his microphone. "Did you get it all, Ali?"

The cameraman nodded. "When do we go to the base?"

Ullah looked into the hills and pointed with his AK-47 at two sets of headlights. His son Jasim was in the lead vehicle with Hamid Qadeer, who spoke perfect Americanized English.

"They are coming out of the mountains now," he told them. "Those are two American Humvees. My informant said there would be a total of about two hundred soldiers. The arrival of the Humvees means the rest are now in place nearby. Once the Humvees get inside the base, their plan is to silently kill the soldiers in the guard tower and open the gates. The rest is inevitable. Get into my car. I will drive you closer. We must go slow and without headlights. You will be able to film the action outside, and after it is over, you will be the first to record the results of the horrible massacre."

CHAPTER 72

The Isle of Pericles

EVERYONE IN THE LIBRARY of Gold was focused on Preston, who was standing inside the door with his M4 and thick bath towels and listening to a message on his radio. As Eva watched, he strode to Chapman and spoke quietly into his ear.

"Gentlemen, we may have visitors," Chapman announced with relish. "Take out your pistols."

Swiftly the men laid their weapons on the table beside the illuminated manuscripts. Although they had obviously been drinking, their hands and gazes were steady, and they moved with authority. There was an undercurrent of enthusiasm, too, Eva thought. They were looking forward to shooting their guns.

She exchanged a worried look with Yitzhak.

The sommelier advanced with bottles of brandy. He poured into Chapman's glass first, emptying the bottle, then poured from a fresh one into the glasses of the other men.

As the sommelier returned to his bureau, everyone looked at Chapman.

Eva and Yitzhak had answered correctly seven of the eight tournament questions. The competitive excitement among the men around the banquet table was almost tactile as they waited for the final challenge—from the director, Martin Chapman.

"Jesus of Nazareth; known as the Rabbi and later as Jesus Christ, 7 to 2 B.C. to sometime between A.D. 26 and 36," Chapman said. "Jesus was the leader of an apocalyptic movement, a faith healer, a rabble-rouser, and with John the Baptist, the founder of Christianity. The consensus of scholars is the four canonical gospels about his life—Matthew, Mark, Luke, and John—weren't recorded by any of the original disciples or first-person witnesses, although they were probably written within the first century of his death. Your challenge is to find in the library where Jesus tells one of his disciples he 'will exceed' the others and learn 'the mysteries of the kingdom.'"

Eva did not remember either quote. She looked at Yitzhak, and he shook his head worriedly. They turned away to study the list. There were three possibilities: One was St. Jerome's early fifth-century Vulgate Bible. The second was *Vetus Latina,* which was compiled before the Vulgate. The third was even earlier, the title translating to *The Old Gospels.* They read the descriptions.

"He's trying to fool us by referring to Matthew, Mark, Luke, and John," Yitzhak whispered.

She had reached the same conclusion. "Do you think it's in the Gnostic book of Judas?" The only known text of the Gospel of Judas had been written seventeen hundred years before, discovered in fragments in the Egyptian desert in 1945 and assembled and translated from the Coptic language in 2006, which was when she had read it.

"I do."

"Then the third one, *The Old Gospels*, is the only choice," she said, "although it predates the Gnostics."

"Dazzle them." Anger flashed in his eyes.

She turned back to the table. The brandy glasses glistened. The men's calculating eyes watched her.

She paused. "In the New Testament, Judas Iscariot betrays Jesus to the Romans for thirty silver coins. The Gospel of Judas says the exact opposite—that it's Jesus' idea, and that he asks Judas to do it so his body can be sacrificed on the cross. If Jesus did ask Judas to do that, it's logical he might've encouraged him by saying he 'will exceed' the other disciples and learn 'the mysteries of the kingdom.' Therefore, the quotation is from *The Old Gospels*. According to the list we were given, the book contains quite a few, including those of James, Peter, Thomas, Mary Magdalene, Philip—and Judas."

Was she right? She could read nothing in Chapman's face. Yitzhak was already walking along the wall. Following him, she passed a section on the Koran and other early Muslim works. Next to it Bibles and Christian literature were shelved.

Yitzhak stared at a manuscript covered in hammered gold. At the center was a simple design—small blue topazes in the outline of a fish. Gingerly he picked up the old book and carried it to Chapman.

Eva's lungs were tight. She forced herself to breathe.

"Damn you." Chapman took the book. "You're right. *The Old Gospels* is an original, written on parchment pages that Constantine the Great ordered rebound and covered in gold in the early fourth century. It's pre-Gnostic, composed in the first century A.D., during the time the books of Matthew, Mark, Luke, and John were recorded. It can arguably be considered as accurate as the New Testament." He stroked the book. "The power of this is considerable. It explodes the myth of monolithic Christianity and demonstrates how diverse and fascinating the early movement really was."

There was a round of enthusiastic applause—for Chapman, not for them. He stood the illuminated manuscript on the table next to his pistol and smiled at it.

The men raised their brandy glasses.

"Good question, Marty," said one.

"Hear, hear."

They drank.

As Chapman swallowed and put down his glass, he frowned at Eva and Yitzhak and gestured behind him to Preston.

Immediately the security chief was at his side, his M4 in one hand, the towels in the other.

"Now?" Preston asked.

"By all means."

Preston leaned the assault rifle against the table and took his pistol from the holster at his hip. The men's gazes were riveted as he advanced toward Eva and Yitzhak with the two towels.

"The later Assassins." Yitzhak backed up. "That's what the towels mean. They covered entrance and exit wounds to control the mess that spraying blood makes."

CHAPTER 73

JUDD, TUCKER, AND ROBERTO hurried along the quiet hallway toward the stairwell. Judd saw instantly both elevators were descending. Passing them, he yanked open the stairwell's door and heard feet pounding down from high above, echoing against the stone walls. They sounded like a battalion.

"Run!"

With Tucker and Roberto following, he hurtled down the steps to the fourth level and peered through the window into a formal anteroom. Assault rifle in both hands, he slid out, Tucker on his heels. No one was around.

Tucker pulled Roberto from the stairwell, locked and bolted the door, and shoved the small man into a corner beside a tall cabinet, where he would be out of range.

Judd nodded at a huge carved-wood door. "The Library of Gold." But before they could breach it they still had to face the security teams in the elevators.

"Looks like it," Tucker agreed.

Judd dropped flat, facing one of the two elevators.

Tucker lay prone in front of the other. They aimed their M4s.

Tucker's elevator arrived first. Four guards were standing inside. Tucker sent a fusillade of automatic fire across them, the noise thunderous. Completely surprised, they'd had no time to aim.

As they grabbed the walls and each other and fell, Judd's elevator door started to open. This time gunfire exploded from the cage, but aimed high, where men should have been standing. Immediately Judd returned fire, ripping rounds across the five men's torsos. They staggered and sank, blood pouring from their chests. The air filled with a metallic stink.

Judd and Tucker jumped up and disabled each elevator.

Roberto was already at the library's big wood door, his eyes wide, his gaze determined.

"Don't go in there," Tucker snapped from across the room.

A guard appeared at the window in the stairwell door and yanked, trying to open it. Other guards were behind him, up the steps. The guard saw Judd and Tucker. As he shot through the glass, they sprinted. The rounds splintered across walls and into mirrors.

When they reached Roberto, there was sudden silence—they were beyond the guard's view, with only seconds before he broke through the door. As bullets exploded again, Judd exchanged a look with Tucker. Tucker put Roberto behind him and readied his assault rifle.

Judd opened the massive carved door a crack, realizing instantly its core was solid steel, the hinges hidden, the movement pneumatic. It was a vault door. No way anyone could shoot through with an M4, and there was no lock to pick.

They slid inside, low, weapons leveled. As Tucker

slammed the bolts behind them, sealing out the guards, Judd stared at eight pistols aimed at them by men standing around a large dining table. He quickly took in the room.

To the right was a shocked sommelier cringing in front of a wine bureau, his hand inside his tuxedo jacket, clasping his heart. Farther along the same wall Yitzhak crouched, sweat greasing his bald head. Eva was sprawled on the floor near him. Oddly, both were dressed in tuxedos. Preston lifted his pistol from Eva to train it on Judd and Tucker. Wearing jeans and a black leather jacket as he had the last time Judd had seen him, he let two towels fall from his hand.

"Judd, what a pleasant surprise," Martin Chapman was saying. "I thought I wouldn't have the pleasure of seeing you again." Tall and genteel, he stood before the banquet table, his thick white hair flowing, his blue eyes sparkling with amusement, his pistol calmly pointed.

Judd stared at his father's old friend. "You're the one who had Dad killed? You son of a bitch." As a wave of fury rolled through him, he felt Tucker's restraining hand on his arm.

"Actually," Chapman said, "Jonathan did it to himself. I tried to talk him out of it, but you know what a hothead he could be. He was completely unreasonable. I'm sorry we lost him. All of us liked him a great deal."

He gestured with his free hand at the other men around the table. They came out and stood in a line on either side of him, their weapons never wavering as they aimed at Tucker and Judd.

Judd studied the men in their expensive evening clothes. Each was at least six feet tall and ranged in age from early forties to late sixties. Perfectly groomed and with strong athletic bodies, they had an unmistakable air of pride and confidence. Their uniformity was chilling.

"Yitzhak." Roberto ran around the outside of the room, passing the sommelier.

The sommelier watched, his eyes enormous. A man in his sixties, he had deep wrinkles and a bulbous red nose, a man who enjoyed wine far too much.

"Shh," Yitzhak warned.

Roberto dropped to the floor beside the professor. As Preston glanced in their direction, Eva lashed out a foot at his leg.

Preston stepped back and pointed his pistol down at her. "Get up!"

Judd realized several of the tuxedoed men were weaving. Those close to the table steadied themselves on it.

Chapman noticed, too. Puzzled, he looked left and right along the line.

The knees of two buckled, and they fell.

"What in hell—" The oldest grabbed his forehead and keeled over.

"Goddammit." Another stared at his gun hand. It was shaking uncontrollably.

Two more struggled to stay upright, and then all three collapsed.

"The brandy—it must've been poisoned," the youngest said to Chapman.

He and Chapman were the last standing. They swung their pistols toward the sommelier.

With the hand that had been gripping his heart, the sommelier whipped out a 9-mm Walther. In one smooth motion, he fired twice. One bullet struck the younger man in the head, and the other shattered Chapman's gun hand.

Reeling, Chapman grabbed up the M4 with the other hand.

At the same time, Preston shoved Eva aside and was running along the wall of books, aiming at the sommelier. Before the sommelier could swing around to fire, Preston squeezed off a shot that sliced across the top of the sommelier's shoulder. From across the room Judd released three explosive bursts into Preston's chest.

Preston froze. Fury crossed his aristocratic features as he looked down at the blood spreading across his heart. He took two more steps. "You don't know what you're doing. The books must be protected—" He pitched over onto his face, arms limp at his sides. His fingers unfurled, and his gun fell with a metallic *clunk* onto the marble floor.

Ignoring Chapman, the sommelier ran to Preston and grabbed the pistol. "Nice shot, Judd. Thanks." As blood dripped down his jacket, he felt for Preston's carotid artery.

"Damn you all to hell!" Martin Chapman trained the M4 on Judd, his finger white on the trigger.

Judd aimed.

"No!" the sommelier shouted from where he crouched. "We need Chapman alive!"

No one moved. Chapman scowled, his weapon pointed at Judd, Judd's pointed at him. The room seemed to reverberate with tension.

Then Chapman's face smoothed. A twinkle appeared in his eyes, and warmth infused his voice. "You should know, Judd, that your father had always hoped you'd join our book club." With his bloody free hand he gestured grandly at the towering expanse of jeweled books. "These can be yours, too. Think of the history, of the trust your father and I inherited. It's sacred. With Brian dead, we're shy three members now. Join us. It would've pleased Jonathan a great deal."

Behind Chapman, Eva had been watching. Judd kept his eyes apparently locked on Chapman, while noting she was taking off her shoes.

"Sacred?" he retorted. "What you have here isn't a trust. It's god-awful selfishness."

Eva sprinted in stocking feet across the marble floor, her black hair flying, her eyes narrowed. She threw herself forward onto her belly and slid silently under the banquet table.

Chapman gave Judd a wry smile, "As John Dryden said, 'Secrets are edged tools and must be kept from children and fools.' You were raised to appreciate the priceless value of this remarkable library. No one can take care of it—cherish it—better than we can. You have a responsibility to help us—"

Hunching up, Eva threw her shoulders into the backs of his knees. He reeled, then crashed forward with a grunt, landing hard. His M4 spun away. He swore loudly and scrambled toward it.

But Eva scooped it up and rolled, and Judd, Tucker, and the sommelier converged. The four stood over Chapman, pointing their weapons.

Face flushed, he clasped his good hand over his bloody hand against his ruffled white shirt and peered around at his downed companions then back over his shoulder at the dead Preston. Finally he glared up, deep fury and a strange hurt in his eyes.

"Who are you?" he demanded from the sommelier.

"Call me Domino," the sommelier said in a husky voice. He had a wide face and a stocky figure. "The Carnivore sends his regards. My orders are to remind you that you were warned about his rules. Then I'm supposed to scrub you."

"I'm not dead yet, you asshole. What did you do to them?"

"Gamma hydroxy butyrate, GHB. Tasteless, odorless, and colorless. A date-rape drug. In the brandy, of course, poured from the 'new' bottle. They'll wake up in a few hours with very bad headaches. I heard you talking. Tell us what's going to happen in Khost, Afghanistan."

"Why would I do that?"

Judd had no idea what Domino meant, but he came from the Carnivore, and that was enough reason for him. All four weapons moved slightly, training on Chapman's head.

"Tell us!" Judd said.

Chapman stared around at the guns. "And if I do?"

"Maybe you get to live, you lucky SOB," Judd said. "But if we have to kill you now, that's all right, too. Your friends will wake up, and one of them will talk."

Chapman blinked slowly. Then he sat up and told a tale of a forgotten diamond mine in Afghanistan and the warlord who was going to eliminate Taliban fighters so the army base would be closed and Chapman could buy the land.

"It's too late to do anything about it," Chapman finished. "The action is going on right now. Besides, it ultimately benefits all of us. Actually, the world. You don't want to stop it."

"You goddamned fool!" Tucker exploded. "You think you can trust a warlord to do anything he promises? He's going to do only what he thinks is in his best interest. There could be a dozen different scenarios, and none of them we'd like. Worse than that, the United States maintains those secret bases because Kabul needs us to. This could bring down the government and start another bloody war." He looked around the room. "Where's a satellite phone?"

As Domino handed one to him, the door thudded. All looked at the only entrance to the library. The guards must have finally broken through to the anteroom and were preparing to blast their way into the library. New worry filled the room.

"They may have something with more kick than M4s," Judd said, listening.

Tucker nodded and punched numbers on the phone's keypad, while they stood silently, trapped.

CHAPTER 74

Khost Province, Afghanistan

THE COLD CHILL OF THE KHOST night was getting to Sam Daradar as he stood at the open window of the guard tower with privates Abe Meyer and Diego Castillo. He inspected the headlights of the Humvees approaching, one behind the other, in the far distance. They looked alone and exposed out there in the black night.

"Any sign of trouble?" Sam asked.

"No, sir," Meyer said. "Quiet as usual."

"Get them on the horn."

Meyer flicked on his radio. "Lieutenant, the captain wants to talk to you."

Sam Daradar punched the button on his radio. "Why are you late?"

There was the sound of coughing from the Humvee. "Sorry, sir. I think I'm getting a cold. We did an extra recon around Smugglers' Point. I had a hunch, so wanted to check it out, but there wasn't anyone there or in the valley." His voice was so thick it was almost un-recognizable.

Silently Sam swore. The last thing he needed was illness sweeping through the base. "See anything any-where else?"

"No, sir. Quiet as a grave." The man cleared his throat.

"I want a full report when you get in." Sam ended the connection. "I'm going out."

Climbing down from the tower, he passed sandbags piled against the wall. Nearby were the Sea Huts that housed the mess and the Tactical Operations Center, and farther were the Butler Huts where his soldiers bunked. The gate unlocked and opened enough for him to slide through.

Hurrying through the light, he reached the darkness and slowed. Letting his eyes adjust, he stared around at the flatlands that rose into hills and then at the high-peaked mountains. To his left was the town. He could barely make out the rough outlines of it. There were a few lights. Nothing unusual. Moonlight shimmered down on the shrubs and clumps of trees around the base. A wind had risen, sighing. He looked for move-ment, listened for sound, sniffed for odors. He was getting to be as much sixteenth century as the other inhabitants around here.

Turning on his heel, he hurried back inside and up into the guard tower. As he took up his post at the win-dow again, he noticed movement coming from the di-rection of town. It was a vehicle of some kind, the moonlight illuminating a silvery surface. Strange that the headlamps were not alight.

He put infrared binoculars to his eyes and stared. Dammit, it was Syed Ullah's Toyota Land Cruiser. As he watched, it stopped, and three people climbed out—one was Ullah. They peered at the base and talked. Then one lifted something to his shoulder, aiming it. Sam stared hard. It looked like a movie camera. What in hell was going on?

When the Humvees were about fifty yards from the base, he ordered the gates opened.

The radio sounded. He picked it up, expecting the caller to be the lieutenant reporting he had sighted Ullah, too.

Instead a stranger said, "Captain Daradar, I'm patching you in to Tucker Andersen, CIA. He has important information for you."

Instantly a strong voice announced, "This is Andersen. I've got a story to tell you. I'll make it quick."

Sam listened with growing concern.

When Andersen finished, Sam said, "There've been no attacks in town or at any of the huts in sight of here. I've got a patrol coming in now. I spoke to the lieutenant a while ago, and he said it was quiet in the boonies, too. But Ullah is in the dust bowl near here with two other people, and it looks as if they filmed the base. Maybe they're the Pakistani news crew your informant told you about."

"You know Syed Ullah personally?"

"As well as any outsider can."

"What's he capable of?"

There was no hesitation. "Anything." Sam signed off and snapped to Private Meyer, "Sound the alarm. I want all troops at their stations, and the rest here. Close the gates as soon as the Humvees get inside."

As the alarm blared and orders were relayed over loudspeakers, Sam grabbed his assault rifle and ran down from the guard tower. He waited well behind it, out of view of the gate. The Humvees would stop on the hard-packed dirt in a well-lit area in front of him. Within seconds a lieutenant and a corporal were beside him.

"What's going on, sir?" the lieutenant asked.

"Don't know yet." Sam had a feeling he had the answer, but he did not like it. "Any of the men got viruses or colds?"

The lieutenant and corporal shook their heads.

"Yeah, I didn't think so. I could be wrong about this, but we can't take any chances. I think Ullah's men may be in those Humvees." He told the lieutenant what he wanted him to do.

As more soldiers arrived, the lieutenant directed half to stay with Sam and ran with the rest to the other side of the gate, where they would be out of sight, too.

With a rumble, the Humvees rolled into the base. Sam peered around the edge of the guard tower to check on them. The gunners in the cupolas wore U.S. Army uniforms and helmets. They were dozing over their machine guns. He could not see their faces, and whoever was inside was unseeable, too, through darkened glass. But there were fresh bullet holes in the vehicles. The gates closed behind the Humvees with a clang.

Sam signaled. And four hundred fully equipped, armored, and armed soldiers swarmed out so quickly, the gunners had time only to lift their heads before they were pulled from their turrets and their weapons torn away. It was an overpowering show of force, rows of assault rifles pointed at the Humvees from every possible angle.

For a moment there was no movement. Then the doors opened, and more men in army uniforms stepped out, hands high above their heads, holding army-issue M4s. All were Afghans. U.S. soldiers ripped away the weapons and took the pistols from their belts.

Sam looked up at the guard tower and shouted, "Is Ullah still out there?"

Private Castillo leaned out. "Yes, sir. They filmed the Humvees entering the base, but the light on the camera's off again now."

Sam pushed through his men to reach Ulla's son Jasim, whose tall frame was spread-eagled against the first vehicle. His face was sullen. Sam reached up and grabbed a fistful of Jasim's jacket and tightened it against his throat.

"You want your father to die?" Sam threatened. Then he lied: "I've got a sharpshooter in the tower, and all I have to do is give the order and Syed Ullah is a donkey turd. Tell me what in hell is going on."

The young man's eyes widened. Still he said nothing.

Sam reminded him harshly he was Pashtun. "Your first duty is to protect your family."

In a halting voice Jasim relayed the details of the plan to invade the base and kill all of the soldiers.

Sam hunched his shoulders in fury. He shook Jasim hard once and released him. He barked out an order to his men: "Find out where they left the bodies of our people, then lock him up. Let's move out."

Sam roared out of the base in a Humvee. In other Humvees and running on foot, his soldiers spread in an arc over the flatlands. Ullah's men rose from behind bushes, from holes in the ground, and from behind trees and hotfooted away across the austere landscape. Most would be captured, but not all. But Sam sure as hell was going to catch Ullah.

There was the distant noise of an engine coming to life, and Ullah's Land Cruiser turned in a big circle.

Sam's Humvee and two others lurched over the terrain at a far faster speed than the Land Cruiser, cutting it off as it turned onto the road that led into the hills and to Ullah's villa.

With a bullhorn, Sam blared out his open window, "Get out. Everyone get out! Now!"

M4 in hand, he jumped out of his Humvee and met Ullah and the two others on the dirt road. He was joined instantly by his men, weapons raised.

Ullah's broad face showed surprise, interest, concern. "Captain Daradar, it is very late for you to be patrolling."

"Good evening, Mr. Ullah. There's room in my Humvee for all of you. Your son is asking for you."

At the mention of Jasim, Ullah's black eyebrows raised a fraction, then knitted. It was a small gesture, but from the Pashtun it was everything. With his son in custody, he was not only overwhelmed by force but cornered by the Pashtunwali code.

"Give me your rifle," Sam ordered.

With a flourish, Ullah spun his AK-47, smiled winningly, and handed it over ceremoniously, butt first, the vanquished admitting defeat—for the moment.

What Sam wanted to do was shoot the damn warlord and give the journalists the interview of their lives, but the Kabul government and Uncle Sam would not like that. "Get in. We'll all go back to the base for some *American* tea."

CHAPTER 75

The Isle of Pericles

THERE WAS A FAINT EXPLOSION, and the Library of Gold door buckled. The guards would be inside in minutes. Despite the high-powered ventilation system, the air in the room seemed to thicken. As Eva rose to her feet, and Tucker spoke to Khost, Judd saw something in Domino's eyes.

"What else?"

Domino nodded and pressed his Walther against Chapman's ear. "Give me your satellite phone."

Slowly Chapman reached inside his tuxedo jacket and removed the phone. "You'll never leave here alive," he said.

Ignoring him, Domino snatched the phone. "I can't do this, but you can, Judd. There's a forward deployment on Crete standing by for rapid insertion. A woman named Gloria Feit is waiting for you or Tucker to call. I'm told she had no other way to get in touch with you and she wasn't certain you'd need or want help."

As Tucker's voice droned on the phone in the background, Eva raised her brows in surprise. "How do you know about Gloria Feit?"

"We'll talk about it later." Domino handed the phone to Judd.

"Archimedes!" Yitzhak had been walking along the wall. He pulled down a volume and opened it excitedly. "Good Lord, they have his complete collection."

Judd was already dialing out.

Instantly Gloria answered. "Souda Bay's been alerted," she said into his ear. "Three Black Hawks with fully loaded fast-rope teams. They'll take off in five minutes. Figure a half hour to get there. Maybe longer. Can you hold out?"

"We have to." Judd ended the connection.

As he filled them in, Tucker finished his call and listened.

"Just a half hour is very long to wait," Roberto said worriedly. "Perhaps your people will require more time to reach the island, and then of course we are down here. Very far underground."

Judd's lungs tightened. Suddenly there was another explosion, this time louder. The door distended into the room, and tendrils of smoke curled toward them.

"The table," Tucker said curtly.

Judd, Domino, and Tucker crashed it over onto its side. Glasses and candlesticks shattered against the floor. They spun the table around through the mess so it faced the door. The top was three inches of marble lying on four inches of wood, a decent shield.

"Get behind," Judd ordered. "Not you." He yanked Chapman to his feet. "Eva, you're in charge of Roberto and Yitzhak."

Roberto grabbed Yitzhak's arm and pulled him away from the books and behind the table. Eva followed with Chapman's M4, glancing over her shoulder at Judd. He looked into her eyes and nodded. She gave a tense smile and nodded in return.

Suddenly Yitzhak rose above the table. "You must not harm the library!"

"Not now, Yitzhak!" Eva pushed him down and crouched beside him.

"You take that side of the door." Domino gestured and ran. "I'll hold the other."

Immediately Tucker sprinted. Like Domino, he positioned himself flat against the wall, weapon ready. Forcing Chapman to join Tucker, Judd unhooked a frag grenade from his belt.

With a thunderous noise, the door to the library blasted open, landing on the marble and sliding across the room. Gray smoke billowed past them and curled back into the anteroom. As Judd pulled the pin and threw the grenade high into the anteroom's smoke, gunfire instantly sounded, the bullets streaking blindly past them in fusillades, pounding into chairs, the table, and the books.

"No!" Chapman bellowed, looking wildly back as golden covers exploded and volumes plummeted to the floor. He crashed an elbow into Judd's side, trying to break free. "Hold your fire! This is Martin Chapman. I order you to hold your fire!"

Tucker slammed an arm around Chapman's throat and yanked him back.

A loud burst from the grenade in the anteroom shook the library. The smoke was heavy and bitter. They coughed into the sudden silence. Moans sounded from the other side of the doorway.

Judd nodded at Domino. Crouching, weapons raised, they rolled around and stared at the bodies of a half-dozen men who lay in a tumble across the anteroom floor. Blood splattered the walls. Body parts of perhaps four men had been ripped off and tossed, lying on other men and against the elevators and in front of the stairwell.

"Let's go," Judd stood upright and called back into the library. "Fast!"

Domino was quickly at the stairs, his Walther tucked away, an M4 in his arms. Judd raced around the packed bodies and entered the stairwell as Tucker propelled Chapman into the anteroom. Behind him he heard Eva gasp. Then their quick steps were following him upward.

"Looks to me as if we got rid of ten on the way in," Judd said to Domino's back. "Another six in the anteroom. That leaves about thirty-four."

"Right."

"You figured out the layout?"

"There's a garage on the first underground level. It's past the kitchen, at the end of the hall. They won't realize you'll know about it."

"Safer than going through the house," Judd agreed.

Suddenly heavy footsteps sounded, running down toward them. Judd looked up and saw a large number one painted on the stone wall, announcing they were just below ground level. Side by side, they accelerated to the landing as two security men appeared.

Dropping flat on the steps, Judd ripped off a grenade, pulled the pin, and heaved it. Domino fell beside him, and they covered their heads with their arms. Captured in the stairwell, the blast was deafening. Stone chips pelted down. And they jumped up, stepped through the smoke, and pushed the door open onto a high-tech kitchen. At first it appeared deserted, then Judd saw chefs and waiters cringing against a back wall.

"Get down!" he barked and aimed the M4.

As the men and women scrambled to the floor, Domino ran to a side door and propped it open. Through it a long corridor showed. His head swiveling, he hurried along, studying closed doors as he passed.

Judd opened the kitchen door, listening. More security guards were running down the flight of stairs.

"You in one piece?" Tucker demanded as he shoved Chapman past him.

Chapman's expression was steely, his eyes glinting with outrage. "When my men catch you, I'll kill you myself."

Judd ignored him. "We're fine," he told Tucker. "Give me one of your grenades. Follow Domino."

As they moved off, Eva arrived with Yitzhak and Roberto. The pair were breathing hard and said nothing. Judd did not like the way Yitzhak looked. The professor's round face was gray, and the sweat on his bald head was thick.

Eva gave Judd a too-bright smile and urged Yitzhak and Roberto toward the corridor.

Alone, Judd crouched, his M4 trained on the kitchen staff as he listened to the footsteps descending. As soon as he saw the first pair of feet, he pulled the last grenade's pin, rolled it onto the landing, closed the door, and sprinted. The noise of the explosion followed him across the kitchen. In his mind he added up the number of the remaining guards in the stairwell—a total of two or three, he decided. That was not a large number. He would have thought the entire force would have been sent after them when they heard the initial explosions.

Slamming shut the door to the corridor, he tore down its length toward the garage. At least thirty minutes had passed, he decided. Roberto had been right. Even if the helicopters had arrived, it would be longer. Ten minutes, maybe twenty, for the teams to fight through the remaining guards to find them. He shook off the worry they would not be able to hold out.

He pushed through the door. And froze. Stared. Domino knelt on the floor, clutching his upper chest where a fresh bullet wound showed. His tuxedo jacket was drenched in blood, and his face was battered. Tucker was helping him up, while Eva kept her M4 aimed at Martin Chapman. At the same time Yitzhak sat cross-legged on the floor, collapsed over his stout stomach, panting, while Roberto worriedly rubbed his back. Six security men lay sprawled on the concrete floor, either dead or unconscious. That was a partial explanation of where Chapman's extra men were.

Instantly Judd checked the door. There was no way to lock it.

"They were expecting us," Domino said calmly as he pulled himself up, his M4 dangling from one hand. "Must have some tracking system I didn't know about. Tucker arrived just in time."

"Good work, both of you."

Domino nodded. Rifle ready, Tucker ran across the vast garage space emptied of patrolling Jeeps toward the maw left open by the sliding garage door. Domino limped after him.

Now Judd had one wounded shooter, the professor, who looked so ill he could not walk, and Chapman, who had to be guarded at all times. Inwardly he swore. Suddenly he was exhausted, and he realized the wound on his side was throbbing painfully. He grabbed a loading cart.

"Let's go, professor. You get to ride." He handed his rifle to Roberto and gently picked up the older man and set him on the cart's bed. "Climb aboard, Roberto."

Roberto sat beside Yitzhak. "You are good, yes?"

The professor said nothing, simply dipped his head once. His eyes were dull with pain.

"You first, Eva." Judd looked at her strained face.

"Delighted. Move, Chapman." Then she warned, "I'll be right behind you, and it'd be such a pleasure to shoot you."

"Let me go," Chapman said, his cool gaze assessing their weakened position. "I'll call off my men and get you out of here."

"My ass," Eva retorted. "You're alive. Don't try for more. As Horace said, *'Semper avarus eget.'* That means a greedy man's always in need, you greedy bastard."

She hurried him off, and Judd ran past them, pushing the cart. Tucker was on one side of the big garage door, Domino on the other. Both were peering out carefully. Judd glanced over his shoulder at the door to the corridor to make certain it remained closed and Eva still controlled Chapman.

But as he neared the garage door and felt the night air cool on his skin, he heard the shouts of men out on the hillsides. He parked the cart off to the side, against the wall. That explained the rest of Chapman's men. More would be coming through the house after them.

"Stay there," he told Yitzhak and Roberto. Before they could respond, he joined Domino, who moved aside so he could take the lead. "See anything?"

"They're closing in," Domino said through bruised lips. His jaw was swelling.

Abruptly fusillades of gunfire raked through the garage's opening, whining past and spitting into the concrete floor. Judd dropped, rolled, and came up on his elbows, sending bursts out toward the flashes of light. Instantly Domino was lying beside him, shooting, too. Dark shadows of men were moving down to join the shooters, far more than the number of Chapman's men Judd had thought were left. Had Chapman put on more security than he realized?

In his peripheral vision he saw Eva push Chapman

to Tucker's side of the door. Now that they had arrived, Tucker dropped to fire, too.

As Judd squeezed off bursts, he glanced up in time to see Chapman take in the scene, his gaze calculating. Only Eva was left standing to guard him.

"Eva!" Judd warned. "Chapman's going to—"

Too late. The tall man whirled and lashed out a foot, kicking away her M4. She lunged for it, and he fell on her. Fighting back, she kneed him in the groin, and they rolled, their legs and arms tangled. Judd could not get a clear shot.

Enraged, he jumped up and ran toward her as gunfire continued to slash into the garage. Rounds grazed his back, burning.

Suddenly he heard the door to the corridor behind them burst open. In the shelter of the wall, he turned, firing blindly, raking blasts toward it.

"Stop, Judd!" Tucker bellowed. "It's our people!"

A paramilitary team dressed in black with black combat gear was streaming around the door, crouching, M4s up.

At the same time, Domino announced tiredly, "Your people are wiping out the security guards on the hills, too."

Judd said nothing, looking out quickly as he listened to the blistering gunfire. Fusillades no longer streamed into the garage. The gunshots came from all over the dark slopes, muzzle flashes bright and fast as the paratroopers fought the guards.

Judd sprinted to Eva. "Get off her, you asshole!" But before Chapman could move, Judd kicked him in the head.

THE HILLS WERE QUIET AT LAST. Shadows moved as paratroopers rounded up the last of Chapman's security men. Inside the garage, Eva waited beside Judd, his closeness comforting, as he and Tucker filled in the lieutenant in charge of the operation. At a distance, Chapman sat on the floor, hands cuffed behind him, head cocked as he tried to hear what they said. Blood matted his white hair from Judd's blow. Refusing to speak, he was alert, his expression angry, his lips thin and tightly closed.

A medic had examined Yitzhak and pronounced a profound case of exhaustion. Roberto and Yitzhak held hands in the cart as one of the soldiers pushed them across the floor toward the house.

Domino took off his tuxedo jacket, and the medic ripped his shirt, gave him shots of antibiotics and painkillers, and cleaned his wound.

"Looks as if the bullet missed your lungs, but you've got a broken rib, I think," the medic decided. "I'll bandage you until I can get you to a hospital. The painkiller should be kicking in now."

"Give that to me."

Domino grabbed packets of sterile bandages. Pushing the medic away, he stood, ripped open two, and slapped one bandage onto the entrance wound in back and the other in front.

He looked at Judd. "Let's get the hell out of here."

Eva was about to say something, then thought better of it. She joined Domino, Judd, and Tucker as they walked across the garage. She felt their weariness and was suddenly aware of her own.

"So you work for the Carnivore, Domino?" she asked.

"I do occasional jobs for him. He felt I'd be appropriate for this particular task." He had a calm, untroubled expression now.

"Who is the Carnivore, really?"

He chuckled and ran a finger along his red nose. "He told me you might ask. The answer is he's a man without a face. He employs me only through e-mail." He gazed at Judd a moment. "I owe you for killing Preston. Saved my hide."

"A pleasure, believe me."

"Nevertheless, I won't forget."

They rode the elevator up one floor, to the ground level. The living room showed the effects of a gun battle. Furniture and vases were shattered, and bullet holes riddled paintings. They walked out through the double glass doors onto the marble pathway.

Moonlight shone down, casting the grounds in a soft glow. A half-dozen corpses were laid out beside the tennis courts. Chefs and staff members were sitting on the ground, guarded by two members of the paramilitary teams. Ahead, three sleek Black Hawk helicopters were parked on and around the helipad. One's rotors were turning. Yitzhak and Roberto were climbing on board.

The four passed two cottages.

"This one was your husband's," Domino told Eva. "In case you want to see it."

She stopped and gazed at the white walls, then at the carved wood door, much like the one into the Library of Gold. "Yes, you're right. I'd like to go inside."

"I'll go with you," Judd offered.

"We need to talk about the Carnivore and how you found out about Gloria Feit," Tucker told Domino.

"Of course. I'll fill you in completely, but give me a few moments to rest. How about on the helicopter ride back?"

Tucker gave an understanding nod. "Agreed."

As the pair waited outside, Judd and Eva entered the small foyer of Charles Sherback's cottage and walked into a spacious living room. It had been searched. Books piled haphazardly on the floor, the shelves that lined the walls empty. The cushions on the sofas and easy chairs were upended, and the drawers on the writing desk left open. Eva clasped her throat.

Judd followed her into the bedroom. The cover and sheets on the king-size bed were torn off. Clothes from the bureau and closet lay on the floor. Men's clothes—and women's clothes.

Eva walked up to a framed needlepoint above the dresser. It was a quotation:

I cannot live without books.
—Thomas Jefferson, letter to John Adams, 1815

"I gave that to Charles," she said quietly, her back to Judd. "It was in his office at the Moreau Library. I'd forgotten about it."

Judd had seen no photos in the living room, but there were several hanging on the wall in the bedroom of Charles and Robin—working together in the library, walking on the beach, picking oranges in a grove. He watched Eva turn to gaze at them.

"Maybe he took the Jefferson quotation to remember you," he said kindly.

"Or maybe he wanted it because he liked the quotation. Did I tell you I can needlepoint?"

He put an arm around her shoulders. "I imagine there are a lot things you haven't told me. I'd like to know all of them."

She smiled up at him but said nothing, full of emotions she could not name.

He felt a moment of disappointment, then he led her to the door. They walked out into the night. Another helicopter's rotors were turning, the motor sending waves of sound across the fresh sea air.

"Where are Tucker and Domino?" Judd looked quickly around.

They ran. Tucker was pushing himself up off the ground behind a bush.

"Tucker, what happened?" she said.

"The bastard got me while I wasn't looking." He grimaced and dusted off his trousers. "Obviously he didn't want to answer my questions."

"There he is," Judd said, peering far up the hill behind them.

Domino was a solitary figure, climbing swiftly. He had peeled off his white shirt and was wearing a long-sleeve black T-shirt. With his black tuxedo trousers, he was difficult to see. Then he turned, and moonlight illuminated his face. Cradling his M4, he caught sight of them.

"Come back, dammit!" Tucker shouted.

Instead Domino lifted two fingers and deliberately touched his forehead in a brisk salute. Eva vaguely recalled the gesture . . . And then it was vivid: A moonlit night like this, the Thracian coast in Turkey. She and Judd were sitting inside the small plane, about to take off for Athens, and Judd had saluted back.

The men cursed as Domino's silhouetted form ran off lightly and vanished over the hill's crest.

But Eva felt a strange thrill. "My God, it was him all along. The assassin without a face. There is no Domino. That was the Carnivore."

EPILOGUE

Georgetown, D.C.

EVEN IN THE LONG SHADOWS of twilight the June evening was sultry, typical for a District summer. The sidewalks and granite buildings radiated heat, while the scents of blooming flowers mixed with the stench of oily concrete as Eva Blake hurried along Wisconsin Avenue in downtown Georgetown.

She was full of memories. It had been two months since the discovery of the Library of Gold on the Isle of Pericles, and at last she had a sense of what she wanted for her future. With her conviction for Charles's murder scrubbed, she had collected his life insurance, leased a condo in Silver Spring, and moved to be near Washington.

Headlines had echoed around the world with the revelation the Library of Gold had been found at last. Included in the news was the Greek government's arrests of Martin Chapman and the other surviving members of the book club—all international businessmen—on charges of kidnapping Yitzhak Law and Roberto Cavaletti, the only charges they had a hope of making stick. The men were quickly out on bail, claiming Yitzhak and Roberto had simply been visiting. Since Yitzhak had told his Rome university he was going out of town on business just before he and Roberto disappeared, there was some credence to the book club's defense. In any case, the seven men had a world-class team of lawyers working around the clock for them, while the CIA needed to keep its role secret and was going to be of little help supporting any charges against them. At least Yitzhak and Roberto were back home and safe in their familiar routines.

A footnote to worldwide news, but a headline-grabber in Los Angeles, was that Charles Sherback had been found on the island, dead. Full of curiosity, former friends and colleagues had called, giving Eva condolences. At the same time the media had swarmed, packing her voice mail with pleas for interviews and camping out outside her hotel. She could not go to the drugstore, pick up her dry cleaning, or eat in a café without being peppered with questions. Thankfully here in Washington she was out of the fish bowl.

As was the way of politics in Afghanistan, Syed Ullah was no longer warlord. The Kabul government had sent its army to force him to give his region to an up-and-coming young rival, and now Ullah was running for the next parliamentary election. It appeared as if he would win, but Kabul gave no indication it was worried. Its ties to Pakistan remained tangled. The film of the two Pakistani newsmen had been confiscated, and the Islamabad government had ordered them to forget anything they saw, so the U.S. military base was safe. It was in Pakistan's best interest to keep Afghanistan as stable as possible, at least for now.

As she walked down the busy street, Eva watched

the dusky shadows. She still felt the bone-weary exhaustion of being hunted, of the roller-coaster ride of terrifying failures and exhilarating successes. And she deeply missed her friend Peggy Doty. Several times she had talked on the phone with Peggy's longtime beau, Zack Turner, who remained inconsolable.

She fought back anger as she remembered Charles's faked death, her incarceration, and the still unidentified corpse in Charles's grave. Betrayal after betrayal. She wondered who she had been before prison and the Library of Gold operation. Clearly she had changed. It was time to find out who she was now.

Judd and Tucker were waiting at a table in Five Guys Famous Burgers and Fries on the corner of Dumbarton Street. They sat across from each other, the older academic-looking man in his tortoiseshell glasses and the battered athlete in his sports jacket and turtleneck. She smiled as they spotted her.

Motioning them to stay seated, she kissed each on the cheek. "You have my hamburger. Thanks, Tucker."

"You look good, Eva," Judd said. "Rested."

"I feel rested." She smiled as she sat between them.

The men were already eating, so she dove into the hamburger and fries they had ordered for her. She had not seen Tucker since her return to the United States, and she had been with Judd only when they were being debriefed. His face still looked troubled occasionally. Not only had his father been killed, but he had discovered his deep involvement in the powerful and immoral book club.

"How's your mother, Judd?" Tucker was asking.

"Much better. Busy again with her philanthropies. She doesn't know the truth about Dad and the Library of Gold."

"No reason she should know," Eva said quickly.

Judd nodded. "What's the latest with the book club, Tucker?"

Tucker chewed a moment. "I can't go into specifics, of course, but I can tell you the Justice Department has investigators working in the various countries in which the club members do business. The problem is, the members are effectively out of our control, even if we discover criminal activity—unless it's in the United States or in a foreign country where the government is willing to cooperate."

Judd shook his head in disgust. Then he changed the subject. "Have we made peace with the Greeks?"

Tucker chuckled. "H. L. Mencken wrote something to the effect that nations get along with one another not by telling the truth but by lying gracefully. We made a deal. In exchange for the Greeks' forgetting we sent our paratroopers into their territory, we let them take credit for finding the Library of Gold."

"That explains the news stories. Charles would've been furious." Eva laughed. Greece's renowned government historian Nikos Amourgis had received the credit. "What's going to happen to the library now?"

Finished eating, Tucker pushed his plate away. "It's vanished. The word is it will remain private."

"You don't know where it is?" she asked, surprised. "The Greeks don't?"

"They ended their investigation on the island last month. The next week our flyovers told us it was gone. There are no buildings on the mesa now. The underground levels have been filled in, and a fruit orchard planted. Even the wharf's been carted away. The bottom line is the island's private, and the collection is privately owned, so they can do whatever they want. The library's hardly a national security issue for us, so we won't devote manpower to locating it again."

They were silent with disappointment.

"What about the Carnivore?" Eva asked eagerly. "Did you track him down?"

She knew Gloria had sent out word to all Catapult operatives, asking them or any of their sources who had contact with Tucker or Judd to tell them to phone her for help. That was how the Carnivore must have known to have them call Gloria while they were trapped in the Library of Gold. Then when the Carnivore escaped on the island, Tucker sent paratroopers out to look for him. They reported a small dark speedboat on the west side, taking off into the night. It was possible the Carnivore was on it, but they had needed the helicopters to transport the injured off the island and so had not pursued.

Tucker shook his head. "No. I had Gloria send out another notice to our people after I got back, this time asking whoever had told the Carnivore about us to let us know. No one owned up to it. Frustrating as hell."

"You've got someone in Catapult who knows the Carnivore," Judd said, "or can reach him somehow."

"Right. And no one's talking."

"Still, his help was critical," Eva said. "In fact, I think it's safe to say he was instrumental in saving our lives."

"Yes, and I'm not going to hunt him," Tucker said. "Bad things happen when one goes after the Carnivore, but that doesn't bother me. I just don't see much point to it, at least for now."

"Oddly, I'm glad," Eva said.

Tucker peered around the lively fast-food joint. Two middle-age men had arrived with their burgers and sat at the next table.

"Let's get out of here." Tucker stood and led Judd and Eva out of the restaurant.

As they walked down Wisconsin Avenue, Tucker, between them, glanced at one, then the other. "I know the Library of Gold operation was rough on you. You uncovered very unpleasant facts about people you loved. On the other hand, I've always believed illusions are overrated. Consider a great ballet. From the audience you see extraordinary dancers seemingly light as air, leaping, pirouetting, and generally moving like sylphs in ways most of us can only dream. But if you go backstage you find sweat, torn muscles, and mangled feet. Which is better?" Before they could respond, he went on: "My take is backstage. That's where you learn what it takes to create something extraordinary. It shows the human spirit at its most indomitable. And the next time you sit in the audience the illusion is gone and you start to see that with effort all of us can achieve a sort of glory in our lives."

"Are you talking about Judd's father and Charles?" Eva asked.

"Yes. Both did despicable things, but they did good things as well. Remembering that will help you to live with the facts."

They were silent.

At last Tucker said, "Judd, there's work for you with me whenever you want. I know you're reluctant now, but remember, I can use you. Ivan the Terrible was onto something when he commissioned *The Book of Spies*. Spies have a long if checkered past, and we're still badly needed."

Judd shook his head. "Thanks, but no thanks."

Eva cleared her throat. "What about me?"

The men stared at her.

"What do you mean?" Judd asked sharply.

"Both of you seemed to think I did a good job," she said calmly. "I want to go through the CIA training program. If I get weeded out, so be it."

"But you loved your work as a curator," Judd objected.

"Yes, but I never felt the same commitment, the same sense of doing something that could make a difference. You must've sensed I was heading in this direction, Judd. Otherwise you wouldn't have bothered to teach me so much."

Tucker chuckled. "You're right, Eva. You've got the talent and the brains. I'll make some calls tomorrow." He looked at his watch. "I'll be leaving you here. I'm going to meet my wife at the Kennedy for opera. Her idea. I hate opera, but right now she gets whatever she wants." He pounded Judd on the back and kissed Eva on the cheek. "I know I can trust both of you never to say a word about the operation." He turned and left.

"Is he in charge of Catapult now?" Eva asked as she looked back over her shoulder, watching his energetic gait.

"Hell, no." Judd's gray eyes danced. "My bet is he'll never take the job. Gloria's irritated, but she's living with it." Then he said solemnly, "I warned you not to like the work too much."

She smiled. "Are you going to hold it against me?"

"No. You'll be a damn good addition to Langley."

He reached into his pocket and held out his hand. As he uncurled his fingers, she saw her wedding ring and the necklace Charles had given her.

"You kept them?" She felt a strange emotion.

"Now that life is settling down a bit, I thought you might know more what you wanted to do with them. They're yours, after all."

"The pendant is a Roman coin. The goddess Diana. It was Charles's first gift to me."

"She's the huntress," he remembered.

"Yes, somehow I reminded Charles of her."

"He wasn't wrong about that."

She took the jewelry and the responsibility. "I'll donate them." She slid them into her pocket.

They walked on silently. She was mulling what Tucker had said about illusions.

"Strange how neither of us saw the truth about your father and Charles," she said at last. "Instead what we saw was love. *Ut ameris, amabilis esto.* That's from Ovid and it means that if you want to be loved, be lovable. In their own ways they were lovable. We can't ever forget what they did—but it'd be healthy for us to work on forgiving them."

"I'll call you," he said.

"Yes, we'll talk more."

She smiled at him, and he smiled back, gazing deep into her eyes. A warm intimacy passed between them.

"I'm glad to have met you, Eva Blake." He took her hand. His grip was firm.

She held up their hands and gazed at his. His hand no longer looked to her like the hand of a killer. But then, Michelangelo had been working in marble, and this was the warm flesh of a man. A very good man.

Rome, Italy

THE MONTH OF JULY WAS THE HEIGHT OF Estate Romana, the Rome summer festival. A six-week auditory and visual feast, the festival was a flood of mostly outdoor shows, many set in grassy parks and amid ruins to take advantage of the splendor of ancient Rome. The Carnivore always tried to be in the city for at least a few days to enjoy as much as he could. Tonight was a good night for it, warm but not hot, the stars shining brightly.

Passing the tumbled walls and columns of the Temple of Claudius on his right, he climbed the steep paving stones of Via Claudia and breathed deeply, filling his lungs and expelling air in mighty bursts, savoring his returned vigor, his good health. Escaping from the Isle of Pericles had taken every ounce of strength he'd had. The medic's painkillers had helped, and of course he had long practiced the rule of the cat—never show you're injured, vulnerable.

Jack O'Keefe, Doug Kennedy, and George Russell had been waiting in a high-powered speedboat at the specified location, and within hours they were at the airport on Mykonos and on their way home. The bullet that got him had ripped through large muscles and nicked a rib, so he had taken time to convalesce, then resumed his regime of cardio and weights.

At the wrought-iron gate he bought a ticket and walked onto the grounds of the magnificent Villa Celimontana. The park spread across Celio Hill, one of the city's seven storied hills, south of the Coliseum. Little known, it was an oasis of peace and greenery in chaotic Rome. Across the drive, "Jazz" was projected in colorful letters. The Carnivore strode through the lights, taking in the tall cypresses and centuries-old oaks and pines. The winding pathways were littered with pieces of carved marble and broken classical statues. In five minutes he was at the sixteenth-century villa, a tall two stories and pink in the night's lights.

Turning a corner, he passed an outdoor jazz poster gallery, sculptures, artistic installations, and finally a fountain heralding the venue's entrance. He listened to the jazz sounds of Charles Lloyd's sweet tenor sax.

As the rich music filled the night air, he climbed the wood terraces built for the summer season. Rows of tables decorated with little red lanterns filled the top three levels of the semicircular amphitheater, while concert seating was on the patio below, the chairs facing the stage, where Lloyd was soloing in front of a small jazz band.

He found his table, sat, and reached for the beer that

was awaiting him—a chilled blond beer from Birra Menabrea, perfect for the warm night.

"Good to see you, Uncle Hal." Bash Badawi was out of his usual shorts and T-shirt, dressed for the occasion in worn jeans and an open-necked purple shirt rolled up at the sleeves. Both were cellophane tight against his muscular body. Despite the late hour, wraparound sunglasses sat on his straight jet-black hair, and his dark eyes were smiling in his golden face. He looked completely modern Roman.

"How's your mother?" The Carnivore drank. Bash was not really his nephew, but his first cousin once removed—his mother's sister's grandchild. It was complicated, but then they came from a large Italian family.

"Mom's good. Making pasta as if we were all still living at home. I told her she should start selling on-line, but she got all bent out of shape. The pasta wouldn't be *fresh*—but I was for suggesting it. That woman can still swing a killer wood spoon. You know what I mean, with the long handle and the hot spaghetti sauce dripping from the bowl. Painful." Grinning, Bash assessed him. "You look pretty good for a guy who had his entrails toyed with."

"Just muscle." The Carnivore drank again, enjoying the young man who reminded him of who he might have been. Then he asked the question that had drawn him here: "Anyone looking for me?"

"Just the usual rogues, wannabes, and historians. Seriously, I think you're safe. I can't give you the details about how I know—national security and all that—but the fellow you met on the island, Tucker Andersen, has called off the hunt."

The Carnivore only nodded, but he was relieved. He had liked Andersen and Blake, and now he owed Judd Ryder.

"You going to be in trouble over this?" he asked.

"Hey, no prob. You did us a favor, and I'm keeping my mouth shut. Secrecy's what they trained me for." Bash raised a muscular hand, two fingers displayed, signaling for more beers. "So are you on downtime now? Got any exciting jobs?" he asked casually.

The Carnivore gazed over the parapet at the vistas of Rome. The city's lights sparkled around the massive ruins of the Baths of Caracalla. Today it was a shell of bricks, but at one time it had sprawled across twenty-seven acres and accommodated sixteen hundred bathers at a time. He remembered that Emperor Caracalla, who had built the baths in the third century A.D., had been a cruel, ruthless ruler. Traveling from Edessa to begin a war with Parthia, he had stopped to urinate on the roadside and was assassinated by one of his own—a frustrated and ambitious officer in the Imperial Guard.

The Carnivore chuckled. "Drink up, boy. The night is young, and for the moment I'll pretend I am as well. As for my plans, secrecy's what I was trained for, too."

AUTHOR'S NOTES

THE MYSTERIOUS HISTORY OF
THE LIBRARY OF GOLD

THE SEARCH FOR IVAN the Terrible's lost library—occasionally called the Byzantine Libreria—in the labyrinthine tunnels under Moscow has continued for some five centuries, capturing the imaginations of emperors, potentates, and the Vatican. Joseph Stalin stopped the hunt in the 1930s because he feared that searching the tunnels would leave him vulnerable to attack from beneath, while Vladimir Putin, in a gesture signifying Russia's new openness, allowed the quest to resume in the 1990s.

Today a host of scholars, scientists, historians, and amateurs pore over old, incomplete maps and request official permission to investigate. Joining the pursuit are vine walkers who claim to use bioenergetic powers to locate metal; psychics who act as security against "dark forces" that might be guarding the hidden tomes since past searchers have been prone to accidents, disease, blindness, or death; and the Diggers of the Underground Planet, a group of urban spelunkers with a cult following, who drop through manholes and pry open forgotten iron doors to reach the unexplored passages.

My interest in the library dates back more than twenty years. On June 28, 1989, I was reading the *Los Angeles Times* when "Kremlin Tunnels: The Secret of Moscow's Underworld," by Masha Hamilton, caught my attention.

> It was a summer evening in 1933 when the two young men found what they were searching for: the entrance to a centuries-old underground tunnel within sight of the red Kremlin walls. As they crept underground toward Moscow's seat of power, lighting their way with a lantern, the men believed they might find Ivan the Terrible's legendary library of gold-covered books. Instead they found five skeletons, a passageway sometimes so narrow that they had to file through singly and, within a few hundred yards of the Kremlin, a rusted steel door they could not open.

I was enthralled by this "library of gold-covered books," which immediately became in my mind the Library of Gold. Kremlin officials stopped the young pair's exploration and swore them to secrecy with the implied threat of death, then Stalin ordered a swimming pool built over the area, putting a conclusive end to anyone's quest.

The story of the fabled library is one of geopolitics, an arranged marriage, madness, and the enduring love of books. And it begins more than two thousand years ago in the Greco-Roman world of emperors, scholars, warriors, and the wealthy.

An intentionally chilling ancient Roman tombstone has this inscription: *Sum quod eris, fui quod sis*—"I am what you will be; I was what you are." Public and private libraries were assembled by the ancients to enjoy, to educate, and to display affluence and privilege. But in the largest sense they were created to preserve knowledge. Remarkable international library centers in Alexandria, Pergamum, Antioch, Rome, and Athens thrived for centuries. Tragically all were obliterated, sometimes in war, sometimes with avarice, sometimes purposefully to destroy history and culture.

The last great repository in that long-ago Western world was the royal library in Constantinople. Founded in about 330 A.D. by Constantine the Great, the city grew up on the site of a Greek town called Byzantium. At the time, it was known as the Roman Empire, though today it is referred to as the Byzantine Empire. By 475, the royal library had 120,000 volumes, probably making it the largest in that era. Over the following centuries the library was burned several times, vaporizing multitudes of priceless works, including, some claimed, a piece by Homer lettered in gold on a twelve-foot-long snakeskin.

Still the imperial collection constantly rose from the literary ashes. In the 1400s the Spanish traveler Pero Tafur described it thus: ". . . a marble gallery opening on arcades with tiled marble benches all around and with similarly crafted tables placed end to end upon low columns; there are many books there, ancient texts and histories."

The final blow came on May 29, 1453, when Mehmed the Conqueror and his Ottoman Turks brutally seized Constantinople. The English historian Edward Gibbon wrote, "One hundred twenty thousand manuscripts are said to have disappeared."

Six years later the survivors of the Byzantine royal family escaped as the Ottoman Turks invaded Morea, the rich Greek Peloponnese peninsula ruled by the emperor's heir and nephew, Thomas Paleologus.

Accompanying Thomas on the small Venetian galley were his wife and children—two young sons and a daughter, Zoë, about twelve years old. She would play a critical role in the Library of Gold.

They made their way to Italy, where Pius II took them under the papal wing, and the Vatican provided a palace and stipend. The pope had a vital political and religious goal—to enthrone Thomas at a recaptured Constantinople. Thomas and his family were Greek Orthodox, but they had promptly converted to Roman Catholic once they reached Italy. If the pope succeeded, Thomas would rule over a Christian New Byzantium, Western in outlook, uniting Catholic and Orthodox—and under the religious control of Rome.

The Venetians, who were making fortunes in trade with the Ottoman Turks, were less than happy about it. When Pius tried twice to mount a Fifth Crusade, this time against Constantinople, the Venetians dithered. Finally they delayed their fleet so long that the last attempted attack fell apart, and the pope died.

The next pope, Paul II, feinted. He looked east again, but this time his target was the widowed Ivan III, the Grand Prince of Moscow, soon to be called Ivan the Great. The Russian Orthodox Church had long flourished in Moscow. Hoping to acquire Ivan as a military ally against the Turks, as well as his consent for the Union of Churches, the pope offered Zoë's hand in marriage in 1472. She was now about twenty years old.

Moscow was the strongest of the Russian states and the fastest growing power of the times, although it was still under the Muslim yoke. Ivan accepted the proposal, and the royal pair married in Moscow before the year was out. Zoë took the name Sophia.

We know Sophia traveled with a large retinue by land and sea to Moscow. Her arrival was accompanied by Italians and Greeks, who settled there, too, and became influential, even rebuilding the Kremlin in a Russian-Italianate style. This is the point where the legend begins.

According to several commentators, Sophia brought with her to Moscow priceless illuminated manuscripts from the Byzantine imperial collection. "The chronicles mention 100 carts loaded with 300 boxes with rare books arriving in Moscow," according to Alexandra Vinogradskaya, writing in The Russian Culture Navigator. Another version is this: "The princess arrived in Moscow with a dowry of 70 carts, carrying hundreds of trunks, which contained the heritage of early cultures—the library collected by the Byzantine emperors," explains Nikolay Khinsky on WhereRussia. com, the Russian National Tourist site for International Travelers.

What is undisputed is that Sophia did bring the Ivory Throne of the Byzantine emperors on which Russian monarchs were crowned ever after, as well as the double-headed eagle, the imperial symbol of the Byzantine Empire for a thousand years, which became the Kremlin's for nearly another five hundred years. She introduced the grand court traditions of Byzantium, too, including ceremonial etiquette and costume. Even before the wedding, Ivan had assumed the title of czar—Caesar—and then added *grozny,* "formidable," a reverential adjective common in Byzantine autocracy, since the sovereign was considered the earthly image of God and empowered with all His sacred and judicial powers.

Since Sophia carried so much of Byzantium with her, it is very possible illuminated manuscripts were among her gifts. As Deb Brown, bibliographer and research services librarian for Byzantine studies at Dumbarton Oaks, wrote me: "There seems to be nothing in the (published) contemporary sources that testifies to books in Zoë/Sophia's possession, but I'm not convinced that she did not carry books with her. The silence of sources has to be weighed against the nature of the sources, which are few and concerned with matters of state and monies, not much else. There are plenty of indications that she was literate and well-educated."

Ultimately the Vatican's geopolitical gamesmanship partially succeeded. Sophia was the one who persuaded Ivan III in 1478 to challenge the Golden Horde. "When the customary messengers came from the Tatar Khan demanding the usual tribute, Ivan threw the edict on the ground, stamped and spat on it, and killed all the ambassadors save one, whom he sent back to his master," according to Gilbert Grosvenor in *National Geographic* magazine. Over time his armies beat back Khan Ahmed's soldiers, and Moscow was never seriously threatened by them again. One of the longest-reigning Russian rulers, Ivan tripled his territory and laid the foundations of state, based largely on the autocratic rule of Byzantium.

Where the Vatican failed was that the Chair of Peter was not unified with the throne of Constantine—upon her arrival in Moscow, Sophia had promptly endorsed Orthodoxy again.

The Library of Gold would have passed from Sophia and Ivan to their son Vasily III, and from him to his son Ivan IV. In 1547 at the young age of seventeen, Ivan IV outwitted Kremlin plots and crowned himself "Czar of All Russia." Eventually he, too, became known as Grozny—Ivan the Terrible—infamous ever since for his cruelty, slaughters of entire cities, and pleasure in torture. At the same time, a hundred years before Peter the Great was credited with doing so, Ivan opened Russia to the West. He frequently corresponded with European monarchs, including Elizabeth I of England, exchanged diplomats, and nurtured international trade. He not only extended Russia to the Pacific Ocean, but he also introduced the printing press to Russia.

"How many Oriental manuscripts does the monarch have?" asks Khinsky, referring to testimony describing Ivan the Terrible's library. "Up to 800. Some he has bought, some he has received as gifts. Most of the manuscripts are Greek, but many are Latin. The Latin I've seen include histories by Livius, *De Republica* by Cicero, stories about emperors by Suetonius. These manuscripts are written on thin parchment and bound in gold."

From his letters we know Ivan was familiar with the Bible, the Apocrypha, the Chronographs, which dealt with world history, and tales from *The Iliad*. He received books as presents from foreign envoys and visitors, had books written, and ordered others to be copied into Russian for his use.

"Historians know about the existence of the library because Ivan the Terrible instructed scribes to translate the books into Russian," says an article in *The Times* of London. "According to legend, the library once filled three halls and was so valued by Ivan the Terrible that he built a vault to protect [the books] from the fires that regularly swept Moscow." But the vault, allegedly hidden under the Kremlin, might also have been the result of Ivan's mental instability and growing paranoia.

News of the library spread across Europe. "The Germans, English, and Italians made many attempts to persuade the Russian czar to sell the treasure," writes Vinogradskaya. "But a man of considerable literary talent himself, Ivan the Terrible was an eager collector of rare books and fully aware of the high value of his collection. He refused to sell anything."

Ivan was also fascinated by spies and assassins, and used them frequently. His top spy and security chief had instant access to his bedchambers through one of the tunnels under the Kremlin. And Ivan created the feared Oprichniki, his clandestine personal armed force, who conducted espionage and assassinations. Chillingly, they dressed completely in black and rode black horses.

Begun in the 1100s and added to over the centuries, the tangled, endless underground tunnels were originally intended as escape routes, to give access to water if the Kremlin was besieged, and to move comfortably from one building to another during the harsh Russian winter. Reaching depths of twelve stories, the tunnels contain streams, dungeons, and secret chambers.

"Legend has it that all his [Ivan's] gold was hidden in one tunnel," writes Khinsky, "paintings and icons in another, and manuscripts from the Byzantine library in another. All the hiding places were carefully bricked up." Salt is a good preservative, and apparently natural salt basements have been found in Moscow's netherworld.

After reading his will in the morning and calling for his chess set in the afternoon, Ivan died in 1584. The will, which might have listed his library, mysteriously vanished. When his body was exhumed in 1963, traces of both mercury and arsenic were discovered, but not at high enough levels for the cause of death to have been poisoning, although it's a popular belief he was indeed poisoned.

According to Khinsky, sixteen years after the monarch's death, a Vatican envoy arrived to find out what had happened to the library. Old archives and book depositories were searched, and exploration parties sent out to dig. "The existence of the library is first mentioned in documents from the period of Peter the Great's rule, which began in 1682," according to Hamilton of the *Los Angeles Times*.

Ivan was the last known owner of the Library of Gold. "Historians, archaeologists, Peter the Great, and even the Vatican have searched fruitlessly for the missing library for hundreds of years," says *The Times* of London. In the seventeenth century most of the oldest tunnels were already out of use and forgotten, and the passage of time has made the hunt increasingly difficult because of weakened fortifications, landslides, flooding, and incomplete maps.

"The Kremlin is the dwelling of phantoms," wrote the Marquis de Custine, who visited Russia in the early nineteenth century. "It feels as though the underground sounds born there were coming from the grave."

It's not surprising that this vital collection of books, perhaps the most important to survive in history, remains the subject of gripping interest. In the course of various explorations, the sprawling mass of subterranean tunnels has yielded very old treasures, including a hidden arsenal of Ivan the Terrible's weapons, the czarina's chambers where Peter the Great spent his childhood, the city's largest silver coin hoard, gold jewelry, documents, and precious tableware and dishes, many of which have been put on public display. The Archaeology Museum is the site of some of these unique finds.

"Fear me, Giant Sewer Rodents, for I Am Vadim, Lord of the Underground!" is the title of an article written by Erin Arvedlund in *Outside* magazine about Vadim Mikhailov and his eager band of subterranean explorers—the Diggers of the Underground Planet. Their dream is to find the Library of Gold. Instead they have turned up skeletons, mutant fish, fugitives, clouds of noxious gas, ugly grass, albino cockroaches, and an underground pond once used as a site of mass suicides. On a more helpful note, they also discovered 250 kilograms of radioactive material under Moscow State University, which perhaps explains the long anecdotal history of illness, hair loss, and infertility among its students and faculty. The government removed the material.

An eighty-seven-year-old Moscow pensioner, Apollos Ivanov, who had been an engineer in the Kremlin and studied the underground structures of Moscow, believed the Library of Gold was in one of the branches that stood above an extensive catacomb network, which he had seen. He revealed his secret to the mayor in 1997, who quickly authorized the hunt. Many were convinced the missing collection would be unearthed at last. Ivanov had gone blind, and according to legend, anyone coming close to discovering the library lost his sight. But Ivanov was wrong, and the library remains missing.

The pursuit continues enthusiastically today, with new searchers bringing increasingly modern equipment. After all, the magnificent royal library of the Byzantine Empire was the last hope of the long-ago Western world, rich with the wisdom and lost knowledge of the ancients, and unrivaled today even by the Vatican Library. To think the Library of Gold, the crème de la literary crème, may lie sleeping quietly in Moscow's mysterious underworld is irresistible.

LITERARY TREASURES THE LIBRARY OF GOLD COULD CONTAIN

This Book is fiction, of course, but all the historical references and anecdotes are either factual or based on fact. For instance, the Emperor Trajan did erect the awe-inspiring monument to his successful wars, Trajan's Column, between two peaceful galleries of Rome's library, which he also built. And Cassius Dio Cocceianus, a Roman administrator and great historian, wrote *Romaika*, the most important history of the last years of the Roman Republic and early Empire. It encompassed eighty books, but only volumes thirty-six through sixty survive. If Cassius Dio wrote about Trajan's Column, I postulate the story would have appeared in book seventy-seven.

At the same time all of this is true: Julius Caesar did receive a list of conspirators planning to assassinate him—but never read it. Hannibal did rampage across Rome's countryside, destroying everything except Fabius's properties. As a result, Fabius had his hands full with a near-mutinous Rome. And in his send-up play *The Clouds,* Aristophanes does depict the revered philosopher Socrates as a clown teaching students how to scam their way out of debt.

The one major exception is the volume I call *The Book of Spies.* However, since Ivan the Terrible had books created and was intrigued by spies and assassins, it's possible he would have ordered such a work compiled.

History is available to us only through oral tradition and the written word. What was lost over the millennia from war, fires, looting, wanton destruction, deliberate obliteration, and censorship is tragic. Our history is the history of lost books.

If I could have my wish, the Library of Gold would exist, would be discovered, and not only would the lost books I name in the novel be found in it, but at least the work of these early six would, too:

- **Sappho** (c. 610 B.C. to c. 570 B.C.) was the lauded Greek poet whose life is recounted in myths based upon her lyrical and passionate love verses. The pinnacle of female accomplishment in poetry, her surviving work was collected and published in nine books sometime in the third or second century B.C., but by the eighth or nine century A.D. it was represented only by quotations in other authors' works.

- Classical Athens had three great tragic playwrights, all contemporaries—Aeschylus (525 or 524 B.C. to 456 or 455 B.C.), Sophocles (c. 495 B.C. to 406 B.C.), and Euripides (480 B.C. to 406 B.C.). The father of modern drama, **Aeschylus** wrote more than eighty plays, lifting the art of tragedy with poetry and fresh theatrical power. He introduced a second actor on stage—thus giving birth to dialogue, dramatic conflict, and dramatized plot. The Athenians had the only copy of his *Complete Works* and loaned it for copying to Alexandria, where Ptolemy III had other ideas—he ordered it left untranscribed and not returned. Scholars flocked. Centuries passed. Then the Alexandria libraries burned, and the scrolls died in flames. Only seven of Aeschylus's plays have survived.

- The author of 123 plays, including *Oedipus Rex,* **Sophocles** used scenery, increased the size of the chorus, and introduced a third actor, significantly widening the scope and complexity of theater. Sophocles said he showed men as they ought to be, while his younger contemporary, Euripides, showed them as they were. Only seven of Sophocles' plays survive.

- Dressing kings as beggars and showing women as intelligent and complex, **Euripides** used traditional stories to display humanity and ethics. He wrote more than ninety plays, which were remarkable for realistically reflecting his era. Reading them would tell us much about Athens. Only eighteen survive.

- **Confucius** (551 B.C. to 479 B.C.) was venerated over the centuries for his wisdom and his revolutionary idea that humaneness was central to how we should treat one another. He wrote "Six Works": *The Book of Poetry, The Book of Rituals, The Book of Music, The Book of History, The Book of Changes,* and *The Spring and Autumn Annals*, which formed a full curriculum of education. But the perfection of his vision is incomplete, since *The Book of Music* has disappeared.

- The first Roman emperor, **Augustus** (63 B.C. to A.D. 14), was one of the globe's finest administrative geniuses, reorganizing, transforming, and enlarging the reeling Roman Republic into a powerhouse empire with easy communications, thousands of miles of paved roads, and flourishing tourism and trade. A cultured man, he supported the arts and wrote many works. Most have vanished. A particular tragedy is the loss of his thirteen-volume *My Autobiography*, perhaps containing the inside views of the man who oversaw and directed one of the world's greatest civilizations during a long and critical period of history.

SELECTED BIBLIOGRAPHY

FOR THE LIBRARY OF GOLD

Around the Kremlin: The Moscow Kremlin, Its Monuments, and Works of Art. Moscow: Progress Publishers, 1967.

Arvedlund, Erin. "Fear Me, Giant Sewer Rodents, for I Am Vadim, Lord of the Underground!" *Outside* magazine, September 1997.

Backhouse, Janet. *The Illuminated Page: Ten Centuries of Manuscript Painting.* London: The British Library, 1993.

Basbanes, Nicholas A. *A Gentle Madness: Bibliophiles, Bibliomanes, and the Eternal Passion for Books.* New York: Henry Holt and Company, 1995.

"Blind Man 'Has Key to Tsar's Secret Library.'" *The Times* of London, September 17, 1997.

Canfora, Luciano. *The Vanished Library: A Wonder of the Ancient World.* Berkeley: University of California Press, 1990.

Cockburn, Andrew. "The Judas Gospel," *National Geographic*, May 2006.

Ehrlich, Eugene. *Veni, Vidi, Vici: Conquer Your Enemies,*

Impress Your Friends with Everyday Latin. New York: HarperCollins, 1995.

Grosvenor, Gilbert H. "Young Russia: Land of Unlimited Possibilities," *National Geographic*, November 1914.

de Hamel, Christopher. *The British Library Guide to Manuscript Illustration: History and Techniques*. London: The British Library, 2001.

Hamilton, Masha. "Kremlin Tunnels: The Secret of Moscow's Underworld," *Los Angeles Times,* June 28, 1989.

Holmes, Charles W. "Unsolved Mystery: What Happened to Ivan the Terrible's Library?" Cox News Service, October 31, 1997.

Holmes, Hannah. "Spelunking: And Please, No Flash Pictures of the Blob." *Outside* magazine, March 1995.

Ilinitsky, Andrei. "Mysteries Under Moscow," *Bulletin of the Atomic Scientists*, May/June 1997.

Kelly, Stuart. *The Book of Lost Books*. New York: Random House, 2005.

Khinsky, Nikolay. "Secret Treasures: Moscow's Caches," WhereRussia.com: Russian National Tourist site for International Travellers, www.WhereRussia.com, 1990s.

de Madariaga, Isabel. *Ivan the Terrible*. New Haven, Conn.: Yale University Press, 2005.

Panshina, Natalya. "Archaeology Expert Hopeful About Library of Ivan IV," *Tass*, September 18, 1997.

Polastron, Lucien X. *Books on Fire: The Destruction of Libraries Throughout History.* Rochester, Vt.: Inner Traditions International, 2007.

Severy, Merle. "The Byzantine Empire: Rome of the East," *National Geographic,* December 1983.

Sheldon, Rose Mary. *Espionage in the Ancient World: An Annotated Bibliography*. Jefferson, N.C.: McFarland & Company, Inc., 2003.

————. *Intelligence Activities in Ancient Rome.* New York: Routledge, 2005.

Simpson, D. P. *Cassell's New Compact Latin Dictionary.* New York: Cassell & Co., Ltd., 1963.

Stewart, Deborah Brown. Bibliographer and research services librarian, Byzantine Studies, Dumbarton Oaks Research Library and Collection, Washington, D.C. E-mail to author, August 7, 2007.

Vinogradskaya, Alexandra. "A Map of Moscow That Does Not Exist," Russian Culture Navigator, VOR. RU, November 9, 1999.

————. "The Mysteries of Underground Moscow," Russian Culture Navigator, VOR.RU, April 12, 1999.

————. "The Mystery of the Byzantine Library," Russian Culture Navigator, VOR.RU, January 18, 1999.

Yevdokimov, Yevgeny. "Possible Whereabouts of Famous Library Revealed to Mayor," ITAR-TASS News Agency, September 16, 1997.

Look for these other pulse-pounding reads from
New York Times bestselling author

GAYLE LYNDS

THE LAST SPYMASTER
ISBN: 978-0-312-98877-7

THE COIL
ISBN: 978-0-312-98876-0

MASQUERADE
ISBN: 978-0-312-98603-2

AVAILABLE FROM ST. MARTIN'S PAPERBACKS